Praise for
Drawn into Darkness

"Fast-paced, dangerously sexy, and full of fun! Annette McCleave has created a world where good and evil fight for the possession of human souls, and love is found despite seemingly unbeatable odds. *Drawn into Darkness* will keep you turning pages and anxious for more!"
—*USA Today* bestselling author Kathryn Smith

"Deliciously dark and spellbinding! Annette McCleave weaves magic so powerful, you'll believe in immortals. *Drawn into Darkness* is sexy, fast-paced, and intense. Readers be warned—the Soul Gatherers sizzle on the page."
—Allie Mackay

"A phenomenal debut! A refreshingly unique and vividly realized world with dark dangers and richly drawn characters. I loved every word. McCleave more than delivers!"
—National bestselling author Sylvia Day

DRAWN INTO DARKNESS

A SOUL GATHERER NOVEL

ANNETTE McCLEAVE

A SIGNET ECLIPSE BOOK

SIGNET ECLIPSE
Published by New American Library, a division of
Penguin Group (USA) Inc., 375 Hudson Street,
New York, New York 10014, USA
Penguin Group (Canada), 90 Eglinton Avenue East, Suite 700, Toronto,
Ontario M4P 2Y3, Canada (a division of Pearson Penguin Canada Inc.)
Penguin Books Ltd., 80 Strand, London WC2R 0RL, England
Penguin Ireland, 25 St. Stephen's Green, Dublin 2,
Ireland (a division of Penguin Books Ltd.)
Penguin Group (Australia), 250 Camberwell Road, Camberwell, Victoria 3124,
Australia (a division of Pearson Australia Group Pty. Ltd.)
Penguin Books India Pvt. Ltd., 11 Community Centre, Panchsheel Park,
New Delhi - 110 017, India
Penguin Group (NZ), 67 Apollo Drive, Rosedale, North Shore 0632,
New Zealand (a division of Pearson New Zealand Ltd.)
Penguin Books (South Africa) (Pty.) Ltd., 24 Sturdee Avenue,
Rosebank, Johannesburg 2196, South Africa

Penguin Books Ltd., Registered Offices:
80 Strand, London WC2R 0RL, England

First published by Signet Eclipse, an imprint of New American Library,
a division of Penguin Group (USA) Inc.

First Printing, September 2009
10 9 8 7 6 5 4 3 2 1

To T.A.M.

ACKNOWLEDGMENTS

I'd like to thank my agent, Laurie McLean, for being my champion and my go-to person for every question under the sun. I'd also like to thank my editor, Kerry Donovan, whose wonderful insights and suggestions coaxed this book into a far finer state than its humble beginnings.

My writing has been greatly enriched by the support of my colleagues in the Ottawa Romance Writers Association, both past and present, and I can honestly say I would never have made it this far were it not for the many hours of advice and the enthusiastic cheerleading I received from my friend Sylvia Day. You are a goddess, Syl.

On the home front, my eternal gratitude goes out to my family for the many meals, hugs, and nuggets of encouragement—most of all to Taylor, who never once stopped believing. Thank you.

1

Even in death, she was beautiful.

Morning mist shimmered on her pale skin, a subtle bloom of radiance at odds with her tragic fate. Her face, rendered unforgettable by a strong nose and regal chin, was like an opal amid the burgundy turbulence of her hair. With her eyes closed, she looked peaceful and perfect, save for the small chicken pox scar at the corner of her mouth.

Lachlan MacGregor ran a finger along the curve of her jaw and grimaced. The outer serenity was a lie. Dark bruises would soon fan across her neck, a vivid and gruesome portrayal of her last moments.

Lying in the reeds at the water's edge, shadowed by the arch of the concrete bridge, the body was barely noticeable in the thin light of an emerging fall day. Only a pair of green jogging shorts, discarded in a damp heap on the gravel, marked the spot. Her attacker had leapt from the bushes and dragged her down to the secluded shoreline, making her the city's fifth fatal rape victim in a fortnight. Grim proof that all was not as it should be in quiet San Jose.

Gentle waves stirred the woman's hair, and with it, his thoughts. Did a man wait for her at home, eyeing the clock, growing steadily more troubled over her delay?

Was an ugly sense of failure beginning to knot his gut? Would he soon regret sleeping through her departure, missing out on his chance to say good-bye and forfeiting their last kiss?

Lachlan scrubbed his face.

Vehicle traffic over the bridge was thickening with every passing minute and rail commuters would soon clog the pedestrian undercrossing on the other side of the water. Lingering was foolish.

His gaze fell to the pearly white mark upon the dead woman's cheek—a fine, three-ring spiral visible only to a Gatherer; visible only to him. Tucking the hem of his frock coat back to keep it out of the water, he leaned over the woman and placed a hand upon her cool, wet throat.

Instantly his fingers tingled and feathery tendrils traced up the flesh of his inner arm—the familiar sensation of a soul leaving a defunct body. Airy, benevolent warmth accompanied the soul as it wrapped around his heart, and Lachlan's chest eased. God, not Satan, had claimed this soul. His duty was the same either way, but if he had a choice . . .

With the woman's soul now under his protection, he flipped open his cell phone, dialed 911, and waited for the dispatcher to respond. He ignored the prompts for specific information and said only, "Almaden Lake. There's a body under the Coleman Road Bridge."

Then he stood. The timing was unfortunate. Emily Lewis's school bus would cross this very bridge in ten minutes, offering the school-bound teens an unpleasant view of the crime scene. But it couldn't be helped.

As he slid the phone into his pocket and turned toward the park exit, a short snap of electricity flashed in the air before him. Lachlan paused. Normally, a visitation this close on the heels of a gather was a good thing.

It meant he could go home, relax, and finish the Sunday crossword.

But that flash had been red, not blue.

The air in the shadowy alcove crackled and hummed, and in quick succession three more brilliant forks shot from the ground at his feet to the cement bridge. He felt, rather than saw, the transparent shield form around him, blocking a forty-foot dome from human view. Anyone peering over the bridge to catch the light show would spy nothing but a quiet emptiness.

Lachlan reached behind his neck and tugged his sword from the leather baldric buckled under his suit jacket. The blade made a reassuring zing as it cleared the metal ring at the top, a familiar prelude to battle that injected adrenaline straight into his veins. No sooner had his sword completed its carefully controlled arc than the air around him suddenly blazed with unbearable intensity. His nose burned with the sharp odor of brimstone and his ears made a soft popping noise.

He blinked . . . and found himself staring at five sturdy young men wearing the unofficial high-tech uniform: jeans, golf shirt, and sneakers. The nearest fellow, a clean-cut, congenial blond, grinned and pointed to Lachlan's black suit and distinctive white collar. "Nice duds. Not many folks would question you hovering around dead bodies in that outfit."

Lachlan didn't return the smile. "The human authorities are already on their way."

"Then we'll have to make this quick, won't we?"

"Bugger off."

"Sorry, bro, not going to happen."

"This soul is no' yours."

A car horn bleated as a truck rumbled along the road overhead, signaling the start of morning rush hour. Lachlan's heartbeat, already thumping heavily, sped up.

All it would take was one human to wander into this dome and there'd be difficult explanations to make. Discovery wasn't an issue for the demons—they could escape in a blink of an eye—but *he* was trapped.

"Maybe," the blond demon responded, "but we're here and the other team isn't, so give it up."

"Sorry, *bro*, no' going to happen."

The demon's eyes narrowed at the parroting of his words. As his hellmates spread out, circling their prey like the craven scavengers they were, he shrugged. "Your funeral."

Lachlan rolled his shoulders, loosening the muscles in his neck. This week his gathers had been very disagreeable, including two blood-soaked murders and a horrific Friday night pileup on the freeway. Today's death of an innocent woman only spurred the primitive howl in his blood. A fight suited him fine—as long as it was short.

"Five against one?"

Reaching deep, finding the cool white power that pulsed at the very center of his being, he stoked it. An icy flare radiated from his chest to his forearms and down to the lethal edge of his blade. The sword responded with a low, eager hum. Although medieval in design, the weapon had been forged by a modern-day master . . . who was also a mage.

"Very unsporting, lads."

Blondie smiled and responded, "What can I say? Ambush 101 is a prerequisite for the demon merit bad—"

The demon's head toppled off, landing on the gravel with a dull thud and a splat of steaming blood. Lachlan's sword brightened with eerie luminescence as demon gore ran along its fine edge, and he displayed the glowing green blade to the other four with a grim smile.

For one advantageous moment, they simply stared.

Hastily positioning the concrete bridge at his back,

he invoked a shield charm. When the demons regained their aplomb, snarling their rage and strafing him with red-hot flame balls, he was ready. The charm kept most of the bombs from burning through to his skin, but not all. A few fireballs breached the shield, forcing him to twist and parry with exhausting regularity. Not normally a problem, given his heightened senses and seasoned battle skills. But one of the demons, standing back from the others, was repeatedly using a dissolve primal to eat away at his shield.

Taking the bastard out became a priority.

Thirty seconds later he got his chance. The demon lifted both arms to deliver another wave of energy, and Lachlan stepped in with a swift, decisive slice. A choked gurgle, a spurt of vivid crimson, and the demon fell to his knees.

But the damage to Lachlan's shield was already done.

He found himself on the receiving end of a fiery strike that seared through the tattered remnants of his protective charm, ate away his sleeve, and wormed its way down to the bone.

Pain exploded inside his bicep, radiating through every nerve ending and snatching his breath. But he refused to succumb, refused to drop his arm. Instead, shunting the agony to the back of his mind, he focused on finding weaknesses in his attackers' defenses. Parry, shift, parry, twist, parry.

There.

A judicious downward cut, and the odds improved again. Two to one. Bolstered by an exultant dose of adrenaline, Lachlan's arm strengthened. He dispatched the smaller of his two remaining foes with a carefully aimed thrust between the ribs, then ducked and spun to the right.

Only one demon remained—a steroid junkie with tree

limbs for arms. Unfazed by the demise of his cohorts, the hulking creature continued to pitch fireballs. Lachlan's feint to the right proved ineffective and another hellish orb slipped past his defenses, this one blasting him in the chest.

Pain clawed into him, wriggled, and dug deeper.

If not for the beaten-silver cross around his neck, which absorbed the brunt of the strike, the blow might well have been lethal. Sweat beaded on his brow and his fingers clenched around his sword hilt, but Lachlan parried the next bomb, and the next. Falling back on his defensive skills, he rode out the agony and regained his momentum.

That's when he heard the screams.

High-pitched, youthful screams accompanied by the harsh grind of something huge punching through a barrier, a brief rumble, and then a heavy splash.

On the opposite side of the bridge, out of view, a vehicle had plunged into the lake.

His beefy opponent halted his attack, grinning broadly. Then, in a wink of garish red light, he vanished. The dome collapsed along with him, all evidence of the demons' presence sucked back into the lower plane. Gone. As if the battle had never been.

Lachlan's heart dropped into his belly.

Mother of God. Emily's school bus.

Even as fear splintered his thoughts, he instinctively began muttering a series of complicated, barely remembered verses. Drawing upon the very limits of his abilities, he conjured twin puffs of vapor to his palms, whipped them into dazzling plumes, then flung the effluvium into the air. Blinding shards of primal power danced away in all directions, spinning, curling, weaving through the atmosphere ...

... briefly halting human time.

Intended only to allow a Gatherer opportunity to rescue a soul before the body was lost to disaster, the time-halt had a very short life: two minutes, no more. It would have to be enough. He dashed across the short stretch of land that separated him from Almaden Lake, tossing his coat, sword, and shoes helter-skelter into the bushes that lined the shore. Without pause, he dove in.

Ice formed in his veins even before he hit the algae-clouded water; the last thing he saw before he plunged in was the tail end of the yellow bus sticking out of the water, its journey to the depths of the lake momentarily suspended.

Humans died every day, a painful reality he'd finally learned to cease resisting. Death visited everyone, placing her glowing white spiral upon cheek after cheek, caring not one whit for the importance of human lives or the fate of those left behind. No one escaped her ruthless mark.

But the teens aboard the school bus wore no such mark. They were not slated to die this day. Satan, not Death, had rolled the dice today, entwining their fates with that of Emily Lewis.

Emily.

Lachlan plowed through the water, his route straight and sure. But the battle with the demons had taken a huge toll. His wretched immortal body kept stealing his energy, redirecting it into the healing process and away from the steady cleaves of his arms through the water. He was still thirty feet from his target, his muscles numb and sapped, when the bus resumed its perilous drive to the bottom.

The water churned and roiled. Terrified screams rent the air. One courageous student flung open the rear door and panicked teens scrambled out, falling atop one another in their hysterical haste to reach safety.

Lachlan summoned a last flurry of desperate strokes,

took a deep breath, and dove deep. The children most at
risk were at the front, not the back.

Through the murky water, the bright yellow paint
acted as a beacon, and he found the windows with little effort. Inside, the water level was rising quickly. Six
teens struggled to keep their heads above the bubbling,
seething water, while two others hovered beneath the
surface, unable to breach the kicking and flailing of their
bus mates.

No sign of Emily.

He latched onto a partially open window and yanked.
Nothing happened. The bus continued to slowly roll down
the lake wall, the tail end about to submerge, and panic
gnawed at him. He gripped the window with stiff fingers and slammed a knee into the glass, breaking it. The
safety glass crumbled, water sluiced in, and he squeezed
through the hole. In the moiling water, he searched for
Emily, diving between the seats at the front of the bus.
But she was nowhere to be found. Time was running
out. He grabbed the shirts of the two submerged teens,
whose struggles were weakening, and kicked up toward
the rear exit.

Then, out of the corner of his eye, he saw her: a crumpled heap of black clothes and blond hair streaked with
black highlights ... floating between two bench seats
closer to the back of the bus. Eyes closed, face slack.

Lachlan's fingers clenched around the boys' clothing.

With a heavy metallic groan, the last few inches of the
bus finally sank below the surface, and a powerful gush
of water poured in through the open exit door, thrusting
him and the two thrashing teens down toward the bottom. Limp and unconscious, Emily tumbled along with
them.

The faces of his two panicky teens were turning purple, but Lachlan had no choice. He had to rescue Emily,

and only one solution came to mind. He pressed his lips to each of the boys and blew into their mouths, sacrificing what little oxygen remained in his lungs.

After all, what does an immortal man need with air?

Squeezed by the absence, his chest ached and strained. His heart pounded in protest. Despite his every effort not to give in, primitive impulse took control. His mouth opened and he sucked in the green-brown water of Almaden Lake. Pain tore at his throat, seared the lining of his lungs, and ripped at his guts as he drowned.

Except he couldn't die.

All he could do was absorb the insufferable pain. Weather it, survive it. And keep going.

Blinking hard to clear his vision, Lachlan reached down, grabbed Emily's black leather vest, and then kicked toward the exit door. He pushed two other trapped teens out before him, thrusting them toward the ever-dimming surface. Then he wriggled his unwieldy group through the aperture, and from there, shot toward the surface.

It took an eternity. A burning, agonizing eternity.

His legs were jelly, his arms so heavy that they only awkwardly did his bidding. When the surface neared, bright and shining, he gave one last push, forcing the children's heads above the water. They choked and gasped, and he kicked until they reached the shore. Someone—he couldn't say who—freed the teens from his tightly curled fingers and began resuscitation efforts on Emily.

Lying half in and half out of the lake, Lachlan coughed up several cupfuls of brackish water. It should have been a blessing to breathe again; instead, he relived the agony of drowning as air slowly replaced the liquid in every miserable bronchiole.

Emily. He had to see to Emily.

Throat raw, droplets of water choking his lungs, he dragged his heavy body out of the water and over to her still figure.

"Is she . . . ?" he asked the Good Samaritan who was draping his shirt over her.

"Breathing," the man responded, nodding. He tucked the cotton cloth around her shoulders. "Close call, though."

Lachlan flopped on his back in the grass, unable to stand. He covered his face with his arm and worked to steady the staccato beat of his heart. The how and why of this insanity needed sorting out, but not this second.

Right now, he just wanted to rest and forget.

But it was not to be. Rescuers splashed about in the water nearby, searching, and sirens shrieked all around him as police and emergency vehicles descended on the scene. Voices called out, some calm, some not. Against the background clamor, the scuff of one set of footsteps gained amplitude.

"Excuse me, Father," said a tentative female voice to his left. "Did you . . . ? Was there anyone left on the . . . ?"

Lachlan called up the last image he had of the bus before he swam for the surface: the blobs of algae, the sea of gritty silt, the fine, lacy edge of a pink sweater.

He sighed, heavy with regret. "The driver. I'm sorry, I couldn't reach her."

A light breeze swept across Almaden Lake, rippling the surface of the water and ruffling Drusus's hair. He smiled at the flashing lights on the opposite shore. His hunch about the girl had proven correct. MacGregor was indeed protecting her, which would please his liege to no end. A soldier of Death assigned to preserve a human life could only mean—

"Detective Roberts?"

Drusus spun around to face the crime scene investigator: an eager young pup who hadn't a clue that he was speaking to a glamoured demon rather than a paunchy, middle-aged cop. A paunchy, despondent cop who, a mere forty minutes ago, had put the barrel of his service revolver in his mouth and pulled the trigger. With a little help, of course.

"Yes?"

"Coroner's ready to take the body to the morgue. Wanna speak with him before he heads out?"

"Did he set a TOD?"

"Around six a.m."

Drusus nodded. Not a bad guess. He'd choked the life out of the jogger's pretty green eyes at 6:07. It had been a thoroughly enjoyable experience—almost as enjoyable as seeing the look on MacGregor's face when he spotted her body. The weeks spent searching for the right shade of red hair had definitely paid off. "Then don't hold him up. I've got enough to go on for now."

The investigator glanced at the bushes hugging the water's edge. "Find anything useful?"

"No, I'm afraid not. You?"

"Coupla shoe prints—that's about it."

"Maybe you'll find something on the body," Drusus said, hiding a smile. Wouldn't matter. He'd been wearing the guise of a local homeless man at the time. Any evidence would lead the police to a bewildered derelict who would pointlessly protest his innocence.

"We can hope, right?"

The young CSI walked away, and Drusus allowed his gaze to fall to the sword and coat lost beneath the arching branches of coyote brush. They lay twenty feet beyond the official crime scene and hadn't been noted. As much as he wanted to cause MacGregor grief, the items would provide no viable fingerprints or DNA to the police, so there was no point in disturbing them.

Besides, there'd be no satisfaction in defeating the immortal warrior if the wretch could claim he'd been less than fully armed. No, this time MacGregor would not escape a proper end. This time he would die the way history had intended—hard.

Crossing the apartment building's lobby to the elevators, Rachel glanced at her daughter's heart-shaped face and flashed back to the image of the waterlogged school bus being pulled from the depths of the lake. She squeezed Em's hand. It could all have ended so differently. It could have been Em the paramedics laid on a gurney and zipped into a body bag instead of that poor bus driver.

"I'm fine." Em shook off Rachel's hold. "Why are we taking the elevator? It's only one floor."

"Because you're in shock."

"Gimme a break."

"You almost died."

"Exaggerate much?" She sighed dramatically. "Come on, Mom. The elevator's too slow, and I'm soaking wet. Can we please just take the stairs?"

"Fine."

Annoyed by how easily guilt chewed into her, Rachel tugged Em to the stairwell. She flung open the steel door and promptly rammed into a warm, solid barrier. A man wearing a dark suit bent over. If she hadn't steadied herself with a hand on his backside, she might have flipped right over the fellow.

"Oh! I'm so sorry."

He straightened. "My fault. I dropped my cell phone."

Rachel blinked. Black suit, plus white collar, equaled . . . *priest*. She snatched her hand away. Not just any priest, but the very one the emergency workers had pointed to as her daughter's saintly rescuer.

Those two facts alone should have placed him in the untouchable category, but her flustered hormones didn't seem to care. As she eyed all six-feet-plus of his muscular frame, her heartbeat skittered. Honestly, if more clergymen looked like this, the churches would be full.

He held her gaze for a brief moment—a strangely palpable moment—then shifted his attention to Emily, who slouched indifferently at her side, black streaks of mascara and eyeliner running down her face. "You okay?"

Em shrugged.

"Yes, she is," Rachel jumped in, embarrassed by her daughter's attitude-laden response. "Of course she is. Thanks to you. I wanted to come over and say something at the accident scene, but the police and the press had you cornered."

Was it a sin to think a priest was a hunk? That classically handsome face, blunted by just a dash of weary experience, made her breath hitch. Even with his black suit wrinkled and stained, and his short brown hair a spiky mess, he looked absolutely amazing.

His gaze came back to her. Blue-gray eyes, steady and very perceptive. "Glad I was there."

Heat rushed into her cheeks. Hugging a stiff-shouldered Em, she said weakly, "Yes. We are, too."

She ought to say more, but what? How do you really thank someone for saving your daughter's life? Words just didn't seem enough, so she settled on an introduction.

"I'm Rachel Lewis, and this is Emily."

He stared at her extended hand for a moment, then took it in his. "Lachlan MacGregor."

The warmth of his lean, square-tipped fingers sent

an unexpected tingle up her arm, and Rachel had to focus to produce a level voice. "Are you Scottish, Father MacGregor?" When he didn't answer right away, she added, "I mean, your name and that slight accent, I just assumed . . ."

"I haven't lived there for many years, but aye, I'm originally from Glen Lyon." He dropped her hand.

There was an awkward pause as Rachel debated what to say next. Tell him they were originally from Connecticut? Admit that they didn't go to church? Invite him to dinner? No, she couldn't invite him to dinner. What the hell could she possibly say to a priest for an hour?

"I've always wanted to visit Scotland," she said lamely.

A faint glimmer of something shone in his eyes. Amusement? "It's a fine country, well worth the trip. Especially in late August when the heather blooms."

His gaze drifted to Em, who stood staring at the floor with her arms folded tight to her chest. Maybe he saw her shiver, because he waved a hand at the stairs. "I believe we could all use a hot shower right about now. After you, Mrs. Lewis."

Mrs. Lewis. Ugh. Even when she and Grant had been starry-eyed newlyweds, she'd hated being called that.

"Rachel, please. I'm divorced." She flushed, suddenly recalling that most religions tended to frown upon divorce. "Em's father and I married too young—"

"No need to explain."

His smile was gentle, and her embarrassment receded. At least, it did until she realized her admission to being divorced might be interpreted as a come-on. Biting her lip, she hustled Em up the wide, tiled stairs. Having lascivious thoughts about a priest might not be a sin, but coming on to one . . . ?

No doubt about it. She was going to hell.

* * *

Lachlan stared at Rachel's arse. To be fair, it was damned hard not to, climbing the stairs immediately behind her. As sweetly rounded as it was, he'd have to be a saint not to have noticed. And he was definitely not a saint.

Rachel.

To this point she'd only been Emily Lewis's mother, but now that he knew her name, it seemed as if he'd always known it. It suited her—old-fashioned, yet earthy and sensual. A biblical name went well with the long waves of mahogany hair and fine, creamy skin. Maybe less of a match with the bedroom eyes and full lips, but he wasn't complaining.

She and Emily paused at the door to the second floor and turned. "Thanks again, Father MacGregor." Her gaze was warm and genuine. "Really."

"You're welcome."

Then the door swung shut, and they vanished.

Lachlan climbed the remaining steps to the second-floor landing and wrapped his palm around the steel doorknob. Faint traces of her warmth still lingered in the metal and her floral perfume hung in the air.

He breathed deep.

Amazing. Every inch of him hummed with awareness, just as it had the first time he spied her by the pool, chatting with one of the older tenants. His eyes had been drawn to her by something he couldn't name, a slightly brighter aura, perhaps. And then she'd smiled—not at him, at her companion—and her face lit up, sparkling with humor. In a blink, that fresh, unbounded grin reached through the layers of his grief and stirred him to life, like rain to the parched desert of his soul.

Lachlan released the knob.

But his focus should be on Emily, not Rachel.

The bus crash was no accident. The driver had purposely rammed the barrier, intending to take herself and her busload of students to a watery grave. Murder-suicides were almost always the result of a demonic lure, but the timing of this one was suspect. Was it a coincidence that he'd been so close to the crash site? Or that Emily had been on that particular bus?

Lachlan turned and continued up the stairs.

Un-bloody-likely. Unlocking his third-floor apartment, he entered the cool sanctuary of his private quarters. Claret walls and black trim abounded, even in the kitchen to his right. Only the rich caramel of the hardwood flooring relieved the somber color scheme. His shoulders eased as he descended the steps into the furniture-barren living room and surrounded himself with the medieval weapons scattered about the room.

Home.

An angel would arrive soon enough to collect the soul he'd gathered, but for now he was alone. Lachlan shrugged out of his frock coat and tossed it over the windowsill. Thanks to the more newsworthy bus accident, the investigation into the redhead's death had been contained. When he'd returned to the bridge to collect his belongings, his sword had still been lying in the bushes, waiting patiently for its owner. A lucky break.

He unsheathed the weapon and returned it to its place of honor, a velvet-backed display above the fireplace. Then, grabbing a Stone Pale Ale from the fridge, he made his way out to the small, sunny balcony that overlooked the garden courtyard . . . and Rachel Lewis's apartment.

Her balcony hung directly below his, and if he leaned over, fragments of her life were visible, teasing him. Every apartment in the complex had a balcony, but Rachel's was unique.

Flower boxes hung off all three whitewashed sides,

spilling over with a profusion of colorful blooms and leafy green ivy. Inside the six-by-twelve-foot space sat a red wooden deck chair, a small table, several potted bushes, and a fishpond. The pond lay beyond his view, but the soft trickle of a fountain and the occasional ripples of swimming fish conjured up a vivid image.

A retreat. One she often sought after a long day.

He didn't expect to see her there now, not given the disturbing events of the morning, but he could imagine her, and he did. Reclining in her chair with a book in hand . . . her long bare legs extended, the dark waves of her curly hair spilling over her shoulders.

Lachlan poured cold beer down his throat, wishing it were something more potent. Hadn't he stopped doing this? Hadn't he decided three months ago that spying on her was pointless, that he was behaving little better than a crazed stalker? He had. And giving up the fantasy had been relatively painless—then.

But everything was different now.

A simple handshake had upended his world. As his palm lay against hers, as their hearts beat in tandem and their heat mingled, a sense of completion had stolen over him. It was as if his body recognized hers. A crazy notion, perhaps, yet the effect was indisputable. The need to hold her in his arms, to feel every inch of her against him, had escalated to a visceral ache. He craved to be welcomed into her embrace; to experience the closeness, family, and normalcy she offered; to feel eager and hopeful again.

But he'd forfeited all that. He had no right to ask for a moment in Rachel's arms. He had ninety-one years of penance left to serve, and then he'd meet his fate— probably in hell.

Lachlan pivoted and reentered his apartment. Almost blindly, he found his way to the small bedroom that housed his sofa and TV. He sank onto the leather sofa, leaned his head back, and squeezed his eyes shut. The shades were drawn and in the dimness he could almost pretend he didn't hear the screams anymore. Not the screams of teenagers trapped on a bus, although there was an echo of that, too. No, the screams that haunted him were the pleading cries of his family. The shrill notes of horror, the terrified wails, and the strangled sound of his name upon their lips as they were brutally murdered by the raiders who had entered his keep by the secret water gate.

The very gate he'd told them about.

2

The summons came at noon the next day.

When the first gloomy notes of the bell tolled through the apartment, Lachlan instinctively stiffened. But he shook off the tension and calmly ate the bacon and tomato sandwich on whole wheat he'd prepared. Then he rinsed his plate in the sink and dried his hands on a kitchen towel. Only when he was confident he'd pushed his luck to the absolute brink did he close his eyes and allow the summons to transport him to Death's cathedral-like abode in the ice caves of Antarctica.

His breath frosted as he opened his eyes and slowly took his bearings: vaulted ceilings, a thousand tea lights recessed into the ice, watery-blue walls gilded by the gold of flickering flames, and a soft gray mist that hugged the floors. Eerily beautiful.

Just like Death herself.

She sat regally on her high-backed onyx chair, draped in a sleeveless black satin gown, her long white hair piled in artful curls upon her head. Her blue eyes were fiercely alert, her pale skin smooth, and her age impossible to determine.

"You try my patience, Gatherer."

Lachlan offered his liege a scant bow, then strode up the scarlet carpet, halting mere feet from her exalted person. Not one of her six cadaverous bodyguards proved witless enough to block his path. "I do no' answer to the jangle of bells."

"Of course you do. Whether you choose to acknowledge it or not, MacGregor, your soul belongs to me."

"I gave you my allegiance," he agreed. "But I died a laird, no' a gillie. I serve no one."

Death rose, the inky fabric of her gown pooling in a shining puddle at her feet. Her face reflected a pristine emptiness. "Your attitude is dangerously bold of late. Are you hoping that in my anger I'll slay you and end your term prematurely?"

Lachlan said nothing.

"Foolish man. If anything, my wrath would see me extend your term another five hundred years. You are unsurpassed in your extermination of demons, and the angels constantly praise your respectful collection of souls. I've nothing to gain by releasing you early"—she descended the three steps to the mist-shrouded floor and swept by him in a cloud of cool, crystalline scent—"even when the temptation to smite you is strong. You violated the Gatherer code, halting time for a living soul."

He pivoted, keeping her in view. "Did you no' ask me to keep her safe?"

"I did, and despite your illicit effort, you very nearly failed me." Scooping a handful of dried fruit from the dinghy-sized silver bowl on the ebony sideboard, she picked through it with the elongated white fingernail of her right index finger—the same finger with which she marked her chosen.

"I can't be in two places at once." He watched a piece of pear disappear between her bloodred lips. "If you wish me to play the nursemaid, release me from my gathering duties."

"Impossible."

"Then prepare for further disappointment."

She pinned him with her icy gaze. "Do not caution me. You can do more than you are currently doing, and I demand your all. Get closer to the family. Every moment you are not gathering should be spent watching her."

"Why?"

Her eyes narrowed. "You do not need to know why. Just keep her out of Satan's hands and inform me of any unusual events."

"Is Satan aware of her importance?"

"Did I say she was important?"

Resisting the urge to snort, he said, "Dragging your finest warrior halfway around the world to babysit says enough."

"Finest? Ha! A few months ago, I'd have happily accorded you that distinction, but no longer. You've lost your ruthless edge, MacGregor. You're making me regret my investment in you."

An ineffective red herring. For more than four hundred years, he'd buried himself in cold, single-minded purpose, honing his skills without pause and shunning the world to focus on his duties. He let nothing stand in the way of his gathering, and that dedication had lifted him to the pinnacle of the Gatherer world. His reawakening at Rachel's hands changed nothing . . . except the pain.

"I find it curious," he said, "the lengths to which Death is willing to go to keep a single human child alive."

"Curiosity is not a virtue in a Gatherer."

The muscles in his sword arm twitched at the heavy note of disdain in her voice. "If I understood her value, I would know better how to protect her."

"Ridiculous. It is simply a matter of slaying demons, a task you already perform with great proficiency."

"Slaying demons is no longer a simple task, even for a seasoned warrior. The rifts are allowing Satan's henchmen to break through to the middle plane with increasing regularity. The flimsy portfolio of tools you provide leaves the Gatherers disadvantaged. We're losing."

"Indeed." Death fingered the ruby necklace at her throat. "A shame. I've lost some talented minions."

The term *minion* did not sit well, nor did her casual acceptance of his brethren's slaughter, but Lachlan held on to his temper. "Then strike back."

"Why? The rifts are temporary. They will pass."

"So you've repeatedly said. But you won't say what's causing them, and despite your assurances, the situation continues to worsen—Gatherers continue to perish."

Death met his gaze for a moment, then shrugged.

Goaded, he snarled, "For God's sake, woman, take charge. Equip your warriors to better battle the demons, or approach the Lord and insist that Satan be reined in."

His outburst failed to rattle her. "There's nothing to be gained by bending God's ear. Chaos on the middle plane works for all of us."

"It doesn't work for the Gatherers."

Adjusting the gauzy black shawl that hung over her thin shoulders, she smiled. "No, I suppose not. But I've neither the time nor the inclination to better equip them."

"Then reach out to the Romany Council. Use the mages in an organized fashion."

"I think not. Insidious troublemakers, the Roma. Every Gatherer who partners with one eventually becomes unmanageable."

It was a sly dig, best ignored. "Their magic is all that stands between me and failure."

"Nonsense."

"The mages are extremely valuable," he said. "Those of us who've happened upon the Council count ourselves blessed. But working alone, with no formal communication system in place, most Gatherers are unaware of their existence. You can remedy that. Easily. Give me access to the Gatherer database and allow me to train them."

"Absolutely not. I cannot have you distracted from your mission." She waved a hand over the flat ice wall before her. Tendrils of fog crept up the wall from the floor and swirled, morphing into a kaleidoscope of brilliant colors. A huge map of the world formed out of the psychedelic haze, populated with clusters of tiny black dots. "Training is a waste of time when Gatherers are so easily replaced. These days, most humans live selfish lives, happy to dance the fine line between good and evil to get what they want. There are plenty in purgatory to choose from."

She tossed him a wry look. "And there are always a few who actually *beg* for the chance to serve me."

Lachlan stiffened.

"Now, away with you, MacGregor. I've work to do. And remember, every moment you are not gathering ..."

It was probably too simple to blame the bus accident.

Rachel sat on Emily's rumpled bed, gnawing the nail of her left index finger down to the quick as her daughter crawled in through the window. But ever since the crash, her life had become a nightmare.

She waited until Em had pulled her heavy-soled combat boots over the sill and straightened her black mini-skirt before she spoke from the shadows.

"I'm thinking, grounded for a year."

Her daughter jerked, bumping her elbow against the

sturdy, particleboard desk and knocking a pile of papers to the floor. The shock of being discovered didn't last long. Em's shoulders quickly resumed their defiant, don't-give-a-damn slouch. "For what? Walking in the dark?"

"Going out after curfew."

"Curfew's bullshit. I wasn't doing anything."

"You're fourteen, Emily. Way too young to be out wandering the streets at one in the morning." Rachel stared at the budding woman before her. Not very long ago, her daughter's favorite color had been baby blue; now she wore thick black eyeliner, gobs of mascara, and a silver spider screw in her nose. Once, they'd talked for hours about every subject under the sun. Now, conversations were as rare as ten-carat diamonds. She no longer knew her own daughter. "It's not safe."

"Nothing happened, did it?"

"That's not the point. Something *could* have happened. Accidents are never really accidents. They're mistakes. They happen when you don't think things through."

"What was there to think about? It was a walk."

"Oh, for God's sake, Em. It's the middle of the night."

"Whatever." Em shrugged. "The grounding thing's lame, anyway. You're never home."

The jab struck deep. Rachel typically woke up at seven, dressed, made the lunches, and prodded her daughter out the door in time to catch the school bus. Then she drove to work for nine and didn't get home most nights until after six. Em was on her own at least three hours every day. "I'll get Mrs. Mendelson to sit with you."

A snort. "Yeah, right. That old bat's a hundred. If I decide to ditch her, there's no way she could stop me."

"You're not just going for walks."

Em's head cocked. "Yeah?"

"Yeah." Rachel tossed the hardcovered book in her hand to the floor at Em's feet. It slid to a stop among the empty gum wrappers and discarded clothing. "I read your diary. You're meeting some boy who owns a motorcycle."

Em stiffened. "You read my *diary*?"

"Yes, I did."

"Hullo? What planet are you from? Diaries are *private*."

"I wouldn't normally intrude," admitted Rachel, flushing in the darkness, "but you've given me no choice. Ever since the bus accident you've been acting weird. Not answering your cell phone when I call from work, drawing bizarre images, and now going out after curfew. I didn't know what to think."

"Ever think to ask?"

Rachel shot to her feet. "*Ask?* Believe me, Em, I've tried. But every time I start a conversation, all I get are mumbles, shrugs, and eye rolls. You haven't been making this very easy."

Em bent to untie her boots. "You don't give a shit about my opinion."

"That's not true. I always—"

"Sure, whatever." She kicked her boots into the corner and dug through the pile of clothes on the floor until she produced a pair of black silk boxers and an oversized black T-shirt emblazoned with a white skull. "I'm tired. I'm going to bed."

"No. Don't shut me out, Em. I want to understand; I really do. Just tell me why you're doing all this, why you're going out in the middle of the night, why you're seeing this guy."

Her daughter straightened. "You don't get it."

"Don't get what?"

"Me, my life, anything."

"Then explain it to me." Rachel put a hand on Emily's arm. She remembered the days when a much younger Em would rush home and blurt out everything that had happened to her at school. "Please."

Em shrugged off her touch. "Nice try, but five minutes once a month doesn't count as mothering."

A spark of anger flashed in Rachel's chest, but she snuffed it. Her work had been very demanding lately and maybe she deserved that. "We could spend time together on the weekend, like we used to. See a movie, go shopping. Whatever you want."

"I've already got plans to hang with Sheila."

"If you want me to understand you, you need to let me in, Em. Cut me a little slack. I'm trying."

Her daughter tugged the baggy T-shirt over her head, then threw herself on the bed. "Try all you want."

"What's that supposed to mean?"

"Nothing."

"Nothing? I hardly think—"

"Jeez, enough with the lectures already. Leave me alone."

This time the fire couldn't be contained. "You want alone? Fine. Forget going to a movie. Forget going anywhere with Sheila. You're grounded for two weeks. And since you've convinced me you need a jailer, Mr. Wyatt next door will be sitting on your ass the whole time."

"Nice." Em's voice dripped with sarcasm.

Goaded, Rachel threw in a parting shot. "Oh, and I'll be calling the police to report this boyfriend of yours, too. Until you're eighteen, messing with you is called statutory rape."

Emily stilled. All hint of teenage softness disappeared

from her face, leaving behind an unrecognizable, malevolent stranger.

"I hate you," she said.

Regret clawed at Rachel's gut. "Em, I—"

"Get out."

"Really, I'm so—"

"Close the door on your way out."

Rachel held Em's gaze for a moment, uncertain. Ending the conversation on such a sour note made her stomach heave. But there was no room for maneuvering in those frigid blue eyes, no hope of breaking through to make amends.

"I love you," she offered helplessly.

To the same cold stare.

Rachel stepped back, chest aching. She slowly pulled the door shut, acknowledging her defeat.

Lachlan's sword hit the brass-studded targe with a loud *whomp*, sending a heavy shudder down his adversary's arm. He followed up with two more fierce strikes before his dark-haired foe stumbled.

"Christ! Enough already," Brian groaned. "My arm is falling off."

Lachlan dropped his weapon to his side and pitched his barely sweating opponent a look of disgust. "How the blazes do you survive, Webster? Any half-formed demon could kick your arse."

"When the going gets tough, I do what any sane Gatherer would do." Brian eased his arm out of the targe's straps and gingerly flexed his bicep. "Use a speed primal and get the hell out of Dodge."

"Running won't save you if you're surrounded." Lachlan wiped his practice sword with an oiled cloth and leaned it up against the stone fireplace. "This would be much easier had you begun training when you were a lad."

"Yeah, well, I was too busy skateboarding and blowing my eardrums out with Pearl Jam, so that wasn't an option."

"Your combat skills need a lot of work."

Brian deposited his sword and shield on the floor. Looking more like a walking sportswear advertisement than an immortal warrior, he used his arm to wipe the faint sheen off his brow and gave Lachlan a rueful smile. "All those years of corporate backstabbing and deep-sixing the competition don't count, huh?"

"No."

"But I'm young and I'm agile. You told me that when we started. And last week, you said I'd come a long way in five weeks. So why the long face?"

"Because you know just enough to get yourself killed."

"Hey," the former stockbroker protested, "I thought you said I had good instincts."

"You need more than good instincts. You need skill." Lachlan rubbed his shirt front to halt the trickles running down his chest. "And you need more bloody endurance. You should be training every spare minute."

"No way. Unlike you, MacGregor, I have a life."

"Read the cards, Webster. Things have changed."

"Yeah, yeah, I know. A year ago, the chances of being ambushed were one in fifty and now it's more like fifty-fifty. But I'm already doing my bit. I work out with you three times a week. That's more than most Gatherers can say."

"Three hours a week is not enough."

"Why not? I'm learning from the best." Brian smiled. "Word on the Gatherer grapevine is that you once single-handedly took down a pair of martial demons."

"Don't believe everything you hear."

"Oh, come on. You were ambushed by elite soldier

henchies from the inner rings of hell and lived to tell the tale. I know it's true; admit it. With you as my coach, there's no question I'll eventually own some demon ass."

Shaking his head at the young man's bravado, Lachlan strode into the kitchen.

"So …," Brian said, following him. "Given any thought to my idea?"

"No." He grabbed two bottles of water out of the fridge and tossed one to the other man.

"Why not?" Brian popped the cap on his water and downed half the bottle in a single, long swallow. "I know at least a dozen Gatherers who'd be here at the drop of a hat if you agreed to train them."

"I don't run a school."

"You trained me."

"A momentary lapse in judgment. I felt sorry for you."

"And you don't feel anything for the other Gatherers, stuck with the crappy shield primal the boss provides?"

"No."

"Bullshit, MacGregor. I've seen you giving freebie advice on the street. I know you don't want to see the rest of them get creamed. What's holding—" Brian broke off as a knock sounded on the apartment door. Arching a brow, he asked, "Expecting someone?"

"No."

There was a pause, then another sharp rap.

"Aren't you going to answer that?" the younger man prodded.

"No."

"Why not?"

"Because I'm no' expecting anyone."

With the finesse of a basketball player, Brian lobbed his water bottle into the sink, then strode toward the

door. "Yeah, but you never know, it could be some su-
perhot babe who wants to jump your bones. . . ."

"Webster," Lachlan warned.

Brian obligingly halted, but only long enough to
glance through the peephole. Then he grinned, tugged on
the doorknob, and swung open the solid wood portal.

Lachlan's breath snagged.

It was Rachel, looking limp and weary from a long
day at the office, but still as lovely as ever in a softly
flowing purple top and beige slacks. Her gaze flicked
between him and Brian. "Uh, if this is a bad time, I can
come back."

"Nope, come on in," offered Brian generously, waving
her inside. Over the top of Rachel's head, he mouthed,
See? Hot babe. "I was just leaving."

Rachel's eyes remained hesitant. They darted from
Lachlan's face to his sweat-dampened gray T-shirt, and
back up. "Are you sure?"

No, he wasn't the least bit sure. Having her in his
apartment—seeing her gaze linger on the breadth of his
chest—did uncomfortable things to his pulse, but turning her away was bloody well impossible.

"Aye," he reassured her. "My friend Brian was indeed
on his way out."

The other man returned his stare. Hard. "I'll be back
later, when you've had time to think on my proposal."

Lachlan didn't respond. The succinct comeback on
the tip of his tongue wasn't fit for polite company.

The door thudded closed, and Rachel advanced into
the apartment, looking around. "This is the first time
I've ever been in one of the three-bedroom suites. Very
nice."

Ridiculous. Just the word *bedroom* spilling from her
lips sent a wave of heat crashing over him. "Can I offer
you a drink? Water, juice, tea?"

Her eyes brightened. "Tea would be terrific."

He filled the kettle and put it on the stove. "How is Emily doing? Recovered fully from the accident?"

"Funny you should ask," Rachel responded dryly. "She's why I'm here." Then she flushed a charming shade of rosy pink. "Probably inappropriate of me, but I asked around to find out which apartment was yours. I hope you don't mind."

"No' at all."

Mind didn't begin to describe the turmoil in his gut. He wanted to be pleased that she'd sought him out, but a host of old memories rose up right along with his male pride. Memories of what it felt like to have a woman desire him, to win her love, to have his heart ripped out when she died—which all living things eventually did. He took two cups and a teapot out of the cupboard.

"What's the problem?"

"It's kind of hard to explain." She wandered over to the stone fireplace, eyeing his sword with curiosity. "You've got quite the collection of medieval weapons. Are they real?"

"No, they're replicas. The real thing would be worth an arm and a leg in today's market." And he certainly wouldn't keep treasures like that in this poorly secured apartment. In a specially sealed vault at the bank, perhaps, but not here.

Her gaze drifted over the furnitureless room. "There are other priorities for your funds, I guess."

The temptation to dispute his lack of wealth was powerful, but Lachlan kept his mouth shut. An explanation would almost assuredly involve showing her his well-appointed den down the hall, which was too close to his king-sized bed for comfort.

The kettle whistled, and he poured boiling water over

the tea bags. "Tell me about Emily," he encouraged. A nice, safe topic.

Rachel crossed the room and climbed onto one of the stools at the breakfast island. As she leaned over the granite countertop, the silky material of her blouse stretched tight across her breasts.

Lachlan abruptly turned away.

She sighed, then confessed, "I don't know what's got into her."

As he fetched the milk and sugar, she explained her daughter's wayward behavior and challenging attitude. Weariness tugged at her mouth and created tiny furrows between her brows—a sight he responded to by handing her several sugar-dusted shortbread cookies, which she ate absently, between words.

When she got to the part about Em's late-night jaunt, he winced. Just his luck. The night before last, while he was out on a gather.

"I've been to the police," Rachel added. "They say there's nothing they can do unless they catch her out after curfew. If she's not doing something illegal, it's pretty much up to me to keep her and this boy apart. . . ."

"And you have to work." He shared Rachel's frustration. His haphazard tracking of Emily between gathers hadn't turned up any sign of this new beau. Clearly, he'd have to start following her home from school.

"Exactly," she agreed, offering him a faint smile.

She had a dimple, just one, on the left side of her mouth. Lachlan couldn't keep his eyes off it. He'd never wanted to do anything as badly as he wanted to kiss that dimple. He handed her a mug of tea. "What is it you'd like me to do?"

"Talk to her."

"About what?"

"Death. She's always been a bit curious about it, but

ever since the accident, she seems *obsessed*. It's as if her near-death experience opened a door to some mysterious new world." She bent and retrieved some papers from her purse. "These are the symbols she used to draw."

She showed him a circle inset with a six-pointed star, an ankh, the eye of Horus, an upside-down crucifix.

"Nothing too shocking," he said. "Goths love symbolism. It doesn't mean anything sinister."

"I know. Em's been Goth for almost a year, and after I did a little research into the culture, I let this stuff slide, figuring it was just her way of developing her own identity." She tugged another piece of paper from the bottom of the pile. "But in the past week, her drawings have gotten a lot darker."

The paper bled with black ink. Edge to edge, it was filled with a series of gruesome images: dripping knives, dead bodies, writhing snakes, trios of sixes, and short, heavily outlined phrases such as "Death is Bliss" and "The End."

"These seem less like a discovery of personality than a trip into hell." Rachel glanced at him, seeking confirmation. "I'm not crazy. Some of these images *are* satanic, right?"

Lachlan's heart pumped heavily. The paleness of her face urged him to hug her, hold her, soothe away her fears. But despite Death's encouragement to get closer, he rebelled at the notion of reaching out to Rachel, of comforting her. He knew without ever having wrapped his arms around her that she would fit into his embrace like no other woman had ever done, and that terrified him. His interest in her was too visceral. Once he crossed the invisible line he'd drawn between them, stopping at a hug might not be possible. "She's a very talented artist."

"Runs in the family, I guess."

He peered at her.

"I'm a graphic designer. I work for a software company here in town."

"Ah." An artist. That explained the haven she'd cultivated from a sterile concrete balcony. Artists saw things in terms of potential—what they could be, not what they were. He picked up the paper and pretended to study it. "The imagery does seem disturbing. Perhaps you should consult a mental health professional."

"Yeah, I'm trying to get her to see a shrink, but so far, she's been very resistant. I was hoping—" Her gaze lifted to meet his. "I know she didn't show it, but she's pretty impressed with you. Credits you with saving at least five kids. I think she'd listen to you."

The squeeze of his chest was almost unbearable.

Rachel sighed. "She sure doesn't listen to me."

"Maybe her father . . . ?"

"No. Grant has trouble talking to her for longer than five minutes, and he phones only about once a month. He wouldn't have the foggiest idea what to say."

"I see." Actually, he didn't. He'd never had any trouble talking to his own children, and he would give anything to . . . The paper in his hand rattled, and he quickly set it down. "You want me to tell her that dying isn't all it's cracked up to be, that life is where the good stuff happens."

"Pretty much, yes."

"I may no' be the right person to tell her that."

"Why not?" She took the drawings back, folded the bunch into a tight square, and tucked them into her purse again. "Because you believe in the hereafter?"

"No." The hereafter wasn't the issue. The issue was the *herebefore*, his very ugly past. "Because Goths tend to reject organized religion. Any advice coming from a priest is likely to get discounted just because of the source."

"But I don't think she sees you like—"

"Perhaps no'," he interrupted. "Still, it would be best if you found someone else to speak with her. A friend or a relative."

Rachel's expression stiffened. She stood, hooking her purse over her shoulder. "Okay."

Lachlan stared at her, noting the telltale glimmer in her eyes. *Bloody hell.* This was fast becoming a disaster. One tear, that's all it would take. One tear and he'd be on his knees begging her to let him help, tossing aside every strident warning his battered heart was drumming out.

Please, God, don't let her cry.

Rachel's chin lifted, and she stuck out her hand. Her eyes didn't quite meet his. "Thanks for your time, Father."

Taking her hand in his, he gave it a gentle squeeze. Then he walked her to the door. "Sorry I couldn't be more help."

"Me, too." Head high, she sailed out into the hallway.

He closed the door behind her with a light snap and leaned against it. His legs felt numb and his skin felt itchy and uncomfortable, as if it didn't fit properly. And no wonder. Even a rough Scottish knight with more brawn than brains would have leapt at the opportunity to aid such a beautiful woman in distress.

Apparently, his chivalry had died along with his body.

3

A shadow darted out of the whitewashed apartment building and under the sprawling arch of a jacaranda tree. Lachlan easily tracked the dim figure from the vantage of his third-floor balcony. Victorian gas lamps dotted the flagstone path with soft circles of incandescence, but Emily carefully skirted them, keeping to the darkened edges of the courtyard garden.

A very determined young lass.

Only moments after the light in her mother's bedroom window winked out, here she was, making a daring escape. At two in the morning. This lad she was seeing must be something special indeed.

Dressed in her usual black canvas mini, black stockings, and black, long-sleeved tee, Emily was little more than a murky outline as she navigated the flower beds, passing under one tree and hugging the trunk of another.

Her narrow face tilted up, and he froze.

As her gaze paused on the balcony immediately below him, he wondered what was running through her mind. Second thoughts? A modicum of guilt, perhaps? Whatever it was, it didn't last long. A moment later, after expelling a light sigh, she slunk along the east wall of the building, rounded the corner, and vanished.

Lachlan gripped the wrought-iron balcony railing in anticipation of following her, but a flicker in the corner of his eye halted him: a second shadow, this one taller and not nearly so skilled at stealth. Rachel. He sighed as he watched her elegant silhouette, minimally disguised in black jeans and a sweater, dash through the garden in pursuit of her daughter.

Perfect.

Now he had two people to watch out for, not just one.

After one final check to ensure the coast was clear, he leapt over the railing and landed in an easy half crouch on the manicured grass thirty-five feet below. Jogging to keep up with his targets, he followed them out to the parking lot. There, just as he expected, Emily was hopping onto the back of a motorcycle, behind a leather-clad, helmeted figure.

Thumbing his keyless entry, he unlocked the door of his black Audi S6 and slid onto the charcoal leather seat. At the first turn of the key, the powerful engine purred to life, and his heartbeat surged with it—a primitive thrill his centuries-old body seemed incapable of taming. He glanced in the rearview mirror before he backed up and saw the motorcycle turn right on Coleman Road, followed quickly by a red compact.

So much for his hope that Rachel had forgotten her car keys.

The city streets were nearly empty at this hour, and exhibiting a surprising level of restraint, the red car stayed well back of the motorbike. Lachlan kept Rachel's taillights in view. They turned left at Santa Teresa, sped past the Oakridge Mall, and merged into the Guadalupe Parkway. On the freeway, increased traffic and Rachel's single-minded focus on Emily allowed Lachlan to close the gap between the cars and slide into the lane behind her.

This afforded him a clear view of her vehicle.

If you could call it that.

The rear ornament labeled it a Datsun 210, but years under the hot sun had faded the red paint to a mottled rose, rust had pockmarked the trunk lid to the point that the latch no longer held it shut, and the left-rear tire shimmied. Judging from the persistent growl and occasional burp of the engine, the exhaust system needed a major overhaul. Add to that the faint blue smoke and the smell of burning oil the car exuded as it ate up the miles, and you had the epitome of a clunker.

His hands flexed on the steering wheel.

Hadn't the last Datsun rolled off the production line sometime in the eighties? Where in hell had she found this horrific piece of junk? Just thinking about her driving it to work every day made him cringe.

Up ahead, the bike exited at Curtner Avenue, and Lachlan eased off the gas pedal. Moments later, just beyond the cemetery, Emily and her beau made a right and entered the Santa Clara fairgrounds. The gate hung wide open, not a lock or guard in sight. The deep-throated roar of the motorcycle engine died off not long afterward, hinting at an easy walk.

To his immense relief, Rachel chose not to follow the bike, parking instead in front of the betting house. He snorted as she locked the doors of her rickety antique.

Who would steal the damned thing?

Waiting until she disappeared around the corner, he quickly parked the S6 in the shadows of Gateway Hall and cut between the buildings to reach the garden area. With a protective cluster of trees and several picnic tables, the greenhouse was the most likely tryst spot.

His guess proved accurate.

As he crept through the trees toward the light above the greenhouse door, he spied Emily's slim figure perched on a wooden picnic table. She was surrounded by five men and two women, all attired in black clothing, all painted with the same liberal dose of eyeliner, and all with an open bottle of beer in hand. A few were smoking and, judging by the glazed eyes and bucolic smiles, not just tobacco. Only one of the young men wore a leather jacket—understandable given the warm weather—so pinpointing the motorcycle driver was easy enough.

Lachlan glanced around for Rachel.

She had approached the group from the opposite side of the gardens and stood deep in the gloom of the wooded copse. She hadn't noticed him; her eyes were locked on the defiant group lounging around the picnic table. Alcohol, cigarettes, drugs—a mother's worst imaginings come to life.

The conversation was impossible to discern from his current position, so Lachlan carefully wove through the trees to narrow the gap. The higher-pitched tones of Emily's voice firmed into identifiable sounds soon after.

"School is such a fuckin' drag."

One of the lads mumbled something agreeable in return.

"They make you do the same shit over and over again, like you're not smart enough to figure it out the first time."

Lachlan halted behind a wide, lichen-dotted tree trunk and stole a quick look at the group, just in time to see Emily's beau stiffen. For a heartbeat he thought it was *his* movements that alerted the young man, but the lad's gaze swung in the opposite direction, toward Rachel, snapping precisely to the shadowy niche where she stood.

Fear ripped through Lachlan's veins.

Although his warrior instincts urged him to leap between Rachel and the possibility of danger, he resisted, remaining stationary, his eyes trained on the young man's thin face. His heart pounded. Spotting Rachel's cloaked figure in the pitch-dark woods was beyond a human's visual acuity. He knew that because he could barely see her himself.

Which meant Emily's swain was not the twentysomething human he pretended to be.

He was a demon.

Indeed, though he couldn't place the firm jaw and heavy brows, Lachlan was certain he knew the creature. Which was strange, because few demons he battled ever got the chance to walk away. In fact, during the four hundred nine years he'd been a Gatherer, he could recall only three, and that included his hulking friend of the other day. This fellow was none of them.

But the sense of familiarity deepened when the demon smiled faintly and turned his head to stare directly into Lachlan's eyes.

When the young man's gaze shifted away, Rachel released an uneven sigh of relief. Her slim view of Emily had implied this spot was well hidden and his pointed stare had rocked her. And not just with the fear of discovery. She'd suddenly realized how tenuous her position was, out in a deserted fairground with seven hooligans, five of them men, all drinking.

Maybe it hadn't been the wisest decision to follow Em out here alone. But she was still glad she had.

The question was, what to do next? The angry part of her wanted to stomp over there, grab Em by the ear, and haul her ass back home. The calmer part pointed out that Em had prudently declined their offerings. Still, the girl must be crazy. These were not your average pimply-faced teens. They were delinquents, maybe even felons.

Had every warning she'd given her daughter over the years gone in one ear and out the other?

Her hand tightened around her car keys.

This boy she was dating wasn't even a *boy*. The gauntness of his aristocratic face and the dark stubble on his chin placed him in his twenties. There was also a hard look about him that suggested he knew a helluva lot about the seedier side of life—more than she ever wanted Em to know.

Almost as if her fears had prodded him into action, the young man shifted, leaning toward Em with a smile. As Rachel watched with mounting horror, he slanted his head, threaded his fingers through the long strands of her black and blond hair, and tugged her close for a kiss.

Not a casual kiss.

A *deep* kiss.

And not a kiss Em was expecting, either. Her slender hands fluttered in the air above his shoulders, uncertain about what to do.

Rachel's stomach roiled. A girl's first kiss should be a memory she treasured forever, the sweet, starry-eyed pinnacle of a schoolgirl crush—not some crass mating of mouths. This wretch was taking advantage of her, stealing her innocence.

Hackles up, Rachel stepped around the tree trunk, only to have her path blocked by a very big and very formidable . . . Lachlan MacGregor.

"Don't," he said quietly.

His sudden appearance in the dark should have frightened her. Instead, the sight of his handsome face, etched with obvious resolve, filled her with a feeling of deliverance so intense she was tempted to throw her arms around his neck and kiss him. Of course, she didn't. Despite the ease flooding her chest, she huffed her dis-

agreement and attempted to dodge around him. Someone had to stop that creep from kissing Em.

He blocked her advance. "He knows you're here.
He's just doing it to goad you."

"How do you know that? She's only *fourteen*."

"Trust me."

He took a firm step toward her, forcing her to back up,
but also conveniently occluding her view with his large
body, protecting her from a sight he knew would upset
her. Constrained by darkness, with only a few visual elements to focus on, her senses clung to other things. Such
as his scent, subtle and free of cologne. It was a breath-
taking swirl of warm wool and spice—very sexy . . . and
damned inappropriate for a priest.

"He looked right at you," Lachlan pointed out. "And
it's pretty obvious he's never kissed her before. It's just
a show."

"How can you be sure?"

"I can't," he admitted. He took another step, again
encouraging her to retreat. "But I've learned to trust my
gut."

Rachel dug her heels in, refusing to let him herd her
any farther away from Em. He closed the gap in one
decisive stride, his broad shoulders towering over her,
crowding her. But if his intent was to intimidate, he
failed. Despite his size, she felt no fear. "I can't leave her
here. Not with them."

"I suspect they won't hang about much longer, but
just to be certain, I'll go back and watch them." He
stared into her eyes with an oddly intimate look, as if
they shared more than just a common goal to protect
Emily. It made Rachel's heart pound. "I need you to go
home, Rachel."

"But—"

"You'll want to be home when she gets back."

Or face the consequences of Em finding out she'd followed her out here. Valid point. Still, she squirmed. "If he—"

"If he goes further than a kiss, I'll take care of it." He brushed a lock of hair back from her face, tucking it behind her ear. "I promise."

Before she could point out there were seven of them and only one of him, he was gone.

The alarm went off at precisely 6:55 the next morning.

Rachel whacked the OFF button and rolled onto her back with a low groan. The grit in her eyes felt like gravel. Even after she got home, she'd lain awake, tense and worried, until Em had returned to the apartment. Thankfully, Lachlan had been right about the timing. Em had been right behind her.

Lachlan.

She grimaced in the dark. When had she gone from thinking of him as Father MacGregor to calling him Lachlan? If she wasn't careful, she'd slip up while talking to him, and how embarrassing would *that* be? No matter how attractive he happened to be, you didn't call a priest by his first name unless it was preceded by the title Father.

Married to God, remember? Celibate.

She snorted. It was almost impossible to imagine a guy who looked as hot as Lachlan MacGregor abstaining from sex. How the hell did he manage it?

She squeezed her eyes shut.

None of her damned business, that's how.

She should be mulling over what to say to Em, not dwelling on the sex life of a man who was as off-limits as you could possibly imagine. She needed to sort out whether to play tyrant mom, or to say nothing for now. Should she wait to find out more about last night's escapade, or just bar the windows and lock her daughter in her room?

Rachel pulled a pillow over her head, breathing in the scent of lemon-fresh Tide. Where was the book on parenting that dealt with this stuff? The one that taught you to stay completely calm in the face of heavy doses of attitude and late-night joyrides with beer-swilling, drug-smoking strangers?

Because, honestly, she wasn't sure she could pull off *calm*.

Worry was already burning a hole in her chest, and she had to face Em over a bowl of Cheerios in a few minutes, look her in the eyes, and smile. How the hell was she going to do that when the next words that spilled out of her mouth would probably poison their relationship forever?

As it turned out, she needn't have worried.

Em greeted the morning with glazed eyes and an unusually pale face, sleepwalking through breakfast and the trek out to catch the school bus. Chin drooping, she barely acknowledged Rachel. Exhaustion, combined with the natural self-involvement of teenhood, saved the day.

Rachel's coworkers, lined up like zombies before the coffee machine, weren't much more on the ball. No one commented on the dark circles under her eyes—not even Amanda.

"Keep your head low," Mandy muttered as she grabbed two mugs from the cupboard and handed one to Rachel. "She's in a foul mood."

Rachel nodded absently as she reached for the coffeepot. *She* referred to their boss, the company's creative director, Celia Harper. A difficult taskmaster at the best of times, in a bad mood, she was Satan. The trick to pleasing her was to stay out of her way as much as possible, while miraculously producing the exact imagery she envisioned in her head.

Rachel poured herself a cup and brought the steaming mug to her nose, savoring the rich, nutty aroma. Already anticipating the jolt of energy she'd get from the caffeine, she groaned. "There really is a god, and his name is Coffee."

Mandy grinned. "Better hope he grants you superpowers or a bulletproof vest. We've got Creative Review in five minutes."

Rachel's heart skipped a beat. A quick glance confirmed that Mandy had her leather portfolio tucked under her arm. Today was Thursday. How had she forgotten that?

"Damn," she said.

"That about sums it up," agreed Mandy. "See you in the conference room."

Rachel tore out of the lunchroom and down the hall to her cubicle, oblivious to the trail of coffee slops she left on the dull green carpeting. Her computer was off and she scrambled to boot it up, then waited an eternity for the screen to populate with icons.

It took seven excruciating minutes for the color printer to spit out her designs. The phone rang several times, but she ignored it. When she finally had everything she needed, she scooped up her papers and spun around, almost bowling over the waiflike brunette standing right behind her.

"Rachel, I need—"

"An urgent graphic for the annual report. I know." She pitched an apologetic smile at the assistant to the CFO as she dashed down the hall to the boardroom next to Celia's office. "Call me later. I'm late for a staff meeting."

"It's really important," the girl called after her.

It always was.

The CR was already in progress when she carefully pushed open the door and entered the crowded room. The keeners, who always arrived ten minutes early, had appropriated the chairs. Everyone else leaned against the walls, trying to look small and unremarkable. A vague smell of fear permeated the overheated room.

Celia stood at the front, a sophisticated vision in maroon and gray, her sleek blond hair pulled tightly back. Her gaze pinned Rachel's for a moment, but she didn't pause to comment on her tardiness.

"... at the product readiness meeting," she was saying. "Imagine how good it felt to have the group product manager label every one of your designs as *garbage* ... to hear him complain that the internal design department was completely out of step with Chiat Day's sophisticated and very expensive packaging."

Silence fell as she glared into the faces of her staff, one by one. No one had the courage to doodle, let alone speak.

Rachel could have pointed out that the product packaging had changed twice in the last six weeks, and that Celia had signed off on every piece of creative before it went to the product manager, but she didn't have a death wish. She needed this job. Grant Lewis and child support were words that rarely ended up in the same sentence.

"So listen up," Celia snapped. "I want at least three new graphic sets on my desk by Monday morning. Every splash screen, every sample file, every goddamned icon. The final beta release is in two weeks, and I am *not* going to be the fall guy for a date slip. I don't care if you have to camp out under your desks all weekend. Get it done."

Every head in the room was bowed. Even Nigel's

smooth, café-au-lait pate. As Celia's favorite, he was normally exempt from this sort of castigation. But not today. The lead designer on a project had no choice but to accept a measure of blame. Of course, the instant Celia retreated to her palatial corner office, the shit would run downhill.

"Now," the creative director said, "let's see what you maggots have produced this week."

Nigel eased to his feet, expecting to lead the briefing. But Celia's cool gaze sliced across the room to the people standing near the door.

Rachel held her breath, crossed her fingers, and prayed. Presenting in front of the group always made her nervous. She tended to fidget and talk way too fast, and that was on a good day, when she didn't look like something the cat dragged in.

"Rachel, I'm guessing your late arrival means you have some lavish, slow-printing designs to show us. Why don't you go first?"

Crap.

It took five men, several ropes, and a solid slam of a sword pommel on the head to subdue him, and even then Lachlan continued to struggle. Shrill screams and the clanging sounds of battle echoed throughout the slate-roofed manor house, and in the air the acrid smell of burning wood mingled with the thick, ugly scent of spilled blood.

The spilled blood of his kin.

Tormod Campbell, his most hated enemy, hauled his wife before him by her long, dark red braid, uncaring of the way her feet tripped in the hem of her torn and sullied gown.

Elspeth, brave and true as always, refused to weep as Campbell thrust her to her knees amid the rushes. But

Lachlan knew her sweetly freckled face better than anyone, and he could see fear etched in the tiny lines around her mouth—not fear for herself, but fear for their three wee bairns, dragged from their pallets moments before and taken outside to the bailey.

"Yer soul will rot in hell for this," Elspeth spat at her captor.

Campbell shook her until tears shone in her blue eyes.

Lachlan roared at the abuse and strained against his bonds. "Unhand her. Your grievance is with me, no' her."

His flailing earned him Campbell's bitter regard. "Ya thought to take what was mine, MacGregor, and now ya shall pay the price."

A chill seeped into Lachlan's belly, threatening to consume his vitals. "This has been MacGregor land since MacAlpin was king," he argued. "I took naught that wasna mine."

"Yers?" The Black Campbell sneered his opinion of Lachlan's claim. "The glen was ceded to the Campbells centuries ago. The charter our laird received from the king in March merely inked the truth into history."

"We ceded nothing. The land was stolen."

Campbell's brows collided with the force of his frown. He jerked Elspeth's head up, near lifting her from the floor with the strength of his arm. "I took pity on ya, wretch. I allowed ya to build yer home on the shores of this loch, and in return ya killed my kin. Take whatever pleasure in yer possessions as ye may, MacGregor, for they shall no' pass to any beget of yer flesh."

The chill reached Lachlan's heart.

"Yer sons are dead."

Elspeth cried sharply, her eyes finding Lachlan's, hoping against hope he could dispute Campbell's claim.

But he couldn't.

His enemy raised his right hand, displaying the palm. Every crease and callus on his hand was painted a vivid crimson, and the saffron of his sleeve had a large stain that looked almost black. "Dead by my own hand," he said.

"No," keened Elspeth, her lips suddenly bloodless. She sagged, unmindful of the ruthless hold Campbell had upon her hair.

Her captor shook her again. "Aye, and the lass, too. They cried for their da to save them, but he didn't come."

Lachlan couldn't breathe. The cold was so severe now, he felt as if the sun had been snuffed out. Wee Jamie was still in swaddling. Mop-haired Mairi had wept for her maither as they dragged her away. And Cormac . . . young Cormac had been staunchly brave faced as they hauled him off. Trying to be like his da.

Now they were gone.

The soft, anguished sobs of his wife filtered through his ears, but Lachlan could no longer find the strength to try to reach her. His limbs were frozen, his chest a block of ice. He had failed her—failed all of them.

"Today," continued Campbell, "yer line will end, Mac-Gregor. There shall be no future for you, no hope for yer kin. Even yer brothers have been run through."

The sound of a knife leaving its leather sheath was subtle, but Lachlan recognized it and immediately understood the significance. His eyes flew up to meet Campbell's, and he bucked against his restraints.

"No," he cried hoarsely. "Take me! It's me you want."

But his words had no effect.

Campbell wrenched Elspeth's chin up, exposing her slender neck. Her wide eyes stared at Lachlan, willing him to save her, begging him to do something, anything. And he tried. Dear God, how he tried. But to no avail. The coarse hemp of his restraints bit deeply into his wrists, and his skin wore raw and bloody, but no matter how hard he strained, no matter how much pain he endured, he couldn't break free of the ropes. Campbell sliced her throat with his gleaming blade, and blood poured over her bosom, soaking her gown. The light in her pretty blue eyes went out immediately, and Lachlan's heart shattered.

He shouted to her, hoping to leave her with one last enduring thought, "I love you, Elspeth."

Campbell dropped her limp body to the rushes, his eyes on Lachlan. "It willna be my soul that rots in hell, MacGregor. 'Twill be yers. Ya brought this upon yerself, with yer hunger for power, with yer unholy greed."

The words were a bitter blow, a ruthless echo of Lachlan's own thoughts. Overcome by grief, enervated by the sapping anguish that flowed through his veins, he barely heard the stomp of boots across the wooden floor. But when they stopped before him, he found the strength to lift his head.

Before him stood a lanky young man with long blond locks and a tawny beard. The face he knew only too well: handsome, with green eyes and heavy brows. This was the man he had foolishly entrusted with his very soul.

Clearly untroubled by the chaos and bloodshed around him, the filthy cur stared directly into Lachlan's eyes and smiled.

Lachlan jerked to a sitting position on his bed, blinking, only vaguely aware that he had slept away a good portion of the morning. Cold sweat covered every inch of his skin. Dear God, was it possible . . . ?

"Drusus," he croaked.

4

Lachlan scooped up his keys and his wallet, then jogged downstairs to his car, mentally mapping the fastest route to San Francisco. Not once since he'd moved to San Jose six months ago had he made the drive into the city. It had seemed wiser to keep his distance, to avoid leaving a trail.

But everything had changed now.

Fifty minutes later, he pulled into the small parking lot of St. Aquila the Redeemer Church and climbed the back stairs to the rectory. To the elderly nun who answered the door, he said, "Father MacGregor to see Monsignor Campbell."

"Oh yes, Father, he's expecting you. Come in."

She escorted him up another flight of stairs and led him to a sparsely decorated room at the end of the hall. The door was open. Inside, next to the narrow window, stood a middle-aged priest, his hair a peppery gray but his stance still strong and firm. He turned his head as Lachlan entered, smiling.

"That was quick."

Lachlan thanked the sister who'd escorted him and crossed the room to take the man's hand. "Thank you for seeing me on such short notice. I hope you weren't put out by my request?"

"Of course not. These are the very moments I prepare for."

Lachlan studied the man's calm face and resolute brown eyes. He'd seen similar expressions on warriors about to step into battle. "You know who I am? *What* I am?"

"Indeed, yes. The Protectorate keeps very accurate records. Sit down and tell me what's led you here," the older priest said, waving at the foot of the neatly made single bed. He took the stiff wooden chair for himself. "I take it you believe the Linen is in jeopardy?"

"I do." Although his watch ticked the passage of each second with grim persistence, Lachlan sat. The mattress was firm, the wool blanket scratchy. "The man who plotted the demise of my family was no' a man at all. He was a lure demon."

Campbell's brows rose. "Are you certain?"

"I saw him again, just yesterday."

"And because a demon was involved, the attack no longer seems random. You think your brother was the target all along."

"Aye," Lachlan said.

"Your brother died that day." The monsignor fingered the white agate rosary around his neck. "If the Linen had been the demon's goal, surely he'd now possess it?"

"William was mortally wounded in the attack," Lachlan acknowledged. "But the night before, he had a dream. In it, he saw himself run through and the Linen purloined. Certain he'd had a vision of the future, he came to me in the wee hours of the morning and begged me to take the Linen and hide it, somewhere unbeknownst to him."

Campbell nodded. "We're taught to take such dreams very seriously."

"Later, as my brother was gasping his last breaths, he

made me vow to protect the Linen with my life. He told me to seek out a man of pure faith and pass the Linen on. I did so."

The older priest's expression turned wry. "And kept a wary and watchful eye upon it ever thereafter, I see."

Lachlan shrugged off the compliment. The truth was far less kind. "I gave my oath."

"Which is what brings you here today. You think this lure demon of yours has tracked the Linen to San Francisco. Possibly to me."

"Aye. The time has come to destroy the wretched thing."

Campbell leapt to his feet, rocking his chair back on two legs. "Absolutely not. Did you not just tell me you gave your oath to protect it?"

"I gave my oath when I thought the Linen was a sacred relic, possessed of a powerful capacity for good. If a demon seeks it, there can be only one reason: It's a dark relic, capable of delivering vast evil."

"Dark or not, the Linen is every bit as valuable a relic as the Shroud of Turin. Destroying it would be blasphemous."

Lachlan stood, too. "We're talking about the cloth Pontius Pilate used to wipe his hands after ordering the execution of Jesus. Its very existence is blasphemous."

"No. Pilate may have been a weak man, but he was not a soulless one. God forgave him. The Linen represents an important stage in the journey Jesus made to save us." The older priest put his hand on Lachlan's shoulder. "Your own brother gave his life to protect the Linen, MacGregor. What would destroying it do but make his sacrifice a waste?"

Lachlan glanced away, rejecting the gentle sympathy he saw in Campbell's eyes. He didn't deserve it. "Had the cloth been destroyed at the start, as it should have been, his life—and that of many others—would have been preserved."

"I will not allow it to be destroyed."

"Then I fear for your life, Monsignor. This is no brattling demon who hunts it. If I'm correct, he's an ancient, one of the first demons Satan cultivated. Drusus once told me he can trace his history back to Roman times."

"Are you suggesting this demon and the Linen are of a like age? That he might be the very demon that drove the Protectorate to hide the Linen?"

"It's possible."

"Well, that's disturbing." The older priest walked to the window and peered outside. A new wariness gripped his shoulders. "Still, I can't allow you to destroy the Linen. I've sworn a sacred oath to protect it, and protect it I will. With my dying breath, if necessary. Even against you."

Lachlan glared at the other man's back. "I'm no' the one you need worry about. I have a conscience. Drusus does no'."

"Then let's focus on the demon. What do you know of him?"

"No' much, save what he told me himself, and that is suspect. I was rather hoping you'd have additional details."

Campbell turned to him with a frown. "The records of the Protectorate are full of useful information, but I'm afraid they won't be much help in this case. Specific demons were rarely named in the old parchments; to quote their names was thought to give them power."

"Don't the records contain details of what happened before the Linen was hidden away?"

"Oh yes. Any who touched it instantly denied Christ, which is half the reason it's now kept in a hermetically sealed case."

"Do the old parchments mention anything of the demon who attempted to steal it?"

"Only that he was both charming and brutal. Not only did he very nearly sway Peter into giving him the cloth, he's credited with the gruesome murders of at least two guardsmen. Eyes burned out, entrails spilled, that sort of thing."

Lachlan briefly closed his eyes. Perhaps he should be grateful it was Campbell who stole the future of his three wee bairns, not Drusus. "Why does he want it?"

"Well, a lure demon could use it to tempt large groups into depravity. But that's not the worst-case scenario, I'm afraid. In Satan's possession, the Linen's sway could be extended to incite thousands upon thousands to turn away from God."

"Inviting sin into every corner of the world." A surge of hot frustration fisted Lachlan's hands. "Explain to me again why we wish to preserve it?"

"Because—"

He put up his hand. "No, don't bother, I understand. But I still believe this is madness."

"Why? Don't you battle demons every day? Isn't that part of what you do? Surely, all you have to do is slay this one hellion and we can rest easy."

But Drusus wasn't your average demon. Not only was he invested with power gained from two thousand years of existence, he was the very sword master who had taught Lachlan to properly wield a blade.

"Just to be safe, Monsignor, maybe you should leave town."

The last traces of the sun dropped behind the trees and Drusus shivered at the sudden chill. When the door opened, he gave the elderly nun his most devastating smile and pushed his way into the lemon-scented alcove.

The astringent rasp of hallowed ground immediately began to chafe at his flesh, but he ignored it. He didn't plan to be here long.

"My name's Alistair Rose," he said, laying on a thick brogue to match today's glamour of an elderly Scottish laborer. "From Dumbarton, Scotland. I've been told a priest from the old country resides here. Is that true?"

Beneath her wimple, the nun frowned. "Well, there's Monsignor Campbell. His family originally came from Scotland, but as far as I know he's lived in the United States all his life."

"Campbell? Would that be the Glen Lyon Campbells?"

"Oh, I have no idea about that."

Drusus nodded. Of course not. The woman had been born in Illinois and never once ventured off the continent. "I wonder if I might speak briefly with the monsignor, to see if he's the man I'm seeking."

She hesitated. "It's after six."

"I promise not to take more than five minutes of his time." Drusus smiled again, deeper and longer this time, diving through the protective layers of her conscious mind. Devout believers could not be possessed, but they could be influenced. All it took was a firm, gentle touch.

The nun's shoulders eased and she beckoned him farther inside. "Can't see the harm in that. Come, I'll show you to his room."

He followed her up the stairs, flinching as he narrowly avoided bumping his shoulder on a large wooden crucifix on the wall. The scent of lemons was harsh now, burning his nostrils, clawing at his skin, but he pushed on. Everything worth having demanded a high price. And he was close to his prize; he could sense the faint undercurrent of the relic's power.

The old nun smiled shyly at him as she waved him

into the sparsely furnished bedroom at the end of the hall. Feeling magnanimous, he returned her smile.

Then he faced the priest.

Like the other Protectors he'd encountered over the years, this one recognized him immediately, despite the intricate human veneer he'd adopted for the occasion. Something in the eyes, perhaps. No matter, it simplified his task. He shut the door.

"Let's get to the point, shall we? The Linen, if you will."

"You're too late," the priest responded. "It's gone."

The words snatched the breath from his lungs, their meaning instantly clear: Although there'd been nothing but confusion in his eyes last night, at some point Mac-Gregor had experienced an epiphany. He'd stolen the Linen. Again. "When did he come?"

The rosary in the priest's hands slid from one bead to the next as he prayed, silently weaving a powerful shield. "Just after lunch."

Six hours. Six miserable hours wasted knocking on the doors of other churches. Six hours of enduring the burning air of consecrated ground, fighting for every breath, feeling his flesh crawl under the ghostly touch of holy spirits. All of it made bearable by the knowledge that he was closing in on his long-sought-after prize.

Only to have it stolen from beneath his nose.

"Credo in Deum Patrem omnipotentem, Creatorem caeli et terrae . . . ," the monsignor began firmly.

The Apostles' Creed. In Latin.

Red-hot rage sluiced through his veins at the familiar words, words that would focus the priest's faith and imbue him with incredible power. Every blessed object in this room would become a weapon. But even a Protector was breakable. He'd proven that himself, several times. Neither God nor all the faith in the world would save this miserable wretch now. He'd live just long enough to regret giving the Linen to MacGregor.

"Et in Iesum Christum, Filium Eius unicum, Dominum nostrum . . ."

The scent of lemons thickened, every molecule of air now a droplet of acid. Drusus glanced at his hands. The skin was peeling away, leaving his flesh red and raw. On second thought, spilling the blood of a single holy man wouldn't be satisfying. Not this time.

"A pity MacGregor chose to desert you," he murmured, as orange flames sprouted from his ravaged fingertips. He'd kill all five of the pious souls living here. Slowly. Singe by painful singe, sear by screaming sear. Using just enough heat to roast the flesh from their bones, he would drag the event out for several hours and truly savor the experience. He'd do the old nun last, so he could watch the light dim in her cowlike eyes. "He's going to miss one hell of a party."

He tossed the first fireball.

There'd be plenty of time to deal with MacGregor.

Later.

"Goddamn it."

Rachel threw her stylus onto the desk, shoved her chair back, and stood. The blank white screen of her computer illustration program danced in front of her face, mocking her with its vacancy.

Most days, her job was awesome. There was nothing in the world like getting paid to do what she would willingly do for free. But at moments like this, she wished she had more control over the process, that her creativity could turn on and off when needed, like a light switch, instead of being stifled by her worries.

She glanced down the hall.

A classic example of why she had focus problems,

right there. The sign on her daughter's bedroom door still read EMILY'S ROOM — KEEP OUT, but at some point the teenage banner of independence had gotten a makeover. Bats with fangs had consumed the cute little daisies, and the simple black lettering now had a heavy, bloodred outline, complete with gory drips.

What the hell was she going to do about Em?

She'd called the police again and told them about the rendezvous at the fairgrounds, but other than a promise to check the gates regularly to ensure they were locked, the officer she'd spoken to had little to offer.

The microwave beeped and Rachel padded barefoot into the kitchen. Doing her best to ignore the digital clock that glowed 12:12 a.m., she opened the door. Nuked coffee. Yum, just what the doctor ordered. She took a couple of sips from the steaming mug, deriving a primitive comfort from the warmth it left in her belly. Then, just like a rubberneck drawn to a grisly accident scene, she swiveled toward the dining room table.

Crumpled sketches, a sea of eraser dust, and a handful of HB pencils littered the dark blue tablecloth. Her leather portfolio lay open at one end of the table, the plastic sleeves glaringly empty. Several balls of discarded paper had escaped onto the floor, hiding their shame behind the curved table legs.

Her work wasn't giving an inch.

She'd have to spend a big chunk of the weekend at her computer, doing her utmost to catch up. Celia had rewarded her presentation with more work: a whole series to do on her own. The assignment made her five thirty departure from the office almost criminal—the rest of her colleagues had ordered dinner in, expecting to burn the midnight oil. Lots of high-tech companies allowed their employees to work from home, but Celia was a stickler for coming into the office. She insisted that a designer's creativity needed the spur of other creative minds, and honestly, Rachel agreed.

If she weren't a single mom—a single mom with a teenage daughter who currently needed to be bed checked every half hour—she would have stayed.

There was a sharp rap on the apartment door, and Rachel jumped, spilling her coffee down the front of her baggy DKNY nightshirt. Visitors during the day were strange enough, but in the middle of the night . . . ?

Heart thumping, she approached the door and peered through the peephole—and immediately eased.

Lachlan MacGregor.

Rachel grimaced at her very unattractive sleepwear, now adorned with an even more unattractive coffee stain. The shirt covered her well enough, coming almost to her knees, but it was old and shapeless, and hardly what she wanted to entertain a hunky guy in.

Then again, Lachlan wasn't a hunky guy; he was a priest—off-limits. Maybe it was better this way—to eliminate all hope of an admiring glance.

She tugged open the door.

And sucked in a short breath.

Seeing him in person had an unexpected, forceful impact. He wore his usual clerical suit, but his short hair looked as if a tornado had ripped through it, and the shadow of a beard darkened his chin. He still had that aura of supreme confidence, but tonight it was mixed with something else, something that swirled in his stormy blue eyes and hinted at . . . vulnerability?

Whatever it was, it was devastating. The shiver that ran through her was so keen, the surface of her coffee rippled.

"I apologize for the late hour," he said, his gaze flickering to her bare legs and back up. The storm in his eyes gathered intensity, which cranked up her internal thermostat and spawned all sorts of naughty imaginings. "But I noticed your light was still on and took a chance."

Rachel forced herself to admire the burnished, beaten-silver cross he wore around his neck. *Priest, remember?*

"May I come in?" he prompted gently.

She flushed, and widened the door. "Of course, sorry."

The moment he entered, however, she regretted the decision. He dominated the small foyer in a way most men could only dream of. When he raked a hand through the tangled waves of his hair and shot her a rueful look, Rachel almost melted on the spot.

"I've changed my mind," he said gruffly.

She blinked. About what? Being a priest?

"About helping Emily."

Heat rushed into Rachel's cheeks, and she plopped her mug down on the hall table, her arm suddenly incapable of holding it. "Oh."

"If you still want me to, I'll talk to her, try to get her to break it off with"—he paused, his gaze dropping to the hardwood floor—"with the motorcycle lad."

The implications of what he offered suddenly sank in. This was it, her answer. He was giving her a chance to reach Em, convince her to see reason, without destroying what little mother-daughter rapport they had left. "Really?"

He nodded.

"Really?"

At the excited pitch in her voice, his lips twitched. "Aye, really."

"Oh my God, thank you." Unable to hold back, Rachel launched herself at Lachlan, flinging her arms around his rock-solid, divinely scented warmth. "You have no idea how much this means—"

He froze.

She leapt back. "Sorry, that was totally off base. It's just that—"

"No." He took a slow, deep breath, then quirked a smile. "No' off base, just a surprise."

His words implied all was forgiven, but his eyes didn't quite meet hers, and Rachel read between the lines: Hugging a priest was a giant no-no.

Given her wildly erratic heartbeat and damp palms, she'd have to agree. "Anyway, that was meant to convey huge thanks. You're a lifesaver. I was completely out of ideas."

She took another step back.

Lachlan forced his gaze up, heart thumping. He fought for composure, but it was a lost cause—the vivid memory of her soft body mashed against his just wouldn't let go. Curvy. Braless. Perfect. His hands remained at his sides, but he couldn't stem a flare of his nostrils as he tried to capture a lingering wisp of her sweetly feminine fragrance.

And the struggle didn't end with controlling his body.

The harder task was controlling the sense of satisfaction he got from making the furrows of worry on her brow disappear, even for a second. He could ease her burdens. He could lift a portion of the weight that bowed her shoulders. Look how simple it was. All he had to do was play the knight, behave just as his instincts told him to—protect her and care for her. All he had to do was risk the pain of becoming attached and then watching her die while he stood helplessly by.

No problem.

"I should go," he choked out.

Rachel bit her lower lip. "But I never offered you a drink or anything."

"It's late."

"No biggie. I'm pulling an all-nighter."

"An all-nighter?"

She waved a hand at the computer desk jammed into one corner of the cluttered dining room. "We're behind on a project at work and my boss has cracked the whip. I've got to produce a whole new graphic series by Monday, or else I'm in deep shit."

As the last word trailed off, the worry lines crept back onto her face. "And here I thought *my* boss was tough," he said dryly, determined to banish the lines once more.

Rachel's hazel eyes danced. "I think you've got me beat. Mine can't summon a flood to wipe all the sinners from the earth, though I'd bet she sure wishes she could."

That wasn't the boss he'd been thinking about, but the result was the same, so he smiled.

"Seriously," Rachel said, coaxing, "I can make a fresh pot of coffee. I really don't mind. Reheated caffeine wasn't quite doing the trick, anyway."

He glanced at her Daffy Duck mug. Looking at the cup was a lot wiser than continuing to stare at the enticing mounds of her breasts as they swayed under that loose shirt. "Is that what you're drinking? Reheated coffee?"

"Yes. Nothing like a little homemade turpentine."

"I'll stay only if you let me make the coffee."

After a brief attempt to convince him that she was the hostess and he was the guest, she yielded him the kitchen and returned to her desk. He watched her as he filled the coffeemaker and set it to brew. Curious. If this was the way most artists worked, it was a miracle they created anything—the entire time the coffee dripped into the pot, she just stared at a box of software sitting on the desk and chewed on the end of her pencil.

"Seeking inspiration?" he asked, handing her a fresh cup.

She nodded. "Unfortunately, it's sadly lacking." She took a sip, then glanced at him, startled. "How did you know what I take in my coffee?"

"I tasted the turpentine."

"Smart man. Very analytical." Cocking her head, she considered him. "Maybe you could help me."

"How so?"

"What do you see when you look at this box?"

He reluctantly turned his gaze from the dusting of freckles on her nose to the package she held out. Mostly white, it had a large collage of imagery at the top and a bold, shimmery blue product name splashed across the bottom: MaskWeave. "Water."

"Okay," she said slowly, tapping the mangled pencil against her bottom lip. "Anything else strike you? What would you guess this product does?"

"Something technical." He pointed to one side of the collage. "These lines look like architectural drawings."

"Any particular feelings surface when you look at this?"

"You're asking a man to describe *feelings*?"

"Just go with it."

Lachlan examined the picture in more detail, absorbing the colors of sea and sky, the sandy tones, and the dichotomy of flat and fully formed graphics. It reminded him of the beach. "Uh, peace? Freedom?"

"Freedom." Rachel jumped up. "Oh, that's good."

She snatched her sketchpad from the dining room table and began rapidly drawing. Lost in translating whatever was in her brain to paper, she hunched over the pad. Her mahogany hair fell forward, partially covering her face, and her toes curled around the stainless steel chair legs. Her fingers skimmed over the paper, the strokes sometimes airy, sometimes firm.

A series of images took shape on the paper—all elements of nature shaded into three dimensions with an inspired balance of light and dark. Fascinating. But not nearly as entrancing as the expressions that flickered over her face as she drew, permitting him a brief insight into her thoughts.

She lived to draw.

The truth was written all over her. Graphic design wasn't just her job; it was her calling. And the radiance of her creativity seduced him, urging him to capture a tiny bit of it, to touch . . . and to taste.

Lachlan closed his eyes. What was he doing? He had to focus. Not on Rachel, as appealing as that was, but on the bastard who had ripped his life apart—on Drusus.

"Thanks for the coffee, but I should get going," he said, his voice crisper than he intended. "I'll drop by tomorrow to talk to Emily."

She lifted her head. Those tiny worry lines between her brows returned. "Okay. Come for dinner at six thirty and you can talk to her then."

He swallowed. An intimate dinner with Rachel and her daughter . . . sitting at her table, exchanging smiles and teasing comments . . . flirting like the lover he could never be. *God, no.* "I'm afraid I've other plans. Unless you object, I'll speak with her after school."

Her face lost its glow. "No, I don't object."

He looked away. "Good night, then."

"Good night."

Lachlan drank in one last, lingering picture of her in that clingy cotton jersey, then escaped the apartment. With more than four hundred years as a Gatherer under his belt, he'd been confident he'd already endured the worst of what purgatory had to offer.

He'd been wrong.

Despite a sleepless night spent reliving his visit with Rachel, Lachlan rose early. He quickly showered and drove out to Stefan Wahlberg's house, fourteen miles south of San Jose.

The Romany mage displayed no surprise when Lachlan parked his Audi in the dusty yard. Indeed, he handed him a six-foot-long wooden box the moment he alit from the vehicle and acted as though they'd had an appointment.

"Come in, come in," he said, waving him into the sweltering three-walled smithy. With curly black hair falling over his eyes, a large belly, and his habitual ensemble of heavy twill overalls and rubber boots, the mage presented a friendly and innocuous image. But Lachlan knew better. Hidden behind that affable smile was the most powerful mage he'd ever had the good fortune to meet ... and a very shady history. The two previous Gatherers Stefan had worked with had died—inexplicably.

He studied the brass-hinged mahogany case, but didn't open it. "What's this?"

Donning thick leather gloves, Stefan shrugged. He thrust a long piece of hammered steel in the hottest part of the fire. "A gift."

Lachlan placed the box on a nearby workbench. "Thank you, but I don't accept gifts." Especially unexpected gifts from mystics with rumored dark connections.

"Shame. It's custom-made for your height and weight, so if you don't take it, I'll have to scrap it."

A seed of curiosity sprouted in Lachlan's mind, but he ruthlessly trampled it. "I need you to forge me a half-dozen new blades. Basic arming swords."

"Why?"

"I'm training some of the other Gatherers."

The blacksmith glanced up. "Death is finally agreeable?"

"No' exactly."

Stefan arched a brow, but didn't delve further. "I assume you want the usual shield-pierce and demon-blood-enhancement spells? And baldrics warding them from human perception?"

Lachlan nodded.

"Easy enough. I'll have them ready by Friday night."

Digging ten crisp one-hundred-dollar bills from his wallet, Lachlan tossed them on the table. Then he turned on his heel. He hadn't gone two paces when Stefan called him back.

"Take the sword, MacGregor. If you must, you can pay me for it. But you'll need it."

Lachlan spun around. "Why?"

The mage pulled the red-hot steel from the fire with a pair of tongs and picked up his hammer. "Murder-suicides and mob-mentality crimes are way up; church attendance is way down. Isn't it obvious?"

"No."

Stefan said nothing for a while, hammering at the steel strip with precise, powerful blows. When he had returned the cooled steel to the fire, he pushed his safety glasses up on his forehead and looked at Lachlan.

"Strange things have been happening for months: friendly visits from the dead, sandboxes that wriggle, multiple lightbulbs exploding. You know the stuff I mean. Definite crossovers from the other planes. But a spike in the murder-suicide rate is unique to a lure demon."

"And this bothers you because ... ?"

The mage put down his hammer and tugged off his gloves. "Most demons can't spend more than a few minutes on the middle plane before they become exhausted," he said, "but lure demons both create and feed off human despair. They're able to set up camp here for extended periods."

"I know that."

"Do you also know what the Gatherer-versus-lure-demon record is?"

Sensing a trap, Lachlan shook his head.

"Zip to eight hundred forty-six," Stefan said, completely serious.

Lachlan frowned. "No Gatherer has ever defeated one?"

"No."

"Why no'?"

"Well, for starters, the blasted creatures are next to impossible to kill." The mage dragged a hand through the sweaty locks of his hair. "In addition to that neat trick they have of manipulating thoughts, they draw power from their liege."

"What kind of power?"

"The unending kind. When a lure demon tires, he renews his strength by pulling energy from Satan—who, as you already know, pulls *his* power from the innumerable souls who've been damned to hell. Trying to slay a lure demon is the same as trying to slay the Deity of the lower plane himself. Impossible."

"Then what good will a new sword do me?"

"Honestly, I don't know. But it can't hurt. Mystically speaking, it's the most powerful sword I've ever made."

Lachlan returned to the long wooden box and unfastened the brass latch. Lifting the teak cover, he stared at the gleaming weapon inside. His heart pumped a little more heavily at the familiar sight. "A *claidheamh mòr*."

"Not a perfect replica, of course. This one is high-tensile steel and titanium, and weighs only five pounds.

Those ancient Ogham markings up the blood gutter will ensure your aim stays true, the peridot in the pommel will ward off his negative sway, and I've augmented the demon blood–enhancement spell. With any luck, it'll do the trick."

"I'd rather no' depend on luck," Lachlan said, lifting the weapon out of the case. From tang to tip, the sword ran more than five feet.

"Then stay out of the lure demon's way."

Lachlan replaced the sword and latched the box. He had no intention of running from Drusus, unquenchable power or no. His honor demanded he face the bastard.

"And if I can't?"

Stefan grimaced. "Hope like hell the sword is enough."

5

At lunchtime, Rachel strolled out to the corner hot dog vendor. Normally she ate at her desk, but the mood in the office today did not encourage relaxation. Stressed-out designers, each of them battling the clock to come up with fresh material, were swearing, popping Tylenol like breath mints, and snarling at the mail girl whenever she added to their in-boxes.

Getting out of the building kept her sane.

"Chili dog and a Coke," she ordered, smiling at the rotund man under the striped umbrella. Then she recalled her pledge to lose a few pounds. "Uh, make that a Diet Coke."

For once, a nice breeze blew in from the coast, and she peeled off her khaki three-quarter-sleeve jacket as she grabbed a sunny spot on a nearby bench. She'd give anything to sit in on Lachlan's chat with Em this afternoon, but there was no hope of that. Not today. Celia stalked the halls like a lion, pouncing on the slightest pause in activity.

Leaning over the napkins spread across her lap, she bit into her meal. A big blob of chili plopped onto the paper.

"I love those things," a low male voice said.

She glanced left . . . and almost choked on her hot dog.

Sprawled on the bench next to her was Em's guy friend from the fairgrounds, smiling as if they were best buds. His short haircut created a disarming cap of blond curls upon his head, and his clothing bore the casual stamp of American Eagle, but all Rachel saw was the hard, polished look in his green eyes.

She swallowed a lump of food.

"Unfortunately," he added, wrinkling his nose, "they don't love me. I get heartburn every time."

Doing her damnedest not to let on how much his sudden appearance disturbed her, Rachel placed her chili dog carefully in her lap. "Do I know you?"

His smile deepened. "Yes, of course you do, Rachel. I'm Drew, Em's boyfriend."

What was she supposed to say to *that*?

"I know you followed us out to the fairgrounds the other night. I saw you in the trees."

She glanced away.

"I confess you intrigue me, Rachel. I don't remember my own mother, so this notion of going to great lengths to protect a child is fascinating. And when I look at you"—his eyes briefly dropped to her chest—"I don't think *mother*."

Rachel decided to ignore the sexual undertones. "How did you find out where I worked?"

"Em told me." His eyes lit with humor. "She tells me everything."

"I'll bet," Rachel muttered. "Since you're here, let's be frank. I don't like my daughter hanging out with you. You're way too ... old ... for her. I want you to stay away from her."

"I can't." Drew sat forward, resting his elbows on his knees. His expression took on a serious air, and his eyes met hers with steady strength. No hint of subterfuge or lie. "I know this is hard to believe, but I truly love her.

She's the brightest, sweetest girl I've ever met, and she accepts me for who I am. You have no idea how liberating that can be."

"What a crock." Rachel glared. That genial air came naturally to him, and it was easy to see how Em had been charmed. But she was not Em. Her experience with Grant had soured her on boyish charmers. "She's still a child, while you're—what—twenty?"

"Twenty-two."

"Twenty-two and taking advantage of a girl eight years younger than you . . . Are you crazy, or just criminally stupid?"

He sat back, smiling. "I see where Em gets her vibrant personality. I like you, Rachel."

"Well, the feeling's not mutual. I want you to stop seeing Em and get out of our lives. Go find a girl your own age."

"Not too many of those around, I'm afraid. And none as fascinating as Em."

The unyielding note in his voice set Rachel's chest on fire. If it weren't for the curious people strolling past, she might have been tempted to grind her chili dog in his face. "What do you want? Is it money? We don't have a lot, but I—"

"I don't want money."

"Then what?"

"I told you. I love Em."

"And I told you I don't believe that bull. No twenty-two-year-old—no *sane* twenty-two-year-old—falls in love with a kid her age."

He reached out and traced a narrow finger along her jaw.

Rachel jerked back, almost upending the chili dog on her cream-colored slacks.

Her recoil didn't bother him. He continued to study

her with a mix of curiosity and admiration. "MacGregor must ache when he's with you."

The world tilted, and she nearly fell off the wooden bench. MacGregor? Did he mean Lachlan?

"The warrior in him would respond to your courage, the same way the warrior in me does. We share a fondness for strong women. Always have."

Unsure how to respond, Rachel said nothing. The urge to flee was intense, but she resisted. He wouldn't try something here, in front of all these witnesses. Would he?

"Sadly, we're not having the meeting of minds I was hoping for," Drew said, sighing. He got to his feet. "I usually do much better, especially with women. I wonder if it's the protective mother thing? At any rate, I have other work to do. Places to be, people to see."

He offered her a wry smile. "I'm disappointed that you didn't warm to me—I'm fond of the arts, and I have a colorful past that I think would intrigue you." Like an actor out of an old movie, he took her hand and sketched an elaborate bow. "But we'll get other chances to deepen our acquaintance."

Empowered by relief over his imminent departure, Rachel snatched her hand back and snorted. "Not if I can help it. Stay away from my daughter or I'll sic the cops on you."

Drew chuckled. "The police can't stop me, Rachel. To have any hope of severing my romantic ties with Em, you'll have to send MacGregor after me."

She stared at him.

"Be sure to tell him I dropped by, will you?"

With a gracious nod, he sauntered away.

An hour later, Rachel scuttled out the back door of her office building with one hand clutched to her still-queasy stomach. In hindsight, the chili dog had not been a wise choice.

She had tried to focus on her designs after lunch; she really had. Work nearly always calmed her down. But dismissing her encounter with Em's boyfriend had been like trying to hold off a tsunami with a spatula. There was something decidedly not right about the guy, something she could only label as . . . ugly. Knowing that he had a relationship with Em, knowing he touched her—that he'd *kissed* her—made Rachel want to vomit.

Lachlan was the only person who'd understand how she felt.

It would have been easier if his number had been listed in the phone book, though. She could have made a quick call from the office instead of begging Mandy to cover her for an hour while she snuck out to talk to him.

She turned the key in the ignition, carefully pumping the gas pedal. The starter gave a frenzied effort, but the engine barely turned over. She tried again.

Of course, there was that whole issue of Drew knowing Lachlan's name. Suggesting Lachlan was the only one who could stop him made it seem as if they shared some history.

She blushed. Crazy thought. Hiding something that important would be tantamount to a lie, and priests didn't lie. Really, whom was she going to trust, a punk who harassed teenage girls or a man of the church who rescued drowning kids off a school bus?

On the third try, her car roared to life.

Thanks to the sparseness of midafternoon traffic, the drive to the apartment took less than ten minutes. A shade after two p.m., she knocked on Lachlan's door.

He answered with a frown on his face and a cordless phone to his ear.

Rachel froze.

No shirt, no shoes, just tailored black pants and a truly magnificent expanse of bare chest. Nicely toned pecs and a sprinkle of crisp, dark hair. A cornucopia of honed muscle, combined with the tumble of wet hair and a fresh, soapy scent. Was it any wonder her brain detoured into a mouthwatering vision of him standing naked in the shower?

Breathe, Rachel, breathe.

"Rachel? Is something wrong?"

"He came to my work," she blurted, struggling to rein in her wild imagination. *Priest, priest, priest.*

"Who did?"

"Em's boyfriend, Drew."

His frown darkened and he opened his mouth to speak, but then he abruptly put up a hand to halt her next words. "Thank you for checking on that, Bishop Marley," he said into the phone. "I'd be honored to participate in the Mass. Monsignor Campbell was a fine man. I'll see you on Saturday."

Thumbing the phone off, he stood back and allowed her to enter. "When?"

"About an hour ago, when I was at lunch." His face was uncharacteristically bleak, and she suspected the phone call was to blame. "Are you okay?"

"I'm fine." He shut the door. "Did he speak to you?"

"Yes." Rachel focused on the living room to avoid looking at his naked chest. Still no furniture. In fact, it looked like a gym with all the water bottles, weights, and towels lying around. "He told me he loves Em. How crazy is that?"

"Completely crazy." There was a wary edge to his voice that drew her gaze back to him—almost as if he were waiting for her to drop a bomb.

So she obliged. "I tried to convince him to leave Em

alone, but he refused. Said the only way I could stop him was to send *you* after him."

Lachlan had a terrific poker face. Other than a slow blink, she got no clue to his thoughts. But his very lack of response set off alarm bells in her head, and for the first time she experienced a twinge of unease over her faith in him. Shouldn't he look surprised or confused?

"He seemed to know you," she added carefully. "Told me to tell you he dropped by."

That got a reaction. Lachlan's right fist clenched, the muscles of his forearm rippling under his tanned skin. But his voice was still amazingly calm. "Did he?"

An icy lump landed in the pit of Rachel's stomach. "You know him, don't you?"

He replaced the phone in the charger. "Aye."

"You know the slime bucket who's involved with my daughter and you didn't think that was important enough to mention?"

"I didn't recognize him at first."

"But you knew last night, when you offered to talk to Em," she accused, suddenly certain, suddenly dizzy with the knowledge.

"Aye."

"Why didn't you say something?"

"It's complicated."

"Complicated?" A harsh laugh escaped her lips. "Terrific, I can't wait to hear this. What? Is he your long-lost brother or your ex-lover or something?"

"No." He sliced her a reproving look. "I didn't tell you I knew Drusus, because I didn't want to worry you."

"Worry me? How?"

"Some time ago . . ." He paused. His gaze flickered to an oil painting of heather-covered hills that hung in the hall, then back to her face. A heavy sigh preceded his next words. "Three years ago, I caught him dealing ecstasy."

Ecstasy? The blood left her head in a huge rush. "You're telling me he's a drug dealer?"

"I'm afraid so. At the time, he seemed genuinely repentant, and promised to clean up his act, so I didn't turn him in. Suffice it to say, I now regret my decision."

"Oh God." She stumbled back a step.

Lachlan grabbed her arm, apparently sensing the puddinglike consistency of her legs. He half carried her to the kitchen island, lifted her onto a bar stool, and quickly retrieved a bottle of water from the fridge. Twisting open the cap, he handed it to her.

"Drink this."

She took a swallow, but only one. Her mind was whirling. "D-do you think he's got Em addicted to that stuff? Is that why she's been acting so strange?"

"I saw no sign of ecstasy use at the fairgrounds," Lachlan said, crouching beside her. His hand covered hers, squeezing gently. "And she declined the pot they were smoking. Let's assume the best for now."

"No, let's call the police and have him arrested."

"Based on what? A hunch? We've no proof of wrongdoing. That's why I must speak with Emily. To find out what she's seen and heard."

"I need to do something." She grabbed Lachlan's hand, her fingernails digging into his flesh. "I need to keep her from ever seeing him again."

"What are you going to do, Rachel? Lock her in her room? Stop her from going to school? Stay home day and night to make sure she doesn't leave?"

"If that's what it takes."

He shook his head. "No, Drusus is the one who needs to be stopped, no' Emily."

"How? He doesn't seem too easy to scare off."

"He wants me to come after him, so I will. I'll find him and . . . talk to him. Maybe his interest in me will deflect him from Emily."

"Talk to him? Do you really think *talking* is the answer?"

His gaze, steady, met hers. "Maybe no'. But it's a start."

"You do know he's dangerous, right? I mean, you just have to look in his eyes to see he's not your average creep."

He didn't answer for a long moment. Then he reached up and grazed a calloused thumb over her bottom lip. "Trust me, Rachel. I won't let you down."

She leaned into his hand and closed her eyes. "Okay."

As the heat of her chin seeped into his hand, Lachlan's gut twisted into a vicious knot. He'd asked for her trust, and with one simple gesture she'd given it to him. But he wished, more than anything, he could make her take it back.

What had he been thinking?

She couldn't trust him. Not one bit. Not only had he lied about the drug dealer nonsense, he'd assured her he could handle Drusus, which, so far, wasn't matching the facts. Yesterday, the bastard had burned the rectory housing Monsignor Campbell to the ground, killing everyone inside. Today he'd brazenly dropped by Rachel's work to talk about his undying love for Emily. It was clear who had the upper hand—and it damned well wasn't him.

Yet here he was promising not to let her down.

Was he mad?

Rachel sighed, her warm breath drifting across the

skin of his wrist. Oh yes. Definitely mad. With desire. He desperately wanted to fall into her arms, sink into her body, forget the real world. Need pounded at him, and right now, with her mouth only inches away, the impulse to snatch her up and toss her over his shoulder was fierce.

Not all of his primitive urges had been tamed.

But if he succumbed, if he gave into temptation, he would give her expectations he could never fulfill. A relationship between them was impossible. He would end up hurting her. And for what, a temporary sating of the ache in his heart? No, he couldn't do it.

Regretfully, he said, "You should go back to work."

There was a palpable pause as she digested his words.

"Mandy's covering for me," she said softly. Her eyes held a note of encouragement, as if she'd sensed his craving and shared it. Her body swayed toward him, loose and open. Willing.

Lachlan swallowed. *Bloody hell.* Could this be any more difficult? "Then it wouldn't be fair to leave her for long."

A shadow flitted across her face, and she pulled away.

He wanted to protest the sudden emptiness of his hand . . . but couldn't. As miserable as it felt, distance was better, for both of them. And he didn't deserve even a moment in her arms.

"Go," he insisted. "And stay late if you want. I'll pick up Emily from school and keep her with me until you return."

She frowned. "Are you sure?"

"I'm sure. Go."

"Okay." She leapt from the stool and gave him a smile that didn't quite erase the rejection in her eyes. "Thanks."

The door clicked shut, and Lachlan closed his eyes. It took a solid minute to talk his legs out of chasing after her. Then he dropped his arse to the hearthstones and fisted his hands in his hair.

Drusus. By God, he hated that wretched bastard. It was becoming increasingly clear his involvement with Emily was no ordinary lure. There was a definite element of taunting in his actions—all aimed at Lachlan. The red-haired rape victim, the bus crash, and now this brazen visit to Rachel. He was begging Lachlan to pursue him.

And the demon was going to get his wish.

A blue spark arced across the room.

The familiar crackle, followed by the resounding crash of one of the practice swords hitting the hardwood floor, drove Lachlan to his feet. The pleasant tang of lemons floated in the air, and then a sudden pop produced an eightysomething, wiry little man. Little more than five feet tall, the fellow stood in the middle of his living room, dressed in a brown tweed suit with a bright yellow vest.

"Ah, there you are," the elder said, smiling.

"You're late," Lachlan grumbled. He was not in the mood for niceties. "Again."

"I am?" The angel blinked.

"Are there no clocks in heaven? I gathered the soul more than three hours ago."

The tweed-clad man scratched his nose. "Really?"

"Aye."

Pulling a tiny spiral-bound notebook out of his satin vest pocket, the angel flipped through the pages until he came to the one that interested him. "Jeffrey Walsh? Died in the Good Samaritan Hospital? Of congestive heart failure?"

"Aye," Lachlan confirmed, exasperated.

"Three hours ago, you say?"

"Oh, for chrissake." God's messengers had always been a little out of step with time on the middle plane, but this was unbearable. "Are you aware that a Gatherer cannot eat while holding a soul?"

"I am."

"And you know that while I carry this soul, I can't collect another unless it's headed to the same final resting place?"

"I am."

"Then what in blazes keeps you away?"

"I come as soon as I'm able."

Right. Without a thought to the Gatherer who perishes while he takes his sweet bloody time. After all, what's the loss of one dishonorable man in purgatory? "Never mind, just take the soul and be gone. I've other things to deal with."

The angel's brows soared. "More important things than seeing a worthy soul into heaven? Surely not."

"No' more important, perhaps," Lachlan said, frowning at the hint of disparagement. "But clearly more urgent."

"Fine," the old man said, himself a little crusty. "Let's get to it, then. Hand or heart?"

Lachlan debated. Both options were effective, but shaking hands took longer. "Heart."

The angel advanced without further comment, reached up, and placed his wizened hand over Lachlan's heart.

Gentle warmth leached into his chest. Then his entire body tingled with a sensation he could only compare to the feeling of joy: sweet and cool, airy and divine. But in a heartbeat the transfer was over, leaving him feeling bereft.

The angel stepped back. "A shame."

Lachlan glanced at him. "What?"

"Were it not for the manner in which you died, you might have walked through the pearly gates and joined us in the upper plane."

"Unlikely. I'm guilty of greed, as well."

"Hmmm." The old man tilted his head and studied Lachlan for a moment. "There's an excess of anger in you and an abundance of self-deprecation. But also great courage and self-control."

"I trust you have a point?"

"Why, yes. Those finer qualities could help others. Becoming a mentor to a middle-plane soul would please the Lord and improve your chances of redemption. Do you know anyone who suffers the same flaws as you?"

An image of Emily's sullen face popped into Lachlan's mind, but he dismissed it. Helping one teenage girl could never outweigh his past sins. Redemption was impossible. "No."

"Keep it in mind." The angel consulted his notebook again. "How many souls have you gathered in your term with Death?"

"I'm no' certain. More than two hundred thousand."

"Really? That's quite remarkable."

Lachlan shrugged. Wasn't much more than one per day.

"And is it true that you've never given up a heaven-bound soul to a demon thief?"

"Aye."

"Hmmm." The angel scratched his nose again. "A fine record. Fine record indeed."

Frustration returned, searing Lachlan's blood. His time was better spent searching for Drusus, not engaging in meaningless conversations about records. No wonder angels were always late. "When you return to heaven, tell God I'm growing impatient at these needless delays."

Mild rebuke again shadowed the angel's eyes. "Do you not trust him to do what must be done?"

"No' when my brethren suffer for his lack of effort, no. The situation is dire and I would see him intervene before more good men are lost. Impress upon him the necessity for action."

"Assuredly, I will." Once again, the old man flipped through the pages of his notebook. "But first, I'm supposed to be in—no, I did that one already. Ah, yes—in Beijing."

Unable to help himself, Lachlan rolled his eyes.

The angel failed to note the gesture, however, as his tweed-clad figure had already vanished in a flash of brilliant blue light. Hopefully, on his way to China, and hopefully before the Gatherer at the other end was swamped by demons.

Really, given the quality of the hired help upstairs, it was a miracle any souls made it to heaven at all.

Lachlan flicked the switch that lowered the passenger-side window. "Emily, may I offer you a lift home?"

The two girls halted beside the car and peered in the window. Both wore the ruthlessly black attire of Goth queens and had graffiti-covered knapsacks slung over their shoulders. Emily tossed him a wary frown, then glanced at her friend.

He recognized the other girl from the fairgrounds—a rather chunky lass with short black hair and three silver rings in her lip.

"It'll be faster than the bus," he pointed out, adding weight to his offer. "And I have air-conditioning."

After a brief, wordless consultation with her friend, Emily returned her gaze to him. "Can Sheila come along?"

Daily school attendance pretty much ruled out the

possibility Sheila was a demon, but it wouldn't hurt to observe her on the drive home. "Sure," he agreed.

"Cool."

The girls clambered in, Emily in the front seat, Sheila in the back. Their knapsacks were tossed without a care for where they landed, and Lachlan winced as something metallic hit the window glass.

"Nice car," Sheila said, smoothing her hand over the gray leather bench seat. "Is it fast?"

"Faster than I'll ever need it to be," he acknowledged, winking at her through the rearview mirror. Her black-rimmed eyes held no sign of guile, just awe. "I drive mostly in the city."

"You should drag it. There's races on Cooper Street every Saturday night."

"Perhaps no'," he said dryly, running a finger under his white collar. "Don't think the bishop would approve."

Both girls laughed.

Dredging up his rusty social skills, he kept them amused until he pulled up in front of the seventies-era, biscuit-colored bungalow where Sheila lived. The grass hadn't been cut in several weeks and children's toys littered the yard. A tight expression replaced the humor on Sheila's face as she eyed the off-kilter screen door. Then she crawled out of the car, dragging her bag with her. "See ya Monday, Em."

Em nodded. "IM me."

Lachlan watched as the young girl approached the house. Before his eyes, her shoulders curled and her chin dropped to her chest. If she was a demon, she must have been an actress in her former life. "Is everything all right with Sheila?"

Emily's face was carefully neutral. "Her dad's a drunk."

A spark of anger flared. "Does he beat her?"

"Not usually. But she has to do *every*thing, including make dinner, and her baby brothers are a pain in the ass. Her dad just sleeps in front of the TV."

Although reluctant to leave Sheila to whatever fate lay in store for her, Lachlan put the car in drive and swung back onto the road. "What about *your* dad? What's he like?"

Her eyes softened. "My dad's great. He's funny and a hoot to be with. We get along really well."

A description at odds with Rachel's feedback. He'd gotten the impression the fellow had little interest in playing the father. "See him much?"

"Not since my mom moved us to San Jose," she groused. "When we lived in San Diego, I saw him all the time."

"Does he drive up to see you from time to time?"

"My mom doesn't want him to. She hates him."

"Has she said that?" he asked, curious.

"She doesn't have to. You should see the look on her face when he calls."

"I see." The tension in Emily was palpable and Lachlan decided to take it down a notch. He pointed to a sign just past the next light. "Can I interest you in an ice-cream sundae?"

Emily rolled her eyes to suggest she was far too mature to be bought with a sundae. But to his surprise, she said, "Okay." Unable to resist one last dig at her mom, she added, "But you'll have to explain to Mr. Wyatt why I'm late, 'cause I'm grounded."

"Actually, I mentioned to your mom that I'd be picking you up from school. There's no Mr. Wyatt tonight."

She skewed him a suspicious stare. "Huh."

"Is that okay?"

Arms crossed over her chest, she sat back. "I guess so."

Despite that inauspicious start, the ice cream break was a success. He treated her to a plain vanilla cone—her choice—and for the next half hour he was reminded that despite her tough attitude and inch-thick eyeliner, Emily was still a kid. She licked the drips running down her cone with unrestrained glee, laughed when Lachlan got whipped cream on his nose, and blushed twelve shades of pink when she asked for his cherry.

Lachlan stifled a grin as he handed her the maraschino.

She popped it into her mouth and chewed. Once the blush had receded, she looked him in the eye and asked, "Are priests allowed to get married?"

"Some," he hedged. "Depends on the church they belong to."

"Are *you*?"

"Technically, yes." Technically, he wasn't a priest, so it was a moot point. "But I've made a choice no' to wed."

"Why?"

Getting Emily to open up would require giving a little of himself, uncomfortable as that might be. "I was married once, when I was younger, and my wife died."

"Oh."

She seemed a bit disturbed by his response, so he bypassed the moment with a few questions of his own. "What about you? What's your take on marriage?"

"I plan on getting married someday," Em admitted. "Not until I'm, like, twenty-five or something, though."

He smiled. "So Drew's no' the one?"

Her painted eyelids dropped to cover her thoughts. "I dunno, maybe." Then her shoulders stiffened and her gaze lifted. "Did my *mom* tell you I was seeing him?"

"Aye."

"Did she also tell you she read my diary?" Emily leaned across the table, suddenly alive with righteous anger. Her black-tipped fingers twisted her napkin into a pretzel. "I mean, jeez, that's like a priest blabbing every-thing he heard in confession. You just don't do that."

"She's worried about you."

"Bullsh—" She blushed again. "I mean, no, she's not. She's just freaked-out that I've got my own life. She's never liked Sheila, she hates the way I dress, and of *course*, she's dissing Drew—he drives a motorcycle."

Lachlan squelched the urge to leap to Rachel's de-fense. He was walking a fine line between earning Emi-ly's trust and alienating her. She wouldn't believe he was sincere if he didn't display the expected opinions of an adult, but she'd stop talking if he came down too solidly in Rachel's camp.

"I think it's his age that has her freaked-out, no' the motorcycle," he said with a faint smile.

She shrugged. "Whatever."

"Obviously he possesses some redeeming qualities, or else you wouldn't have given him the time of day. What's the appeal?"

"He's cute."

"That's it? So, you'll date any good-looking lad who comes along?" he teased.

She grinned. "Of course not. I have standards."

"Which are?"

"Smart, but not a geek. Funny, but not a goof. Cute, but not a prep."

"And Drew meets all those requirements?"

She nodded. "He thinks I'm hot, and he listens to me. Really listens. You have no idea how many people talk right over you, so full of their own shit they can't hear a word you say." She blushed again as she realized she'd cussed, then threw him a quick smile. "You don't."

"That's a relief. Being a snoring bore is no' a good trait in a priest."

Emily laughed.

But Lachlan barely heard her. He was remembering the early days of *his* relationship with Drusus. How he had stumbled across the lad, badly beaten and near death in the moors. How he'd opened up his home, arranged for a healer to tend his wounds, and treated him as a comrade. How as the weeks passed and Drusus mended, they'd grown as close as brothers.

"It's no' just how kind he is that appeals to you," he said softly. "It's the wild, untamed part as well, isn't it?"

Her eyes met his. "He's fun," she said, a tad defensively.

"I know."

"And he's different. He's not just some jerk pretending to be a badass to impress the chicks, you know? He's deeper than that."

"How so?"

"I don't know, exactly." Then she suddenly brightened. "Okay, like, he wears this cool thing around his neck. Not your typical cross or medallion, but a hollow tube of glass with these rockin' symbols etched on it. He calls it a relic or something, and says it contains the souls of these four people from ancient Scotland. A mother and three children."

Lachlan froze. He had difficulty forming the words, but managed to ask, "He wears a reliquary?"

"Yeah, a reliquary. That's what he calls it." Emily caught his expression. "I know, sounds gross, right? But it's not like it's *real*. I mean, come on, it can't be. But the whole idea is just neat, you know? Keeping someone's soul next to your heart?"

A spike of dread tapped deep into his chest. "Did he say why he wears it?"

She wrinkled her nose. "Not really. He says he's planning a family reunion, but I don't know what that means."

Lachlan forced himself to breathe.

He understood. Perfectly. Drusus wore a reliquary around his neck containing the souls of Elspeth, Cormac, Mairi, and Jamie, four souls destined for heaven, but cruelly snatched and imprisoned in an amulet. If he failed to destroy Drusus, if he proved too weak for the task, the consequences would not be limited to the loss of Emily or the Linen—the souls of Lachlan's family would be lost forever to the depths of hell.

His *family*.

The anger that had been building inside him since he first spotted Drusus at the fairgrounds suddenly broke free. Fury surged through his body with such force that the metal sundae spoon clutched in his hand bent in half.

Jamming the warped utensil into his pocket, he stood.

"Drew sounds like quite an interesting guy. Can't wait to meet him."

6

Rachel fooled everyone.

She answered the phone, whipped up two new sample files, squeezed in an emergency banner for tomorrow's employee blood donor drive, and coached a colleague on the fine art of object modeling. But her mind wasn't on her work at all. Nope. She was stuck in a loop, replaying that breathless moment when Lachlan's hand had cupped her cheek, when she'd looked into his eyes and saw desire.

No, take that back. Desire was too mild a word to describe what she'd seen. It was more like lust.

For her.

Even though single motherhood had left little time for a social life since her marriage fell apart, she recognized the signs. Taut, eager muscles. Heat radiating from him in waves. An added edge to his rich, masculine smell. Oh yeah. He wanted her, all right. And the feeling was mutual. One look into those smoky eyes and her bones had melted like baked Brie. There was nothing more erotic than being thoroughly, desperately wanted.

The priest thing was a bit of a sticky issue, though.

Not for her, for him. From the start, she'd had trouble seeing him as a sexless clergyman, and as time passed, that white collar was becoming less and less of an impediment. But for him, it must be a pretty big deal. Priestly vows were not the kind you made in haste and then repented at leisure. Priests studied for years before taking the plunge. And yet here she was, leaning into him, encouraging him, hoping that he'd bust down the wall between them and just kiss her.

Did that make her immoral?

If he hadn't reminded her about work, she was convinced they would have ended up on the floor, wrapped around each other and oblivious to everything but finding satisfaction. There was no doubt in her mind that the kiss would have been spectacular. Hell, if she closed her eyes, she could almost taste it.

"I must say I'm very impressed."

Rachel's eyes popped open.

Nigel, looking remarkably fresh and crisp in a periwinkle blue shirt, stood next to her desk, one hand slung over her cubicle wall, the other propping his glasses on his forehead. Fortunately, his owl eyes were on her computer screen, and not on the rising heat in her cheeks.

"Your nature series is positively stunning. The drawings scanned in beautifully and I love the drama you've created with the light source."

"Thanks."

"You're very talented, Rachel. And smart. I heard you created the wire-frame object models we're using in the designs."

She shrugged. "It was easy."

"Don't be modest. MaskWeave is a very complicated program. The rest of us are in awe." His plump face creased in a thoughtful frown. "I noticed you've checked in eight new illustrations already."

"Yes."

"Hmmm. Matt is a little behind in the pop art series. I wonder if you could take on a few of those as well?"

Rachel stiffened. Every moment of her weekend was already accounted for. She had eight more sample files to complete, and a daughter who was headed for serious trouble if Rachel didn't spend more time with her. "I don't know. . . ."

"You're so fast," Nigel said, cajoling. "It's a gift you have, working so quickly. Matt can't keep up. But we're all in this mess together, and if one of us fails, we all fail."

The mail room girl tossed an elastic-bound stack of new requisitions, production proofs, and documentation blues on Rachel's desk as she sailed by, all of them demanding some kind of attention before the day was done.

Damn. She already felt squeezed between a rock and a hard place, but if she didn't help out, the project would suffer. Her stressed-out coworkers would end up with even more work on their plates. "Okay, I'll do two. Where's his creative spec?"

"On the server." Nigel, his purpose fulfilled, straightened. He minced down the corridor in his stovepipe check pants and Italian shoes, leaving behind a gagging cloud of Boss cologne. "Thanks, sweetie. I knew I could count on you. If you have any problems, come see me in the morning."

Rachel opened her mouth to break the bad news that she wouldn't be coming in over the weekend, then closed it with a snap. Why ruin a good moment? Maybe they'd all be so busy, they wouldn't notice her absence.

She could dream, couldn't she?

Rachel's feet were literally dragging by the time she got home from the office at eleven. Forty-one hours of wakefulness had taken its toll. Her pointy-toed pumps cinched her swollen feet like miniature iron maidens, and all she could think about as she hobbled up the stairs to the second floor was planting her face in her pillow.

But her weary discomfort evaporated the moment she unlocked her apartment door and pushed it open. Why? Because Lachlan MacGregor lay on her living room sofa, his socked feet crossed over one armrest, his right arm folded behind his head.

Sound asleep.

She carefully closed the door, eased her feet out of her torturous shoes, and tiptoed over to look at him.

He overwhelmed her plump chintz sofa as if it were doll furniture. His feet had pushed the glass bowl of apple-cinnamon potpourri to a precarious perch on the side table, and one of his hands had fallen off his chest to the moss green area rug. He looked younger, less burdened. Furrows of experience still lined his brow, but sleep had softened them, and Rachel was suddenly struck by how long his eyelashes were.

And by how absolutely gorgeous he was.

His big chest rose and fell with one deep breath, then two. As she watched, his nostrils flared and his eyes blinked open, instantly homing in on her face. His smoky gaze pinned hers, a turbulent eddy of dark, sultry thoughts.

"Hi," she said breezily, trying to ignore the responsive shiver that ran down her spine. "Looks like—"

She never got a chance to say more.

He grabbed her wrist, tugged sharply, and toppled her over the sofa, onto his chest. He gave her the briefest of moments to protest; then his broad hand dove into the waves of her hair, cupped her head, and yanked her lips to his.

Rachel melted against his solid, spicy warmth. All memory of being tired and disheveled and ready to sleep was swept away by his kiss.

And what a kiss it was.

His firm mouth slanted over hers in a primitive male claim: roughly insistent, hot, and possessive. His tongue swept along the seam of her lips in a blatant demand for entry, and with a soft mewl, she opened her mouth. The tangle of her tongue with his earned her a short groan of satisfaction from Lachlan, and almost immediately, a gentling of his siege.

He adjusted his body beneath her, fully taking her weight and easing the awkward angle of her hips. It was both a thoughtful gesture and a mind-blowingly sensual one. Pelvis to pelvis, it was impossible to miss the hard ridge of his arousal against her belly. His hand slipped under her silk shirt and grazed up the length of her spine, the rasp of his calloused fingers on her sensitive skin sending sweet, delicious ripples along every nerve ending.

Her breath shortened and her nipples puckered. Her belly quivered and her skin grew feverish.

So lost in sensation was she that she barely noticed him release the clasp of her bra with one deft flick. All she knew was pleasure. For the first time in forever, she felt attractive and desirable—a woman. As his warm hand slid around to cup her naked, aching breast, she moaned into his mouth.

Lachlan suddenly broke off the kiss, his breathing ragged. He stared at her for a long moment, the look in his eyes raw and dark . . . and heart-stopping. His hand shifted to a safer spot at her waist.

"You were supposed to slap my face and send me packing," he said huskily.

"Nuh-uh. Not buying that." Still throbbing with fiercely awakened needs, she kissed his chin, nibbling upward along his jaw, reveling in his musky scent and the rough texture of his skin. "I made it pretty clear earlier this afternoon that I was interested, and I know you're a smart man."

A low chuckle rumbled through his chest and into hers. "You say that as if you believe a male brain actually functions around a beautiful woman."

She grinned. And then, because he indirectly called her beautiful, she kissed him again, this time on the lips.

"Perhaps," Lachlan murmured against her mouth, "this would be a good time for me to mention that Emily is in her bedroom and, as of ten or fifteen minutes ago, was still wide-awake."

"Oh, crap."

Rachel swung her feet around and leapt to her feet, glancing over her shoulder at Em's bedroom door. The door was firmly shut, thank God. She hastily shoved her hands under her shirt and refastened her bra.

Lachlan sat up.

"How to be a great role model," Rachel said, grimacing as she smoothed her hair into a vague semblance of order. *"Not."*

"You're doing a fine job with Emily."

"A little two-faced of me to tell her not to go around kissing some black-clad stranger she barely knows, though, don't you think?"

He opened his mouth to speak, then closed it again.

"So," Rachel said, diving onto the velvet chair across from him and folding her hands neatly in her lap. She studied her fingers, amazed that they looked so prim and proper when they felt so hot and tingly. "How did the talk go? Learn anything?"

"Aye."

His tone was suspiciously flat, and Rachel's gaze darted up to meet his. "What? Is it bad?"

"Drusus has successfully wormed his way into Emily's affections. She likes him a great deal. It's going to be very difficult to keep them apart."

"Did you ask her about the drugs? Is she using?"

"Yes, I asked her, and no, no' yet."

"That's good, isn't it? Maybe he won't—" Rachel's hands clenched, gaining more from the look in Lachlan's eyes than she got from his words. "You think it's just a matter of time, don't you? That he's just slowly reeling her in."

"Aye."

"Aye? *Aye?*" An image of her precious Em, wild-eyed and emaciated, desperate for another hit, invaded her mind, seeming all too possible. Her chest clamped so tight she could barely breathe. "How can you be so calm? He's *manipulating* her, and the path he's leading her down will probably end up kill—"

"Rachel, stop." Lachlan tugged her to her feet, his voice soft. "It's okay, trust me. A visit with Drusus is next on my to-do list."

"Talking isn't enough. We have to *do* something."

"Don't worry." He folded her into his arms. "I won't let him walk away, not this time. You have my word. I'll do whatever it takes to ensure he's punished."

His pledge, low and unequivocal, left no room for doubt, and she eased. Wriggling deeper into his embrace, she turned her nose to his broad chest and inhaled a swirl of his reassuring fragrance. "I'm being a stupid, hysterical mom, aren't I?"

"You love her."

"The funny thing is, I never thought I'd be like this. You know, the hovering, overprotective, smothering type. *My* parents gave me plenty of rope to hang myself on—they even let me fly off to study art in Paris when I was twenty." Her gaze found the maple smoking pipe displayed on the mantel, the top of the tobacco bowl darkened by frequent use. Her dad's.

"Life changes you," Lachlan said.

"Yes, it does." Marriage to Grant had certainly changed her. She'd fallen hard for that lazy charm and irresistible smile, only to meet disappointment. Unwilling to give up his bachelor lifestyle and feeling strangled by their commitments, he'd disappeared into the city every weekend, leaving her to shoulder their burdens alone. Rachel shuddered.

Lachlan's arms tightened around her.

"Guess the pendulum swung a little too far in the opposite direction," she said wryly. "Now I'm so tightly wound, I can't let go and I'm pushing her away."

"Your caution is warranted. Drusus is a genuine threat."

She glanced at her daughter's door. "I wish I could convince Em of that."

He stood back and looked her square in the eye. "Give it time." Then he grazed her lips with his, a brief but promising kiss. "I have to go, and you should get some sleep. We'll touch base again in the morning."

"Okay."

Then he slipped on his shoes and was gone.

Rachel stared at the apartment door with eyes that grew wearier by the second. She wished the evening had ended a little differently, but sleep sounded awfully damned appealing. *One date with soft pillows and cool cotton sheets, coming right up.*

Then she groaned—right after she checked Em's room to make certain there was a warm body still under the covers.

It took seventeen minutes of ruthless meditation to clear his mind enough to perform the summoning chant. The sweet taste of Rachel on his lips refused to die easily, and for that, he had no one to blame but himself. The look in her eyes when he woke—the one that suggested he was a man worthy of her interest—had brought him to his knees. He'd known precisely what would happen when he kissed her, and he'd done it anyway.

He'd claimed her.

Like some raiding warrior of old. Now the primitive part of him insisted she was *his*; insisted that he had the right to hold her, make love to her, to never let her go.

An impossible reality.

He slammed a mental door on his folly and carefully tried the summoning again. This time, he got a response, though it wasn't the one he had hoped for. Death sent one of her anorexic bodyguards in her stead.

He scowled at the gray-faced ghoul. "This is an official request. I've followed proper protocol. Get your scrawny arse back there and tell her she *has* to see me."

The milky-eyed guard stared at him for an interminable moment, then nodded abruptly and disappeared.

Ten seconds later, Lachlan was yanked through the frigid chill of time and space without any warning, and without the standard allowance for preparation. It was a damned good thing he was alone in his apartment.

"This had best be important, MacGregor, or I may claim an ear for my irritation."

Lachlan thawed enough to open his eyes.

Death stood before him, staring into a long, garishly lit vanity mirror, powdering her already-pallid nose. Today she wore black stiletto pumps, diaphanous black stockings, and a crisp, stylish black suit. Her white hair was smoothed back into a tight knot, emphasizing the fine bones in her face.

Her eyes met his in the mirror. "Speak."

Lachlan glanced around. They appeared to be in a public restroom—judging by the fixtures, somewhere in

Europe. Two of her guards blocked the door. "I need a tool with which to defeat a lure demon."

Her laugh was a trickle of water over ice. "You can't be serious."

"The girl's soul is at stake. Give me what I need."

Death closed her powder compact with a snap. She tucked it in her purse and then spun around to face him, folding her arms across her chest. "This lure demon has her ensnared?"

"Aye."

Her long white nail tapped her suit sleeve. "By the venomous gods, I hate that bastard."

Lachlan blinked.

"Selfish to the core, a blackguard of the worst kind. He has no reason to interfere, no reason to stand in my way. He's doing it merely to spite me."

It seemed impossible that she would curse at a lowly demon, even an ancient one like Drusus, so Lachlan hazarded, "Satan?"

"Who else?"

"Then arm me properly, and we'll see him and his hellspawn thwarted."

She snorted. "Do not attempt to play me, MacGregor. What do I gain if I give you the wherewithal to seek out and destroy one of Satan's favorite bootlickers? Trouble, nothing more."

"Does the girl's safety no' concern you? The danger is real; derailing the demon's efforts will be difficult."

Death turned back to the vanity and picked up her purse. "I will be most displeased if you fail. You require nothing extra. The tool you need to defeat the lure demon is already within your grasp."

Lachlan's heart slowed to a heavy pound. If true, that was a very valuable piece of information. "No Gatherer has ever slain a lure demon."

"Yes, well, think of it as yet another record you can break." She strode toward the door, her stiletto heels clicking on the white ceramic tiles. As she reached for the handle, her two bodyguards shimmered and evaporated. "Your allotted time is up, I'm afraid. I've got a very important date with a workaholic executive from British Telecom."

"Wait," he barked, annoyed that she would dare to leave him hanging. "What is this mighty weapon of which you speak? The one I apparently possess?"

She tossed a look over her shoulder and smiled.

"You're a smart man, MacGregor. Figure it out."

"Find a spot along the wall and put your back to it," Lachlan ordered briskly. "Slide down until your knees are at ninety degrees and hold your position until I call halt."

All six of his new students complied without protest. Or, to be more accurate, they said nothing until the first minute had passed and their muscles began to quake. Then they grumbled. After the full five minutes, most of them were moaning.

"Halt."

They collapsed to his living room floor amid pathetic sighs of relief.

"Now find a partner." He waited for them to roll to their feet and pair up. "One of you will stand with your feet shoulder width apart, knees slightly bent, buttocks tight. The other will attempt to knock you to the floor. After five minutes or a takedown, whichever comes first, switch places. Everyone clear on the exercise? Good. Go."

Everyone obeyed—except Brian.

"I don't have a partner," he complained.

"You and I have done this exercise many times."

"Yeah, and you always win. Come on, let's spar. It's

my day to introduce your ass to the cold hard floor; I can feel it."

"No' today."

"Why not? Got something better to do?"

"Aye." Like figuring out why everyone kept insisting he was smart when he was actually stumbling about in a bloody fog.

"What?" Brian peered over his shoulder at the notes he was making. "More exercises?"

"No."

The younger Gatherer waited for Lachlan to add to his terse response, but his patience went unrewarded. "You know, MacGregor, you're one closemouthed son of a bitch. I doubt what you're working on is a state secret, so why the hell won't you just fess up?"

"Because it's none of your business."

"Maybe I could help."

"No, you can't."

"Are you sure? I saw the word *persuade* written there in your girly, old-fashioned handwriting, and thought I'd remind you I was the top salesman in my brokerage firm before I wrapped my Lambo around a tree. I know a thing or two about persuasion. Come on, MacGregor, try me."

Lachlan put down his fountain pen. "All right. I'm working out a plan to defeat a two-thousand-year-old lure demon. Got any experience with that?"

"What's a lure demon?"

Lachlan snorted and returned to his notes. "Point made."

"No, wait. What's he after, this lure demon?"

"Why does that matter?"

"Because the key to swaying a person is figuring out what he wants and then giving it to him. In a manner of speaking. What's this creep want?"

Well, the Linen, for one. But as for why Drusus had targeted Emily . . . "Still a question mark. But the plan involves seducing a fourteen-year-old girl."

"A what?"

"You heard me."

"That's sick."

"Webster, stay with the conversation, please. Obviously, I need to keep him away from the girl."

"No," Brian said, with a thoughtful shake of his head. "You need to convince the girl he's not worth having. You have to sell her something better, something she needs more than she needs your demon."

Lachlan arched a brow.

Brian pivoted and studied the six Gatherers who, red-faced and sweaty, were wrapping up their assigned exercise. He pointed to a lean yet muscular young man over by the window, and said, "You need to sell her *him*."

"He's a Gatherer."

"Yeah, but to her, he could be Prince Charming."

Lachlan sighed and rubbed a rough hand over his face. "This girl doesn't want Prince Charming. She wants a very suave and debonair Dracula."

Brian choked back a laugh. "Seriously?"

"Seriously."

"Then that's what we'll give her."

"She's already got one."

"Maybe," Brian said, smiling, "but we'll make this one better. Can I assume this girl belongs to the hot babe I met here the other day?"

"Aye."

"And Mom disapproves of our lure demon, right?"

"Aye."

"Why?"

"He's eight years too old and rides a motorbike."

"Excellent." Brian waved at the young man near the window. "Carlos, buddy, come here a sec."

The young man crossed the room with a typical teen-age swagger and Lachlan eyed him carefully. He was slimly built, Hispanic, with long black hair and a tattoo of a cobra on his wrist.

"How old are you?" Brian asked Carlos.

"Eighteen."

"You've been a Gatherer for only a year, right? Think you could pass for a sixteen-year-old high school student?"

The lad shrugged. "Sure."

"A bit of makeup, some black clothes"—Brian beamed at Lachlan—"and there you have it, Something better. Younger, with no motorcycle. Bad boy, but not too bad. A charming Dracula she can invite home for dinner."

"It might work."

"Come on," Brian prodded. "Admit it, the plan has legs. What's the downside to giving it a whirl?"

"Discovery."

"Don't sweat it. I'm well aware that the devil is in the details. I'll coach him personally."

"You are the farthest thing I know from a Goth teen," Lachlan pointed out. "How can you possibly coach him?"

"I have my sources. Trust me, we can do this."

Thoughtfully, Lachlan studied Carlos. The lad was young and inexperienced, but also confident and diffi-cult to read. Putting him into play was a risk, but how great a risk? "Are you sure you want to do this, Carlos? What's at stake here isn't a short stint in juvie hall; it's oblivion."

The lad shrugged. "In my old life, I played for the same stakes every day."

"And lost. That's why you're here."

"I'm a bit smarter now."

"Maybe, but this time your soul could go to hell."

"My five-year-old brother died right alongside me, man. I'm already in hell."

Lachlan could have argued that it wasn't the same, but the bleak look in Carlos's eyes told him there was no point. "Fine, we'll go with it. Get him decked out and enroll him in Emily's school while I try to figure out the demon's next step." As Brian turned away to lecture Carlos, Lachlan grabbed him by the arm. "Don't be a hero. Either one of you. If Emily displays the slightest suspicion, back away."

"You bet."

Lachlan nodded and turned back to his notes.

The truth was, the Carlos plan might be risky, but it was also convenient. Having someone else interrupt the relationship between Drusus and Emily would allow him to focus on winning back the souls of his family. He could concentrate on finding Drusus and crushing him.

But first he had to figure out what weapon in his arsenal was powerful enough to kick the demon's arse permanently back to hell. The most obvious contender was the new sword Stefan had made for him, the *claidheamh mòr*. The replica of his old war blade offered him both enhanced magic and a familiarity born of many successful battles. There would be a certain justice to using it to bring Drusus down: an old blade for a very old crime.

A ghost of memory shuddered through him.

"We done for the day?"

He glanced up at Brian. "Aye. Be back tomorrow at eight."

"In the *morning*? On a Sunday? Doesn't three hours of brutality today entitle us to sleep in tomorrow?"

"No. From now on we train every day."

"But—"

"That's the deal, Webster. Take it or leave it."

"I've created a monster. This training gig is definitely not rounding out your personality the way I'd hoped."

Lachlan didn't rise to the bait. He simply returned Brian's stare until the other man shrugged and followed the other Gatherers out the door, leaving Lachlan to his thoughts.

Drusus had disappeared nine days before the attack on the manor house, during the massive raid on the Campbells that had won the MacGregors their land back. Everyone had presumed him a casualty. Elspeth had even wept over the poor lad's tragic loss.

The fountain pen in his hand snapped in two, and blue ink sprayed over the countertop.

Lachlan had known the truth—that Drusus was alive and well—and the blame for what happened next lay squarely upon his shoulders. He deserved every moment he'd spent in purgatory, forced to relive the events in excruciating detail for five hundred years. He'd likely end up in hell for his part in his family's horrific demise, and rightly so.

But Drusus was far from blameless.

How fitting it would be for a *claidheamh mòr*, a weapon out of their mutual past, to bring the filthy bastard down. But he wouldn't rely solely on the sword. He'd brush up on his magic, as well.

One way or another, justice would be served.

7

"Where's Emily?" Lachlan asked.

Rachel smiled and opened the door wider. "In her room. Why?"

"I need to speak with you, and I'd prefer we were alone."

Rachel ushered him inside the apartment, then turned to face him. She wore a snug green T-shirt and a pair of faded blue jeans, leaving her feet delightfully bare. Her gleaming hair hung loosely past her shoulders, a graceful tumble of soft dark curls.

"Alone sounds good," she said. "Except that I'm supposed to be working, and you're hell on my concentration."

He pinned her gaze. His entire body had responded instantly to her scent, his blood pumping hot and heavy through his veins, insisting she was his to claim. He let her catch a glimpse of the burn it caused inside him. "How curious, you have exactly the same effect on me."

Rachel gave a gusty laugh and glanced away, shoving her hands into her pockets. "You know, that doesn't help at all."

"Sorry," he said. Except he wasn't. "Can you take a short break to answer a question?"

"Is it important?"

He nodded. "Yes."

"One question?"

"Just one."

"Couldn't you have done that over the phone?"

"Aye, but had I called you on the phone," he said quietly, "I wouldn't have been able to see your naked toes, or smell your shampoo, or watch you lick your lips and wish you were licking mine."

She stared at him, the pulse in her throat beating like a hummingbird's wings. Then she closed her eyes and groaned. "God, what was I thinking? I should never have opened the door."

With her chin tilted slightly upward, her eyes closed, and her body open to him, Rachel was a lure too enticing to resist. Lachlan bent and stole a brief, hard kiss.

"I'm glad you did," he murmured as he breathed her in. Sweet and warm, like honeysuckle on a summer's eve.

She leapt back. "I'm trying to be good here, and you're not making it easy."

"Sorry," he lied—again.

"Sure you are." She retreated into the apartment, cheeks flushed. "Go sit in the armchair."

"Will that really help?" he asked, doubtful. To his mind, nothing short of putting the Pacific Ocean between them would help.

Her eyes narrowed, and she pointed. "Go."

Lachlan did as he was told.

Rachel stomped into the kitchen and grabbed a pitcher of tea from the fridge. He smiled faintly when he saw her double up the ice cubes in one glass, leaving almost no room for tea.

"Hoping to cool me off?" he asked, accepting the iced tea.

"Stop smirking and ask your question." She stood a safe distance away and sipped at her drink.

"What are you cooking?"

"That's your question?"

"No, I'm just curious. Your apartment smells delicious." The savory scent of meat in the oven, the quiet background music on the radio, the lit candles, and the family mementos on the fireplace mantel . . . it all felt wonderfully inviting. Homelike.

"Roast chicken," she confessed, giving a quick smile of pride at his compliment.

A pang of loss hit him hard then. It had been a long time since he'd let himself think about a home or a woman's cooking, about plying compliments intended to tug smiles from reluctant faces. He'd been quite good at that once.

With a slight wobble in his hand, Lachlan set his glass down on the side table. "My real question is, what's the one thing Emily wants most?"

"Why do you need to know?"

"If Drusus is intent on sucking her into his view of the world, he'll attempt to give it to her, to win her confidence."

Rachel stilled, her oval face pensive. "I have no idea."

"Take your time."

Her eyes met his, filled with genuine pain. "No, you don't understand. I really have no idea. I used to know her so well, but now . . . I haven't a clue."

"Didn't you say you read her diary?"

"Yes. Pages upon pages of dark angst over school and friends and boys. Nothing about her deeper wants and desires. Half of it was in code, anyway, people's initials instead of their names."

"Is there a dream she wants to fulfill, an impossible item she's always wanted to purchase?"

She grimaced. "Not that I know of. I mean, she makes

the usual oohs and aahs about the stuff she sees on TV, but minutes later, it's forgotten."

"Okay," he said, getting to his feet. "Keep thinking on it. Let me know if you come up with something. It'll help us figure out what he's planning next."

"Can I ask Em?"

"I'd rather you didn't. If she shares the discussion with Drusus, he'll be on to us."

"Okay."

The look of failure on Rachel's face was too much to bear. Lachlan tugged her into his arms and rested his chin in the soft cloud of her hair. Standing here like this, with their bodies loosely entwined and the urge to protect her a warm burn in his chest, he could almost fool himself into believing a future together was possible.

"You know her better than you think," he said gently. "The Goth outfit hasn't changed the girl beneath. What's important to Emily now is likely the very same as when she was a child. Dig a little deeper and it'll come to you."

She gave him a grateful squeeze, and then laid her cheek against his chest. Her sigh was barely audible, not intended for his ears, but he heard it.

"Can I keep you?"

He closed his eyes. His heartbeat was an echo of the very same question. Unfortunately, he knew the answer.

After he had gone, Rachel returned to her illustration, but it was a waste of time. Lachlan's question kept ringing in her ears: *What's the one thing Emily wants most?*

Wow. What kind of mother doesn't know what her child dreams about? She often accused Grant of not knowing his own daughter, but was she any better? At least *he* had an excuse—he lived in a different city. She lived with Em day in and day out. Saw her at breakfast every morning. Ate dinner with her. How could she not know?

But she didn't. Not even a decent guess.

At age six, Em had dreamed of growing wings and becoming a fairy. And at nine, she'd desperately wanted a pony. But now? Her spoken desires amounted to little more than a plea for hot concert tickets or a new pair of earrings. Or that damned tattoo she'd asked for last month. But it couldn't be something as simple as a tattoo.

Rachel flicked on the oven light and peered in at the chicken. Starting to brown. Time to start thinking about the rest of the meal.

She set the burner under the potatoes to high and opened the fridge. All the ingredients were there for a salad, so she pulled them out, plus butter and milk for the potatoes. The milk carton was almost empty.

Leaning around the kitchen wall, she called, "Em."

No answer.

She shook her head, trod the four feet of hallway, and turned the doorknob. Em lay on her bed, reading a book with her MP3 player hooked into her ears. To compensate for the attention barriers, Rachel upped her voice level. "Em, I need you to run down to the 7-Eleven for me."

"I'm reading."

"I can see that. But we're out of milk. Don't you want to get out for a few minutes?"

Em chewed her lip.

It was day ten of the two-week grounding, and other than the trip to the fairgrounds that night, as far as Rachel knew, Em hadn't been anywhere except school. The attraction of leaving the apartment, even for a chore, had to be high.

Sure enough, Em tucked a bookmark into the latest installment of her urban fantasy saga and crawled off the bed. "Okay."

Five minutes later, alone in the apartment, Rachel was chopping up tomatoes and cucumber for the salad. The grandfather clock chimed the half hour, and just like that, an idea popped into her head—one she couldn't seem to shake.

She had a brief opportunity to peek into Em's bedroom.

Everything Em claimed as her own ended up in that room: her coat, her shoes, her schoolbag—everything. If it was Em's, it went into the cave, sometimes never to be seen again. If she wanted to find a clue to what Em desired most, wasn't that the best place to look?

Rachel put down the paring knife and wiped her hands on a tea towel. Taking a deep breath, she returned to her daughter's bedroom and pushed open the door.

Standing on the threshold, she slowly swept the room, absorbing the familiar, post-apocalypse flavor. Clothes and garbage were strewn everywhere. The picture on the dresser caught her eye: a family shot—Christmas Eve, maybe five or six years ago—with all three of them sitting in front of the holly-decked fireplace of their home in Connecticut, hugging and laughing as if their lives weren't on the verge of falling apart. A handful of loose change, one lone earring, and a bottle of black nail polish littered the dresser top, but there were no magazines or notes that might serve as clues.

The big double bed stood against the far wall, its black cotton sheets rumpled and the lightweight comforter balled up against the wall. Above the bed, tacked to the wall at crazy angles, hung posters of several Goth bands and singers, including Siouxsie Sioux, the Cure, and Lycia.

The walk-in closet displayed racks of untidily hung black clothes, with a pile of mismatched shoes at the bottom. Even the knee-high lace-up leather boots Em had promised to keep in pristine condition were tossed onto the heap.

Rachel stepped into the room.

She dodged the clumps of scattered clothes on the floor and crossed to the desk. Unearthing a couple of magazines from beneath the junk food wrappers around the computer, she searched for dog-eared pages and open spreads—anything that would suggest interest. When that turned up nothing, she dug through the drawers.

And found a knife.

Not just any knife, one of her ebony-handled Shun steak knives—razor sharp. Rachel picked it up, frowning. Why would Em have a knife in her room?

"What the hell are you doing?"

At the low snarl of Em's voice, Rachel spun around, her heart ricocheting against her rib cage. Her daughter stood at the door, MP3 player in hand, betrayal a dark stain in her eyes.

Oh God.

At a loss for anything else, Rachel went with the truth. "I feel as if I'm losing you, Em. I came in here looking for a sign, I guess, of the person you've become. Something that would help me talk to you."

Em yanked open the dresser drawer and dug for a spare battery. "Or maybe you just wanted another go at my diary."

"I didn't read your diary."

"Why not? Did I come back a little too soon? How inconvenient of me to interrupt Mommy on her little spy mission."

"It wasn't like that," Rachel said defensively.

"Not really feelin' the love here, Mom. Groundings, room rousts. Christ, next you'll be putting bars on my windows and a lock on my door."

Flushing, Rachel quickly changed the subject. "Why do you have a steak knife in your room?"

"Why does that matter?" Em's shoulders hunched. "I was probably eating something."

"Em, listen to me. I'm just worried about you, that's all. This whole thing with Drew has me freaked-out, I'll admit it. He scares me."

"Oh yeah, he's really scary. He wears a black leather jacket and drives a bike."

"There's more to him than that." Rachel needed to believe that a piece of the old Em still existed. The bright, straight-A student who questioned everything. Surely if Em knew what kind of person Drew really was, she'd do the smart thing and walk away? "He's not what you think he is, Em. Lach—Father MacGregor used to know Drew, and he told me he was involved in something pretty bad."

At the mention of Father MacGregor, Em grew still, and Rachel knew she had a chance. Although she didn't want to frighten Em, the truth had worked so far. . . .

"He sells drugs, Em."

As soon as the words were out, a shutter fell over Em's face. She gave a harsh laugh and sauntered over to the window. "Wow, he was right. He said you'd dredge up some over-the-top story, that you'd go out of your way to make him look bad. I didn't believe it, but hey, here we are."

"It's not a story. It's true."

"Really? Better get your facts straight, Mom. I talked to Father MacGregor about Drew, and guess what? He *understood*. He totally got it. He never once tried to convince me Drew was some evil, despicable drug dealer."

Too late, Rachel realized the trap she'd fallen into and she backpedaled. "He didn't want to frighten you."

"Nice try, but guess what? I don't buy it."

"Em, I—"

"Know what the funny part is? I defended you. Drew told me he went to see you, to tell you all about himself, but that you wouldn't listen. He insisted that you ordered him to stay away from me and threatened to sic the police on him. I told him my mom wouldn't do that. I told him that as much as I get pissed off at you, you were basically okay. You just wanted me to be happy, and you get things screwed up a bit, trying too hard. But now, I can't help but wonder if he was right. Did you do that, Mom? Did you threaten him with the police?"

Rachel swallowed. "I—"

"On second thought, don't answer. Life sucks enough as it is. I don't need to know that my mom is a bitch."

Although the word was purposely cruel, it was delivered in a very quiet and controlled manner. Em had retreated behind her icy wall. She tossed her spent batteries on top of the dresser, then shoved the drawer shut.

The family photo wobbled, but didn't fall, and Grant's laughing face wagged at Rachel in a smug taunt.

"I'm going to get the milk."

Early Sunday morning, Lachlan decided he was ready to confront Drusus.

Three a.m. seemed a natural time to find a lure demon intent on perverting weak souls, and a dark, foul-smelling alley behind a graffiti-decorated apartment building seemed the perfect place to perform a locator spell.

He carefully intoned the words of the spell, ensuring his pronunciation was clear, and then scattered the necessary handful of scorched rat bones. A misty circlet formed in the air above the bones, glowing faintly. In the center of the circle, images began to appear, drop by drop, like paint splatters on a canvas. Each image showed a location around the city. Some he recognized; some he did not. As new drops wiped out old, the images came faster and faster, until his eyes could no longer keep up.

Then they suddenly stopped.

But not in a helpful spot. Instead of the usual pinpointed landmark, all he got was a four-block radius in which to search, just west of where he stood.

With a heavy sigh, he waved the damp mist away and crouched beside his latest gathering assignment.

A gut-shot punk in a black silk jacket lay sprawled amid the rubbish, a small bag of white powder floating in the blood next to him. He placed his hand on the dead man's throat. A drug dealer. How apropos.

The familiar feathery tendrils danced up his arm, but this time there was no balmy warmth, no gentle tranquility—only the slimy ooze of a rancid soul snaking around his heart. As usual, the sensation evoked a low wave of nausea.

No more than an instant after the ooze leached into his blood, the air around him crackled and dried like mud under the desert sun. Not unexpected, of course. Unlike angels, Satan's henchmen were never late picking up a soul.

Pop.

Still squatted next to the body, Lachlan glanced up . . . just as a ball of brilliant orange fire plowed into his right shoulder. He reacted instinctively, rolling back and drawing his *claidheamh mòr* as he regained his feet. But the severity of a fireball hitting him full on, without the mitigation of a shield spell, brought tears to his eyes and blood to his lip as he bit down to diffuse the pain.

"Hello, MacGregor."

A wave of undiluted agony shuddered through Lachlan, and his voice broke. "Dru-sus."

"Those hurt like hell, don't they?" the lean, blond demon said, pointing to the writhing, blackened flesh of Lachlan's shoulder and smiling at his own joke. "I don't normally lower myself to collect souls, but I thought since you were looking for me, I'd oblige."

"Nice of you," Lachlan gasped as he wove a belated shield charm. He blinked until his opponent came into focus.

Drusus walked around him in slow, measured steps, his sharply angled face a study of youthful arrogance.

"I see you're sticking with the tried and true. Nothing modern man has created quite surpasses an excellent blade, does it?" A soft whoosh, and then he, too, held a sword in his hands: a gladius, shorter than Lachlan's sword and engraved up the length with his name in Roman script. "I'd forgotten what it feels like to hold one."

Deep in the shadowy gap of the demon's zippered jacket, a thick gold chain shimmered, a chain strong enough to support a heavy glass reliquary. Lachlan's gut twisted.

"Perhaps you've also forgotten how to use it."

Drusus swung the gladius loosely in front of his body. "You could hope for that, *baro*. But if you recall, it was I who taught you everything you know about fine swordsmanship."

"No' everything."

"I can still picture your face the first time I disarmed you. You, a mighty clan chieftain, and I, nothing but a spindling lad. You were galled."

"I'm less vexed now that I know you cheated."

"Cheated?"

"Demon versus human is hardly a fair fight."

The demon's eyes hardened into shiny beads of jade. "Immortal versus immortal would seem to be a battle of equals, though. What do you say? Shall we engage in a contest?"

"Aye, let's duel. The point of my sword is eager to meet your belly."

Drusus snorted. "I admire your confidence, Mac-Gregor. But perhaps we should get our business out of the way first, on the off chance it's you who perishes and not I. Where's the Linen?"

"I destroyed it."

"Nice try. Unfortunately, destroying a relic of such consequence would leave a mystical residue of mushroom cloud proportions." He glanced up at the sky. "I don't see one, do you?"

That would have been nice to know. Yesterday. "You don't really expect me to tell you where it is, do you?"

"Of course I do. You owe it to me." The demon's eyes glittered. "We had a bargain. You were to let me in the back gate so I could steal the Linen. Hiding it was never part of the arrangement."

"Any bargain we struck was voided the moment you invited the Campbells into my home. The deal did no' include the slaughter of my family."

"Actually, it did. I just never told you that part."

Lachlan stiffened. Even now he knew Drusus was a demon, it was surprisingly hard to accept that the young man who'd once carried an adoring young Cormac on his shoulders had watched dispassionately as Tormod sliced the boy's throat.

"Apparently, there were words left unspoken on both sides," Lachlan said. "Had you bothered to speak to me before running my brother through, you'd possess the Linen today. Despite the promise I made to protect it, I intended to give the cloth to you."

The demon's face darkened. "You lie."

"Nay, I was your puppet, properly enthralled. But watching my wife's throat cut before my very eyes and listening to Tormod Campbell crow about slaying my bairns shook me free of your clutches, hellspawn. I vowed then you'd never touch it, and I happily did the unthinkable simply to see you thwarted."

Drusus grimaced. "Indeed, I never expected you to entrust it to the very clan that wiped out your family. I could have saved myself several hundred years of searching, had I considered that possibility."

"There you have it—the Linen eludes you because of your own mistakes."

"Not mistakes. Just the one. My only error was with you."

Silence fell between them as Lachlan absorbed the significance of that. Irrational or not, being the only one in two thousand years to hoodwink Drusus induced a twinge of pride. Perhaps it boded well for this encounter, too.

"And tonight," Drusus added, "I get the chance to redeem myself. We'll battle, you'll put up a good fight, but I'll win. I'll get the whereabouts of the Linen, and you'll finally get a respectable warrior's death. It'll all end well."

"I'm already dead."

Humor softened the harsh lines of the other man's face. "Yes, well, you know what I mean."

And then, without warning, he lunged. The point of his sword drove accurately at Lachlan's heart, his attack swift and sure—only to be deflected by the *claidheamh mòr*.

"Oh, bravo," Drusus said, unfazed. "I would have hated this to be a one-sided affair."

Lachlan had been about to toss a blinding spell, so it

would hardly have been a one-sided affair, with or without his excellent reflexes. But he didn't bother to debate that. He was too busy executing a fierce downward slice toward the lure demon's neck.

Drusus parried it. At the same time, he brought his own flavor of magic to the fight. A dustbowl of swirling red miasma rose up from the damp pavement, encircling the two of them as they dueled. Spinning madly, the crimson tornado lifted higher and higher, until it obliterated every star in the night sky. Then white-hot fireballs began to rain down on Lachlan.

His shield charm took a heavy beating. In a disquietingly short time, the hellish fury pitted the protection spell to rice paper density. But Lachlan had little time to spare for repairs.

He was battling an expert swordsman.

Had he been the same rough soldier Drusus had manipulated all those years ago, his defeat would have been quick and brutal. The demon held nothing back, hitting his blade with powerful, bone-rattling blows, the kind of blows one avoids in practice sessions for fear of irreparably damaging a blade.

Fortunately, though, Lachlan was no longer a backward Scottish knight who only hacked and thrusted. With the help of Italian and Spanish masters, at whose feet he had studied for a hundred years after his death, he'd honed his talents to a lethal edge. Those talents now served him well.

He cut and thrust with smooth, almost effortless technique. He broke through the demon's defenses twice, slicing through the leather jacket and biting deep into flesh. His new sword glowed green with the taste of demon blood.

But victory eluded him.

The sword was not enough. Not only did his opponent's wounds heal with incredible speed, allowing Drusus to continue fighting without respite, but moments after Lachlan scored his second successful slice, the beleaguered shield charm collapsed, leaving him dreadfully barren of protection. He swiftly called forth another, but it was whisked away before it was fully formed, with no more exertion than a horse swatting a fly.

The swirling red vapor dissolved, carried away in wisps on the night breeze. Drusus paused, staring curiously at Lachlan's heaving chest and sweat-drenched brow.

"You Gatherers are little better than humans," he observed, sounding disappointed. "This is hardly the challenging duel I'd hoped it would be."

Lachlan responded by whipping a restraining spell at him, roping the demon in thick white cords and pinning his arms to his sides.

Drusus broke the binds with a single in-drawn breath. "Very rudimentary stuff, that. There's a much better spell in the *Book of Gnills*. Where's the Linen?"

As the tattered remnants of the binds fell away, the gap in the demon's leather jacket widened, and Lachlan caught a glimpse of a faint golden glow about his neck—the reliquary. A bitter dose of failure poured into his throat, choking him. Drusus could crush him, right here and right now, if that was his desire—not without a fight, of course, but slowly, inevitably, courtesy of the indefatigable power the bastard borrowed from Satan. And when he fell, the souls of his family would be cast into hell, never to be recovered.

No. He could not let them down. Not again. He drew deep on his powers and straightened to his full height.

"Fuck you."

His nemesis smiled coldly. "Don't be foolish, MacGregor. Put down the sword, or I'll be forced to wring the location of the Linen from you. Bit by agonizing bit."

"Go ahead, try."

"That confidence is born of ignorance. You can't begin to imagine the pain I can inflict." He paused, eyeing Lachlan's firm stance and grip. "Tell me where the Linen is."

"No."

"Tell me where it is, or I'll be forced to take my anger out on Emily."

Unease crept into Lachlan's muscles, numbing the pain of his exertions and slowing his breathing to a barely discernible flow. The demon could jump to Emily's room in an instant. "You won't harm her."

"Are you certain? Are you willing to watch her suffer just to spite me?"

"You've spent a lot of time setting up this lure," Lachlan said. "You won't risk the end result by allowing her to see the real you now." Not when the corruption of a pure soul offered Satan twice the power of an ordinary soul.

"Fine, you're right." Drusus shrugged. "But that still leaves me with the lovely Rachel to play with. And don't bother to deny she means something special. I *know* you."

Her name upon the lure demon's lips was an abomination. It ate away at his insides like acid, but Lachlan successfully reined in his bitterness.

"The man you once knew is dead, inside and out," he said. The words rang with quiet honesty—not too surprising, as he'd endured four hundred years of that truth before waking to Rachel's siren call. "I feel nothing."

"Come now, MacGregor. Death is not a fool. She does not lock a Gatherer's feelings away with his soul. She'd end up with an army of passionless drones, were that the case."

"Death didn't rob me," Lachlan agreed. "I believe that honor is yours."

There was a short pause, then a deep rumble of laughter. "By Satan's glory, are you pandering to my ego? Trying to manipulate *me*?"

"Believe what you want."

The flatness of Lachlan's comment tugged the demon's heavy brows together. "Shall I fetch Rachel and see?"

"It won't matter. I still won't tell you where the Linen is."

"She's a fine woman, your Rachel. Beautiful *and* strong. The sort who quickens your pulse the moment you spy her. Admit it, *baro*, you care for her."

And give the demon a reason to harm her? No. Lachlan drained every speck of emotion from his voice and buried his feelings for Rachel in the deepest vaults of his mind. "I will no' admit what I do no' feel."

"Then I take it you won't mind if I cut in? I have a sense she'll be even more enjoyable than Elspeth was. Did I ever tell you your lovely wife gave herself to me in a desperate bid to save your life?"

Lachlan closed his eyes. The image of Elspeth's torn and sullied gown returned to him in painful clarity, along with the tears on her face and the pallor of her cheeks. His inability to save her shuddered through him once more.

"Bastard."

He dove at the demon, sword swinging.

And the fight began anew. Lachlan's fury served him well, for a while. He successfully landed a spell or two and broke through the demon's powerful defenses to score blood several gratifying times. But every Romany magic spell drained his energy. With Drusus wielding his full repertoire of primal energy and Lachlan bereft of protection, the outcome was inevitable. In the end, the sheer longevity of the battle brought him to his knees.

Drusus grabbed his hair and yanked his head up. "Tell me where the Linen is."

"No."

The iron pommel of the demon's sword struck him in the face. "Tell me."

"No." The word, though slurred by his split lip, was still forceful.

"So be it."

Drusus showed no mercy. He hacked and sliced until Lachlan reached the very precipice overlooking oblivion, until the roar of the express train to hell rushed past his ears, until there were no more twitches of resistance. Only then did the demon cease his attack.

"This isn't over, MacGregor," he snarled.

Battered, bloodied, and racked with pain, Lachlan barely felt the bastard put a hand on his heart and snatch the drug dealer's soul.

8

Night still held the sky when Lachlan opened his eyes—one of them, at any rate; the other was completely swollen shut.

It was survival instinct that roused him. His subconscious mind registered the nutty aroma of coffee and the rumble of human voices, dragging him from the deep stupor his wounds had left him in and forcing him to wake. Less than fifty yards away, two men, paper cups in hand, approached the entrance to the alley, shuffling along at a gait that suggested they were still half asleep. In a moment they would be upon him. They would spy the sliced ribbons of his clothing, gasp over the pools of blood, and run shouting for the police.

Unless he moved.

Now.

Fighting the numbing fatigue of a body desperately struggling to recuperate and the biting protest of multiple bleeding wounds, he tossed his sword into a nearby pile of garbage. Then he reached out a hand, clawed at the tarmac, and dragged himself farther into the alley. He resisted the urge to moan, his focus solely on his goal: a shadowed doorway some three feet away. Huddled there, he'd appear nothing more notable than a homeless vagrant.

The men were twenty yards off.

He pushed with his feet, slipping, straining, feeling a bone-deep gouge on his leg part and leak more blood. Knowing he injured himself further with every kick at the pavement, yet willing to pay the price to reach safety.

And thankfully, he did.

The pair of McDonald's employees traipsed by in the darkness, unaware that the dark wet patches on the sidewalk were blood, unaware that only a few feet away lay a body nearly drained of essence.

Survival now assured, the adrenaline-induced tension in Lachlan's muscles drained away. His chin nodded toward his chest as a black fog once again strove to claim him, to protect him, to heal him.

Rachel.

He sucked in a deep breath and jerked his head up.

He had to find her, make sure she was okay, *warn* her.

His head wobbled on his neck as he squinted at the weathered brass knob above his head. Lifting his very heavy hand, he extended it an incredible distance—miles, it seemed. But he never reached the knob.

Somewhere between here and there, his immortal body decided it required lights-out, and he fell headfirst into a vast pool of emptiness.

Rachel sighed as she tugged her wide portfolio out of the backseat. Despite her best efforts, the morning hadn't gone much better than the weekend. Em still hated her. Breakfast had been fifteen minutes of stone-cold silence, punctuated by glares. Frankly, the drive to work had been a reprieve.

She locked the car doors. The only parking spot she'd been able to find had been way at the back, next to a big blue garbage Dumpster. On the plus side, the nearby cluster of maples would shade the car in the afternoon and alleviate the sweltering heat of the drive home. Oh, to have air-conditioning.

"Rachel."

She spun around to face the trees.

There, leaning against a sturdy gray trunk, partially cloaked by shade, stood Lachlan MacGregor. But not the take-charge, confident version she was used to. This one was hunched over, head bent, one leg supporting the bulk of his weight.

She took a tentative step forward, a little afraid of what his sagging appearance meant. But as she drew closer, details became visible and Rachel gasped. His unshaven face was deathly pale, one eye sported a large purple bruise, and his nose had a lump that hadn't been there before. There were a dozen places on his body that looked singed, and those slices in his black suit . . . were they *knife wounds*?

Portfolio banging against her legs, she ran to him. Her shaky fingers grazed along the shredded edges of his jacket, feeling a crusty dampness that her thumping heart told her was blood. Up close, she saw more cuts—on his arms, his chest, everywhere. "Oh my God, what happened?"

"Drusus and I had our little . . . chat."

"Since when do chats involve knives? His gang sure did a number on you—you're bleeding all over the grass."

"It's no' as bad as it looks."

"Really?" she said, trying to sound calm, doing her best not to think about just how much blood he'd lost. With so many cuts, it must be gallons. "You look like you were run over with a lawn mower."

"Oddly enough, that's exactly how it feels." He smiled,

a jumbled expression of amusement and confusion. His leg gave out and he slid down the trunk of the tree to sit in the grass.

Rachel dug into her purse, her fingers suddenly nerveless. "I'm calling 911. You need to get to a hospital."

"No." He covered her hand with his.

"Lachlan, you could *die*."

A short chuckle escaped his dry, cracked lips. "Trust me, I'm no' going to die. Drusus was very careful about how far he went. See for yourself, the bleeding has almost stopped."

Rachel shook her head, but she put the phone away. He was right; the bleeding had definitely slowed. "Why did you come here, you idiot? You should've gone straight to a hospital."

"I needed to see you," he said, his voice low. His dark eyes unerringly found hers in the dim light.

"Why? D-did he threaten me?"

"I'm just a worrier." Lachlan shifted, pushing up with one hand, straightening against the tree. "I'll be back on my feet soon enough, but in the meantime, don't talk to him, don't listen to him, even if it involves Emily. Promise me."

"This is getting out of hand. We should go to the police. One look at you and they'll lock him up."

"No, they won't. There weren't any witnesses. It'll be his word against mine."

One cut on his thigh, an ugly red gash nearly six inches long, oozed blood at his movement, and concern overrode Rachel's budding anger that Drew might go free. "I'm driving you to the hospital. Now. That cut needs stitches."

"I'm fine."

"Don't argue. Get in the car."

"All right." He reached for a low branch and hauled

himself to his feet—an action that brought sharp lines of strain to his brow.

If his easy acquiescence wasn't enough to make her hurry, she didn't know what was. He was weak as a kitten, and given Lachlan's penchant for exercise, that couldn't be a good thing. She unlocked the car, then darted back to Lachlan's side to help him walk. But when she went to put an arm around his waist, he jerked upright.

"I told you, I'm fine."

"But—"

Displaying more energy than she thought him capable of, he yanked open the car door and slid awkwardly onto the seat. "Just drive, Rachel."

She grimaced. Men and their stupid macho bullshit. She joined him in the car, backed out of the parking spot, and zoomed toward the gated entrance. "O'Connor Hospital is the closest. I can have us there in a couple minutes."

"That's if this death trap of a car doesn't kill us first."

She glanced at him.

His head lolled on the headrest and his eyes were closed, but he was smiling faintly.

"Was that a joke? You must be hurt worse than I thought."

He opened his eyes. "Are you accusing me of having no sense of humor?"

"You *are* a bit serious," she pointed out.

His smile deepened. "Only a bit?"

Rachel stared into his unsettling gray-blue eyes a tad too long and almost rammed into the back end of a bright green Volkswagen Beetle. When she slammed on the brakes, pitching them both forward, Lachlan grunted.

"Sorry," she said, wincing at his pallor. "Uh, we're here."

As she flung open her door, Lachlan said, "No, don't get out. I'll walk in on my own."

"Are you nuts?"

He grabbed her arm, preventing her exit—amazingly strong for a guy on death's door. "It's ten to nine."

Rachel bit her lip. If she left now, she could still make it to work in time for the assessment meeting with Celia, the meeting to decide whether the launch date of the product would slip. "I can't just leave you here."

"Yes, you can. It's only a couple of feet to the Emergency Room door. I can make it on my own—I swear."

With her having been MIA at the office all weekend, no one would know how many designs she'd completed. People would be panicking. "Promise me you won't faint from lack of blood before you get there."

"Okay." He smiled and tucked a wavy lock of hair behind her ear. "Promise me you won't talk to Drusus."

"Okay. But what do I do if he shows up?"

"Call me. My cell phone number is—"

"Wait." Rachel opened her purse and dug deep, pulling out a handful of markers, elastics, paperclips, and coins. She selected a fine-point black marker and thrust the rest back in. "Ready."

She wrote the number on her palm.

Stiffly, he maneuvered out of the car and shut the door, then limped around to her open window. "Thank you."

Taking a deep breath, she tried to settle her thoughts in preparation for the meeting. But her eyes kept straying to Lachlan's pale face.

"Are you sure you're going to be okay?"

"Go."

She sighed at the fatigue etched into the corners of his mouth, and giving in to a rather possessive urge, grabbed his chin and planted a firm kiss on his lips. "Don't die on me, Lachlan MacGregor, or I'll be very angry."

He smiled, his eyes impossibly gentle.

She dug into her purse again, pulled out a bottle of Tylenol Extra Strength, and thrust it into his hands. "In case ... I don't know, just in case."

Then she put the car in gear and roared away.

"What the fuck happened to you?" Brian asked.

Lachlan grimaced as he opened the taxi door and slid onto the seat. He'd asked himself that very question a thousand times while waiting in front of the hospital. "What took you so long?"

"Don't drive, remember? So I had to call a cab. And when you called, you neglected to mention you were bleeding all over the sidewalk." Brian quoted Lachlan's address to the cabbie, then sat back and studied the patchwork of burns and slices. "Seriously, you look like shit. What happened?"

"I got my arse kicked."

"I see that. The other guy's a stiff, I assume?"

"No." Unfortunately, Drusus was alive and well. Lachlan dug a black thread out of the coagulating wound on his leg. Most of his injuries had already crusted into scabs, but not the one on his thigh.

"You lost a fight with a demon?" The enormity of Brian's surprise was mollifying. "And you're still around? I don't get it."

Debating the best response, Lachlan stared out the window as the taxi coasted down the semicircular drive of the hospital and onto Di Salvo.

"Jeez, did you *run*?"

"No, I bloody well did no' run," he said, glaring at the younger Gatherer. "The bastard spared me."

"Why?"

"Because he wants me to suffer as much as possible."
And there was a damned good chance he'd use Rachel
to do it.

"Ah," Brian said, the light of understanding finally
shining in his eyes. "You got punked by the creepy pe-
dophile. Well, I've got some news that might make you
feel a bit better."

"What is it?" The cab hit a pothole, and he winced.

"Uh, you need us to pull over?"

"No."

"You're looking a little green."

"Just get to the point, Webster."

"I mean it; you look like you're going to—" Brian
caught Lachlan's eye and halted. Still, incorrigible pup
that he was, he reached across and cracked Lachlan's
window open before saying, "We made first contact this
morning, and I think it went pretty well."

"Carlos met with Emily?"

"Yeah. I signed him up at the school this morning and
made sure they bumped into each other at lunch. We're
taking things slow, natch, but things are headed in the
right direction."

"Did they talk?"

"Not exactly. Unless you count talking with their
eyes."

Lachlan rubbed at his unbruised eye with the heel
of his hand. "Relationships can take weeks to develop,"
he said with a heavy sigh. "I'm no' sure this is worth the
risk."

"Come on, even gathering is a huge risk these days. I
say we run with Carlos for as long as we can."

"There are other avenues to pursue."

The taxi halted in front of the whitewashed apartment building, and the two men rolled out. After he paid
the driver, Brian turned to Lachlan.

"Those avenues involve me and the other guys, right?"

"No. This is between me and Drusus."

"Uh, looked in a mirror lately? I'll let you in on a little secret: The one-on-one thing was a botch."

No doubt about that. But if anything, the severity of his thrashing only confirmed how senseless it would be to pull the other Gatherers into his troubles, and how unbelievably foolish and risky his budding relationship with Rachel was. He was going to get her killed. "It's no' your fight."

"Sure it is. He's a demon, and we fight demons."

"Let it go," Lachlan said wearily. His head was throbbing, and he was not in the mood to argue.

"No, I won't let it go. Don't count us out, MacGregor. I'm telling you, you're going to need all the help you can get taking this whack-job out."

"I'll keep that in mind."

"You do that."

Twisting the cap off Rachel's bottle of Tylenol, Lachlan tossed back two caplets. Speaking of whack-jobs, another visit to Stefan was definitely in order.

"Sorry, buddy." Brian patted Lachlan's arm with exaggerated care. "I've got a gather scheduled, or I'd come upstairs and make you some chicken noodle soup."

"Sod off."

The other man grinned. "If you're lucky, maybe your hot babe will show up and give you a cuddle."

"And if *you're* lucky and you leave quickly, you'll avoid the drubbing I'm still very capable of giving you."

Brian laughed.

But he also made a hasty retreat down the driveway.

Which was wise, because between Lachlan's pounding headache and the tempting but impossible thought of cuddling with Rachel, his mood was souring at an exponential rate.

*   *   *

Rachel hung up the phone, frowning. Lachlan wasn't at the hospital. In fact, the emergency triage nurse said they had no record of him at all. Which meant what? That he'd let her drive him all the way to the hospital and then gone home without seeing a doctor?

She grimaced. Idiot. He needed help. She could call him on his cell phone and warn her she was coming, or . . . just show up.

"Mandy, can you check these files in for me?"

"Sure, Rache." Her friend accepted the disc, then, curious, tilted her stylishly tousled blond head. "But why can't you do it yourself?"

"I'm leaving early."

Her response was met with silence.

"They really liked my nature set," Rachel said brightly, avoiding Mandy's reproving stare. "And I finished off two more of Matt's sample files."

"Yeah, but Celia was royally pissed that you didn't come in on the weekend, and the group as a whole is still behind. If we hadn't squeezed more time out of the printers, we'd be in deep shit. We have three more days, that's it."

"Yeah, when I told Nigel I needed to leave, he freaked. Then he made me promise to finish off the rest of Matt's sample files by tomorrow night."

"Yikes! Are you crazy?"

"A friend of mine is really sick," she said. "I have to go check on him."

"Him?" Mandy spun around in her chair and favored Rachel with a sly look. "I hope this *friend* is worth the six extra files. Is he cute?"

"Cute? No," Rachel said wryly. Lachlan would probably choke over that description. And he definitely hadn't looked cute the last time she saw him—not with a whopping bruise around his eye and that nasty bump on his nose.

"What's his name?"

Sensing the questions were going to continue until Mandy got a juicy morsel of gossip, Rachel smiled sweetly at the other woman. "Father MacGregor."

"A priest? Oh, come on. You're pulling my leg."

"No, I'm not."

Mandy gave a defeated huff and turned back to her computer. "You really gotta get a life, Rache."

"Trust me, I'm working on it."

All the way home, Rachel mulled over her last throwaway comment to Mandy. Was she really working on getting a life? Or just setting herself up for further grief? A couple of kisses did not add up to a relationship. Hell, she didn't even know if a relationship was possible. Some priests could marry, of course, but was Lachlan one of them?

Not that she was signing up for marriage again, of course. One drive around that block was plenty.

She parked the car in her usual spot and took the stairs. The object of her internal debate opened his apartment door after only one knock, looking anything but cute, but undeniably heart-stopping.

"Rachel."

He stood there, staring at her. No naked chest this time, but his short-sleeved clerical shirt allowed her to admire the ropy muscles of his arms and imagine them wrapped around her. An event was probably not in the cards today, given his injuries, although he did look a lot healthier. The bruise had faded to a greenish yellow and he even had a bit of color in his cheeks.

"Are you going to invite me inside, or leave me standing in the hallway?"

His long pause was hardly flattering.

"Come in," he said finally.

She glanced around as she entered. "Am I interrupting something?"

"No."

The terse response sent a ripple of unease through her, and she whirled to face him. Had she made a mistake coming here? Misinterpreted his kisses and the warmth in his eyes? "Did I do something to annoy you?"

"No."

"Then, what's with the chilly greeting?"

He released a slow breath. "I'm in a foul mood, Rachel. No' really fit company right now."

Concerned, she reached out to touch his face. "Are you in pa—?"

He leapt back, bumping his shoulder against the wall and wincing. "Bloody hell."

Watching him straighten, his skin gray and his lips in a tight slash, she grimaced. "You should be in bed."

"That's the last place I need to be."

"Those cuts—"

"Are healing just fine. Take my word for it."

"Lachlan, you're hurt worse than you're willing to admit. I mean, look at you, you just swore. Priests don't do that, not healthy ones at any rate."

"I'm no' a priest."

"What?" Her laugh came out a little broken, and her gaze darted for reassurance to the beaten-silver cross hanging around his neck. "Of course you are."

"No." His eyes met hers, hard, daring her to argue further. He plucked at his black shirt. "This is a disguise."

A dribble of fear mingled with her confusion. "B-but why? Why would you need a disguise?"

"To keep people away. I live alone and I like it that way. This charade helps me maintain my . . . privacy."

Rachel stared at him for a long, stunned moment,

then dropped to the short stairs leading to the living room, suddenly exhausted—suddenly convinced. He wasn't a priest. It matched what her instincts had been telling her all along. "You'd rather live a lie than let people get close."

"It's easier."

"On who?"

He was silent.

"So, you're not a priest. Great. That makes pretty much everything I know about you a lie. Is Lachlan even your real name?"

"Aye."

She wasn't sure what to make of his terse response. No hurried assurances that the rest of what he'd told her was the absolute truth, probably because it wasn't. "You know this calls into question your story about Drew, don't you?"

"No, it doesn't. Trust your instincts, Rachel. I shared nothing about my history with Drusus until you came to me, already frightened. Discount my words if you choose to, but don't discount what your gut is telling you. You know he's dangerous."

Yes, she did. The sick feeling in her belly settled a bit. "What do you do, then, if you're not a priest? For a living?"

"I have a few investments."

"Enough to cover the rent on a three-bedroom apartment in Southern California and the lease on an Audi."

Again, silence.

"A sane woman would doubt every word that spilled out of your mouth at this point. Me? I'm a sap. I look at your stupid, beat-up face and I believe you." She glanced at him. "Why are you telling me this now?"

"Because I haven't been fair to you, Rachel. I'm no' the man you think I am, and I'm giving you expectations

I can never meet." He raked a hand through his cropped hair. "Your coming here this afternoon is proof of that. You want something I can't give you."

"And what is that, Lachlan? What is it you think I want?"

The look in his eyes softened. "A partner."

Her shoulders responded to the word, instantly easing. It was a mute and unassailable acknowledgment of the truth, but she shook her head. "I tried the partner thing once. Didn't work."

He crouched beside her and lifted her chin with a gentle hand. "He wasn't a real partner. If he had been, it would have worked."

The certainty in his voice and the quiet sympathy in his gaze brought tears to Rachel's eyes. "What would you know about it?"

He didn't respond; he just stared into her brimming eyes.

Rachel turned her head, hating what she saw in his gaze—an intuitive knowledge of her pathetic past, even though she'd never told him a word of it. She blinked the tears away. "Maybe you're reading way too much into my visit. Maybe I'm just looking for sex."

He froze.

Encouraged by the subtle edge of anticipation in his stillness, Rachel added, "No strings attached, down and dirty, wild crazy monkey sex."

A short breath hissed from his lips.

"Single moms don't get out much, you know," she went on, gaining momentum with every increasingly excited heartbeat. Nothing she knew about Lachlan was real . . . except the attraction. Maybe she was crazy, but salvaging something out of this train wreck—even if was only the sexual romp she'd been imagining ever since she bumped into him in the stairwell—had tremendous

appeal. She was tired of going to bed alone and unsatis-
fied. "It's been a while since I had a screaming orgasm
without the help of my vibrator."

She heard him swallow, hard.

"Maybe I just want you to help me with that."

Finding courage she didn't know she possessed, she
looked into his clear blue eyes. "If that were the case,
would you still push me away?"

9

Lachlan was afraid to breathe.
   He was terrified that if he moved even a single muscle, if he so much as twitched, the moment would drift off into hazy nothingness, the way all of his dreams did.

Sex with Rachel.

Christ.

His entire body clamored to say yes. It ached with the need to have her soft and yielding beneath him, to hear her gusty pleas for release echoing in his ear, to feel her clenching around him as he drove her over the edge. By God, his blood was surging so relentlessly in the direction of his cock, it was making him dizzy.

Struggling to focus, he stared into Rachel's eyes.

Her beautiful hazel eyes. Those delightfully expressive eyes told him far more than she probably wanted to tell him: that she was lonely and wounded; that she needed to believe, if only for a few moments, she was still an attractive woman.

Her question hung in the air, hesitant, expectant.

Fearful.

And every instant that passed without a response from him summoned shadows into her eyes. He saw them grow and deepen, and hated himself for being the cause.

Yet how could he say yes? Sex was a very intimate act. Even if they kept it light and friendly, they'd walk away with a new, more profound knowledge of each other. And if Drusus sensed that deeper connection . . .

No. Sex was impossible.

Only a bastard would endanger her that way.

But only a bastard would turn her away, too. It was just one afternoon and, on his part at least, the connection was already dangerously deep. He had the power to do some good, to wash away those lingering doubts about being attractive, to give her some genuine pleasure. It wouldn't cost him anything. Except, perhaps, a little more damage to his already pulverized heart.

"Screaming orgasms I can help with," he said, offering her a quirk of a smile. "How much time do you have?"

Rachel sucked in a sharp breath, and then another.

He said yes.

Holy shit, he said yes.

"I didn't mean today," she said hastily. "I mean, you're not really in any shape to—"

"Are you changing your mind?" he asked softly.

It sounded like a challenge, but his tempered expression told her he'd let her walk away without a fuss if that's what she really wanted. But it also told her this was a one-shot deal, a limited opportunity. If she walked away now, he wouldn't be leaving the door open for a repeat visit.

"No," she breathed.

"Then come with me." He stood and extended his hand.

Heart skipping random beats, Rachel studied his lean, square-tipped fingers. Sneaking home from work for a little afternoon delight was so not her. But right at this moment, she didn't care. She placed her hand in his.

He tugged her easily to her feet and led her down the hall, past walls hung with moody Scottish landscapes, past a den populated with a brown leather sofa and a massive home entertainment unit, down to the huge bedroom at the end, a room faintly marked by a masculine blend of soap and cologne.

Those *few investments* sure paid healthy dividends.

She felt as if she'd walked into an old English manor. Heavy cherry woods dominated the room, layered with moss green velvets and red plaids. The huge, drapery-hung four-poster bed ate up most of the space. A wing-back chair stood in one corner, a rolltop desk in the other, and a thick-piled Oriental carpet visually pulled them together in wall-to-wall luxury.

More evidence that Lachlan was not what she had originally assumed him to be. Not a priest, not short of funds. And she knew just by looking at the mask of solemn reserve on his face that she'd only scratched the surface of his deception.

She must be crazy to trust this man.

He tightened his grip and drew her all the way into the room. Testing her resolve with his steady gaze, he lifted her wrist to his lips and kissed the delicate and very sensitive flesh there. His warm breath sent a flurry of tiny shivers up her arm.

Rachel wanted to give in to the exhilaration.

But as madly desirable as Lachlan was, she couldn't stop thinking that mad was exactly the right word to describe her decision to do this. He was a stranger, a man she barely knew, and he'd already admitted he was a shadowy composite of lies. She should never have left work. Em would be home in two hours. This was reckless, and rushing into things always had disastrous consequences.

She stiffened.

His tongue drew a delicate pattern on her wrist. Combined with the heat of his hand seeping into her skin and the heady effect of his musky scent, she tingled—all over.

"Is it difficult?" he murmured.

"What?"

"Being the sole provider for your family, always having to be responsible, never being able to take more than a moment for yourself, even when you need it?"

Her breath caught.

"Sometimes," she whispered.

"Then take advantage of me, Rachel. I can't offer much, but I can offer this one afternoon. Let me take care of you. For a few short hours, let go. Lean on me."

The promise behind his words—a brief respite from being mother, employee, and chief decision maker, a brief opportunity to indulge herself without any worry—blew her away. She stared into his eyes and a huge weight lifted from her shoulders.

God help her, she did trust him. Despite what she'd discovered about him, despite her certainty that there were more unknowns lingering in those smoky, mystery-shrouded eyes, she didn't feel that he was trying to con her. He wasn't offering her the world, just one afternoon. And crazy or not, she trusted him to give it to her.

"Okay."

He smiled. "Good. Close your eyes."

"What?"

He threaded his fingers with hers and tugged her off balance, leaving her no choice but to fall against his solid strength. "Close your eyes."

She did as she was told.

And was almost immediately bombarded by feedback from her other senses: his incredibly delicious smell, of course; the sultry heat radiating from his body;

the fluid steel of his muscles; the absolute dependability of his firm stance. She felt very much the small, soft female in the arms of a big, hard man ... and was totally turned on by the physical disparity. Her head fell back, exposing her throat, silently begging for a more intimate exploration.

He obliged.

His mouth, nibbling and sucking, found the soft skin just above her collarbone. Little flirty dances across her flesh made her head swim. Her breasts responded to the proximity of sensation, plumping and swelling, her nipples budding.

"I can feel the beat of your pulse against my lips." His voice was low and husky, a gravelly testament to his need. "I want you so bad, I ache. Do you ache, too, Rachel?"

"God, yes."

"I'll happily soothe that ache, but there's a price." His fingers slid beneath the hem of her shirt to caress bare skin. Every place he touched, fire leapt along her nerve endings. "You have to let go. You have to let me take charge, completely." His lips found their way to the underside of her jaw, his tongue tracing small circles on her flesh. "Do as I bid, follow my lead, no questions asked. Can you pay?"

Rachel's pulse skittered. A thin thread of fear wove through her excitement. Could she? Could her fragile trust in him really stretch that far, to allowing him to dominate her?

She hesitated.

His capable hand found the button at her neckline and unfastened it. As the silky material of her blouse parted, a single finger slipped down, trailing lightly over her flesh, raising goose bumps. A second button gave way ... and molten need poured over her body, a damp wave that rolled down between her breasts and pooled in her belly.

"Say aye, Rachel."

"Aye," she groaned. With a deep breath, she sank limply against his chest. Her arms slipped around his middle, her fingers instinctively finding the waistband of his pants and edging in, searching for bare skin.

"Hold on, love." He snagged her roving hands, thrust them behind her, and backed her toward the bed. His eyes burned so intensely, she shivered. "You do what *I* say, remember? Nothing else."

She bumped into the bed.

"Lie down, Rachel."

Amazed by the thrill that trickled down her spine at his firm order, she followed his direction, first lifting herself atop the high mattress, then reclining on the sinfully soft velvet comforter. Her eyes devoured his lean, handsome face.

Now that she knew he wasn't a priest, the sexy masculine vibes he gave off made sense. She didn't doubt for a second that he knew his way around a bedroom ... or a woman's body. His expertise was evident in the hooded depths of his eyes, in the predatory way he studied the rise and fall of her chest and then slipped lower.

As she watched, he reached behind his neck, unbuttoned his black clerical shirt, and pulled it—and the silver cross—over his head, leaving behind a finely honed golden chest and two long, red scabs where he'd been sliced by Drew's knife ... nowhere near as serious as she'd first thought, but still a grim reminder of his injuries. He was hurt.

His gaze met and held hers.

One of his hands lazily reached for the button on his black wool pants and popped it free. Guilt nagged at her, but not enough to tell him to stop.

"Take off your blouse," he demanded hoarsely. His fingers dragged the zipper of his slacks down, but his eyes remained locked on her. "Let me see you."

The scrape of his zipper shortened Rachel's breaths to shallow pulls and sent her heartbeat into overdrive, which in turn made her hands tremble. Still, somehow, she managed to unfasten the rest of the buttons and free her arms of the lilac silk.

As she lay flat again, she caught a glimpse of how easily she moved him. The mere sight of her bare midriff and lacy black bra darkened his eyes and brought a faint flush to his cheekbones.

With a groan, he bent and nuzzled the valley between her breasts. "You're so damned beautiful," he said against her skin, his breath hot. "So sweet to taste, so soft to touch. I've dreamt about kissing you here, Rachel."

Light-headed and breathlessly eager, she welcomed the unhooking of her bra. His hand slid around and cupped the eager flesh of one breast, and Rachel arched into his palm, gasping.

"And here," he whispered. "I've dreamt of having your beautiful breast in my mouth, sucking at you hard, watching your eyes widen as the ripples reach your toes."

Oh God.

He tugged her bra off, and pulled back a bit to stare at her. Her nipples budded to painful intensity under his admiring perusal. He didn't say anything, but she saw the storm gather strength in his eyes.

She held her breath as he drew closer, and closer.

And then his mouth was on her breast.

Gently at first, little flicks of his tongue over the engorged tip of her nipple, and then just as he'd promised, hard and sucking.

Rachel thought she might die.

Darts of keen sensation, heightened by anticipation, shot from her breast straight to her womb, creating a restless ache between her thighs that she needed to soothe. Somehow. With Lachlan.

"Touch me," she begged. "Please touch me."

"Where?" He turned his attention to her other breast, suckling until that one, too, was full and wet and swollen. "Where do you want me to touch you?"

Writhing upon the bedclothes, unable to summon coherent words, she touched herself, pressing the heel of her hand against the throbbing between her legs.

"Here."

His hand followed hers, covering it firmly, rocking in a slow, rhythmic samba of pressure. Rachel relished the rising heat of her own arousal against her palm, melted under the firm guidance of his hand, and shuddered as his tongue rolled her nipple. Everything felt so incredibly good.

But not . . . enough.

She wanted more, everywhere: skin to skin, every limb entwined, every aching inch of her able to feel every incredible inch of him.

A whimper of need escaped her lips. "Please . . ."

"Please what?" he rasped, letting her nipple slip from his mouth. "Do this?" His lips feathered down to her belly, the soft, steamy kisses making her quiver and tremble. His hands worked at her pants until they gaped open, a vee of pale flesh exposed to him. "Or this?"

One hand slid beneath her own hand, into her panties, threading through the curls, all the way to the damp heat that at this moment was the center of her universe. His calloused finger slipped slowly into her, while his thumb circled, played, drove her mad.

Her eyes closed involuntarily, succumbing to the hot flames spreading up her chest. She arched into his hand, wanting him deeper, needing him to ease the restless throb.

There was a groan, but Rachel wasn't certain whose it was.

"So wet, so tight. It'll feel so damned good to slide into you, Rachel. Imagine me there, pumping deep inside you."

That moan was definitely hers.

"I want you, Rachel." Displaying amazing agility for a man who had one hand fully occupied, he shucked his pants and cotton boxers. Then he was on the bed alongside her, taking her hand and guiding it to his erection. "Feel how much I want you, how much I need you."

Her hand wrapped around his hard length, feeling his searing heat, feeling him pulse, feeling him grow harder under her fingers. His rich, musky fragrance deepened with her touch, filling her nose, caressing her skin in return.

"You need, too, Rachel," he said, his voice low and guttural. "Tell me what you need."

Pale memories of other sexual encounters, of Grant and the brief relationships since, slid over her. Most of them had been quick and fast and not nearly satisfying enough.

"I need—" A sudden flush of shyness came and, under the expert ministrations of his hand, went. "I need to explode. Shatter into a million pieces. I need you to make me come until my legs wobble and I can't see straight."

"My pleasure." He separated her hand from his erection and kissed her fingertips. "We'll come back to this part later."

Then he tugged her slacks and her lace panties down her body and off. Gently but firmly, he spread her legs. Trailing his fingers up her inner thighs, he sent a shiver of raw anticipation through her. "I love hearing you moan and gasp as I touch you. If I make you come, will you scream for me, Rachel?" His head slowly lowered.

"Ye-sss."

Her response was half word, half gasp as his steamy, hot mouth sought and found her center. He flicked his tongue and suckled, and sweet shocks sizzled through her, making her womb clench, flooding her with wetness, easing the thrusts of his finger, allowing it to go deeper.

"Oh *yes*."

He'd barely even started, and already her muscles were tightening and quivering in an orchestral prelude to mind-blowing bliss. Rachel had never felt so electrified, so incredibly on fire, so ready for release. Partly for him but mostly for herself, she moaned. Her hands dug into his short hair, holding him, encouraging him. Her breaths grew ragged and harsh, even to her own ears, and her blood pounded so loud that thinking beyond raw sensation was impossible.

He was relentless, reaching deep into her with one finger and then two, tonguing her with such consummate skill, her brain went woolly. She stopped wondering how many women he'd practiced on. The tension in her body mounted . . . building, climbing, soaring.

"Don't stop," she begged. Higher. Tighter. Just a little bit more. She reached for and grasped the edge of the precipice with both hands . . . then everything flew apart.

As she spun into ecstasy, she screamed, "Lachlan!"

The sweet burn that swept through him as Rachel screamed his name was so intense that Lachlan had to squeeze his eyes shut and strain to hold on. Her delightful, high-pitched squeal rang in his ears and echoed in his chest, in that cold, empty space that only she seemed able to fill.

She was so incredibly responsive.

A few words, a few touches, and she'd fallen hard.

He wasn't foolish enough to take her wonderful response personally. She'd just needed to come, just needed an outlet for that surplus of passion she kept bottled up inside. And he'd simply been in the right spot at the right time.

That's all it was.

He was convenient.

Shaking off an irritation that he had no right to feel, he nibbled his way across her flat belly and over the three cute little moles on her hip—claiming every inch of her, if only for this one impossible moment. He licked away the faint traces of perspiration he found between her breasts, savoring the salty taste of her smooth skin. Leaving a trail of wet kisses up her neck, he kissed the underside of her jaw and then lifted himself enough to look into her face.

Her eyes were closed, her lips slightly parted. The creamy skin of her cheeks was flushed, and the pulse at her throat beat like a wild thing trapped in a cage.

He'd like to remember her just like this. Loose and sexy and sated. With any luck, the image would be enough to sustain him through the remaining ninety-one years of his servitude, as she went on to live a full, happy life, and he merely existed, as his heart slowly shriveled.

Reaching across her to the nightstand, he opened the drawer and dug for a condom. The expiration date had long passed, but it wouldn't matter. His seed was as dead as the rest of him. On his knees, using the lingering play of emotions on Rachel's face as an aphrodisiac, he pumped a hand up and down his cock, and then rolled the condom on.

"How many times were you hoping to come?" he asked, leaning over her once more.

Her eyelids lifted, displaying dark pools of spent passion. A very lazy, satisfied smile curved her lips. "Just keep going until I faint."

He chuckled. "I'll do my best."

She traced a delicate finger along one of the thin scabs on his chest, down his abs to the line of hair that began on his lower belly. "You are without question the best-looking guy I've ever seen without a shirt on."

His blood heated at her compliment, renewing the ache in his balls and sending a squeeze of pressure to the base of his erection. He wanted to be the only man she saw without his shirt on, the only man she coveted, but that wasn't to be. A little angry, he dug into the silky tresses of her hair, imprisoned her head, and kissed her on the lips, hard.

At the same time, he ground himself against the apex of her thighs, shuddering at the pleasure that rippled through his body, reveling in the subsequent flare in Rachel's eyes.

"Open for me," he said roughly against her mouth.

Her knees were already lax, but she spread them wider, lifted her ankles, and wrapped them around his waist, inviting the most intimate connection possible of their bodies.

Her heat and her wetness called to him, urging him to take her. "I'm going to fill you, sink as deep as you can take me, ride you long and hard," he whispered, resting his damp forehead against hers. "Is that what you want, Rachel?"

Her breath came in soft pants.

"Do it," she urged.

He shifted, finding the entrance to her body, the honeyed slickness of her, and slid in—slowly—testing her ability to take him, adjusting to her every mewl and moan. The deeper he sank, the more Rachel wriggled and squirmed and lifted her hips, her excitement escalating, her patience failing.

"Please."

The tight grip of her around him and the slow, synchronized throbbing of their heartbeats were almost more than he could bear. When he was fully seated, buried inside her as deep as he could possibly go, he stilled.

The words that filled his heart were ones he could never utter, so instead, with his throat constricted, he kissed her tenderly, reverently.

"You feel unbelievably . . . perfect," he said.

Rachel's hands clutched at his shoulders, her fingernails digging into his flesh, urging him to move, inciting him to do as he'd promised and ravish her until her legs wobbled.

He began to move in and out, slowly at first and then, as their bodies aligned and found a rhythm, with more vigor. Sweat beaded on his chest and on his brow, hot blood pooled in his groin, and the thick scent of their mingled arousal filled his nose.

The torrent of physical sensations stole his sanity, blurred the pain of the past, and grounded him in the here and now. In this moment. In this one afternoon. With Rachel. He could pretend, however briefly, that this was all there was and all there need be.

"Come for me, Rachel," he begged hoarsely.

Her hazel eyes fluttered open, softly focused, almost green against the flush of her cheeks. Every pleasurable impact of his body against hers was reflected in their depths. But her sigh was regretful. "I'm not sure I can."

Immediately, he paused.

But it cost him. Dear God, it cost him. The rush in his head and the pulse of need in his groin were so bloody overwhelming, so damned ferocious, that his abs and biceps shook badly under the strain. His heartbeat railed against his rib cage.

"What's wrong?"

"I'm sorry. I caught a glimpse of my watch, and then I thought about Em and work and . . ." She sagged. "I lost it."

"Emily is still at school. Everything is fine." He kissed her brow, and then her nose, and finally her lips, trying desperately to ignore the insistent and almost painful ache of his erection inside her. "You need to be here. With me."

She returned the kiss, gently, still a tad reticent. "I know."

"Let go, love."

Mutely, she stared back at him. Big eyes, damp curly hair. So beautiful against the green of the bedcovers.

"I lead, you follow. That was the price, remember?" He kissed her again, harder this time, bruising the tender flesh of her mouth. "Today, those are my worries, not yours. Forget them. Forget everything but me. Because I intend to make you come again and again . . . and again."

He swiveled his hips, grinding deeper, searching for that magical spot that would enhance her experience. At the same time, he gathered her hands and yanked them above her head, exposing her fully, emphasizing her vulnerability.

"Do you want me to *make* you come, Rachel?"

The answer was there in her eyes, but she spoke anyway. A choked word that was laced with excitement. "Yes."

He kissed his way across her throat to her ear and bit on the lobe, enjoying her needy moan. Then he proceeded to tell her in very rough, very explicit words what he intended to do to her and precisely how her body would respond.

The moan became a whimper, and Rachel thrust up against him, a silent demand for fewer words and more action, which he agreeably met.

Keeping his own desires severely in check and chasing the worries from her thoughts with the sheer intensity of his sensual attack, he made love to her as he had never made love to a woman in his lengthy existence—with everything he had.

He stole every kiss from her lips, seized every moan. He demanded, insisted, seduced. He rammed into her, teasing her relentlessly with the intimate slap of their bodies, ensuring the steady, heady mix of friction and pressure did precisely what he said they would do. Tracking her every shiver, her every quake, her every tensed muscle, he coaxed her to the pinnacle.

Then he wrapped his arms tightly around her, pressed his mouth to hers, and took her over the edge.

10

It was unbearably hard to let her go.

Against his better judgment, he sought lingering last touches and soft sweet kisses, trying to drag out the experience as long as he could. But he was very careful not to speak of the future, very careful not to allude to a repeat encounter.

And Rachel made no attempt to prompt such a discussion.

She smiled shyly, kissed him firmly on the mouth, and then, rumpled and disheveled and still swollen from his kisses, left the apartment.

Lachlan closed the door and sank to the tiles, dressed only in a pair of knee-length gray sweat shorts. His heart ached, but this was just the beginning of the torture, and he knew it. Even if he managed to survive his next encounter with Drusus, he'd have to endure ninety-one years of remembering today.

Remembering Rachel.

He glanced down at his chest, at the ever-thinning wounds from last night, the grim reminders of his unequivocal defeat. Neither the sword nor his current repertoire of magic had been enough to triumph over the bastard, but something Drusus had mentioned made him think winning was still possible.

The *Book of Gnills*.

He pushed himself to his feet and returned to his bedroom, a bedroom redolent with the scent of spent sex and . . . Rachel. Giving in to temptation, he bent to the pillows and inhaled deeply, pulling her earthy aroma into his lungs and trapping it there for a long moment.

Then he slowly released the breath, entered the bathroom, and turned the shower on full blast.

With cool water.

An hour later, he parked the Audi in Stefan's long, dusty driveway and unfolded himself from the car. The smithy behind the house glowed with the incandescent heat of an active forge, but there was no sign of Stefan in the small wooden building, and Lachlan, wary, turned to study the front door of the mage's house. Not once in the seven months he'd known him had he been invited inside Stefan's home.

Home being a very loose word, of course.

It was actually the modern-day equivalent of the Romany caravan—a large brown and white fifth-wheel with slide-outs. The cedar strip skirt erected to hide the wheels and the well-tended flower garden did little to banish the air of impermanence.

Lachlan wended the stone path between mounds of pink and white flowers, climbed the steps, and rapped on the thin metal door. How did anyone live in such cramped quarters day in and day out?

A short black-haired woman with riveting dark brown eyes opened the door. Stefan's wife, Dika. He'd met her once or twice before. She gave him a rueful smile, then stood back to let him enter.

"He's in the back," she said, gesturing to the far end of the trailer, where a purple velvet curtain divided the room.

The trailer was amazingly luxurious—maple cabinets

throughout, leather furniture in the living room, and stainless steel appliances in the kitchen. A big pot of spaghetti sauce bubbled on the stove, filling the trailer with a spicy tomato aroma.

"Am I interrupting?" he asked Dika.

"No, he's expecting you."

He traversed the length of the trailer and pulled back the curtain to view Stefan's private domain. As he stepped over the threshold, however, the heavy material slid out of a suddenly limp hand.

Gone were the smooth glass windows, the beige carpet, the cream-colored walls. In their place stood dank stone walls lit by masses of dripping candles, heavy oak tables covered in dusty, leather-bound tomes, and a plethora of small earthenware jugs labeled with curious names, such as beetle wings and spiderwebs. The thick smell of mildew and fatty tallow wax hung in the air with a medieval authenticity he remembered all too well.

But the décor didn't startle him as much as the size of the room. A fifteen-foot square could not possibly fit inside the forty-by-ten-foot dimensions of the trailer.

Stefan lifted his gaze from the book he was reading and arched a brow at Lachlan's black jeans and pale gray oxford shirt. "You've given up the priest's robes."

Lachlan shrugged. "They weren't helping."

"Still, haven't you worn them since your bro—?"

"I'm no' here to discuss the past. You told me there was no way to defeat a lure demon."

Stefan's eyes narrowed. "Yes."

"Then why did Death assure me I could do so?"

The mage closed his book, sending a curl of dust into the air. "Did she? How interesting."

Lachlan was tired of being played, first by Death and her mysterious words, and now by Stefan and his carefully neutral response. He closed the gap in one easy stride and snatched hold of the man's tan shirt. Yanking him off the stool, he lifted the swordsmith until his toes barely touched the wood-planked floor.

"Do no' test the sharpness of my mood, mage. I need answers and I need them now."

Stefan did not struggle for release. Nor did he invoke any of the many protection spells he was capable of. "What makes you think I know what she was referring to?"

"Because you're keeping secrets."

"What secrets?"

Lachlan lifted him a bit farther and shook him slightly, enjoying the wince that flickered over the other man's face. "The *Book of Gnills*, for one. According to Drusus, it contains powerful spells that could aid me, yet you've shared nothing of that particular tome."

Stefan blinked through the inky locks that now hung over his eyes. "I see."

"Well, I don't, and I'm weary of being trifled with."

He gave a slow nod. "Let me down, and I'll tell you what I know."

For several angry heartbeats, Lachlan's fingers remained tight. But curiosity finally won him over, and he released him.

"Leave nothing out."

The mage tucked his wrinkled shirt back into his overalls. Then he grabbed a stool, positioned it against the south wall, and reached for a shelf of large jugs above his head. From behind the jugs he drew two books, both remarkably unnoteworthy, both bound in simple black leather with no exterior markings. As he jumped down, a waft of damp decay assailed Lachlan's nose.

"The *Book of Gnills*," Stefan said, sighing as he dropped the larger of the two volumes upon the table-top with a dull thunk. "And the *Book of T'Farc*."

The second book made no sound when he dropped it. Not even a whisper.

Lachlan stared, suddenly uneasy. "What are they?"

"The *Book of Gnills* is a compendium of shade magic, gathered and recorded by my ancestors in the time before we were Roma, during an age when the deities walked more freely on the middle plane."

At the question in Lachlan's eyes, he enlarged. "The magic you currently use is entity magic—magic that comes from within, magic that is stoked by the wielder's own strength, passion, and intelligence. Shade magic is something else. It draws from the environment, from the very fabric of the plane itself."

"And this other book? The *Book of T'Farc*?"

"Void magic. Magic that draws upon the concentrated power of the human soul, draining all those within reach, killing them instantly. God has outlawed the use of void magic, and has sworn vengeance on anyone who uses it."

"Do no' God and Satan draw upon the power of the human soul? Is that no' the source of *their* power?"

"Yes, but the souls they draw on are the souls of the dead. Even so, with the deific skills they possess, they never exhaust a soul completely. Casual wielders of void magic unfortunately lack the skill to prevent that tragedy."

Lachlan grimaced. Of course. Drusus, who would feel nothing but glee at the notion of killing to strengthen himself, had the ability to draw on the power of a soul, while a man of good conscience was doomed to defeat because he could not do the same.

"What happens when you use shade magic?"

With a wave of his hand, Stefan conjured two steaming mugs of coffee and handed one to Lachlan.

"No," he said with a smile, "that wasn't shade magic.

But I could have used shade magic to do the same thing if I'd been willing to sacrifice something else. All magic is basically a trade, an exchange of one form of power for another. Had I used shade magic instead of my own root energy, I'd have had to give up something in our physical environment. Stones from the wall, or a book, maybe."

Lachlan studied the dark brown liquid in his cup, thinking. "Not such a terrible repercussion."

"Except that extinguishing a physical object using shade magic leaves a hole in the plane, an area of instability, the size of which depends on the intensity of the spell that was cast. Strange things begin to occur around those holes, things we can't control. Random disappearances. Freakish weather. There's even been tales of creatures coming through from the other side."

"Havoc demons?"

"Worse."

Havoc demons, the unscrupulous accident-inducers that occasionally broke through the barrier to the middle plane, were bad enough. He wasn't sure he wanted to know what *worse* might entail. "Are shade spells stronger than entity spells?"

"Yes, and void spells are stronger than shade. The power used to generate them is deeper, more focused."

Taking a sip of his coffee, Lachlan digested that. "You lied when you told me you knew of nothing that could destroy a lure demon."

"I didn't lie. I haven't read either of these books."

The rumors said otherwise. "Ballocks. Your reputation among the Roma is as questionable as these books. You've read them."

Stefan arched a brow. "You're aware of the gossip?"

"I am."

"Then why agree to work with me? If the stories are

true, you risk your very existence by putting any faith in my skills."

"Because you're also the best."

Stefan smiled. "And you're arrogant enough to believe vigilance can prevent your demise."

Lachlan said nothing.

The mage shook his head. "Accept the truth or do not: I've never read either tome. The Romany Council outlawed them, insisting the consequences far outweigh the rewards. I agree with their assessment."

His next sentence hung in the air, unspoken: Lachlan should turn his back on the spell books. Yet how could he? He kept seeing the golden glow of the reliquary tucked inside the lure demon's jacket, kept seeing Emily laughingly licking ice cream from her cone, and his insides burned.

"Surely there's a way to work around the problems."

The mage's face darkened. "No, there's not."

"Damn it, Stefan, how can you be so certain?"

"Because my father succumbed to curiosity and read both grimoires cover to cover. After seven years of study, did he ever attempt even the smallest of spells? No. In the end, he hid the blasted things away. My father died, like many Romany mages before him, at the hands of a vicious demon ... using only entity magic in his defense."

Lachlan regretted causing the lines of grief on Stefan's face. Still, unable to accept that the battle might be over before it had truly begun, he plunked his mug down, sloshing coffee onto the dusty oak tabletop.

"There *must* be a way. The lure demon must be defeated."

Stefan shook his head. "Not with these books."

"My only chance lies with these books."

"Weigh the consequences, MacGregor. Are the lives

you're trying to save worth the damage that will be done? And I don't just mean damage to the fabric of our world or the loss of human lives, though those are certainly enough to convince *me*. I mean the damage to your honor as well. You've spent the last four hundred years trying to redeem yourself so you can join your family in the upper plane. Are you willing to throw that all away?"

Lachlan dragged his fingers through the short locks of his hair, a dull ache throbbing behind his eyes. "My family never made it to the upper plane. Their innocent souls are guaranteed to burn in hell if I do no' succeed."

A heavy silence fell.

When the pause grew uncomfortable, the mage released a sympathetic sigh. "Then all I can say is, may God have mercy on you."

It happened quite by accident.

Em was sitting in the assembly hall thinking about Drew when the three lame-ass geeks seated one row ahead got the best of her. They kept turning in their seats to look at her, rolling their eyes and snorting. First it was just annoying. Then her head began to pound.

She closed her eyes in an attempt to stop the dull throb, but it just kept hammering.

Irritation fermented into anger. The more the geeks bobbed and giggled and snorted, the angrier she got. Waves of dark thoughts poured over her, and an image of them hanging limp in a tree, necks broken, popped into her head—along with a surge of incredible pleasure. The pencil she was holding in her hand cracked and a sliver of wood bit into her palm.

Shocked by both the intensity of her feelings and the stab of pain, she dropped the pencil.

But the damned thing didn't fall to her lap. Nope. It

hung in the air, hovering about an inch off her thighs, bent at an odd angle and decorated with a bright smear of blood.

Through the strands of her hair, Em quickly checked to see if the geeks were watching. They weren't. Miraculously transformed into good little sheep, they sat straight in their chairs, listening intently as the principal presented the school's new safety policy.

Frowning, she stared at the floating pencil. But even as she debated how to get rid of it, the problem took care of itself. The pencil disappeared. Vanished. No puff of smoke, no flash of light. Nothing. Just gone.

Em sat a little straighter on her folding metal chair. Wouldn't it be cool if she could follow it? She closed her eyes and concentrated, but when she opened her eyes, she was still surrounded by brainwashed idiots.

Oh, well. It was a thought.

Watering the copious plants in her balcony flower boxes should have been a relaxing chore for Rachel—it usually was. The sun on her skin and the soft trickle of water in the fountain normally made her a bit sleepy. But as the afternoon breeze dried her freshly showered hair, she found herself glancing repeatedly at the balcony above, wondering if Lachlan was thinking about her as much as she was thinking about him.

She set her copper watering can on the table, and put her palms to her burning cheeks.

Was he reliving the damp rub of her skin against his, the intoxicatingly perfect fit of their very different bodies, and the incredible way they'd found release at precisely the same time? She wondered, because *she* couldn't stop thinking about those things. She blushed every five minutes, half embarrassed, half turned-on by the racy memories.

She plucked a wilted pink plumeria blossom from its stalk and tossed it over the balcony.

It still amazed her that she'd had the courage to go through with it. Sex just for sex's sake, no strings attached. Except for one wild year at college, which was almost too long ago to remember, her sex life was pretty conservative.

Of course, today's lovemaking didn't compare at all to those crazy, almost thoughtless couplings in college. Maybe she was just being stupid, reading something into his actions that hadn't really been there, but honestly, she'd never been made love to with such an obvious dedication to her pleasure, or with such a potent mix of authority and tenderness.

An incredible experience.

An incredible, *never-to-be-repeated* experience.

The cordless phone on the Adirondack chair trilled, and Rachel's heartbeat surged with hope. But the number on the call display brought her daydreams to a crashing halt. She mentally braced herself as she brought the phone to her ear.

"Hello, Grant."

There was a brief pause, then, "Uh, hi, Rachel."

At two in the afternoon on a Monday, he couldn't have been expecting her to answer the phone. He'd obviously planned to leave her a message—which meant . . .

"Is my check in the mail?"

"Jeez, Rachel, do we always have to dive right into the money stuff? Can't you ask me, just once, how I'm doing?"

Rachel grimaced, unwillingly drawn back into the game they always played: Rachel bad, Grant good. "How are you, Grant?"

"Rotten. You won't believe my life right now. My 401(k) is in the toilet, I'm knee-deep in a merger, working seventy-hour weeks, and my car just blew up. It's going to cost me a bomb to repair."

"So, you aren't sending us a check," she concluded.

"If I do, I've got no car. I'll send the alimony check next month, when things have settled down a bit. Not that you need it with that fancy high-tech job of yours."

Her grip on the phone tightened. "It's child support, not alimony. The money you send goes directly to Em. It pays for her dentist bills, her clothes, and her clarinet for band. Please remember that."

"Yeah, well, you could cover that stuff by yourself, especially if you sold a couple of your paintings. People seem to like them."

"I have only two left," she said. "You took the rest and sold them behind my back, remember?"

"Don't rag on me about that. We weren't divorced then, and I needed to pay the credit card bill. Hell, I don't know why you make such a big fuss about it. Just go paint some more."

"I haven't painted in years." Her gaze swung to the open glass doors to the living room, where she could see the edge of her easel peeking from behind the TV unit. Dusty.

"That's not my problem. You did a complete one-eighty after we got married, never wanted to do anything fun anymore."

"My mother was sick, and we had a baby, Grant."

"I remember when I first met you, on the flight to New York. I thought you were this wild, sexy artist chick, hip enough to fly off to Paris for a year, wicked enough to get drunk on airline booze. I was totally bowled over. I had no idea you were in the process of turning into a psycho over your dad's death. If I had, I'd have run for the hills."

A dozen responses rose to her tongue, but she squashed them all. There was no point arguing. Grant always had glib answers. She scooped a dead leaf out of the oak barrel fishpond and sprinkled goldfish food on the sun-sparkled water.

"What time will you get here on Friday?"

"I can't come. Friends have invited me to their beach house to go boating."

"Grant, you promised. Can't you go boating another weekend? Em's going through some tough stuff right now."

"Love to, but this weekend is a once-in-a-lifetime opportunity. Look, I gotta run. Give her a hug for me."

The line went dead.

Rachel set the phone down with an arm that felt as heavy as her heart. The payment for Em's band trip was due this month and she didn't have the cash to ante up. Em had been looking forward to that trip for two years. It was the only reason she stayed in band—five days of living in hotels, shopping, and hanging with her Goth friends—all far away from her tyrannical mom.

Rachel had really been hoping that, for once, Grant would come through, but no such luck. And, of course, she was the one left breaking the bad news.

A thrill raced across the back of Em's neck, whisking away the last of her lingering thoughts about the pencil. She glanced over her shoulder. Sure enough, four rows back, seated among a bunch of his sophomore classmates, was the new guy. He was staring at her—not in a creepy way, but in a quiet, serious way.

Carlos.

Could be the principal's droning speech about the school's zero tolerance policy on bullying had put him into a stupor and his gaze had landed on her purely by accident, but she didn't think so. Once could be an accident. Three times, no way.

Pleased, but determined not to show it, she threw him the most bored look ever and dropped her gaze back to her doodling. She inked another gory blood drip on the tip of the knife.

Deeply tanned skin and obvious muscles didn't normally do much for her, but she had to admit that Carlos Rodriguez was a hunk worthy of a few sighs.

Attitude rolled off him in waves, from the just-try-me tilt of his head to the don't-give-a-shit angle of his shoulders. He was a Goth like her, which gave him extra points, and the cobra tattoo on his wrist added a gritty edge to his personality—totally cool. His narrow face came awfully close to pretty, but the white scar slicing through his full bottom lip saved him.

Still, as attractive as the whole package was, it was his eyes that got her. Dark brown and bleak as hell.

There was a world of pain in those eyes. A dark, ugly wound that reached into his soul and ate him up, something Em could empathize with. She knew without ever having talked to him that Carlos was a kindred spirit.

And judging by his interest, he sensed the same thing.

The end-of-day bell would ring in about three minutes. Everyone would shuffle out of the room, make their way to their lockers, and then head home. The question of the day was, would Carlos find an excuse to talk to her in the hallway?

She hoped so.

The principal ended her speech on an impassioned plea to have a safe and untroubled year, and then the bell rang.

Em stood up. Her hands grew sweaty as she gathered up her book bag. It took every ounce of willpower not to give in and peer in Carlos's direction. Better to act as if she didn't give a shit. That way, if he didn't talk to her in the hall, he'd never guess how much it bothered her. She trailed the crowd out of the room and sauntered toward her locker, walking slowly to give him the chance to catch up with her—assuming he was following, of course.

Unable to resist, she shot a quick glance back.

And her gaze collided with a pair of long-lashed, smoky topaz eyes. *Oh my God.* He was right behind her.

"Hey," he said, unsmiling.

"Hey."

She paused in front of her locker, and he stopped, too. Leaning against the next locker, silently watching her, he made her heart race. Which in turn made her cheeks hot. Grateful for the mask of pale makeup that covered her face, Em casually spun the combination on the lock with one hand.

"You take the Almaden bus?" he asked.

Her gaze drifted back to his face. His eyeliner extended into small teardrops beneath his eyes, a simple but angsty touch. He was taller than her by more than a foot, and she liked that. "Yeah."

"Cool, so do I."

He waited for her to pack up her knapsack, then walked with her across the grassy soccer field toward the line of yellow school buses parked on the west side of the school—closer than a casual friend would walk, almost touching.

She snuck a peek at him.

In spite of his height, the hem of his long black trench coat brushed the toes of his black army boots. A very impractical coat for the mid-October heat, but way cool. She nearly sighed when he flipped the hood of his sweat-shirt over his shoulder-length brown hair, blocking out the sun completely.

Em saw several girls in her class toss her envious glares. Even that bitch, Daria, who'd snickered at her hairy arms during gym and called her a troll.

"Whatcha listenin' to?" she asked, nodding to his iPod earbuds.

"Sisters of Mercy."

She nodded, strangely disappointed. Great band, a little on the ordinary side. But hey, she was a rabid Lycia fan and they were pretty mainstream, too. Just 'cause his tastes weren't as unique as Drew's didn't mean he was boring.

And, as much as she was drawn to him, Drew didn't make her pulse dance this way.

They reached the sidewalk in a companionable silence. Em was already thinking about what it would be like to sit next to him on the bus—their bodies occasionally grazing, then pressing against each other every time the bus rounded a corner—when she heard the frantic, high-pitched trumpet of a car horn.

"Em!"

Her head swung toward the parking lot . . . and a mixed sensation of horror and surprise washed over her. Her *mom*. In that rusty, embarrassing shitbox she called a car.

"Em!" Her mom waved from the window. "Come on, I'll drive you home."

"That your mom?"

Em briefly considered saying no, but decided her lie would be outed far too quickly. She pitched Carlos a look she hoped said, *Aren't moms pathetic?* and mumbled, "Yeah."

Something flickered in his eyes, something distressingly close to irritation. "Guess you won't be taking the bus."

Her heart sank. "Maybe we could—"

"See you tomorrow?"

With growing numbness, Em nodded. She watched Carlos swagger off toward the bus, shoulders rounded, his black trench coat flapping. Some other girl would sit next to him. Not her. His first day at school, the day he'd actively be making new friends, and he was getting on the bus without her. He might end up paired with some other girl, maybe even Daria, all because her mom showed up for the first time in *forever* and offered her a ride home.

Un-fucking-believable.

Another example of how life totally sucked.

11

After enduring a flaming argument over the band trip and a bitterly silent trip to Safeway, Rachel had been fairly sure things couldn't get any worse between her and Em. But she was wrong. As she and a very grim Em approached the glass doors of their apartment building, a leather-clad young man rose to his feet to greet them, all smiles.

Drew.

"Let me help you with those, Rachel." He reached for two of the paper grocery bags and took them from her nerveless hands. Hefting the load with ease, he bent and kissed Em, full on the lips. "Hello, sweet."

A tremble rippled through Rachel, chilling her from tip to toe. This . . . this *monster* . . . had almost killed Lachlan last night and yet, here he was, acting as if nothing had happened. Pretending to be a normal young man.

Drew's gaze met hers. His smile deepened with a splash of unrepentant arrogance. "I was hoping to take Em for a short ride this afternoon, Rachel. But I know you're not too keen on motorcycles, so I thought I'd ask your permission first."

"Absolutely not." The response was out before she could stop it.

And it earned her a dark glare from Em.

"I'm a very good driver, and we'll only be gone for a half hour. I won't let anything happen to her, I promise."

Meeting Drew's amused green gaze only fueled her rising panic: He knew precisely what impact he had on her. Every corkscrew twist of her gut, every terrified stumble of her heart, every strangled breath . . . he knew. And it made him smile. Lachlan's warning pounded in her head. *Don't talk to him, don't listen to a word he says, even if it involves Emily.* But his words didn't cover this particular scenario.

She glanced at her hand.

There, still visible in smudged ink across her trembling palm, were ten magical, hope-inspiring numbers: Lachlan's cell phone.

"Hold on," she said, trying to pull off a smooth smile and failing miserably. Stepping onto the grass, she dug her phone from her purse and dialed Lachlan's number. The uncontrollable spasms of her fingers shrank the keypad to an impossibly small area, and she had to start over four times.

Finally, she got it right.

Turning her back to Drew for privacy, she waited for Lachlan to answer. One ring. Five rings. Nine rings. Nothing. She endured fifteen empty rings and numerous hopeful clicks on the line before she acknowledged the dismal truth.

She was on her own.

"We should take the groceries in," Drew said kindly as she pivoted to face him once more. "The ice cream is melting."

Rachel simply stared back at him.

The image of him standing in her kitchen, amiably putting away the groceries, just wouldn't form. Instead, her brain insisted on placing a gleaming silver knife in his hands to go along with the memory of dark red blood oozing from Lachlan's wounds.

"Mom." Em nudged her with her elbow. "Let's go in."

Her daughter's bright blue eyes were intent, her pale face warily hopeful. *Here*, she said silently, *here's your chance to make up for that last painful argument. Let him come in, and all will be forgiven.*

And Rachel truly, truly wanted to. . . .

But with their very lives at risk, how could she agree?

Her gaze found Drew's again, this time a little stronger, emboldened by righteous anger. She could not let this monster into her house. Opening her mouth, she began, "I—"

But he preempted her, his expression very serious, his smile gone. "I can see the concern in your eyes, Rachel, and I understand how hard it is to trust me. I'm a stranger. But I swear to you, nothing will happen to Em. She's very important to me—just as important as she is to you—and you have my word that she'll be safe."

He was speaking directly to her, for her benefit alone, trying to convince her he wouldn't harm Em. But she knew the truth about him and no words from his smooth-talking, deceitful mouth were ever going to convince her he was trustworthy.

"Go away," she said tightly. "Go away and leave us alone."

"Mom!"

At Em's strangled cry, a hint of a smile returned to Drew's face, and Rachel's heart tripped and fell into a rabbit hole. She'd played right into his hand. He'd been hoping that she'd spurn his efforts, counting on her to run roughshod over his impassioned pleas. Everything he'd said was all part of the show, and the show was all for Em.

He didn't bother to respond, just stood quietly and let Rachel's own words do his work for him.

"What the hell's *wrong* with you?" Em snapped, pitching her load of groceries onto the sidewalk at her feet, uncaring of the glass-shattering impact. "Drew's done everything humanly possible to please you and it's still not enough. What does he have to do to make you happy?"

"He's not what you think he is, Em. He's a monster. He and his friends mugged Father MacGregor last night and cut him up very badly. Why don't you ask him about *that*?"

Em halted her tirade, eyes blinking in confusion. Her gaze swiveled to Drew.

"Em, please." Drew threw Em a shocked glance and took a defensive step back. His sudden paleness, widened eyes, and apparent confusion seemed authentic. "I swear I don't know what she's talking about. I don't even know this Father Macwhatever guy. I sure as hell didn't cut anybody up."

Even the desperate timbre of his voice rang true. If Rachel hadn't heard the other side of the story—and if Drew hadn't already admitted to knowing Lachlan—she probably would have bought his act.

"He says you did," she said coldly. "And frankly, I believe him over you."

"Well, maybe your faith in this priest guy is misplaced, because I'm telling you I never mugged him, never mugged anyone. My friends and I like to act tough, but all we do is dress like badasses and ride around on our bikes. Sure, we drink the odd beer and smoke some weed, but we're not criminals. Are you sure this Father MacGregor is telling you the truth?"

He was good. Very, very good.

Even though she *knew* he was using the huge unknowns

about Lachlan to his advantage, she was swayed—just a little. *Was* she sure? Was she truly convinced that Lachlan had told her the truth about the attack?

No, she wasn't sure.

Not about Lachlan.

But she was sure about Drew. Maybe it was a mother's innate ability to sense danger, but she was certain this suave, good-looking young man couldn't be trusted, no matter how convincing his words were.

"I'm very sure," she replied. Snatching the two paper bags back from Drew, she briskly added, "Em, pick up the groceries. We're going inside. Tonight, you can hear Father MacGregor's version of this ugly little story. Then you can decide what the truth really is."

Em hesitated.

"Go ahead, Em," Drew said quietly. "Talk to this guy; it can't hurt. Just remember I love you. I'd never do anything to hurt you, or anyone else."

The burn in Rachel's chest subsided—a bit.

He was backing off, but he didn't seem at all concerned about Em speaking with Lachlan. In fact, he encouraged her to do it. Why would he do that when he knew a brief chat with Lachlan would prove him a liar?

Em's face still held traces of animosity, but she gathered the spilled groceries at her feet and stood, her arm cradling the now-soggy paper bag.

With safety only a few feet away, Rachel jogged up the stairs to the double glass doors, tugged one open, and stepped aside to let Em pass through. Her daughter entered the cool, blue lobby, and immediately Rachel's heartbeat calmed. But it didn't completely settle. It was almost too easy, this escape, as if they were a pair of mice making a mad dash for freedom, unable to see that the cat had them cornered.

Before she followed Em inside, Rachel pitched a parting look at Drew.

He stood exactly where she'd left him, watching her. When her gaze met his, he offered her a slow, lazy smile, implying that everything had gone exactly the way he'd planned.

Then he spun on his black-booted heel and departed.

Lachlan sat back on the hard wooden stool. Rolling his shoulders, he attempted to relieve the tightness that had developed at the base of his neck.

Despite the vast number of candles dripping wax onto the stone floor, the light in the room was annoyingly dim. How sweetly he'd been seduced by modern technology. He could barely believe he'd once accepted this flickering murk as the norm. Add in medieval gall ink faded by time and endless pages of yellowed parchment, and it was no wonder his eyes protested at the abuse, demanding he shut them.

But he couldn't rest.

There was too much to learn. He hadn't yet cracked the spine on either of the two grimoires perched on the corner of the table, but the book of ancient lore he was currently perusing had already turned his known world on its ear.

The gods were not what he thought.

To hear Death talk, one would think her supremely capable and infinitely powerful. In fact, she was weak. While God and Satan were consummate deities imbued with an extensive range of powers, Death was not. She was a lesser deity, a demigod, and as such she had only limited abilities. The Gatherers suffered with a poor portfolio of primals, not because she deigned it so, but because it was all she could provide.

The book was quite fascinating. Indeed, the moment he'd turned the first crinkly page, he'd been enthralled.

He glanced at his watch.

And frowned.

The silver hands on the black face insisted the time was two twenty, but that couldn't be right. That would suggest he'd been lost in the tome for twelve hours. Unlikely.

"Stefan," he hollered.

A moment passed. Then the mage stuck his head around the purple curtain. He was munching on a chunk of crusty bun slathered with butter. "What?"

A tantalizing waft of spicy spaghetti entered the room with him, and Lachlan's stomach growled.

"What time is it?"

"Seven thirty."

"Bloody hell." Not quite as bad as losing twelve hours, but still a shock. "My watch has stopped working."

"Oh," Stefan said, wrinkling his nose. "Did I forget to mention that? In here, none of your modern gadgets work."

"Where is *here*, exactly?"

The mage stood taller, sweeping the room with a proud, fatherly look. "Castle Rakimczyk, Hungary, fifteenth century."

"A *real* castle, in the *real* fifteenth century?"

Stefan beamed. "Yes."

"Impressive. A family inheritance?"

"I guess you could say that."

Lachlan glanced at the darkened arch to the left, the one with a circular stone staircase leading up. "Can someone from this time walk in on us?"

"Not without a lot of heavy digging. The castle above has been burned to the ground. The locals weren't too happy with my ancestors. Blamed them for every milk-less cow and festering boil."

"Why work here? Couldn't you find a more pleasant spot?"

"No choice. The books are spellbound to this room and this time. Can't be moved. If I want to use them, I have to use them here."

"Vexing."

"To say the least. Keeps them safe, though."

Lachlan's nostrils flared as he caught another whiff of spaghetti off the mage's clothes. "Food passes over the threshold with no problem?" he asked as he watched the last of the bread roll disappear inside Stefan's mouth.

"Yes. Clothes, too, as you can see. Seems to mostly affect the electronic stuff." His gaze glimmered with faint amusement. "Hungry?"

"Aye."

"Come out and join us, then. Dika made enough pasta to feed an army, and she'd be pleased to fill a plate for you."

Although the opportunity to dig into Stefan's mysterious life intrigued him, he'd already spent more hours here than he ought to have. For the first time in more than a week, he hadn't trailed Emily home from school, and although he suspected Drusus was lying low after last night's attack, that nagged at him. Luck hadn't exactly been running in his favor lately.

"Thank you for the offer, but I'd best head home."

"Your loss." Stefan shrugged and retreated back behind the curtain. "Dika makes the best spaghetti this side of Italy."

Lachlan slid a dry quill between the pages to mark his spot and glanced at the heading of the next chapter: "The Trinity Soul." According to the first few lines, it was an ancient myth about a rare soul who, in a time of dark conflict among the deities, would be born upon the earth, summoned by God to help him save the world. A bit of useless fiction.

He was about to shift the quill to the next chapter, when his eyes drifted over the sketch at the bottom of the page, and he halted, feather in the air. It was a very simple image—three equal-sized black dots, two on top and one centered below—a motif that probably occurred frequently, naturally, in any multitude of places. Still, the hairs on his neck lifted. He'd seen that exact pattern just this afternoon. Ran his fingers over it, kissed it—a tiny grouping of moles on Rachel's right hip.

With his heart pumping chilly unease through his veins, he peered at the worn inscription below the sketch: *Mother of the Trinity Soul.*

Lachlan stiffened.

He'd never put much stake in coincidence. Yet Emily was the focal point of a large number of coincidences: Death's fascination with a human child; the assignment of her best Gatherer to watch over her; the bizarre request to keep the girl alive that flew in the face of Death's own raison d'être; Satan's interest in that same human child; the assignment of one of his lure demons to sway her; the ever-increasing threat of demon attacks.

Was it possible? Were those three tiny moles on Rachel's hip what they seemed to be? Was Emily this unique Trinity Soul?

And what exactly *was* a Trinity Soul?

Almost afraid of the answer, he bent over the book and read on.

"He's home. Let's go."

Her daughter looked up. She sat at the desk, hunched over her laptop computer, several MSN chat windows and a pinball game open at the same time. A glass of milk and a pilfered box of chocolate chip cookies balanced precariously atop various piles of junk.

"I don't really need to go," Em said, spiritlessly. "I believe you, okay?"

"No. I'm tired of having Drew imply that I'm lying, that I'm just saying all this stuff to make him look bad. I want you to hear the whole sordid mess direct from Father MacGregor's mouth and see the cuts for yourself. Let's go."

Em huffed an exaggerated sigh, typed *brb* into all her open windows, then rolled off the chair. "Fine, but I'm not staying long. I've got things to do."

"Homework, I hope?"

She shrugged. "I guess."

"Don't worry. I'm not planning to stay long, either."

In all honesty, Rachel wasn't sure how eager Lachlan would be to see them on his doorstep, not after her last visit. Although neither one of them had said words to that effect, it had felt an awful lot like good-bye when they parted.

They trod up the tiled stairs to the third floor and paused before a white colonial door identical to theirs, except for the shiny brass numbers, 309. The smoky strains of Michael Bublé's latest hit single floated into the carpeted hallway, and Rachel smiled. A modern take on old-fashioned songs. Yes, that suited him.

She rapped on the door.

A moment later, Lachlan stood before them in all his six-foot-plus glory, and Rachel's vow to remain cool and objective flew right out the window. The fantasy-inhibiting clerical outfit was gone, replaced by coal black jeans that hugged his muscular thighs and a pearl gray oxford shirt, the sleeves rolled up and several buttons undone at the throat.

Relaxed. Casual. And unbelievably sexy.

He blinked at her as if she were the last person he expected to see, which was probably true.

"We need to talk to you," she said, scrambling to repair her businesslike facade. "We had a visit from Drew today."

His gaze slammed into hers, no longer politely distant, but intimate and concerned. He searched her face, then quickly checked her body. With her well-being confirmed, his shoulders noticeably eased and his gaze moved on to Em. "Why didn't you call me?"

"I tried. You didn't answer your phone."

"But I had it—" He halted, rubbed his forehead, and sighed. "What happened?"

"Nothing, he backed off. But he insisted you were lying about last night's attack, and I needed Em to see and hear the truth. From you."

"The truth?"

Rachel nodded. "Can we come in, please?"

"Rachel, I—"

"This will only take a second," she assured him, barreling over his protest and pushing past him to enter the apartment, hoping to forestall any mention of her last visit. "Em and I can't stay long."

He closed the door and trailed them slowly into the open space of the living room, the room that was becoming as familiar as her own. So much so, in fact, that she instinctively adjusted the ornately framed beveled mirror hanging slightly askew on the wall.

Under the soft light of the chandelier, his face looked just as it had the first time she met him—classically handsome—no hint of the bruise around his eye remaining. He descended the steps from the entranceway without a limp—an amazing recovery.

For some reason, her heart was beating a little fast when she said, "Just show her the cuts on your chest and tell her what happened last night. Then we'll be out of your hair."

Lachlan stood very still, his eyes on her face. "I can't do that."

"Why not?"

Em was listening to the exchange with far more interest than she'd shown about coming up here. She'd stopped fidgeting and removed her earphones.

"It's no' possible."

"Not possible? You showed them to me. Why can't you show them to her?"

"Rachel, this is—"

"You don't get it," she said, her shoulders sagging. "She half believes him. He's very convincing. Let her see what he did to you so she can understand what kind of monster he is."

"I can't."

"Do you *want* her to believe him?"

"Of course no'." He turned to Em. "Emily, Drew truly did attack me last night. I saw his face quite clearly."

Em frowned. "But you're way bigger and stronger than he is. How could he beat you?"

"Because they attacked him in a group, that's how," Rachel answered in an angry rush, envisioning the swarming in her mind. "Drew and his whole gang."

"Actually," Lachlan said, with a quick glance at Rachel, "that's no' true. He attacked me alone. Smaller doesn't always mean weaker, Emily. He's a very skilled fighter, and he had weapons I didn't possess."

"Why would he do that? Attack you, I mean? Why would he want to hurt a priest?"

"He knows me. He knows I'm committed to protecting you, and he knows I won't back away easily."

"You knew each other before you came here?"

"Aye."

Em tilted her head. "Did he have anything to do with the death of your wife?"

Rachel's breath caught. *Wife?* What wife?

Lachlan's blue-gray eyes darkened. "Aye."

Em folded her arms over her black leather vest. "You talk a pretty good story, Father MacGregor, and I really want to trust you. But you don't look hurt. If Drew attacked you like you say he did, wouldn't you have bruises or stitches or something?"

Lachlan was silent.

"None of it really happened, did it?"

"Of course it happened," said Rachel, still flummoxed by the news that Lachlan had a wife. "I saw his injuries myself."

"Maybe you're just going along with the game." Em's heavily made-up eyes turned to her, narrowing. "Maybe this is all part of your big plan to get me to split up with Drew."

"Why would I haul you all the way up here if this was just a game?" Rachel retorted. Now more determined than ever to prove her story—and Lachlan's—she reached for the buttons on Lachlan's shirt.

"No, Rachel." He grabbed her hand and held it tight.

She wrenched her fingers free. "Just show her, damn it."

"I can't."

Em slowly shook her head. "He can't show us the cuts because they don't exist. Isn't that right, Father MacGregor?"

"Em, you're being ridiculous."

"Isn't that right, Father MacGregor?" Em repeated, her voice firm and sure.

"Oh, for heaven's sake."

Rachel slapped away Lachlan's hands and began unbuttoning his shirt. Lower and lower, until the shirt was completely unfastened, until his magnificent chest was bared. Rachel froze. There was no sign of the long, narrow cuts that had decorated his flesh a few hours ago. Not a scratch or scab remained.

She lifted her gaze to Lachlan's face, confused.

"How is that possible?"

"Because they were fake, Mom. It was all a big hoax."

Rachel shook her head, remembering the oozing blood, the parted layers of skin, how pale he'd been. "No, I saw them. They were bleeding."

He grabbed her shaking hands, tugging them close to his heart. His eyes were soft gray clouds. "Rachel . . ."

His heart pumped strong and steady beneath her fingers, clearly healthy, clearly uninjured. His bare skin was warm and smooth and, except for a few old white scars, impossibly *unblemished*.

She jerked away, backing toward Em. Betrayal swirled in her belly like a bitter medicine, and hot tears pricked behind her eyelids. She had trusted this man, believed in him. She'd let him make love to her. God, she was such a sucker for a handsome face. "A hoax? You did all this to fool me?"

"It wasn't a hoax."

"Then explain it," she begged. "Where did those cuts go?"

"They healed."

"In less than a day? I don't think so."

"I heal very fast."

"You need to work on that story a little more." Rachel threw him what she hoped was a scathing look. It was hard to know for sure what the net effect was, with her eyes all blurry and her bottom lip trembling. "As it stands? No one's buying it. Come on, Em, let's go."

"Rachel, wait. I need to speak with you. Alone."

Already at the door, Rachel turned. "I think I've

heard enough for one day," she said, her voice as weary as she felt. "Honestly, no matter what it is you need to say, I'm not ready to hear it."

"It's important."

"Really?" She smiled, or tried to. "And here I thought all the *other* conversations we had today were important. I guess I had things mixed up."

Fearing a total and ignominious collapse, she yanked open the door and, with her hand wrapped tightly around Em's, walked out.

12

Rachel took a deep breath and stepped into Celia's office.

"Sit down."

Feeling like a delinquent student dragged before the principal, she did as she was instructed and took one of the two armchairs in front of the kidney-shaped desk. Her clammy palms found comfort in the voluminous fabric of her chambray peasant skirt.

While she waited for Celia to finish reading the single sheet of paper on her desk, Rachel glanced around. A series of bright Chagall prints decorated the walls, and a huge floor-to-ceiling window added a warm touch of color to an otherwise-sterile work space.

Her boss pushed aside the report, leaned her elbows on the desk, and favored Rachel with a cool look. Her wheat blond hair was parted with a swag of bangs draped over one eye. "I'm not pleased that you left the office early yesterday."

"I checked with Nigel before I left."

"So he said. But you know how I feel about my designers working together, spurring each other to new creative heights."

"Yes."

"And still, you left."

"Yes."

"If this was just about you, Rachel, there wouldn't be a problem. You consistently produce the best illustrations in the department and you never miss a deadline. But this is a team, not a production unit of one."

"I understand that."

"Do you? I'm not so sure." Celia's leather chair creaked as she leaned back. "Are you aware that the junior designers look up to you? That they aspire to one day reach your level of talent? Are you aware that your fellow senior designers rely on your expertise to help them leap the hurdles of the software?"

"I help out as much as I can."

"No, you don't. You deliver the files, but not the commitment." Celia sighed heavily. "You're capable of so much more than you're giving us, Rachel. I know it. But frankly, I'm at a loss as to how to get you to live up to your potential."

"I'm a single mother, Celia. I can't put in the same hours as other people. And my daughter was recently involved in a horrible bus accident."

"Yes, but she's fine, isn't she? Back at school?"

"Yes, but—"

"I believe in you, Rachel. You have incredible talent and the ability to calm the most agitated of clients. You can teach without being preachy and you don't get frazzled by pressure. Basically, you have all the qualities I look for in a team leader."

Rachel blinked.

"So, I've decided the best way to cultivate your commitment is simply to demand it of you. I'm promoting you."

No way.

"As of this morning," Celia continued, "you're earning five grand more a year. You'll be supervising Francis, Mandy, Jen, and Matt. Congratulations."

Rachel could hardly breathe. Promoted. Wow. At any other point in her life, she'd be shouting from the rooftops. But today? With her daughter in the clutches of a scumbag drug dealer and dedicated mothering the only hope she had of keeping Em safe, the timing sucked. She needed to spend fewer hours at work, not more.

"Celia, I—"

"No, don't thank me. I'm actually being quite selfish. I need you to help us out of a tough spot, Rachel. If we don't make the cut-off in two days, the Design Department is going to take some serious heat from upper management. That'll mean layoffs, and we don't want that, do we?"

The weight tugged Rachel's shoulders down. "No, we don't."

"I need you to make sure the graphics are not only done, they're done well. Tough job, I know, but if anyone can make it happen; it's you."

"Uh, thanks."

Celia swiveled her black leather chair to face her computer and flicked a slim, manicured hand at the door. "Go get 'em, tiger."

"You still work here?"

Rachel glanced over her shoulder. Mandy was following her down the corridor with a steaming cup of java in hand. "Yup. In fact, I'm now your boss. I thought you'd already know, since you're sleeping with Bill in HR."

"Oh, he's very vocal in the bedroom, no doubt about that," her friend said, smiling slyly, "but nothing about work."

Clapping her hands over her ears and shuddering in mock horror, Rachel laughed. "Ugh. Too much information."

"Well . . ." Mandy waved her keycard over the electronic panel at the entrance to the Design Department, waited for the beep, then pushed open the door. "If I have to have a new boss, I'm glad it's you. No way you'll suddenly become Celia's bitch like Nigel did."

"Thanks for the vote of confidence. I just wish the timing were better. Things are not going well back at the old homestead."

"Problems with Em?"

"Yeah." That, and other nasty stuff.

"My sister says you just need to survive until she's seventeen, and then—poof—one morning you'll wake up to find she's turned into this sweet, well-behaved little lady."

Sliding into her cubicle and taking a seat in front of her computer, Rachel chuckled. "I can hope, right?"

"By the way, are you Matt's boss, too?"

"Yes."

Mandy shook her head. "Well, you better go have a look at the work he's doing. Just my opinion, of course, but I think all of his stuff is crap and has to be redone."

"Great. You know what Celia told me—?" Rachel's phone buzzed, and she glanced at the call display. Reception. She was expecting a package from the printer. "Hold on, I've got to get this."

Mandy nodded, her gaze wandering.

"Hello?"

"Ms. Lewis, you have a visitor. Do you want me to send him up to the fourth floor?"

"A visitor? Who?"

Mandy's gaze darted back to Rachel's face, one delicate eyebrow raised.

Rachel shrugged at the unasked question.

"A Mr. Lachlan MacGregor. He says it's very important that he speak with you."

Rachel frowned. So, he was still on the *I've-got-critical-information* kick. She'd like to tell him to go to hell, but with Drew still stalking Em, could she afford not to listen?

"All right, send him up."

"Him, huh?" Mandy leaned over the wall of the cubby, eyes sparkling. "Would this possibly be the *him* you left early to look after yesterday? The priest?"

Despite an intense desire to keep her cool, Rachel felt her cheeks grow hot under Mandy's curious stare. Someone had gotten looked after yesterday, but it wasn't Lachlan. "Maybe."

"I'll go meet him at the elevator."

"No," Rachel protested, leaping to her feet. But she was too slow. Mandy left her coffee balanced on the cubicle wall and took off like a greyhound out of the gate.

The vivacious blonde returned three minutes later with Lachlan in tow, flirting up a storm and tossing her hair in an open invitation for seduction, her arm tucked in his.

"I was just telling Lachlan how you denied that he was cute," Mandy gushed, "and how I'm in complete disagreement."

Most guys who found themselves wrapped in a buxom little blonde with the shortest miniskirt imaginable would be hard-pressed to stay focused. Not Lachlan. The moment he spied Rachel, he had eyes only for her—unwavering, solicitous, and strangely possessive. As if she were his, and he'd stopped by to remind her of that fact.

She almost forgave him everything right then and there.

Wretch. How dare he look so good in jeans and a T-shirt.

"Hello," he said, his eyes searching hers. "How are you?"

"You came all the way down here to ask me how I am? Couldn't you have done that over the ph—" She halted abruptly, remembering his response the last time she asked that same question—something steamy involving licking lips and bare feet.

Lachlan's wry smile told her he remembered, too, but he was gentleman enough not to mention it. "I'd like to speak with you. In private."

Mandy pouted. "Don't worry. Rache and I are bosom friends. I won't blab about anything you say. Besides, she can't really wander off, not anymore."

"That's true. I'm up to my ears in work. Maybe you could just say what you need to say and then go home."

Lachlan smoothly detached himself from Mandy's grasp, his eyes never once leaving Rachel's face. "I'm prepared to tell you everything, and by that I mean *absolutely* everything. But I need to do it in private."

Everything?

Rachel chewed her lip. Did she really want to know everything about Lachlan MacGregor? She had an uneasy feeling she wasn't going to like his story. His response to what happened to his injuries sure hadn't sat well. Even now, she didn't know what to think about that. The cuts and the blood had seemed so real. Yet they hadn't been.

But the annoying truth was—despite all the lies and wacky stories—saying no to those smoky blue eyes was impossible.

"Okay, come on. There's a small conference room around the corner we can use."

"Rachel? Are you crazy?"

She glanced at Mandy's scandalized face. "Print off

Matt's designs and leave them on my desk. I shouldn't be long."

Spinning on her heel, she led the way down the hall, intent on keeping her distance. Avoiding the curious looks from the other designers, she tugged him around the corner and into the conference room, which felt incredibly small with his six-foot-plus frame in it. Especially with white cotton knit clinging to his perfect pecs and worn blue denim hugging his muscular thighs.

"Okay." She put the table between them. "I really don't have a lot of time, so just spill it. What's your version of the truth?"

"You'd best sit down."

"Now there's an ominous start," she groaned. But she pulled out a chair and sat down.

"There's no easy way to say this. You're no' going to believe me, no matter what words I choose, so I'm going to be blunt."

"Okay."

"I'm dead."

She frowned. "Dead, as in you're in some really serious trouble?"

"No, dead, as in no longer alive."

"Um, you're breathing," she pointed out, not quite able to digest his words and a little afraid to attach meaning to them. "And I've felt your heart beating. Those are usually pretty good signs you're alive."

"My body is not what it seems. I eat, breathe, and bleed, but I'm no longer alive the way you are. My mortal body died in 1603. I now serve as a Soul Gatherer for the goddess of Death."

Rachel stared.

Was he kidding? He must be.

The strange thing was, his story didn't seem as ridiculous as it should have. Maybe it was the matter-of-fact way he spoke, or the unwavering seriousness in his eyes, or even the lingering stupor of her almost-sleepless night, but his story didn't make her laugh.

It just made her numb.

"You're pulling my leg, right?"

"No." He shook his head. "The reason I can survive the sort of wounds you saw yesterday is that I'm immortal. I can be slain, but only by a fellow immortal."

Lachlan's hands fisted seemingly of their own accord, and he looked down at them.

"Drusus is also immortal, and we share a past. He played a significant role in the deaths of my wife"—he paused briefly, then pushed on, his voice less steady than before—"and my three children. All my kin."

His gaze lifted.

And in his eyes, she saw the very depths of him: the lingering sadness, the fierce determination, and a certain resignation about the future.

Words failed her. For once in her life, she truly had no idea what to say.

"I don't expect you to believe me," he continued, "no' really. I know it's a fantastical tale. I'm only telling you because you already think I'm full of shite, and it's very important that you know what you're up against with Drusus. You can't best him on your own. You need me."

He was saying all sorts of words—nouns and verbs and adjectives—but none of them were sinking in. "Do you have a doctor?"

"A what?"

"Someone who prescribes your medications? The little blue pills you're supposed to take but have recently run out of?"

"Rachel . . ." He sighed. "Yesterday, did you believe my injuries were real?"

Her eyes found his face again. "Yes."

"You saw how deep the cut on my leg was?"

"Yes."

"How do you explain the disappearance of such a wound?"

She shrugged helplessly. "I can't."

"That's as good as my evidence gets. I realize it tests the boundaries of what you know to be true, but isn't there room in your belief system for things that you can't explain?"

"You're asking me to believe you're *dead*."

"Aye."

"We made love yesterday, and now you're trying to tell me I screwed a dead guy?"

To her amazement, twin flags of color rose in Lachlan's cheeks. "An honorable man would have told you then, I suppose, but in truth, it hardly seemed the time."

Propping her elbows on the table, she covered her face with her hands. "God, I can't handle this. My brain feels like it's going to explode."

Crouching beside her, he covered her hands with his. They were warm, reassuring. "I never wanted to hurt you, Rachel."

"Bull," she said, jerking away, suddenly angry. "You've been messing with my head since we first met. If all this is true, then you lied to me about Drusus being some kind of drug dealer. And you knew—for whatever reason—that you were majorly unavailable. But you still gave me all those smoldering looks, you still kissed me, you still made love to me. If you didn't want to hurt me, it would have been better just to stay away."

His eyes were steady and clear. "You're right."

"Of course I'm right—"

"When it comes to you, I'm a fool. I do things I know I shouldn't. I stay when I should walk away. It's a mistake to touch you and kiss you and want you, but I can't seem to help myself."

Ah, damn. He had her at *fool*. Who doesn't want the guy they love to admit he's a fool over them?

Rachel's mouth went dry. Wow. Did she really love this madman? This guy who might very well end up in a padded cell at the local mental hospital?

"I would apologize," he added gently, "but 'twould be insincere because I'm no' sorry. I don't regret a moment spent in your company. No' one."

"It wasn't *all* your fault. I could have stayed away, too."

"Could you?"

She met his gaze. "No. Who am I kidding? My willpower is probably one tenth of yours. I'm the one who showed up on your doorstep and begged you to have sex with me, remember?"

"Vividly."

Rachel glanced away, embarrassed.

"It's a memory I'll treasure for the rest of my existence."

The term *existence* rippled through her like a cool breeze, reminding her of his supposed immortal status, of his crazy, unbelievable story. Afraid to buy into his delusions, but desperately wanting to understand, she asked, "What does a Soul Gatherer do?"

He studied her for a long moment, as if debating her ability to absorb more, and then responded, "In the very brief moments after a person dies, a Gatherer collects his or her soul. It's his duty to pass the soul on to a guide who then escorts the soul to its final destination."

"Heaven."

"Or hell."

She winced. "Hell is real?"

"Aye."

"Which means that Satan is real."

"Aye."

"Yikes. Maybe it's time I started going to church."

"Your churchgoing habits do no' determine the destination of your soul. The basic goodness of your soul does that. Avoid the big sins, don't take your own life, and you should be fine."

"Should be?"

He smiled. "I've no fear over where your soul will end up, Rachel. You shouldn't worry, either."

Whew. "If you're a Gatherer, what does that make Drusus?"

"A demon."

"From hell?"

"Aye."

The contents of her stomach did a lurching dance. If she believed his crazy story, then Em was dating a monster. Not a straightforward, regular, drug-dealing monster, but some nightmare out of *The Exorcist*.

Terrified to let her thoughts settle, Rachel asked more questions—about his job, about Drusus, about Em. The one area she avoided was his past. It bothered her more than she was prepared to admit that he'd been married before and had three kids, that they'd all died tragically, and that—judging by the hitch in his voice—he still desperately missed them. Embarrassed by her jealousy, she found it easier just to ignore that part of his tale.

Lachlan didn't volunteer additional details.

Instead, he turned the topic to the reason for Drew's interest in Em. "According to this ancient manuscript, Emily may be what's called a Trinity Soul, a human soul born with the power to manipulate all three planes—heaven, earth, and hell. This soul is destined to act as a sort of . . . ambassador for God."

"Em? An ambassador for God?"

"Aye."

She blinked at him. "Okay, wait. I love my daughter, and to me she'll always be unique and special, but why would God pick *her*? Out of all the people on this planet, what makes her qualified to be this Trinity Soul?"

"I don't know."

"How's she supposed to do the job? She's a teenager."

"She can travel at will between all three planes."

Rachel snorted. "Em can travel to heaven anytime she wants? I don't think so. If that were true, there's no way she'd stick around to clean her room on Saturday mornings."

"She may no' be aware of her ability."

The first giggle bubbled out of her mouth before she could stop it, and another quickly followed. The sheer ridiculousness of everything she'd heard this afternoon overwhelmed her: Lachlan dead, Drew a demon, Em able to fly to heaven. She'd actually started to suspend her disbelief until that part. But Em being some kind of weird superkid was just too much. Another laugh burst free—and another. In a moment, she was laughing so hard, her belly ached and tears were streaming from her eyes.

She laughed until Lachlan swooped in and silenced her hysterics with a kiss—not a hot kiss, an impossibly tender kiss.

He pressed his lips firmly against hers, with enough heat and passion to break through her troubled thoughts, but only just. The rest of the kiss was understanding and acceptance, comfort and contentment—slow and sweet, as if they had all the time in the world.

As if it didn't matter that Lachlan was delusional.

But it did.

"I'm sorry," she moaned against his lips. "I want to believe all this stuff, but I just ca—"

"Hush," he said softly, kissing the corner of her mouth and then the tip of her nose. "I understand."

Weak woman that she was, she let him kiss her and hold her. Just for a moment, she wanted to close her eyes, rest her cheek against his chest, and pretend that everything in her life was normal, that her man was a regular, run-of-the mill guy—an accountant, maybe. Not a priest, or a Soul Gatherer, or a nut.

Other women had normal boyfriends.

Was it too much to ask?

Lachlan reluctantly left Rachel at her desk, silent and frowning, and returned to the visitor parking lot, where he found Death waiting for him.

She leaned upon the shiny hood of his car, dressed entirely in black: slim jeans, a cotton shirt, and a pair of low-heeled leather cowboy boots. A long white ponytail completed the outfit. All she was missing was the pale horse.

"My liege," he acknowledged warily as he crossed the sidewalk. "To what do I owe this honor?"

He couldn't remember the last time she'd come to him. Tasked with marking more than two hundred thousand people every day, she was an industrious goddess, and usually it was the other way around—he had to fit into *her* schedule.

She straightened, standing tall and regal, and judging by the tight slash of her dark red lips, annoyed. "Were my instructions not clear, Gatherer?"

"About what?"

"You were to inform me of any unusual occurrences."

"I remember. If I've failed in that, my apologies. These days, everything seems unusual."

She tossed a glare at him, but it quickly faded, replaced by a more contemplative expression. "How many gathers have you done in the past week?"

"Nine."

"And none of them were . . . odd?"

"No," he said slowly, reviewing them in his head. "Why?"

"Something is afoot."

Lachlan lifted his brows. "You mean other than the ridiculous number of demon attacks and the intolerable delays of the angels?"

"Pah! What the psychopomps are doing is of little concern. I mean something serious. At the monthly tallying of souls, the numbers favored Satan for the first time in two millenniums. I was shocked, but apparently not nearly as shocked as Archangel Michael. He dove across the neutral line, grabbed Lucifer by the shirt, and accused him of cheating. Not your usual fare, at all. Michael is usually the very epitome of civil."

"And you're telling me this because . . . ?"

"Because Michael also mentioned he paid you a—" Death halted, her eyelids slipping down to cover her frosty blue gaze. "Never mind. I need to know everything that's happened of late. Come here. I wish to read you."

Lachlan hesitated. Death could review all of his gathers in detail, simply by placing her hand over his heart. She'd not checked up on him in such a manner since his first few clumsy efforts, and it did not bode well that she wished to do so now. But it was a reasonable request, and he could not refuse.

He stepped closer.

Her hand was frigid, even through his thick T-shirt. No sooner had it touched his chest than chips of ice sped through his veins, chilling every inch of him, numbing every muscle. Basic movements, even breathing, became a chore.

Death's eyes drifted shut and she caught her crimson lip between her teeth. Small flickers of her eyes beneath her lids reflected the rapid pace of her thoughts. A bare instant after she began, her eyes popped open.

He startled at the hungry glow in them.

"By the gods," she breathed, "I was right. She's the one."

Beneath her hand, his heartbeat accelerated. Bloody hell. He had assumed—wrongly—that her ability to read him was limited to his gathers. How much did she know?

"The one?" he asked carefully.

"Emily Lewis is the Trinity Soul."

What little hope he had drifted away like smoke on a breeze. "Perhaps. But she's shown no sign of possessing the Trinity powers described in the ancient texts."

Death ignored him. She stepped back, a cold smile spreading over her face. "The information that led me to her was naught but a faint bread crumb trail through the old testaments. There was no way to be certain it was she. But you've found definitive proof. What an absolute delight."

Delight? Nay, disgust would be a better label for the roil in his gut. He'd read the entire section on the Trinity Soul, and he knew the value Emily represented to Death: a chance to rise up the ladder and become a full god.

"She's shown no sign of possessing the Trinity powers," he repeated.

Death's gaze turned to him. "That's irrelevant."

"She may no' be the one."

"Of course she is. The mark you found upon the mother is indisputable. She simply hasn't matured yet."

Lachlan, who up to that moment believed he'd left his superstitious nature back in the seventeenth century, crossed his fingers behind his back. "Until she fully matures, I assume she's of no use to you?"

"Correct. The more power she controls at the moment I consume her soul, the more power I will absorb." Death's eyes narrowed in thought. "Which means you must be more diligent than ever in keeping her soul out of Satan's hands. I will not tolerate failure, not at this stage."

"Then tell me how to defeat the lure demon."

Her familiar smirk returned. "Haven't you figured it out yet? I'm disappointed, MacGregor. Not as smart as you'd like to think, are you?"

"Apparently no'."

"You've done well for me today, so I'll reward you," she said. "The trade you made with your brother all those years ago—your life for his—was a fair one. He gave you the very tool you need to succeed."

An old fury, still surprisingly bitter, rose in his chest. "Fair? Do no' dare call that trade fair. You were duplicitous. You implied you would save him, when in fact—"

"Cease." She snapped her fingers under his nose. "I lived up to my bargain. Your father's line continues even to this day. Your reluctance to accept the truth has long become tiresome."

Lachlan subsided—with difficulty. It would be a mistake to let the past distract him from the importance of her advice. "What tool did he give me?"

"The holy rood, of course."

"You lie," he snarled, reaching the end of his patience. "I was wearing the cross when I last battled Drusus, and it did nothing to protect me."

"Come now, MacGregor, you must know the rood is simply a physical representation of God's abiding love for humankind. It's nothing but a focusing tool. The power lies in your faith, in God, and in yourself."

"You're saying that any Gatherer with faith can defeat a lure demon? I find it hard to believe none have ever succeeded, then."

She laughed. "Ah, there's the rub. Since the moment God called me into being on the First Day, there's never been a Gatherer arrived upon my doorstep with his faith intact. Spiritually damaged, one and all."

"So, if I—"

"Stop." She held her hands like a shield. "I've given you all I care to. I've many people to visit today. The rest is up to you."

"By God, you're a bloody useless *git*."

But his words were not the defiant bullets of scorn he intended them to be. She'd already disappeared in a brilliant flash of cold white light.

13

Lachlan located Brian in a posh little boutique on Santana Row, trying on a pair of hand-stitched New & Lingwood loafers.

"You can't run in those," he said to the young Gatherer.

"No," Brian agreed as he stood and extended his American Express card to the pretty salesgirl. "But if they catch me, I'll be the best-looking corpse on the street."

"Don't you have a gather to do?"

"Yup. Don't worry, I'm on it. See the poor bugger sitting at that table on the corner, sipping his java and yakking with his pals? He's about to get hit by a 1977 Mercury Marquis. The old guy driving is going to stomp on the brake when he sees the red light, but hit the gas pedal instead."

Peering through the etched glass of the store window, Lachlan studied the coffee drinker relaxing beneath an umbrella: middle-aged, fit, probably a dad. He couldn't see the telltale white spiral glowing upon his cheek, but he trusted Brian to know it was there. "Shite."

"Yeah."

Brian smiled nicely at the salesgirl, accepted his shoe box, and then pushed through the mahogany-framed door to the street. About twenty seconds later, a bilious green land yacht bounced over the curb, mowed down the decorative metal fence, and struck the table, just the way Brian predicted.

Metal shrieked, people screamed and ran, coffee flew everywhere, and the hazy odor of car exhaust was replaced by the ugly stench of blood and fear.

The younger Gatherer thrust his box at Lachlan and dove into the crowd of horrified bystanders, trying to reach his target. But an off-duty police officer took control of the situation, holding unnecessary people back while another man administered CPR. Unknown to those scrambling to keep the man's heart pumping, he was already brain-dead, the back of his head crushed against the pavement. Brian returned almost ten minutes later, looking annoyed.

"Poor bastard. They wouldn't let me near him. He had to stay in that mangled body way longer than he should've, dealing with the mental shock of what happened. Definitely not fun."

"But he's at peace now?"

"Well, that would depend on how you define peace. He's destined to join us in purgatory. Didn't quite live the pure life he should have."

"That's the price we pay for our mistakes."

"Yeah, but I still feel bad. He's got two little kids and another baby on the way. He's leaving behind a lot of sad people, people who need him."

Lachlan didn't answer. Any response would either minimize the man's death or pull them both into a morose bog of empathy. He handed Brian his shoes. "I want you to do something for me."

"Name it."

"Buy the lads some bling."

Brian stared at him.

"To be more specific, Christian bling. Big silver crosses on heavy chains." He tossed Brian a roll of bills. "Buy as many as you think they can comfortably wear."

"Are you serious?"

"Aye."

"Why?"

Lachlan explained what Death had told him.

"How is that good news, exactly?" Brian asked as he and Lachlan strolled up the street. "Drusus almost punched your time clock the other night and you've got more faith in God than the rest of us put together. What makes you think a crucifix or two is going to save *our* asses?"

"Just do as I asked, Webster."

"Okay, okay." He shrugged. "By the way, Carlos said he saw something freaky happen with Emily yesterday."

"What?"

"One second she was holding a pencil, the next she was levitating it. Carlos said it hovered there for a second; then the pencil just vanished."

Lachlan sighed. So much for his hope that Emily wasn't the Trinity Soul. "She's unconsciously shredding the barriers between the planes. He should be careful."

"I'll warn him." Brian nodded, but his attention had wandered to the sign for a Mexican bistro. "Have you had lunch?"

Before Lachlan could respond, a bright red spark arced across the pavement and ricocheted off the black-painted lamppost in the grassy median beside them. A busy street in the middle of the day was a poor choice for a visitation, so he snatched Brian by the arm and hauled him down into the depths of a nearby underground parking garage.

"Hey," Brian protested, smoothing the wrinkles on his navy suit jacket. "This is Armani, pal."

"Did you bring your sword?"

"Yeah." One spark became three, lighting up the dimness in a series of brilliant flashes. Brian's attention finally shifted from his attire. "We're not running?"

"No."

"Alrighty, then." He tossed the shoe box onto the oil-spotted concrete floor and pulled his sword from the baldric under his jacket. "Showtime."

Lachlan drew his own weapon just as the air parched and his ears went pop. Four rapacious demons appeared before them, hungry for a taste of human soul. Having come out on the wrong side of fair play in recent days, he didn't warn them off. He simply whipped up a hasty shield charm and attacked, taking off the head of the closest demon and severing the arm of the fellow next to him with his first swing.

Brian leapt into the fight without hesitation and made a powerful two-handed slice that took the third demon by surprise, gutting him. In less than five minutes the battle was over, with the last demon collapsing the cloaking dome in a desperate bid to save his immortal life. Unfortunately for him, Lachlan split the front of his neck just before he disappeared. Demon gore ran thickly down the *claidheamh mòr* as the dome winked into nothingness.

"How many is that now? Four?" Brian wiped a trickle of sweat from his brow with his arm and resheathed his sword. "At the rate you're saving me from extinction, I may not be able to repay you before your term is up."

"You owe me nothing. We fought as a team."

"I did okay, huh?"

"You did well."

"Wow, was that actually a compliment?" Grinning, the young Gatherer bent to retrieve his new shoes, which had spilled out of the box. He polished the toe of one loafer with his sleeve before carefully tucking it back in the tissue. "I'm going to get a swelled head."

Lachlan studied Brian.

And it struck him then that he might not always be around to guide the young man's development or to convey the things he wanted to convey. He put a hand on Brian's sleeve. "You're a natural leader and a quick study. You've learned a great deal. If the worst should happen, I'd expect you to take charge of the others."

"Christ, don't say shit like that."

"It's no' my intent to expire." Not if he could help it, anyway. "But you must be prepared for every eventuality. If my end comes unexpectedly, promise me you'll find another seasoned swordsman and keep training."

"MacGregor, cut it out. This is bullshit. I'm not going to discuss what I'm supposed to do after you're whacked."

"It's good strategy to review all the possible outcomes."

"No, it's just nuts. How about we discuss all the possible ways we can beat this asshole lure demon instead?"

Lachlan smiled. "Aye, that's also good strategy."

"Score one for the Yale grad. Uh, does that mean you're up for lunch at Consuelo's? I'm starving."

"By God, Webster, do all your conversations eventually come back to you and your superficial needs?"

Tugging the cuffs of his pale blue shirt to adjust the amount showing beneath his Armani jacket, Brian led the way up the ramp to the street. "Pretty much. Got a problem with that?"

Em's brain was so saturated with dark thoughts over the humiliations she'd suffered at the hands of other students that she barely noticed Carlos all day. It took a pointed comment from Sheryl to shake her loose.

"Girl, he is *so* crushing on you."

"Who?"

"The new guy."

She lifted her gaze from her bootlaces and glanced around the school yard. Almost every other kid was scrambling to leave as quickly as he could, either walking briskly home or lining up for the buses. Hands in the pockets of his long black coat, earphones in his ears, Carlos leaned against the brick wall, watching her.

With those deeply soulful eyes.

Keeping her face neutral, she finished tying her boots and then straightened. "He's cool."

"No," Sheryl disagreed fervently, "he's totally hot."

"He's on my bus."

"No *way*."

"Way."

Sheryl pitched her a thoughtful frown. "What about Drew?"

Em blinked. Whoops. Just for a second, she'd actually forgotten about Drew. "Don't worry, I'm not looking for a new boyfriend, just enjoying the attention."

"Oooh, here he comes." Smiling with a shade of jealousy, Sheryl adjusted her books in her arms. "Text me later and give me the scoop."

"'Kay."

Carlos sauntered over, all smooth, silky waves and quiet intensity, and Em's heartbeat fluttered. Most boys carried the distinct edge of body odor on their clothes, but not Carlos. He smelled warm and lemony at the same time.

"Bussin' today?" he asked.

"Yeah."

"Me, too."

Together, without speaking, they lined up in front of the bus, then boarded. There were no empty benches left, only single seats, and disappointment tugged at

Em's lips. But much to her surprise, Carlos silently gathered up her hand in his, stopped beside a bench housing a lone boy, and held up their entwined hands for the kid to see.

"Mind?"

The boy shook his head and scurried for another seat.

Em wasn't sure if the result was due to Carlos's naturally intimidating style or just kindness on the boy's part. To be honest, she didn't give it much thought. She was lost in the sensation of his lean, sweat-free hand wrapped around hers and the tingly feel of his shoulder and thigh brushing against her clothes as they sat.

Okay, not *totally* lost.

A part of her beamed with the knowledge that the other girls on the bus had witnessed his very public claim of her hand. He'd proved the backstabbing bitches wrong with one simple act—she wasn't a lesbo or a troll.

The whole event made her light-headed—so light-headed, in fact, that the short trip to her stop passed in a blur, and in no time at all the bus was squeaking to a halt in front of her apartment complex.

Carlos released her hand. "Tomorrow?"

"Yeah."

Head down, with her long, streaked hair masking her expression, Em strode to the front of the bus and began to descend the steps. But as determined as she was not to act stupid and starry-eyed, she was unable to resist a quick glance back at Carlos before she exited.

He was watching her, just as she expected.

But this time, as their eyes met, the corner of his mouth lifted in the teensiest of smiles, and her heart did a little flip.

OMG.

He really *liked* her.

*   *   *

Searching the Net didn't lift Rachel's spirits one bit. According to Wikipedia, there was something called delusional disorder that fit Lachlan's symptoms to a T. Well, except for the sexual dysfunction, and the tendency to be hypersensitive and argumentative. Okay, so it didn't really describe him at all. She still wasn't able to accept the other option—that he was dead.

So, she typed *Drusus* in the Google search bar instead.

She waded through a ton of useless pages before she found an entry for the son of a Roman general, one S. Cornelius Drusus Magnus, who died of an apparent poisoning at the tender age of twenty-two. The description fit: slim build, blond curly hair, and green eyes. The interesting bit was that he rated as an up-and-coming political star of the time, a brilliant strategist, and a gifted orator.

That explained the glib tongue, but not how he ended up in hell. She tried searching for *Drusus demon*.

Unfortunately, Nigel walked by at that precise moment, caught a glimpse of her computer screen, and practically tripped over the tassels of his Gucci loafers.

"What are you doing?"

Although Rachel alt-tabbed back to her CorelDRAW screen and blended two objects together as though she'd been busy on her graphic all along, lying didn't seem profitable. "Just looking up some info on the Net for a friend of mine."

"Rachel . . ."

She flushed. "It's after five."

Sighing heavily, he backed up two steps and leaned over her cubby wall, his mauve silk shirt a perfect match to his designer eyeglass frames. "Have you reviewed Matt's illustrations yet?"

"Yes."

"And have you met with him to discuss how to improve them?"

"Yes."

"Will he be able to deliver?"

She frowned. "I'm not sure. He's got plenty of enthusiasm but not a lot of originality. His designs are . . ."

"Crap?"

Rachel flushed. "Well—"

"You know you're going to end up doing them all yourself, don't you? Why do you think Celia assigned him to your team? She knew you were the only one who could redo all his stuff in the short time we have left." Nigel clucked sympathetically. "You haven't got time to surf the Net, sweetie. You barely have time to pee. If I were you, I'd get my ass in gear."

To prove her willingness to follow his advice, she tabbed back to the Internet screen and shut down the browser. "I'm on it."

"Good girl." He straightened. "Drop the completed files on my desk before you leave."

Then he was gone, mincing his way down the hall, leaving Rachel with a bad case of itchy fingers. She desperately wanted to keep reading about Drusus, but the clock was ticking and she had a lot of illustrating to do.

Research would have to wait until she got home.

Lachlan closed his e-mail and sighed.

A gather was the last thing he wanted to do right now. With Rachel nervously unsure of him and Drusus preparing to pounce, he should be watching Emily around the clock, not driving across town to tend the dying. But Gatherers could not decline assignments.

He stood, mentally reviewing the details.

A sharp rap at the door interrupted his thoughts.

Crossing the room, he peered through the peephole, then opened the door. A young Asian man stood before him, wearing the green cap and uniform of a local dry cleaner.

"I'm here for a pickup."

Lachlan studied the skinny, five-foot-nothing lad for a moment, then walked to the hall closet and retrieved a zippered suit bag looped with a white plastic tote. This might well be the worst decision of his entire existence. But it felt right. He handed off his three sets of clerical garb. "Make sure you do a good job. They have sentimental value."

"Sure, sure. They get the gold treatment. No problem."

The dry cleaner flung the clothes over his shoulder, skipped down the hall, and disappeared down the stairs. Trying not to read too much into the careless handling of his possessions, Lachlan exited the apartment, locking the door behind him.

The drive to Anselm Brucker's home in Los Altos took only twenty-five minutes. Since he was early, Lachlan parked down the street and studied the large two-story house for a few minutes, deciding on the best entry. Garage roof to the back bedroom window, from the look of things.

If there was an alarm system, it wasn't currently set. No dog, either. All good news. None of those hurdles would have deterred him, but simpler was always better.

Lachlan crossed the tree-lined street with a relaxed gait and strode toward the front door. It never paid to look as if you didn't belong. At the porch steps, he leapt silently from the walkway to the garage roof, crouching low on the tile to minimize his aspect. Four slinking steps along the pink-washed facade and he was around the corner, out of sight. When he reached the window at the back, he found it wide-open, curtains fluttering in the mild breeze.

In the large, masculine bedroom, next to the window, a frail, gray-haired man sat in a wheelchair, his legs draped with a wool blanket.

He smiled as Lachlan ducked inside. "You're early."

Lachlan shrugged off his long black overcoat and tossed it on the bed. It always amazed him that dying people knew immediately what he was. He took the old man's thin hand, which felt thin and cool, like fine porcelain. "Your request for a few moments to discuss the transition was granted. Am I intruding on your private time?"

"No, no, I'm ready to go."

Lachlan studied the wrinkled face and faded blue eyes, and asked, "Are you?"

"More than you know. I've had a good life, full of amazing and wonderful things. And my wife, Marta, passed away last year, at Christmastime."

"You wish to follow her."

"Oh yes. I told her I wouldn't be long." He bent forward and said in a conspiratorial whisper, "She'd never been anywhere on her own before and I didn't want her to worry."

"No doubt your assurances made her passage easier."

Anselm smiled. "She's waiting for me up there."

A feather of disquiet brushed the back of Lachlan's neck. "I'm afraid I can't guarantee—"

"Oh," the old man said with a chuckle, "don't worry about that. I'm going to heaven. God told me so himself."

"Did he?"

"Yes, in September, when I had the stroke that put me in this crazy chair. Death almost took me then, you know, but I asked the Lord if I could wait until my great-granddaughter was born. He agreed. Not too many people get to see their great-grandchildren come into this world."

"True."

Anselm frowned. "You don't believe me."

"It's not tha—"

"What's your name, young man?"

Lachlan held back a grin. Could four hundred thirty-nine really be considered young? "Lachlan."

"Do you pray, Lachlan?"

"Sometimes."

"Do you think he listens?"

Good question. A lot of his prayers over the years had gone unanswered. "Sometimes."

The elder man dug beneath his blanket and pulled out a dog-eared, leather-bound book. His hands shook as he opened it to the first page. "In my darkest hour, my grandfather gifted me this Bible. When he handed it to me he said, *Faith isn't about finding God, Anselm. We know where he is. Faith is about finding yourself.*"

He looked at Lachlan. "He's always listening."

"You sound very sure. How do you know?"

"Because he answers me." Anselm coughed twice, held a trembling tissue to his lips, and then sat back, weary. "I don't always agree with his response, mind you. Sometimes his choice is to leave me hanging, or to make me walk through fire. But I'm a better man for everything that's ever happened to me. Whenever God's tested me, it's been for a good cause."

Lachlan recalled the deaths of his family and silently disagreed.

"Take the death of my Marta, for example," Anselm added. "Cancer. And not one of those quick, relatively painless passings. Oh no, Marta had colon cancer and it ate her up from the inside out. You might wonder how I can still believe in God when I had to watch her go that way."

Lachlan said nothing. But he did wonder.

"I mean, why make us suffer like that? Especially at the end, when we can't possibly learn anything from it?"

Yes, why?

"I'll tell you why. Because the end of our lives on Earth is not the ultimate end. We go on to a whole other existence once we leave here. We keep growing; we keep learning. But it's a very different existence. He wants us to understand that no matter how hard life is, how painful, how short, this time we get on Earth is a blessing. Here, we touch, we smell, we *feel*. Up there, not so much."

"You're saying he wants us to rejoice in pain?"

"I didn't say that," Anselm said, wagging a knobby finger at him. "I actually said just the opposite. He shows us pain so we can rejoice in the other stuff. Even the boring and the mundane. Tell me honestly, do you not relish the good moments you had far more now that tragedy has touched you? Are your memories not that much keener?"

God, yes. Sometimes horribly so. "The pain might be valuable to me," he said, "but how could it possibly benefit a wee bairn, an innocent child?"

Anselm's rheumy eyes met his. "I was a doctor before my fingers became too gnarled to work properly, and I can tell you I met many a child whose wisdom exceeded that of adults. Suffering makes us all stronger, even children. And you must trust God not to leave a child, or an adult for that matter, with more painful memories than he or she can handle."

"Your faith in him amazes me," Lachlan confessed. "But I don't share it."

"Perhaps not. But when the time comes, place yourself in his hands. You might be surprised."

Staring intently into the old man's eyes, Lachlan saw the first stroke hit him, saw the tide of blackness crash over him and then recede. He reached for Anselm's hand and squeezed it.

The old man slumped in his chair, his head rolling back, his gray hair askew. He smiled weakly, a lopsided grin. Only one half of his face showed any emotion, but it was a shining reflection of both hope and fear. The spiral on his left cheek glowed ever so faintly.

"I knew the end was near," he said, his words garbled. "And I prayed for you to be the one to come."

Lachlan frowned. "You don't know me."

"Oh, but I do," he whispered. "You are me. Sixty-four years ago, right after the war. Right after the car accident that claimed my first wife and my twin boys."

Lachlan leaned closer.

Anselm's next words were barely audible. "I was driving."

Lachlan had to force himself to maintain eye contact. Old feelings of guilt churned in his belly.

"My youngest boy lingered for two days, and I sat at his bedside night and day, praying tirelessly. Hoping against hope. When he died, my faith died with him. I went to church, just as I always had, but in my heart, I no longer believed in a caring God. I see that same emptiness in your eyes, Lachlan." Anselm sucked in a shaky breath. Speaking seemed to sap his strength, what little there was left, and he slumped further. "I see me."

A tear rose in Lachlan's eye and he blinked, letting it fall. "How did you rediscover your faith?"

"This Bible. My grandfather left details of his life and his own sins in the margins. I knew him as an honorable man with a generous heart, but he was not always that man. His notations helped me . . . to accept my actions . . . and to understand God's plan. This Bible taught me how to forgive myself." For a moment, the only sound in the room was Anselm's raspy breathing. Then he pushed the book toward Lachlan. "I want you to take it."

"No."

"Take it."

"I can't."

With some effort, Anselm lifted a hand and squeezed Lachlan's arm. "Please."

There wasn't enough time left to argue. "All right. Because you insist, I will. Now rest. You've done enough. It's my turn to look after you."

Anselm's hand dropped to his blanket-covered lap.

"Read it." The old man smiled crookedly. "Find yourself. More importantly . . . learn to . . . forgive . . . yourself."

Anselm's eyes widened, and the last word came out as a thin sigh from a slack mouth. The final stroke was sudden and catastrophic, and his brain succumbed immediately, his eyes dulling. Moments later his heartbeat ceased, too, leaving behind only a gaunt shell of the man who'd used his last moments on Earth vainly trying to restore Lachlan's faith.

But it wasn't an empty shell. Not yet.

He put his hand on the loose skin at Anselm's throat. His nose itched fiercely and he was forced to blink repeatedly as the tickle of soul transfer feathered up his arm and a balmy warmth wrapped around his heart.

Sixty-four years ago, this man had experienced a similar break in faith, blaming himself for the loss of his family, seeing life at its bleakest, a source of only darkness, death, and destruction. Yet, somehow, he'd learned to forgive himself. He'd come back from the brink, and in the process, become a man more committed to God than ever before, more determined to prove himself worthy of a place in heaven.

An admirable man, despite the sins of his past.

One deserving of an honorable end.

Lachlan stood. No filthy demon horde could be allowed to rob Anselm of his eternal joy, no matter how many of the bastards crawled from the bowels of the earth to attack him. Satan would gain an unwelcome surge of power from a soul so pure. It wasn't quite the prize of a corrupted soul, but valuable nonetheless. He strode to the window.

Then he paused and looked over his shoulder. Retracing his steps, he bent and picked up the tattered Bible.

A promise was a promise.

14

Lying on her stomach, swinging her foot to an old David Bowie tune, Em never heard her phone ring. She just saw it light up and start dancing on the black cotton bedcovers. Tugging her earbuds out, she glanced at the number, verified that it wasn't her mother, and picked it up.

"Hi, Drew," she said softly.

"How's my Bella this afternoon?"

She grinned and turned her vampire romance facedown. "Just fine. How'd you know I was reading?"

"I know everything about you, sweet. How did it go yesterday, with your mom and the priest?"

"He's a phony. No cuts, no bruises, nada."

"I told you."

"I know," she responded, recalling his pleading eyes and squirming with genuine regret. Why hadn't she believed him? "She just sounded so convincing."

"I wish I knew why she dislikes me so much. I'm not *that* bad, am I?"

"No," she laughed. A seed of thought sprouted in her mind and, picking up her pen, she began to doodle absently on the closest notebook. Sixes. "I still say it's the motorcycle."

"Maybe. Speaking of motorcycles, I came by the school today to pick you up."

Em flushed. Wow. Apparently, she had been so focused on Carlos, the loud rumble of a motorcycle hadn't made any impact. "Sorry, I must have missed you. I got on the bus."

"I saw."

"You saw?" Her swinging foot froze in midair. What *exactly* did he see?

"You got on the bus with a tall, dark-haired guy."

Enough, obviously. "He's a new kid, just started on Monday. I was being nice."

"Of course you were. Does the new kid have a name?"

Em bit her fingernail. Drew's tone was almost too calm, too offhand. Was he testing her? "Carlos Rodriguez."

"And is he, by chance, showing an interest?"

"In me?" she asked, swallowing hard.

"Yes, sweet, in you."

"I suppose," she hedged. "A little."

"Can't say that I blame him; you're the most beautiful girl in the school. Still, he'll turn out to be just like the others, Em. You know it. Eventually, he'll say what's really on his mind, just like that Daria girl. And that redheaded boy who called you a lesbian in front of the whole cafeteria. Don't get sucked in."

"I don't think he's like that. He seems more like us."

"Sweet, there is no one else like us. We're one of a kind. He'll certainly never understand what we're thinking about doing. Forget him."

The dark vines of gloom creeping through her mind sprang into full blossom. Em drew a decent rendition of Daria's head and put a hangman's noose around her skinny neck. "Yeah, I guess you're right."

"That's my girl. Hey, your dad's coming up this weekend, isn't he? Will I get to meet him?"

Em glanced up at the dresser top, to her favorite Christmas photo. For once, the laughing faces didn't make her feel like crying. Maybe she was getting used to disappointment. "He's not coming."

"That really sucks, Em. I know how much you miss him. Your mom did it again, huh? Discouraged him from making the trip?"

"Yeah." What was that? The fifth time? She sketched a limp body beneath the head—riddled with bullet holes. "She's down on everything lately."

"Everything except this priest guy."

"She didn't have anything good to say about *him* last night, either."

"That's good. He sounds like a nut."

"Yeah." Em's pen paused above the paper. She recalled the afternoon she'd spent with Father MacGregor, the ice cream, the kidding around. He hadn't seemed like a nut. He'd been pretty nice, actually.

"So, can I pick you up tomorrow, maybe take you for a spin out to the fairgrounds?"

"I'm still grounded."

"Come on, Em," he coaxed. "We haven't had any time together lately. Can't you blow off Mr. Wyatt?"

"I only have one more day left, and if I blow him off, I'll end up grounded for *another* two weeks."

"We can't have that, can we?" Dry amusement flavored his voice. "I'll be good. I'll pick you up and drive you right home."

She drew another body lying on the ground beside Daria, and labeled it *Todd*. "Okay."

"You don't sound too sure."

"My mom'll be mad if she finds out."

"Your mom," he said pointedly, "is looking for reasons to hate me. We need to calm her down, let her think we're falling in line. Let me drive you home. Let me get you back safe and sound, and maybe I can score some points with her."

"Okay."

"That's my girl. All right, back to your reading. You've only a half hour left before your mom starts hounding you about homework."

"You know me too well."

"Impossible. No such thing." Then, after a pause, he said, "I love you, Em."

She opened her mouth to toss back an automatic echo of the sentiment, one she'd uttered a dozen times before without a qualm. But an image of Carlos surfaced in her mind, his brown eyes as troubled as her own. The roiling darkness of her thoughts eased, and she hesitated—just for a second. Then she said, "I love you, too, Drew. See ya tomorrow."

"Looking forward to it."

Em folded the phone and placed it back on the bed, staring at the sleek silver shape and wondering why, for the very first time, she couldn't say the same.

The next morning, quite auspiciously, it rained.

The steady drizzle perked up the wilting lawn and brought to Lachlan's mind, however briefly, the soft wet weather of Scotland. Standing on the balcony, with a steaming cup of coffee in hand and his face turned up to meet the fine spray, he almost missed Emily's regular trek to the bus stop.

But the grunt the teenager gave as she hefted her large backpack over her shoulders drew his attention to the stone pathway—and to Emily's straggly hair and black-lined eyes.

And that's when the earth stopped spinning.

Perhaps on a bright sunny day it might not have been so noticeable, but in the overcast gloom, the pearly white mark glowed like a lighthouse beacon, even through the pancake makeup. Even through the rain.

The helix of Death.

On Emily's cheek.

Bile replaced the nutty taste of coffee on his tongue. The fact that he could see it meant that *he* was the one destined to gather her soul. Closing his eyes, he shut out the image of the ghastly, immutable mark, unwilling to accept that it was truly there. It couldn't be. Death had assured him only yesterday that Emily was of no use to her yet, that she still wanted Lachlan to watch over her, protect her.

Why would she do that? Unless . . .

He dragged his eyes open.

She lied. She knew he'd grown attached to Emily, and she knew he'd be honor bound to save her. So the wretched witch had lied. She had said whatever was necessary in order to throw him off the trail, then cold-bloodedly sought out Emily and branded her cheek with a mark that he knew all too well could never be removed—ever.

Emily was going to die.

And there was not one damned thing he could do about it.

Awash in a torrent of bitter regret, Lachlan threw his mug with all his might, smashing it against the white-washed side of his apartment building, watching the dark brown liquid splatter and run . . . and slowly drip away under the fine rain.

Dear God, how was he going to face Rachel?

Desperate for a pick-me-up on a dreary wet day, Rachel indulged in a vanilla latte from Starbucks. As she exited the shop, sipping on her cup and holding her purse over her head, she spotted a man standing on the street corner in the rain—no one she knew, a stranger, a guy in a light overcoat, identical to a dozen other people treading the sidewalk that morning.

Except for one thing: He was talking out loud, to no one.

Not subtly, either, but with plenty of hand gestures and facial expressions, enthusiastic words, and sudden, loud guffaws. He paused occasionally, tilting his head as if he could hear someone responding, then rambled on again.

Obviously the guy was mentally troubled, schizophrenic perhaps.

Nothing like Lachlan. Lachlan not only looked normal; he acted normal. More than normal, in fact. Competent. There was no sign of muddled thoughts, no sign of undue stress, no sign of anything but a sane, rational man. When she compared the two men, it made her assumption that Lachlan was crazy seem . . . *crazy.*

She skirted past the wildly gesturing man on the corner and dove into the Datsun. The little car growled ferociously on start-up, then settled into a low rumble. She really needed to book an appointment with a mechanic . . . someday when she had a few extra bucks.

The sharp rap of a knuckle on her window made her jump, and foamy coffee sloshed down the front of her pale green sweater.

"Sorry."

She glanced up.

Through the trickling beads of water on the glass she recognized the nut brown hair of the young man from Lachlan's apartment. It was Brian, looking very dapper in a charcoal suit; looking very, uh, alive. But if she believed Lachlan's story, this man was also a Soul Gatherer.

She rolled down her window.

"Can I get a lift into town?" he asked, smiling pleasantly. He was much more handsome than she remembered. His eyes matched his silver tie and his cologne smelled heavenly.

"Because you have a . . . *job* to do?"

At her obvious disgust, his smile broadened. "Nope, I'm off duty. Lachlan just asked me to keep an eye on you."

Melting a little under the knowledge that Lachlan was thinking about her, she nodded. When he was in, with the door shut and his seat belt fastened, she pulled away from the curb. "If you're immortal, why bother with a seat belt?"

"It's the law, and I've got better things to do with my money than give it to the cops."

That made sense. "But if you went through the wind-shield, you'd live, right?"

"Yes, although *survive* would be a better term than *live*, since technically, I'm not alive now." He leaned over and flicked on her wipers. "As for the windshield thing . . . been there, done that; don't recommend it."

She glanced at him. "You died in a car accident?"

"Yup. And no, I wasn't wearing my seat belt. I wasn't sober, either. All I can say in my favor is that I didn't kill anyone else on my way out the door."

"How reassuring, they pick morons to be Soul Gatherers."

"Ouch. But for the record, Death doesn't pick morons, just sinners. Morons don't last long in this job."

"Don't all the sinners go to hell?"

"No, believe it or not, a lot of them make it into heaven. God's big on the whole forgiveness schtick. Only the completely unredeemable souls go to hell." He grinned. "I didn't qualify. We Gatherers aren't rotten enough for hell and aren't sweet enough for heaven. We're getting one last chance to prove ourselves."

"I see." Sort of. "But Gatherers are all men, right? What happens to the women who fall into a similar limbo?"

"Doomed to an eternity as high school guidance counselors, I think."

"Very funny."

His eyes twinkled. "Seriously? The odd woman passes muster as a Gatherer, but you're right, most don't. They and the *guys* who aren't natural warriors end up working somewhere in Death's bureaucracy, managing her messaging system, extracting relevant information from the huge volumes of data she collects on humans, giving us our job assignments, that type of thing."

"Ugh."

"Hey, no one said purgatory would be fun. You want to turn left here."

She glanced in her rearview mirror, then darted into the left-hand lane. "So Lachlan's a sinner? What did he do?"

"Not for me to say, I'm afraid. You'll have to ask him."

Nice dodge by a very smooth talker. Once they rounded the corner, she asked, "Do you believe all this stuff about the Trinity Soul?"

"I'm not sure," he admitted. "But I'm probably not the best person to ask. I didn't believe in God or Satan, either, until I ended up on the wrong side of the soul track. One thing's for sure: What happens behind the scenes is a lot weirder than you think."

Pulling to a stop at a red light, Rachel looked at him. "I don't know that I buy any of this."

"Yeah, it's pretty hard to take. I walked around in a stupor for a week after Death handed me my walking-dead papers."

"And now you fight demons every day."

"Not every day. Light's green; you can go."

She grimaced as she took her foot off the brake and accelerated through the intersection with a barely muffled roar. "Let me guess. You no longer own a car."

"Nope, me and driving don't mix."

She turned at the next corner and then right again into the SpliNext parking lot. To her surprise, Lachlan MacGregor was waiting in front of the entry gate—shirt soaked through, hair spiked, a heavy frown upon his handsome face.

"I think that's my cue to bow out," Brian said, tugging on the door handle.

"He doesn't look very happy."

"No," he agreed with a rueful smile as he slid out. "But I wouldn't worry unless he pulls his sword out. After that, all bets are off."

She stared at the intensity of Lachlan's gaze through the thumping wipers, her palms damp, her heartbeat riotous. How could a guy who looked at her like that—as if she were the best thing that happened to him today— be crazy? Wasn't it possible that she was just letting old fears hold her back? That her painful mistake over Grant was clouding her judgment? Wasn't it possible this was the real deal? "He carries a *sword*?"

"Yeah, but trust me, Mrs. L, that's a good thing."

"Don't call me Mrs. Lewis."

Brian grinned. "I wasn't." He shut the door and waved her on through the gate.

"Everything okay?" Lachlan asked Brian as he watched Rachel maneuver through the lot and park her rust bucket of a car near the back fence, several spots over from the big blue Dumpster and the clump of maples.

"I dunno. Did you see Carlos when you followed Emily to the school this morning?"

"No. Why?"

"I didn't hear from him last night."

Rachel scurried across the pavement toward them,

her purse over her head, the edges of her green sweater flapping in the rain. She wore a narrow black skirt today, which hugged her very shapely arse and highlighted her long, slim legs. "Probably out on a gather."

Brian turned up his collar. "Yeah, but he's supposed to check in every night, to let me know how things are going. If you're okay here, maybe I'll head over to his place."

"Fine."

"*Are* you okay here? You seem a little . . . tense."

Lachlan took a deep breath and let it out slowly. It didn't do a damned thing to loosen the tightness in his chest. "Emily has the mark."

"*The* mark? As in lovely white spiral?"

"Aye."

"Fuck." Brian glanced at him, then over at Rachel, who was leaping over a small puddle. "You gonna tell her?"

"I don't know."

"I wouldn't."

"Thank you for the advice. I'll take it under advisement."

"Man, what a freakin' shame. Kind of expected, though, right? Given the lure and all? Do you know how it'll happen?"

"No, I haven't received the job assignment yet."

Rachel reached them and smiled tentatively at Lachlan. "Did I miss anything?"

"No." Lachlan stood there, staring into her big golden eyes, listening to the raindrops plop into the puddles, each one of them a second lost of Emily's life. He ran through several options of what to say next, and discarded them all.

Brian cut the awkward silence. "Well, I'm off. Don't have too much fun without me."

"Call me when you touch base with Carlos."

"Absolutely." And then he was gone.

Leaving them alone.

A droplet of rain slid down Rachel's nose, and though the temptation to kiss it off was very powerful, Lachlan grabbed her arm and led her into the SpliNext foyer, where it was warm and dry. Inside the cave of green marble tile, where even the slightest sound echoed off the walls, he lowered his voice.

"We're running out of time, Rachel."

"You think Drew's going to doing something?"

"Aye."

"Well, I finally have an idea of what she might want. She's been looking forward to a school trip in May, but I had to pull the plug on it yesterday and she's pretty upset." A soft flush of embarrassment rose in her cheeks. "We don't have the cash."

Lachlan slid his hand down Rachel's soft woolen sleeve and threaded her cool, wet fingers with his, squeezing gently. May was a long way off. Any feelings tied to the school trip would be muted, and it was un-likely to give Drusus the jolt of emotion he needed to finalize the lure. But he didn't have the courage to tell Rachel that.

"Good."

He should have said more, soothed her, wrapped her in his arms, and lent her a bit of his strength, but he felt helpless. And his tongue was stuck to the roof of his mouth.

"I've been thinking," Rachel said softly.

Their gazes met.

Her eyes shone. "I've decided to believe you."

She didn't muddy the words with further explana-tions or justifications or excuses. She just let the state-ment hang there, beautiful in its simplicity.

The last bricks around his heart fell.

He didn't deserve her faith, but his blood still pounded with the heady rush of it. By God, what more could he ask for? Despite all the doubts she had, despite his sorry lack of evidence to support his claims, she was putting her trust in him. She was making a leap.

For him.

And she not only believed him; she seemed quite determined to prove it. Dropping her purse to the marble floor with a sharp clatter and leaning against his chest, she dug her slim fingers into the sopping mess of his hair and kissed him—open-mouthed, eager, and unbelievably sweet.

She tasted like vanilla.

The simmering warmth in his blood exploded into a raging brush fire, and miserable cad that he was, he accepted the kiss—then deepened it.

He drank from her like a drowning man, fearful that this might well be the last kiss he ever stole from her lips. Closing his eyes, he slanted his mouth over hers and kissed her as if she were truly his, as if there weren't a huge, dark chasm between them, as if the future held light and promise instead of gloom and despair. Because that's how she made him feel, however briefly.

When he finally pulled back to let her breathe, all she said was, "Wow."

He smiled in agreement, but for the first time, he had difficulty meeting her eyes. "I'm going to stick close to Emily from now on. To make certain Drusus doesn't get an easy shot at her."

"Thank you. I swear, the more I think about him, the more creeped out I get. Did you know he's as old as Christianity?"

"Where did you hear that?"

"I read it on the Internet. He earned a bucketful of

medals as a Roman centurion, then got assigned as a political aide to Pontius Pilate. Pretty fancy career, but it ended on a rather sour note—he was poisoned the same year Jesus was nailed to the cross. By Pilate himself, if the rumors were true."

So, the timing was right for Drusus to be the demon who forced the Protectorate to hide the Linen—not obviously useful information, but worthy of being tucked away just the same.

Rachel grimaced at her watch. "I've got to go."

His fingers tightened around her arm. "Call me if anything unusual happens."

"You'll answer your phone this time?"

He winced. "I apologize for that. I was out of cell range."

"Okay, just don't do it again."

"Rachel, I—"

She tilted her head, her eyes curious. Trusting. "What?"

The words froze in his chest. He couldn't do it. He couldn't look her in the eye and tell her that Emily was going to die. He couldn't admit that he, the warrior who had already failed his family and his brother, had also failed her.

"Nothing."

The rain stopped around noon, the sun came out, and by two thirty not a patch of dampness or gray cloud remained—except in Lachlan's thoughts.

At first, the low chugging sound matched the steady drum of guilt in his head and it didn't register. But as the rumble grew closer, he identified the noise as a motorcycle. Tearing his gaze from the painted red doors of the school, he sought the source, his pulse hammering.

Sure enough, a burnished silver BMW motorbike

maneuvered into a parking spot on the east side of the soccer field, the helmeted rider draped shoulder to toe in black leather.

Drusus.

Lachlan slid out of his car and hit the speed dial on his phone. As he exited, he spotted two familiar faces, one on each side of the grassy field—lads from the fairgrounds, undoubtedly demons. "I'm at the school," he said when Brian answered. "Get your arse over here."

"Hold on," the other Gatherer said, huffing. "Carlos hasn't answered his phone or his door all day, so I'm about to break into his apartment."

"Forget Carlos. Drusus is here—with friends."

"Shit." A heavy whomp and the sound of wood splintering punctuated his words. "Gimme one minute, okay? I've got a cab waiting downstairs. I'm coming. Just don't do anything stupid until I get there."

Lachlan folded the phone and tucked it into his pocket, his eyes locked on Drusus as the demon flicked out the kickstand, dismounted, and removed his helmet. Stupid no doubt included coming within thirty feet of the lethal bastard and his mates, but a desperate need to take a physical stand between the demon and Emily got the better of him.

Drusus pivoted as Lachlan neared.

"Ah, there you are. I assumed you'd be somewhere about."

"Shove off. Emily's no' going anywhere with you."

The demon smiled and fluffed his short curls with a gloved hand. "I think we've already proven that you can't stop me from taking her, if that's what I want."

Scores of cars and minivans surrounded them, each filled with waiting parents, and though Lachlan didn't spare them a glance, he used them to his advantage. "You won't slay me in front of human witnesses."

"And you won't draw your sword. Stalemate."

"Walk away. You gain nothing by killing her."

The demon placed his helmet on the seat of the bike. "Oh, but I do. Her death will garner me the esteem of my liege Lord, and his rewards are well worth any effort, believe me."

"You care nothing about pleasing Satan, you piece of filth. You want the Linen. So why no' negotiate for it?"

"Of course I care. My allegiance to Satan is unassailable. Hell can be an unending misery or it can be an exquisite, sinful pleasure. It all depends on how well I please the boss."

Lachlan stepped closer, coming toe to toe with the demon and taking a raw, primitive pleasure in the fact that he stood some four inches taller. "Just answer the bloody question."

"It's simple." Drusus crossed his arms over his chest and leaned back against his bike. Other than that, he did not acknowledge Lachlan's intimidation effort. "Bartering is not my style. I want it all. You and Em *and* the Linen."

"I'm no' going to let that happen."

Drusus snorted. "You won't have a choice."

The school bell broke the stillness of midafternoon in suburbia, ringing shrilly.

Lachlan paused. In roughly three minutes, the students would collect their belongings and file out. After that, the situation would get harder to control. "If I give the Linen to you freely, will you walk away from Emily?"

"I'm afraid not, *baro*. She's got the lead role in my grand finale, and I've got a killer ending lined up. You won't want to miss it." A smile spread across the demon's face. "In fact, I've saved you a seat at the show. Right next to me, so I can absorb the full impact of your pain."

"I told you, Emily is just a job."

The demon's smile broadened to a smirk.

At that moment, Lachlan's cell phone warbled. He would have ignored it, but the ring tone told him it was Brian. "What?"

"He knows," the other Gatherer said quietly.

"Knows what?"

"About our little matchmaking project."

Lachlan's gaze flickered to the lure demon's blandly smiling face, then across the field to the two demon henchmen. Already anticipating what he was about to hear, he clenched his fingers around the phone. "Carlos?"

"Yup. Deep-fried, poor bastard. Sometime last night. And my money's on your demon pal as the guy with the torch."

Christ. "Where are you?"

"Paying off a cabbie a hundred yards south of you. But heads up, Emily's about to crash your party."

Lachlan whipped around.

15

Em dragged her feet all day.

Although she hated to admit it, she missed Carlos. He hadn't shown up at school this morning, and even though she shared only one class with him, she couldn't stop thinking about him. Was he sick? Or had she scared him off?

Maybe Drew was right; maybe he'd started to think bad thoughts about her, like the others. Hard to believe, though, when she remembered that wonderful bus ride—how he'd held her hand and smiled at her.

By the time the bell rang at two thirty, she had a whopping headache. And the pain in her head only intensified when she exchanged the cool dimness of the school for the sunny outdoors—Drew was waiting for her, just as he promised, but so was Father MacGregor.

"Why are *you* here?" she asked the priest.

"To harass me," complained Drew, straightening. He offered her the spare helmet. "All he's done since he got here is threaten to beat me to a pulp."

Father MacGregor ignored Drew, keeping his gaze locked on her. "You know why I'm here, Emily. To protect you."

"Don't listen to him, Em. He's a liar, remember?"

Father MacGregor didn't protest Drew's slam. Heck,

he didn't even blink. He stood tall and sure, his silver cross hanging around his neck like gleaming proof of his honesty.

"Did my mom send you to spy on me?" she asked.

"She didn't need to. I know what kind of hellspawn Drusus is, and I won't let him hurt you."

"Hellspawn? Jeez, Em. You're not buying this crap, are you? He swore I cut him up, but that wasn't true, was it?"

No, the cuts had been a lie. She sighed.

"Emily, listen to me," Father MacGregor said, his voice low and urgent. "Your friend Carlos didn't show up at school today, did he? Want to know why? Because he's dead. Drusus murdered him. We found the body this afternoon."

Dizziness, dread, pain, and fear all hit Em at once. Carlos? Dead? Her throat closed, and she couldn't draw a breath. "What?"

Pushing past Father MacGregor, Drew grasped her arm. "This is ridiculous. First I'm a mugger and now I'm a murderer. I haven't done a damned thing wrong except love you." He peered into her face, his own expression pale and worried. "You know me better than anyone, Em. You know I live to make you happy. Do you really think I killed this guy?"

Aching for him, she opened her mouth to reassure him.

"Did you mention Carlos to Drusus yesterday, Emily?"

Her breath snagged on the priest's words. She had.

Drew noted her uncertainty and shook her arm slightly. "Come on, sweet, don't be swayed by his bullshit. This is me we're talking about. The one you trust with your deepest, darkest secrets. I've never once lied to you, but he has. Who are you going to believe?"

A man Em didn't recognize jogged up the sidewalk

and halted beside them. He was dressed in a fancy suit and tie, and at first she thought he was someone's dad, but that theory went out the window when he spoke.

"Whatever this A-hole just said"—he indicated Drew with his thumb—"is a fucking lie."

Father MacGregor winced.

Drew snatched up his helmet and jammed it on. "I've had enough. Em, get on the bike. Let's go home."

She hesitated. The important-looking guy in the suit had sided with Father MacGregor, but what did that mean? Did it mean Carlos was really dead?

No, she couldn't accept that Carlos was dead.

Or that Drew had killed him.

"He's just giving me a lift home," she said to Father MacGregor, somewhat apologetically. She tugged on her own helmet and fastened the chinstrap. "You can follow us, if you like."

As she swung her leg over the seat of the motorbike and wrapped her arms around Drew, the man in the suit frowned and reached behind his head. But Father Mac-Gregor grabbed his arm. "No, let them go."

"But—"

"We can't do anything here."

"But—"

"Neither can he, Webster. Stand down."

As the powerful engine of the bike surged to life and vibrated through her thighs, Em watched the two men cross to Father MacGregor's car. Apparently, they were going to take her up on her offer and follow her home.

Was that a good thing?

With Drew's shoulders and stomach stiffer than she'd ever felt them, she couldn't be sure.

Lachlan tailgated Drusus all the way home.

Taking advantage of the Audi's responsive engine, he

wove in and out of traffic as smoothly as the bike, never once allowing a car or a traffic light to come between him and Emily. His blood pumped fiercely and every muscle in his body tensed in anticipation of a sudden and unexpected move . . . but nothing happened.

The drive to Emily's apartment was short and uneventful. The demon dropped her off in the parking lot, stole a quick kiss as he accepted the spare helmet, and then roared off.

"Okay," Brian said. "Maybe it's just me, but I'm confused. If she's got the mark and it's clear she's going to die soon, shouldn't he have tried to nab her?"

"He's still luring her."

"Which means what?"

"We watch and we wait."

"I'm tired of waiting," the younger man said, loosening the knot of his tie with a sharp jerk. "The rotten bastard fried Carlos. Not quickly, either. From the look of things, Drusus dragged the battle out for quite a while, made him suffer. I want to carve his fucking guts out."

Parking the Audi in his usual spot, Lachlan sighed. "As you yourself pointed out, attacking Drusus one-on-one, or even two-on-one, won't work. It's got to be a group effort."

"Then let's round up the guys, find his hideout, and hack him to pieces. Waiting around for him to complete his lure is just asinine."

"Patience, Webster. Once I get the job assignment for Emily's soul, I'll know where and when her death will happen. We'll have all the details we need to hunt him down."

"True." Brian sat back against the leather seat, the tension visibly flowing out of him. He pitched Lachlan a sympathetic look. "So, did you tell her?"

"No."

The younger man nodded, understanding. After a brief pause, he asked, "What's the plan?"

"You stay here and watch Emily's apartment while I go inside and wait for the message."

Brian tugged his BlackBerry free of its holster and glanced down. "No can do, pal. Just got an emergency gather. An unmarked. Poor bastard was hit by a stray bullet during a demon-inspired drive-by."

"Fine. Call one of the others to relieve you."

"Okay." Brian looked exactly the way Lachlan felt—uneasy. "I'm so not liking this," he said as they both got out of the car. "Something doesn't feel right."

"Carlos's death is getting to you. It's one of the reasons Drusus would have taken him out, to shake your confidence. Just stay sharp."

Great advice, if only he could follow it himself.

As Lachlan entered the building and climbed the stairs to the third floor, he couldn't help but imagine Carlos lying on the floor of his apartment, blackened and lifeless. The poor lad hadn't even had a halfway-decent chance to earn his way to heaven, which meant his soul would likely go to hell.

And the burden for that lay with him.

He'd sent Carlos into harm's way.

Lachlan checked his e-mail repeatedly throughout the evening, but the message he was expecting from Death—the one that would tell him the details of Emily's last moments—never came.

Standing, he crossed to the fireplace and lifted the *claidheamh mòr* free of its mountings. He ran his fingers lightly along the flat of the blade, savoring the cool touch of the metal and the thrum of the mystical power beneath. A rigorous training set would relieve the tension of waiting. After all, it might be hours more before the message came, if it came at all. What better way to pass the time?

His gaze swung to the kitchen counter. Anselm Brucker's worn leather Bible lay on the granite surface, right where he'd dropped it.

Reading was another option, of course.

Assuming he could find the courage.

Rachel actually thought twice about doing a bed check that evening. Em hadn't snuck out since the night she went joyriding to the fairgrounds, and tonight they'd actually managed to have a civil conversation at the dinner table. They had talked about going to see the new Ashton Kuchter movie together. It seemed a little unfair not to trust her.

But then she remembered what Drew was. A demon wasn't going to play nice, and that meant she couldn't, either.

She turned the knob on Em's door and quietly pushed it open. The room was dark, and she spent a moment drinking in the warm, subtle scent that enveloped her: Em's scent, still vaguely childlike, reassuringly familiar, and calming.

The floor was littered with the usual evidence of Em's daily existence—discarded clothing and dog-eared papers culled from her school binder. Rachel instinctively bent to pick them up, then remembered the time and glanced toward the bed.

And found it empty.

Her fingers went numb.

Even in the very faint light that spilled in from the hallway, she could see the rumpled cotton sheets, the puffy comforter tossed back . . . and the hole where a sleeping teen ought to be.

She spun around. The window stood open, the slatted blinds pulled into a tight bunch near the ceiling. The balcony ran under the window, but she couldn't see the flower boxes in the dark. All she saw was the breeze toying with the edges of the curtains, gently sucking them out and blowing them in.

Numbness crept up her arms and into her chest.

Em was gone.

Out with *Drew* in the middle of the night.

Heart beating in erratic spurts, breaths short and tight, Rachel tore out of the room and reached the kitchen phone in record time. It was after midnight, but she didn't care. She dialed Lachlan's number, closed her eyes, and prayed.

He answered on the second ring. "Rachel? What's wrong?"

"She's gone."

Further explanation was unnecessary. "Stay there. I'll be right down."

She disconnected, tried another number, and then overcome by dizziness, lowered her head to her knees, battling the black spots that crowded her vision. Fainting would be a really useless thing to do. She needed to get a grip.

"Rachel."

His voice was so warm, so reassuring, so exactly what she needed to hear, that Rachel flung herself into his arms and let all her defenses fall away. She just wanted to lean on him, lose herself in his arms, forget the current nightmare of her life. A sob escaped her lips as she pressed her face into the warm skin at his neck—and then another sob, and another.

He held her gently, rocked her, and let her cry, and he didn't object at all to the big damp patch she left on his shirt. When the storm finally passed and her cries had receded into hiccups, he asked quietly, "Did you try calling her cell?"

"Yes. It's off."

"Any clue where she might have gone?"

"No."

He lifted his phone to his ear. After a moment, someone answered and Lachlan crisply asked, "Who's on watch?"

There was a husky burble of voice.

"Check on him. Emily's gone."

Then he tucked the phone away and peered down into Rachel's face. Whatever he saw there made him press a soft kiss to her lips. "Don't worry, we'll find her."

"How?"

"Let's start with her room." He folded his hand around hers, a solid suggestion of support, and led her down the hall. Flicking on the light, he looked around Emily's room. "Anything missing?"

"Missing? What do you mean?"

"Did she pack a bag, or just take the clothes she was wearing?"

Gripping the doorjamb with every last bit of her strength, Rachel forced her eyes to sweep the room. The bed still looked heartbreakingly vacant. Em's favorite pajamas were not hanging over the footboard. Nor was her purse in its usual spot on the floor. One of the dresser drawers hung open, the contents an untidy jumble of cloth, but that was such a common sight, it was impossible to know if it was significant.

Her gaze lifted.

Coins and elastics and nail polish still littered the top of the dresser, but the pewter picture frame with the old Christmas photo had disappeared. She glanced around quickly to check if it had been moved, but no. It was gone.

"Grant," she whispered.

"What?"

Rachel closed her eyes, reliving all the tears and anger of the split, reexperiencing every disappointment she'd seen reflected in Em's eyes over the past four years as her father repeatedly bailed out on his visitations.

"Oh my God. Her dad. You asked me what she wants most in the world, and that's it . . . her dad."

"You think she's gone to San Diego?"

"Yes."

"Call him." Lachlan thrust his phone into her hand. "Warn him that she may be coming and tell him to keep her there until we arrive."

Rachel blinked. "What do I tell Grant about Drew?"

"Nothing."

"But—"

His eyes softened. "There's nothing you could say that would adequately prepare him."

Rachel sagged against the wall, realizing it was the truth. *Hello, Grant? Just calling to tell you your daughter is dropping by with her demon boyfriend.* Yeah, that would go over well. She'd have to hope Drew wasn't interested in hurting Grant. With amazingly steady hands, she dialed. "I can't believe this is happening."

At the other end, the telephone rang and rang. No one picked up. She was beginning to hate the phone. Why couldn't people damned well be home to answer? Where was Grant at this hour, anyway?

"No answer," she told Lachlan, "and he doesn't have voice mail."

"Keep trying. Let's go."

In the living room, Rachel stopped to pick up her purse and keys. A glance at the softly ticking grandfather clock made her pause. "When will we be back?"

"The drive there will take us roughly seven hours, so sometime tomorrow afternoon, if all goes well."

Rachel's stomach knotted. Sometime tomorrow meant she was going to miss work. And missing work meant she wouldn't be there to guide her team, nor help tackle the huge pile of outstanding graphics. Plus, the illustrations she'd done last night had yet to be handed in.

Dashing off now would leave her department in the lurch and might even jeopardize the release date. People were counting on her, praying for her to save the day, and she'd be letting them down, big-time.

But . . .

This was Em, the sweet-smelling cherub she'd brought home from the hospital bundled in pink flannel, the laughing little girl who'd blown out the candles on her sixth birthday and announced, "I'm going to be a fairy."

This trip to San Diego was probably crazy. But for once, work would have to take a backseat. Tonight, no matter what the consequences were, she had to put her personal needs—her own wants and desires—first. She couldn't continue to shoulder the entire burden for both her company's success and Em's life. She couldn't continue to let guilt split her in two. On the drive to San Diego, she'd leave Nigel a voice mail, explain what had happened, and hope for the best.

"All right," she said, swallowing the lump in her throat and reaching for Lachlan's hand. "I'm ready."

The sun was just creeping over the horizon when Drew and Em pulled up outside of her dad's condo on Sixth Avenue. Although the motorbike was made for touring and was amazingly comfortable for long hauls, her legs shook when she dismounted.

"He might not be up yet," she said into the helmet mike. "It's still pretty early."

"Let's buzz him and find out."

Em removed her helmet and shook out her hair. "Maybe we should go grab breakfast first. My dad's not a morning person."

Brushing a stray lock out of her eyes and peering at her, Drew said, "This is what you wanted, isn't it? To visit your dad?"

"Yeah." She smiled at him. "Thanks."

He kissed her on the lips, cool and quick. "I'd do anything for you, sweet. You know that."

They entered the building holding hands, and Em punched in the call number at the ring station in the lobby. After the third try, she shrugged. "Not home or not up. Let's go to IHOP."

"Try one more time."

She sighed, but did as he suggested.

And got a groggy, grumpy response. "Who the hell is this?"

"Dad, it's me, Em."

"Em?"

He sounded so baffled and dubious that she added pointedly, "Emily, your daughter."

"Oh."

"Can I come up?"

He didn't answer, just hung up. But a second later, the door buzzed, and Em tugged it open. She tossed a weak smile at Drew. "He's not really himself until after he's had a cup of coffee."

The man who opened the door at her knock was a tousle-haired version of the man in her favorite picture. Somehow, dressed in a faded brown T-shirt and blue striped cotton boxers, he managed to look just as handsome as ever. He was still her dad.

She wrapped her arms around his neck, closed her eyes, and breathed in a blanketful of old memories along with his Polo cologne.

"Hi, princess." He hugged her in return, a familiar, exaggerated squeeze that lifted her toes off the floor and made her giggle. Then he released her, glanced at Drew, and frowned. "What's up? Where's your mom?"

Not quite ready to launch into all the explanations, Em shrugged. "Back in San Jose. Her job's keeping her pretty busy."

"Aren't you supposed to be in school?"

"School's a bore. I'm taking a coupla days off."

Her dad glanced again at Drew, more curious than judgmental. "And this is . . . ?"

Em introduced them, then added, "We were wondering if we could bunk here for the weekend. Hang with you, do some shopping, you know?"

"Your mom doesn't know you're here, does she?"

"Come on, Dad. You know what Mom's like, totally freaking out over the slightest change in her schedule. I couldn't tell her. Not until I got here."

"Better call her right now," he said. He strode into his kitchen, paying no attention to the dirty dishes stacked in the sink and old Chinese food cartons on the counter. Digging through a jumble of stuff in the cupboard, he found a tin of coffee and set a pot to brew. "She'll be worried."

Leaving in the middle of the night had been Drew's idea. Em shoved her hands into her jeans pockets, her gaze dropping to the floor. "I don't think she's up yet."

He opened the fridge, sniffed the milk in the carton, wrinkled his nose, then put it back. "Hope not, or I'll have the cops at my door. Black coffee okay for everyone?"

"Dad, I'm fourteen. I don't drink coffee."

He smiled wryly. "Water for you, then. Anyway, princess, this is not a good weekend for me. If you had called, we could have arranged something fun, maybe in a week or two."

"Dad . . . ?"

He glanced at her.

"I miss you," she said. "I just want to be with you."

Tweaking her nose, he smiled. "I miss you, too."

"Can't I stay here? I won't be any trouble. I can do your grocery shopping, clean up the apartment, do the laundry. . . ."

Her dad shook his head. "I told you, honey, this is not a good weekend for me. I'm not even going to be here. I'm headed out of town."

"That's okay. I can get a lot done while you're gone. By Monday, this'll look like a whole new apartment."

Her dad handed Drew a cup of coffee. "*You're* old enough to have caffeine, aren't you?"

"Yes, sir."

"Jeez, don't call me sir. Makes me feel old. Honey, it's really sweet of you to offer to clean up, but you need to be back home with your mom, going to school."

"You dropped out of high school when *you* were fourteen," she reminded him.

"I got kicked out. Trust me, there's a difference. And I went back later and earned a college degree."

"Then maybe I could go to school here in San Diego."

The coffee cup halted just short of her dad's lips. "What?"

"It's not working out with Mom," she said slowly. "I want to come and live with you. Full-time."

His eyebrows disappeared under his mop of chestnut hair and he gave a short laugh. "With me? Here?"

"Yeah."

"No chance."

The stab went deep and Em's shoulders hunched. Outright rejection. Wow, she hadn't expected that.

"You don't want that, princess. Living with me is a bitch, just ask your mom. I'm out a lot. Hell, I barely sleep here."

"I can help you. I won't be any trouble."

"Honey," he said, shaking his head. He sent a sheepish grin in Drew's direction. "No offense, but having a teenage girl living with me would cramp my style. You know what I mean?"

Deep in her pockets, Em's fingers grew cold. She did know ... and yet she so *didn't*. "I thought you loved me."

"I do love you. More than I've ever loved anything in my life. But looking after you full-time? I'm not up for that."

Her blood started pumping again, hopeful. "But that's just it. You wouldn't have to look after me. I'm not a baby, Dad; I'm fourteen."

"You don't get it, princess. Looking after you requires time and money. Money I don't have. Hell, I don't even have a car right now. I'm begging a lift to the beach with friends this weekend."

Em frowned. "You're going to the beach?"

"Overnight at a beach house in Malibu, actually."

This was supposed to have been her dad's weekend with her. It had been planned for weeks. "But you were supposed to be coming to San Jose this weekend."

"That didn't work out."

"Because you decided to go to the beach with your friends instead?" she asked with growing dismay.

"Come on, Em," he said, cajoling. "You're making it sound worse than it is. These are important people, the in crowd. It's not every weekend I snag an invite like this."

"It's not every weekend you get to visit your daughter, either."

"Yeah, but I can see you anytime, honey. This party is a one-time deal. I already told your mom I'd reschedule."

"You'd rather be with your friends than with me."

"It's not like that."

He put a hand on her arm, but Em jerked away. This was not at all how she imagined things would go. All the way here, she'd imagined a sweet reunion, an eager acceptance. But the cozy picture of her and her dad living together, hanging together, having tons of fun, had just exploded in a giant ball of flame.

He was just like the others—a liar.

He didn't love her. She'd been replaced by . . . *friends*.

Backing away from her dad, she reached for Drew. He gathered her against his chest, hugging her, understanding immediately what she needed. At least *he* loved her.

"I guess I made a mistake coming here," she said.

Her dad nodded slowly. "If you had called first, we could've planned something special. Maybe another time?"

"Sure."

"Not Thanksgiving, though. I'm busy that weekend."

Em stiffened. Thanksgiving hadn't even been on her mind, but his words robbed her of breath. Thanksgiving was for families, but her dad would rather spend it with someone else. Not her.

"Okay," she said, completely numb.

Her dad chucked her under the chin, smiled, and said, "Sorry, honey, someone's picking me up in a half hour, so I've got to hop in the shower. Why don't you call your mom, then go grab some breakfast?"

"Sure, great idea."

He kissed her cheek. "Call me next week and we'll make a date, okay?"

"Yeah."

And then he was gone, down the hall to the bathroom without another word—without even waiting to see them out.

Drew dropped a kiss on the top of her head. "Wasn't what you expected, was it?"

"No, it wasn't."

"I'm really sorry about that."

"It's not your fault."

"No, but I feel for you, sweet. I want to take away the pain, make everything right again. You don't deserve to be treated like shit. And this world needs a fucking wake-up call to remind everybody how screwed up it is. I can help you make that happen, Em, if you let me."

Em felt as if she were being sucked into a deep pit of black syrup. She struggled to stay afloat. "They're all phony hypocrites."

"Every last one of them," he agreed softly.

"And everything will be better when it's all over, won't it? We'll be in a better place?"

"You bet. Nirvana, Em. A beautiful haven with no more pain. Eternal peace. I'm ready for it, aren't you? This place sucks."

He tugged her over to the hall closet. "I bet your dad can help, in his own way." He opened the door and reached up.

Her heart beat with the slithery rhythm of a snare drum as he pulled down a scoped hunting rifle, a silver handgun, and several boxes of ammo. "The knife we've been practicing with is good but, really, nothing beats a bullet."

"How'd you know those were there?" she asked.

"They sang to me." He smiled at her. "If you listen carefully, they'll sing to you, too, Em. Can you hear them?"

Strangely, she could. Soft, sweet lullabies that encouraged her to close her eyes. What Drew offered sounded so good, so soothing. It promised a distance from the pain, like an out-of-body experience—a distance she desperately craved.

She stopped resisting and let herself be drawn into the darkness. "Let's do it."

16

He didn't need to be nearby to finalize a lure, but watching the events unfold in person never failed to pump a sweet burning sensation through his veins. Drusus glanced at Emily's pale face as he slid off the bike. "Stay here, sweet. I've got a little business to attend to."

She said nothing; just stared straight ahead.

He smiled, pleased with her level of enthrallment. Then he removed his helmet and crossed to the open door of the gas station. The sun was already beating down on them, heating the air to a balmy hundred degrees. A perfect day.

The gas station attendant lifted his head.

"Drew. What brings you out here?"

"You do, Mark, my friend." Drusus glanced around to make sure they were alone. He sent a primal wave at the surveillance camera, killing the live signal and the footage recorded just prior to his arrival, then another wave at the door to lock it. "You do."

Mark's voice dropped an octave, eager and urgent. "I did it. I injected rat poison into every loaf of bread in the store, and I've sold at least a dozen of 'em so far. Those bastards in town will regret ganging up on me and getting me fired from the bank."

Drusus turned to the long-haired man behind the counter. The portal to his thoughts was perpetually ajar now, after weeks of steady invasion. Drusus slid in without any effort at all, coating everything in dismal gray as he passed.

"Excellent work." He located the idea he'd planted in Mark's subconscious and sparked it to life. "Now it's time to wrap things up."

The fellow's eyes immediately took on a vacant quality, and he ripped open the loaf lying next to him on the counter. "I'll be famous," he said, grabbing handfuls of slices. He stuffed them into his mouth and began chewing. "They'll never forget me."

"You're right about that," Drusus agreed. Tomorrow's headline would be quite spectacular: ELEVEN PEOPLE DEAD, SIX SERIOUSLY ILL IN HOSPITAL. The rat poison he'd given Mark was highly toxic, available only on the Chinese black market, and the local doctors would struggle to cure the sick, losing two more before the week was out. "Especially with that YouTube video you made. Great job."

He watched the attendant's face turn purple and his eyes bulge. He stood back as a spectacular amount of vomit spewed forth, covering the countertop and spilling down the fellow's shirtfront. Violent spasms racked Mark's body, taking him to the floor, a small display of candies crashing to the linoleum alongside him. Drusus waited patiently for the jerking to cease and the light to drain from Mark's eyes. Then he stepped toward the body. When his work was done, he exited the store, slid onto the seat in front of Em, and drove the bike back onto the highway.

Yes, indeed. An absolutely perfect day.

"I can't believe it. He's still not answering." Rachel tossed the cell phone on the dash, frustrated.

"There's your reason," Lachlan said, pointing ahead to several cars parked on the street. "Isn't that him with the suitcase? Next to the red convertible?"

"Yes." Amazing. One glance at her old wedding photo, and Lachlan had him memorized. Then again, Grant's looks had always been his strong point. She clawed at the door handle. "Block the car. Don't let him drive away."

The instant the Audi halted, she leapt out and darted between the parked cars. "Grant, wait!"

Her ex-husband glanced up. The couple in the red Sebring, a middle-aged man and a voluptuous younger woman, looked up, too.

"Rachel."

"Have you seen Em?"

Grant nodded. "About a half hour ago, with her boyfriend."

Rachel sagged. "You let them go?"

"I didn't know I was supposed to hang on to them."

"If you'd answer your goddamned phone, you would know. I've been trying to reach you since midnight."

"I was sleeping. Is that a crime?"

"When it comes to your daughter being in danger, yes, it is. Would it have hurt you to answer?"

"I went to bed late and I had the ringer turned off. So what? I talked to her just a few minutes ago and she was fine. As usual, you're making a mountain out of a molehill. She's not your dad, Rachel. She's not going to die the minute your back is turned."

Rachel's gut knotted at the mention of her father. But she didn't allow Grant to sidetrack her. "Wrong. The guy she's with is a nut. There's a real possibility he's going to hurt her."

"He looked okay to me."

"Really? A guy in his twenties is dating your fourteen-year-old daughter, and you think he looks *okay*?"

"Rachel." Lachlan's deep voice came from behind her.

Her ex glanced over her shoulder, frowning. "Who's this?"

"Lachlan MacGregor. A friend. What kind of father are you, Grant? I said the guy Em is with is in his twenties. Doesn't that bug you at all?"

Grant shrugged. "He seemed to really care about her."

"*Care* about her? He wants to ki—"

"Rachel," Lachlan whispered in her ear, his breath a warm tickle in her hair, "I know he's pushing your buttons, but we need information, not an argument."

He was right. She stepped back until she was leaning against his firm chest. The sense of security that swept through her at his touch brought tears to her eyes. Forcing her volatile emotions to the back of her mind, struggling for a calm voice, she asked Grant, "Do you know where she went from here? Where they were headed?"

"No, I assumed they'd head home. I suggested breakfast, and I did tell her to call you." Her ex studied the lay of Lachlan's arm around her waist. "You two living together? 'Cause if you are, I don't need to pay alimony anymore."

If Lachlan's arms hadn't tightened at that precise moment, Rachel would have leapt for Grant's throat. "*Alimony?* You mean the lousy five grand in child support you've sent me in the last four years, you asshole? Give me a break."

"Rachel," Lachlan reminded her softly.

She sagged against him again. He was right. Her sorry-assed ex wasn't worth going to jail over. He was just an outlet for her worry.

"Grant." Lachlan was calm, yet his voice held a note

of cold steel. "You're responsible for Emily's welfare until she's eighteen, and only deadbeat dads weasel out of paying for basic necessities like food and clothes. If I were you, I'd get it together before Rachel hauls your arse into court."

Then he nodded to the couple in the convertible, took Rachel's hand, and led her back to the car. As he opened her door, he muttered, "Bloody bampot."

She smiled.

"What in blazes did you ever see in that simpleton?"

Rachel's anger evaporated as she watched him close her door with a tightly controlled snap and circle around to his side, still muttering and shaking his head. It felt good to have someone on her side, someone who didn't see Grant's handsome face and charming smile and instantly forgive him. "Uh, did you get a good look at him? That chin, that nose, those baby blues? And he's smart . . . when it comes to engineering, anyway. He's a vice president at his firm. If he didn't party all his money away, he'd be pretty well off."

He flashed her a grimace. "He's lucky he's already out of your life. Otherwise, I'd be forced to do something very unpleasant."

"Really? Like what?"

"Like take my shiny black boot to his arse."

"Hmmm, I thought maybe you were volunteering to cut him into a million pieces with your sword."

A slow smile spread across his face as he started the engine and pulled away. "Sorry, wouldn't be worth it. Blood as weak as his would corrode the blade."

That thought kept a smile on their faces until they reached the next light and the decision to turn left or right—until she remembered they had no idea where to look next.

"What do we do now?" she asked.

Lachlan turned left, heading back toward the freeway. "Find his lair."

"His what?"

"His lair. Lure demons remain on the middle plane for extended periods of time, so they need somewhere to live. Underground, usually, so they can draw on the power of hell."

"How do we find it?"

Lachlan glanced at her. "We do a locator spell."

"A spell? Like magic?" She grimaced. "If you can do magic, why did we need to drive all the way to San Diego? Couldn't you have just transported us here?"

"My mystic skills are very limited."

She suddenly recalled Lachlan's terrible wounds and his explanation that Drew had torn him to shreds single-handedly. "Can Drew do magic, too?"

"In a manner of speaking."

"And are his spells better than yours?"

He slanted her a wary look. "Some."

"Then how do you intend to beat him?"

"Let me worry about that," he said gently. "I have a few aces up my sleeve. You need to focus on Emily. By taking her to visit her father, Drusus will have proven he's the only one she can truly count on. He's now capable of completing the lure. The only way to stop him will be to break his hold on her."

"Oh God." She buried her face in her hands. "I can't even have a civil conversation with her. What chance do I have of breaking through a demon's magic?"

"Don't underestimate your power, Rachel. You're the woman who gave birth to her. If anyone can reach her, it's you."

The cell phone on the dash warbled.

Lachlan reached for it, flipping it open as he merged

smoothly into rush hour traffic. "Aye, Webster, what's up?"

He listened for a few moments, grim faced, and then said crisply, "Go see Stefan Wahlberg. Tell him I need him. Then collect the others. Volunteers only, this is my cause, no' theirs." Folding the phone, he handed it to Rachel. "Well, that makes three. In addition to Carlos and the guard assigned to watch your apartment last night, Drusus killed a gas station attendant just outside of San Jose."

"Why would he kill a gas station attendant?"

"To leave us a message. One of the Gatherers found a note in old Ogham script carved into the poor fellow's chest. He's inviting us to meet him. Tonight, at midnight."

"Where?"

"We're still working on that part."

"And we're just going to show up when he tells us to?"

"Aye."

"Why? I mean, my commando experience is limited to movies, but even I know this smells like a trap," she said, irritated by his lack of initiative.

"It's a trap," he agreed.

She glared at him. "Obviously you have a plan. So stop being a smart-ass and just tell me what we're doing."

He smiled. "Drusus believes I'll come alone. He won't be expecting eight Gatherers, or the mage I'm bringing along to enhance our magic."

"Mage?"

Catching her confused frown, he explained, "A sorcerer."

It sounded like a plan. Sort of. But . . . "Can we really trust Drew not to harm Em before midnight?"

"No. But midnight is the most powerful hour for demons, and he's planning a flashy end. I'm counting on his ego to hold him off."

Rachel turned her gaze to the slow-moving cars outside the window, sighing heavily, her shoulders drooping. A *flashy end* sounded anything but reassuring. "You know, I was a lot happier before I knew about demons and Gatherers and magic. I don't know if I'll ever sleep soundly again."

His hand wrapped around hers and squeezed gently.

"You're tired," he said. Glancing in the rearview mirror, he signaled a right-hand lane change. "You'll feel better after some rest. Since we've got the time, I'm going to find a motel."

"You don't really expect me to nap, do you?"

"You need to be at your best when we confront Drusus."

Dubious about her ability to sleep, but understanding the rationale, Rachel shut up. She let him park in front of a Motel 6, sign up for a room, and direct her toward one of the two brightly colored double beds.

Toeing one Keds off and then the other, she eyed the mattress.

Who was she kidding? Lie down on a soft, comfortable bed? When Em was out there somewhere, trapped by Drew, in very real danger of losing her life? No. It just wasn't possible. Hell, she didn't even want to sit, let alone lie down. She needed to do something—anything—to get her daughter back.

"I can't sleep," she told Lachlan, as he turned to lock the door. "No way, no how. Let's just walk through the plan so I know what to do."

"You've been up all night. If you don't get some rest, you won't be in any shape to help tonight."

Avoiding the bed, she opened the minibar, peered inside, then closed the door. "You've been up all night, too."

He tossed her a wry smile. "Gatherers don't need sleep."

"I'm not tired."

"You may no' feel it, but you are. You're running on pure adrenaline."

"Then I'll keep on running until we get her back. Believe me, even if I close my eyes, I'm not going to fall asleep." She walked to the window, pulled the curtains aside, and studied the nearly empty parking lot, not entirely certain what she was looking for.

He sighed. "All right. Go have a hot shower, then. Relax. Recharge your batteries."

"No. If the phone rings while I'm in the shower, I'll freak." She returned to the bed and slid her feet back into her sneakers. *Empty parking lot.* "I need to be ready to move."

Dragging her fingers through her hair, she walked back to the window. *Empty parking lot . . .* She halted abruptly. "The fairgrounds. Isn't it possible *that's* where his lair is? Why else would he hang out there?"

"Good question." Lachlan made a quick call to Brian, then hung up and smiled. "He's going to check it out."

Rachel tucked her tangled hair behind her ears. "We should go, too. Back to San Jose, I mean." She stuffed her hands in her pockets, then yanked them out.

Crossing the room in two long strides, Lachlan grabbed her fluttering hands. "Rachel, it's okay. Truly. There's nothing we can do until tonight."

"But she's alone. He might be hurting her."

He lifted her chin with a knuckle, looking deep in her eyes, his gaze steady. "I told you he won't do anything until midnight. He wants us to be there. He's too ego-tistical to harm her without an audience. Are you saying you don't believe me?"

She returned his stare, not sure how to answer.

Lachlan saw genuine fear in Rachel's creased brow, a relentless shadow of worry that lingered in spite of his reassurance. But he also saw the glassy, wide-eyed quality of her eyes, proof that her desperate concern for Emily would drive her to exhaustion if he didn't find some way to calm her down.

"I believe you," she said. "But—"

He kissed her. Slow and sweet.

Maybe not the best solution given the impossibility of their relationship, but it felt right. And it seemed to work. Her hands stopped fighting his.

"Have you ever heard the saying *A change is as good as a rest*?" he murmured, rubbing his lips lightly across hers, teasing them both with the subtle, sensual friction.

She went completely still, except for the telltale pulse that thrummed at the base of her throat.

"Here we are, in a quiet little motel room with a per-fectly good queen-sized bed. Hmmm . . . if sleep is out of the question, what else could we possibly do?" He unbuttoned her blouse, one pearly button at a time.

"Lachlan . . ." It came out low and uneven.

"If you're worried about making a quick getaway, I'll let you keep your trainers on." He nibbled his way along her jaw, then down the length of her pale neck to the plump mound of her breast. "And maybe this fine lacy bra."

His mouth closed over the peak.

Although his actions had been motivated primarily by a desire to distract her, the rasp of delicate lace under his tongue, the unbearably sweet scent of her skin, and the exquisite mewl she uttered as he suckled blew every calculated thought right out the window. His blood pounded in his ears and all he could think about was having her supple and sated beneath him.

Fortunately, Rachel was of the same mind. She shrugged out of her blouse, letting it slide to the floor at his feet like a soft sigh. At the same time, she unfastened the clasp of her jeans and slid the zipper down.

"Make me forget," she whispered. "Just for a while."

Releasing her for a brief moment, he yanked his T-shirt over his head and tossed it atop the TV. Then his hands grasped her hips and tugged them against his own. As their groins collided, sending a delicious, mind-numbing jolt through his body, his fingers dug into her buttocks, clenching. "Christ. It always seems impossible that you could feel better than I imagine. But you do."

Her answer was a kiss.

A kiss that started off sweet but quickly dissolved into a torrid mimicry of the sex act they both wanted: his tongue thrusting deep in her mouth, her lips swelling under the onslaught, growing hot and wet.

She wriggled her hips against him in a clear demand for more—hard and fast and furious more.

And he was determined to oblige, but not until he was certain her real need was being met. He broke off the kiss and peered into her face. Shadows still lingered in the purple beneath her eyes, but dark-eyed, flush-cheeked passion had replaced the worry. Her faith in his ability to ease her burdens, to take care of her, shone in her golden eyes. A hot rush of pleasure swept through his body. He lifted her clear off the floor, parted her legs, and encouraged her to wrap them around his waist, her damp heat pressing intimately against his arousal. An arousal that was, at this moment, painfully hard.

"I want you," he said hoarsely against her throat.

"Then take me."

He needed no further encouragement. Carrying her to the closest bed, he tossed her on the garish polyester comforter. He shucked his remaining clothes in record time and almost dove on top of her. Her lacy underwear disappeared in short order, and they pressed into each other, hot skin to damp, hot skin. Unlike the previous encounter, there were no long sighs or hot stares. An edge of desperation laced their touches and their kisses, almost as if both of them knew this was a last hurrah, a moment snatched out of time.

When Lachlan's fingers slid between her legs to her core, he groaned at the wetness he found there.

"Take me hard," she begged, gasping as he plunged two fingers into her and thumbed the ultrasensitive nub at the apex of her thighs. Her fingers dug into his sweat-slickened shoulders, spurring him on.

"For you, *mo cridhe*, anything," he whispered.

Gently shifting her quivering legs, he opened her fully to him, and then in one sure thrust, drove deep inside her, hard, just as she demanded. And he didn't stop there.

Braceleting her wrists, he held her tightly to the bed and devoured her lips. When they were both breathless, their skin alive and eager for more, he began moving inside her, slowly at first, then harder and faster, every thrust a wet slap of joined bodies and a jolt of pleasure so intense that it rippled all the way to his toes. Blood pumped through his veins, sweet and hot.

The edginess inside him grew almost unbearable as Rachel's breathing grew short and raspy, and sweat misted the valley between her breasts. When tiny tremors racked her womb, he knew she was close.

"Please," she begged.

He rotated his hips and slammed into her.

"Oh God, yes."

As a violent shiver tore through her and the elusive crest of her desire swam into view, she whimpered.

"That's it, love. Come for me," he urged hoarsely as he thrust once more. He reached that one perfect spot inside her that trembled on the verge of exploding, and she fell, hard, screaming his name.

"Lachlan!"

Her fingernails dug into his hands, clinging to him as if he were a lifeline. He rode her hard as she climaxed, using her rippling body to spur his own release and giving up a very guttural and undisciplined shout of euphoria as he collapsed atop her.

Aware that his weight was not insubstantial, the instant his muscles had any power he rolled to the side, taking her with him. They lay like that—her cheek damply stuck to his shoulder, her long hair wrapped around his bicep, their limbs still fully entwined—for a long, languorous moment.

His eyes were closed, his nose full of the heady scent of Rachel and sex, when he admitted, "If I could trade the rest of my existence for one extra minute with you, I would. You know that, don't you?"

His confession hung in the air for a breathless moment. It was the closest he could come to telling her he loved her without actually saying those impossible words.

The significance wasn't lost on Rachel. She lay quietly for a moment, her heart beating in tandem with his, absorbing what he had said . . . and not said. "How long do you have left?" she asked. "Of soul gathering?"

"Ninety-one years."

More silence. Understandable silence. She'd be dead by then, buried at least twenty years. And long before that, she'd have grown old and withered and gray. He could almost hear the cogs of her mind turning as she considered the cruel passage of time.

But her next question surprised him.

"Tell me about your family," she said softly.

He stiffened, then expelled a heavy sigh. Rachel deserved to know more about him—if not everything, then as much as he could bear to admit. "Elspeth was a good wife and a fine mother. We barely knew each other when we wed, but we came to love each other over time. Easy enough to do when you share three bonny children."

"What were their names?"

He told her, and went on to describe them, with all the tiny, endearing details he refused to cede to dulling memory.

"It's obvious you loved them very much." Her fingers trailed through the hairs on his chest. "When you spoke just now, your accent got thicker, did you know that? As if you'd actually gone back in time."

Perhaps he had, fleetingly.

"If you *could* go back in time, would you?"

Interesting question. "I'm no' certain. I was a different man then. Full of unwarranted pride and reckless vigor. I craved power, thirsted for land, and believed I was the one warrior capable of returning the MacGregor clan to its former glory. I went to battle against the Campbells for my own selfish desires. As convenient as it might be to do so, I canno' blame Drusus for everything that happened. He merely played to my vanity. It was I who bartered my soul away."

Realizing just how far he'd come, how much he'd changed, he rubbed a strand of her hair between his finger and thumb. The man he'd once been could never have won Rachel's fond regard.

But it was too late. What was done was done.

He'd made a deal with the devil, and there was no way back.

"Tormod Campbell had been generous, as Campbells go, turning a blind eye as I built a small manor on the shores of Loch Lyon and fended for my kin. He raided my home and killed my family out of honest vengeance, because I took that generosity and spat on it. I had many a good reason to despise him, but canno' fault his actions that day, only my own." In that, there was no room for debate. "So, would I choose to return to the past if it were in my power to do so? Only if I could be the man I am today and no' the fool I was then."

"Is that why you ended up in purgatory? Because you attacked the Campbells?"

"No."

She lifted her head to look at him.

"I was judged on two counts," he said. "Greed, which is one of the seven deadly sins, and the crime of taking my own life."

Rachel sat up. "You killed yourself? *Why?*"

His steady gaze met hers. "You don't think causing the death of my wife and bairns is reason enough?"

She shook her head. "I just don't see you taking the coward's way out. Blaming yourself? Sure. Going a little crazy with grief and killing Tormod? You bet. Killing yourself? Nope, I don't see it."

He reached up and cupped her chin in his hand. "Your faith in me is astounding."

She leaned into him. "There's more to the story, right?"

"Aye." At the prod of her elbow, he continued. "After Tormod ran my entire family through, he set fire to the manor house and left me to wallow in my guilt. It began to rain, and at first I mistook the voice for the whisper of raindrops on the battlements. But after a time, I realized the faint noise came from my youngest brother, a friar, lying upon the cobbles, bleeding into the dirt. I went to him and held his head in my lap, hoping to ease his passing."

Lachlan recalled the moment vividly. Starkly. Weeping like a bairn and near puking with regret, he'd begged his brother for forgiveness. Being a better man than Lachlan could ever hope to be, his brother had granted it.

"When he said he saw Death approaching, I had no notion what he saw. Lost in my despair and believing it to be Death herself rather than her agent, I pleaded for her to spare his life and offered my own life in return. No one was more surprised than I when she appeared to me and accepted the trade."

"Wait a second. Death is a *she*?"

"Aye." He smiled at her disgruntled expression. "But to strike the bargain, I had to die. I can't say I was completely without doubts, but watching the blood seep out of my brother made the decision remarkably easy. I took my hunting knife and drove it through my own heart."

"Just like that?"

He nodded. "Just like that."

"Did it hurt?"

"More than you can possibly imagine."

She shuddered.

"But that pain was nothing compared to the agony I felt the moment I realized I hadn't actually saved my brother."

Rachel sucked in a sharp breath. "Death *cheated* you?"

"In a manner of speaking. He didn't die that day, or even from the wounds he received that day. He regained

his health, left the church, married, and had a bairn of
his own. But Death brands all who are destined to die
with a mark visible only to Gatherers, and the moment
I became a Gatherer, I saw it there, an immutable mark
upon his cheek. I knew that one day I'd be called upon
to collect his soul. I fought against it, stayed by his side
every moment of every day, refusing to close my eyes or
sleep. But eventually, despite my efforts, Death claimed
him."

He paused, picturing another white spiral in his
mind.

"You did your best," she offered him with sympathy.
"It's not your fault that she cheated."

"Rachel, I . . ."

"At least he got to fall in love and have a baby. He got
a chance to live a little, thanks to you."

He said nothing, just stared at her.

"I understand why you did what you did," she said,
lying alongside him, hugging him tightly. "So, you're not
perfect. Welcome to the club."

"What, you're no' perfect, either?" he teased, trying
to summon his courage.

"No." She ran her fingers through the dusting of hairs
on his chest. "I killed my father."

Lachlan blinked. "Pardon?"

"Okay, not directly. But I might as well have."

He relaxed. "What happened?"

"I was an only child, like Em, and when I was eleven,
my mom was diagnosed with multiple sclerosis. That
changed everything: To be closer to medical help, my
dad sold our farm, moved us into town, and got a job at
a chemical factory. Then when I was sixteen, he was involved in an accident at work and was blinded. It kinda
fell on me to look after everyone. Not because my parents wanted it that way—in fact, my dad was as indepen-

dent as they come—but out of necessity. I was the only one with a driver's license."

Rachel shifted positions, clearly uncomfortable.

"Anyway, to make a long story short, I won an art scholarship to Paris for a year. One of those once-in-a-lifetime opportunities, and my parents insisted that I take it. I knew it was a stupid thing to do, but idiot that I was, I let them persuade me. I wanted the dream so badly. Three weeks after I moved to Paris, my dad was hit by a car when he was crossing the street. Grocery shopping."

"How is that your fault?"

"Doing the groceries was *my* chore." She grimaced. "I know what you're going to say—that I couldn't have known he'd get hit by a car. Except that I did; I knew what kind of man he was. I knew he wouldn't sit at home and have everything delivered to his door. I knew he'd try to walk to the store. And I still left him alone."

"Rachel—"

"I flew home right away to look after my mom. I met Grant on the plane from Paris to New York and the rest, as they say, is history."

"You are no' to blame for your father's death."

"Nor are you to blame for your family's. You went above and beyond trying to save your brother. You did a very brave thing."

Lachlan closed his eyes and kissed the top of Rachel's head. Her version of the story was so much better than the truth. And brave? Hell no, he was a bloody coward. Again he'd had the chance to tell her about Emily, and again he'd choked over the words.

Rachel had found some acceptance of his brother's death in the knowledge that he'd experienced a measure of life. What had Emily had the opportunity to do? Nothing. She'd never truly been in love. Never finished high school, never attended her prom in a fancy dress. Never discovered her calling in life, whatever that might be. Never married, nor had a child. She'd die unfulfilled, and Rachel's heart would shatter in the struggle to accept it.

Forgive me, he begged silently.

17

When Lachlan and Rachel crested the north peak of Mount Misery, they found Brian and the others waiting. To Lachlan's surprise, not one of his young trainees had bowed out, despite the two deaths of their brethren. In fact, two other men, well-seasoned Gatherers with long years of battling demons under their belts, stood in place of the fallen. Each of the sturdy warriors had a razor-edged sword in his hands and the glint of a heavy silver chain around his neck.

Rachel took one look at Stefan's rubber boots and plump belly and whispered, "Is that the mage?"

"Aye. Good guess."

"He doesn't look very ... powerful."

Lachlan stared at the mage for a moment. "Looks can be deceiving." To Brian he said, "You cut it a little close texting me the GPS location, Webster."

"Yeah, sorry about that, but it took us a while to figure everything out. Rachel was right about the fairgrounds, sort of. It wasn't the actual lair, but it *was* the entrance to some kind of freaky spatial bridge. Your buddy Stefan had a little trouble finding the On/Off switch, but once he tracked it down, he just used a little hocus-pocus to activate it." The younger man pointed to a shadowy cleft in the rocks. "We surfaced there, at the mouth of an underground cavern. Quite the ride, I must say. Fairgrounds to here in one heart-stopping, piss-your-pants step."

Lachlan acknowledged Stefan with a nod. Shady or not, the mage's skills were proving advantageous. "Excellent work. I take it you've already enhanced everyone's shield charm?"

"Yes."

Glancing at his watch, Lachlan called out, "It's eleven. Let's go in." Then he paused, remembering Death's advice. "One thing before we enter. This is the moment to put aside your grievances with God. Whatever your history, whatever your reasons for doubting him, find it in yourself to believe. If you can't summon a pure and powerful faith, you'll be of little use in a battle against one of hell's most formidable demons."

He surveyed the faces before him, one by one, hoping that what he was about to do would be enough. "An oath will center our faith."

Several of the men frowned, but no one backed away.

"Raise your crosses." He raised his and waited until every warrior's hand was lifted and a sea of silver reflected the moonlit sky. "Upon my immortal soul . . ."

Nine voices repeated his words, strong and sure.

"I swear to give my all in the fight for good and God . . . and to forever defend the middle plane against the forces of Satan."

"Amen."

Lachlan's pulse slowed as a familiar, prebattle calm slipped over him. "The goal is to locate Drusus as quickly as possible, enter his cavern, and then spread out, surrounding him. Do no' under any circumstances take him on yourself. Clear?"

The men nodded, but Rachel frowned. "I don't have one. A cross, I mean."

Brian looped a silver chain over Rachel's neck. "All fixed."

She fingered the heavy cross, tracing the Celtic-knot design engraved upon it. "Does this work the way it does with vampires? Burning them?"

"No," Lachlan said. "The power is in your belief. The rood can only channel your faith."

Her gaze flickered up to meet his, a cloud of doubt in her eyes. "Uh, this might be a bad time to tell you, but I'm not very religious."

As much as he understood her doubt, he couldn't let it continue. "You believe in *me*, don't you?"

She nodded.

"Then think on it this way. I couldn't stand before you now if there were no God. I'm here because he's giving me a second chance to prove my worth. Thus, if you believe in me, you must believe in God."

The cloud faded and she smiled. "Okay."

He grasped her hand, holding it tight in his. Bringing a woman—*his* woman—into battle did not sit well, but he had no choice. Rachel's presence would greatly influence the final outcome. Bending, he kissed her firmly on the lips. "Let's go collect Emily."

They entered the dark, uneven tunnel, Stefan leading the way. The taste of dirt and dank and bat droppings closed in on them, and the path almost immediately angled sharply downward, making walking perilous and holding swords a challenge. But none of the warriors complained.

"I can't see anything," Rachel grumbled. "Doesn't anyone have a flashlight?"

"Don't need one," replied Brian. "Gatherers can see in the dark."

"*I* can't."

"Just hold on to the big guy; you'll be fine."

Rachel's grip on Lachlan's hand firmed. He smiled and squeezed back.

"What about the mage? How does he see?"

"He doesn't," explained Lachlan, aware that her need to talk stemmed from a faint sense of claustrophobia. He felt it, too, and *he* could see. "He's following the scent of magic."

They had descended some thirty or forty feet into the bowels of the earth when Stefan suddenly halted. He ran a hand through his hair, muttered a few words, then stood silent.

Lachlan wove his way to the front of the line, Rachel in tow. "What is it?" he asked the mage.

"I'm not entirely certain," Stefan said slowly. "But it's a void spell."

"How do you know?"

"Your body doesn't currently house a soul, so you can't feel the sapping sensation, but I can feel it and I bet Rachel can, too."

"I do. It's cold and somehow . . . exhausting."

Lachlan stared into the dark recesses ahead. Drusus was down there, waiting for him. The demon wouldn't have issued an invitation if he intended to lock him out, so this spell couldn't be that formidable. And it was now twenty minutes to midnight. "Break it."

"I can't. Not without invoking a void counterspell."

"Do it," he snapped.

"No." Stefan turned to him, deep lines etched into his brow. "If you're that determined, you do it. But a void spell requires the sacrifice of a soul, Lachlan. There's only two down here. Who are you asking to die, Rachel or me?"

The sharp stab of the mage's question reached all the way to Lachlan's toes. "Neither." He scrubbed a hand over his face. "What do we do now?"

"We try to pass through it and see what happens."

Lachlan frowned. "That's our best option?"

"That's our *only* option."

"Christ. All right, I'll go first." He tried to shake off Rachel's hand, but she wouldn't let go. "Rachel . . ."

"I'm going with you."

"No."

Her entire body wrapped around his arm, refusing to accept his verdict. "Drew wants me to be part of his sick grand finale; you know he does. He's not going to kill me up here with some stupid magic spell."

The slight tremor in her voice told him she wasn't as certain as she made out, but he couldn't deny the truth of her words. Drusus did want her to be a party to his triumph. And they didn't have the time to argue.

He sighed. "Don't let go of me, no matter how cold you feel or how numb your body gets. I'll pull you through, I promise."

"Don't worry, I'm latched on tight."

They edged past Stefan and continued down the sloping path. Lachlan's sword began to glow a pale purple color and tiny shocks rippled up the blade to his arm. Rachel shivered violently and stumbled over a short stalagmite, but he caught her before she fell. Ten paces farther, the purple glow dissipated, and Rachel's skin warmed under his touch.

"We're through," he called back to the others. "Brian, you next. Bring Stefan."

The young Gatherer didn't hesitate. He grabbed Stefan's arm and strode down the path, sword extended. An instant later, a brilliant flash lit up the cavern and Brian flew backward, knocking over the mage.

Lachlan's heart seized.

A low groan broke the breathless silence and Brian rolled over. "Fuck, that hurt."

"Stefan, are you all right?" Lachlan asked, relieved.

"My hands feel like they're frostbitten. Other than that, I'm fine." The mage got to his feet, dusting himself off. "Well, that clears up any confusion. It's a barrier spell."

Lachlan grimaced. "None but Rachel and I can pass."

"That would be my guess."

"I thought you said he wouldn't be expecting you to bring anyone else along," Rachel said in dismay.

"Apparently, I was wrong."

Lachlan studied the dust and pebbles at his feet, his gut in turmoil. No other Gatherers meant no circle of crosses and no backup. No Stefan meant he'd have to do all his own spells. Basically, unless he managed to pull a rabbit out of a hat, this was going to be a repeat of his first, disastrous battle with Drusus.

"You need to go back, Rachel."

"No."

"Please don't argue," he said quietly. "I won't be able to protect you down there. It'll be a bloody miracle if I save Emily. There's no way I can look after you both."

"I understand." Her voice was equally firm. "But Em is my child, my *only* child. I'm not going to sit back and play it safe while she faces down a demon determined to kill her. You can't possibly believe I would do that. My life is nothing compared to hers. You made the ultimate sacrifice to save your brother, Lachlan. You must know how I feel."

His throat tightened painfully.

"This is different," he said hoarsely. "You have other options. I'm going into battle as your champion, Rachel. I will fight for Emily. I will fight for *you*."

"She's not your daughter, Lachlan."

"Please." The strands of flesh holding his heart in

place ripped a little more with every beat. He closed his eyes to an unbearable vision of Rachel dying in his arms, blackened and burned, just like Carlos. "Don't ask me to do this. Go back."

"I can't. I won't."

"Damn it, Rachel," he spit out angrily. But he'd already accepted the inevitable. She wouldn't turn around and he knew it. They were caught in the same tragic web: she unable to desert Emily, he unable to desert the innocent souls of his family. And even though he knew the end would crush him, he couldn't help but take the next step down the narrowing tunnel.

But first, he gave into a raw, selfish need.

He snatched Rachel to his chest, buried his face in her fragrant hair, and said, "I love you. Whatever happens, don't forget that."

"Okay," she murmured softly, yielding to the embrace. "Uh, MacGregor?"

Lachlan glanced back up the slope at Brian. "What?"

"Stop wasting time. Just get down there and kill the bastard, will ya?"

Brian's back was to him, as were the backs of all the Gatherers. Lachlan could feel their tension.

"What's wrong?"

"Apparently, Drusus was worried we'd get bored while we waited. He left a little party behind to entertain us. A bunch of demons just crawled out of the walls, including the two jerks from Emily's school and a big, badassed guy that reminds me of the Incredible Hulk. Only not as green."

"Can you handle them?"

"Looking forward to it."

Reluctant as he was to leave the others to face a mob of demons—one of which sounded remarkably like his

steroid-junkie friend from the Coleman Road Bridge—
Brian was right. The important battle was with Drusus.
Lachlan grabbed Rachel's hand and dove down the tun-
nel. "Make me proud, Webster."

Brian snorted.

The demon's lair lay deep in the belly of the mountain. Rachel sighed with relief when they entered the
well-lit cavern and warm, dry air replaced the musty
closeness of the tunnel. Stumbling along blindly behind
Lachlan, even after he confessed that he loved her, had
been unnerving.

She squeezed his hand.

He tossed her a quick smile, then swung his gaze to the
center of the room. Under billowing swags of blue and
white–striped silk, a man reclined on a velvet divan.

Drew. But his lazy smile and gladiator costume
couldn't hold Rachel's attention. She quickly scanned
the room for a sign of Em, and gasped. Her daughter
knelt in front of a fiery brass pot, garbed in a white
Roman-style gown, holding the sharp point of a knife
to her breast. Eyes wide open but focused on the flames,
she didn't seem aware of anything around her.

Rachel leapt toward Em, only to be held back by
Lachlan's tight hold on her hand.

"It won't be that easy," he murmured.

"It most certainly won't," agreed Drusus, getting to
his feet. Studded leather armor covered his bright red
tunic and old-fashioned leather sandals laced up his
bare legs. "In fact, saving her is impossible, Rachel. She's
going to die, no matter what you do. You should just accept that."

Rachel glared at him. "Your entire relationship with
Em is built on lies. Pardon me if I choose not to believe
you."

"Fighting words, my dear," the demon said, advancing toward them, the muscles of his thighs flexing with every step. There wasn't a spare bit of flesh on the guy, anywhere. "But I'm fairly certain Lachlan won't echo them. He knows better."

She glanced at Lachlan. His face reflected nothing but grim resolve, impossible to read.

"He's just as determined to save Em as I am," she said.

Drew arched a brow. "Really? Are you sure about that?"

"Yes."

"Maybe you should ask him."

Rachel stiffened at the amused tone in his voice.

"But make your question very specific," Drew advised. "Ask him if he came here to save Em's life, or whether he came here to gather her soul. You do know that's his job, right? Gathering the souls of the dead?"

Her heart knocked like an icy lump against her ribs.

Was it possible?

She shut her eyes, blocking out his mocking face. No. Drew was a consummate liar. He knew exactly what to say to manipulate people into doing and saying what he wanted. She couldn't let his insidious half-truths color her judgment.

"I don't need to ask him. He already told me he would fight for her, that he's ready to die for her."

The demon chuckled. "Oh my, you really do have it bad. Look at his face, Rachel. Read the truth in his eyes. He knows he can't save her. She wears the mark of Death on her cheek, and he can see it."

Rachel didn't need to look. She felt the flinch ripple through Lachlan's body, right down to her fingers.

And despite a desperate need to shutter her thoughts, to keep from panicking, the echo of Lachlan's voice earlier that day rang in her ears: *Death brands all who are destined to die with a mark visible only to Gatherers, and the moment I became a Gatherer, I saw it*. Oh God. That look he'd given her back in the motel, the darkly tormented look of guilt. It had been guilt over Em, not his brother.

She shook her hand free of his.

This time, he didn't try to hold on to her.

Numbness took over her entire body. Em was going to die. Tonight. And Lachlan was going to claim her soul.

"He's not the man you think he is, Rachel. Did he happen to mention how he earned his place in purgatory?"

"The sins of greed"—Rachel glanced at Lachlan, then back at Drew—"and suicide."

Drew smiled. "Let's deal with the greed for a moment. To be specific, MacGregor craved land. He wanted land so badly, he went to battle against the Campbells, killing scores of people to win a piece of land that had belonged to his family a hundred years before."

"He told me."

"Good. Then no doubt he also told you how his hated enemy got inside his heavily fortified manor house to gain his revenge."

Rachel glanced at Lachlan again. His eyes were closed.

"No," she confessed.

"Left that little detail out, did he? Can't imagine why. It's such a touching part of the story." Drew sauntered over to Emily and rubbed a lock of her hair between his fingers. "He let them in."

Rachel's heart skipped a beat.

"Well, technically he let *me* in, but it amounted to the same thing. Against the edicts of his clan, he told a stranger about the secret water gate on the north wall and then purposely left it unlocked. Why? Because we had a deal. He got information about the movements of his enemy that enabled him to win back his land and I got . . . Well, let's just say he never lived up to his end of the bargain."

Drew's gaze lifted to meet hers.

"He traded his entire family for a piece of land, Rachel. Still think he's the kind of man who'd risk his life for yours?"

Her tongue felt swollen.

"Not convinced yet? I've got one more gem to share." He tugged a chain free of his breastplate and held the glass vial at the end aloft. "MacGregor didn't come here tonight for *you*. He's only here to rescue this."

"That's a lie." Lachlan spoke for the first time, his voice crisp and sure.

Drew ignored him, his jade gaze locked on Rachel. "This reliquary contains the souls of his dead wife and children. He's been using you, Rachel. All he wants is to save his family from an eternity in hell, because his guilt is eating him alive. And rightly so."

She stared at the etched-glass tube. Everything he said made a sick sort of sense.

"He's twisting the facts, Rachel," Lachlan said. "Don't listen to him."

"Is it true?" she asked quietly, without looking at him. "Does that thing hold the souls of your wife and children?"

"Aye, but—"

"And did you come here to rescue them?"

He sighed heavily. "Rachel . . ."

For a long moment there was no sound in the cavern except the fluttering of the flames in the brass pot. Rachel clasped her hands together in front of her body, trying not to shiver. She didn't want to believe Drew; she didn't want to believe any of the horrible things he was saying. But Lachlan's response completely undermined her resistance.

What if it was all true?

"Tell you what," Drew said, smiling. "I'll simplify things. I like you, Rachel, so I'm going to be benevolent. I'm going to let you walk out of here alive. Just turn around, go back the way you came, and you can forget this whole mess ever happened."

"I can't leave, not without Em."

"Of course not. Take her with you."

"But—" Rachel studied the frozen figure of her daughter. She had that weird sense again, of being a hapless mouse in the paws of a wily cat—as if the escape were too easy.

Drew snapped his fingers, and Em blinked. Her hands parted and the knife clattered to the stone floor. A dull, unfocused look remained on her face, but she was clearly alive.

Still, Rachel hesitated. She glanced at Lachlan.

"Go, Rachel," he said, his blue eyes cool and empty. "Take Emily and leave. Drusus is right. This has always been about rescuing my family. Cruel of me to worm my way into your affections, I know, but I had to stay close to Emily. So I did what I did. My family has always come first."

Her pulse slowed to a funeral march. His family. Not her. Not Emily.

"I think you knew that, deep down."

She blinked.

He was right. She *had* known—or at least suspected. That's why she'd experienced those heavy twinges of jealousy whenever the conversation turned to his wife and children. She'd sensed the unusual depth of his bond. She just hadn't suspected he'd go to this much trouble—to the point of actually pretending to love her—just to get close enough to rescue them.

How wrong she'd been.

Her gaze slid away from Lachlan's, dropping to the flat stone floor of the cavern. Her chest hurt, as if someone were grinding a knuckle into her sternum.

She was such an idiot, always so engrossed in her own little world that she couldn't see the truth, always seeing what she wanted to see, the picture postcard. Grant had never loved her; he'd loved a woman she could never be. And Lachlan never loved her, either. He had just been using her.

Tears pooled in her eyes.

Damn it. She'd let down her guard, let his calm, sure words gull her into hoping for the impossible. She'd fallen in love with the image, the seemingly dependable facade, only to discover that no matter how many layers she peeled away, there was nothing real about him. Nothing at all. She'd made the same mistake she'd made with Grant—picked the bright bow and shiny paper wrapped around an empty box.

But never again. Handsome charmers could go to hell.

She turned away.

Lachlan watched Rachel escort a dazed Emily out of the cavern, disappearing into the gloom of the tunnel, this time with a flashlight Drusus had kindly conjured. The tears glistening in her eyes had damned near killed him, because *he*'d put them there. But he'd had no choice. She'd been hesitating when she should have run.

And knowing she'd survive almost made it bearable.

When the beam of the flashlight faded away, a familiar chill settled around his heart. She was gone. Once again, Drusus had succeeded in ripping away everyone he cared for.

"Excellent."

He faced the lure demon.

Drusus grinned. "Not quite as much fun as slaying her before your eyes, but a delightful amount of pain, nonetheless. And it'll only get worse for you, my friend. Even if you survive—a highly doubtful scenario—you'll be doomed to watch her from afar. When Em dies, as we both know she will, she'll blame you."

"Better that she blame me than blame herself."

"Hero to the end. Bravo. Unfortunately, you won't be around to save the day tomorrow. Em's been a very bright pupil, a delightful protégé. She's going to go out with guns ablaze. Literally. Taking out at least seven of her fellow classmates before she kills herself. It'll make all the headlines."

And it would destroy Rachel.

But that didn't bear thought. Not right now.

"Did you dress up just for show?" Lachlan asked. He waved a hand down his body, and his jeans and T-shirt were instantly replaced by the rusty red and moss green pattern of the MacGregor plaid. "Or do you actually intend to fight?"

"Shade magic," noted Drusus with a raised brow. "Tsk, tsk, MacGregor. What would the great man upstairs say?"

The reliquary around the demon's neck swayed with every move, taunting Lachlan with its proximity. Somehow, he had to steal the amulet and deliver it to the other Gatherers before Drusus killed him. "Does it matter?"

"To you? Absolutely." Drusus peered at him, his eyes lit with curiosity. "So, I take it you read the *Book of Gnills*?"

"Cover to cover."

"And the other? The *Book of T'Farc*?"

"Didn't have time to read the whole thing. I focused my efforts on chapter nine."

The demon's eyes narrowed.

"That's the chapter on slaying demons," Lachlan reminded him pleasantly.

"I remember." Drusus shook his head. "But you're not fooling anyone, MacGregor. You won't delve into dark magic. Not when every void spell swallows up a human soul. Not when the only souls close enough to sacrifice belong to Elspeth and your three children."

"Are you certain?" He gripped the leather-wrapped hilt of his *claidheamh mòr* with both hands and casually swung it back and forth in front of his body, loosening his viciously tight muscles. "Didn't it occur to you that I might prefer to send their souls into the void than let you take them to hell?"

The demon stilled as the jeer echoed through the chamber. But he quickly recovered. "No, you won't use a spell that invokes God's wrath. I know how desperately you want to walk through those pearly gates."

"Grab a sword. Let's test that theory."

Wariness carved new lines in the demon's brow. No doubt he was weighing Lachlan's confidence against the arse kicking of a week ago. Finally, Drusus nodded.

Summoning his gladius to hand, he said, "You could save their souls, you know. Your wife and children. All you have to do is give me the Linen and I'll hand over the reliquary."

"I didn't bring it."

"Not wise, *baro*. My message on Mark's chest was very clear. You've not only damned your innocent family to hell, you've guaranteed yourself a shitload of pain. This time when I torture you, I won't be lenient. I won't stop until you spill your guts." He smiled at his bon mot.

"Won't do you much good. At best, you'll get a description of the Asian lad I handed it off to. But since I've never seen the man before and I've no idea who or where he is, that information won't get you too far."

The demon blinked. "You gave the Linen to a stranger?"

"After all this time, you still don't know me very well, do you, Drusus?"

The lure demon gathered himself, rising to full height, his muscles thick with anger. "Satan's blood, you're a fool. You'll die tonight, MacGregor. A slow, excruciating death that will have you begging for mercy."

"Unlikely. Death told me how to defeat you."

"And you believed her? There *is* no way to defeat me. Even with void magic, you won't win. At most, you'll manage four good spells, while I have an endless supply of power at my disposal."

Lachlan stared at the swaying reliquary.

Four good spells. Drusus was right; that's all he'd get. But that's all he needed. He knew the words of four particularly potent void spells by heart; he had memorized them with just this moment in mind. They weren't the equivalent of a lure demon's power, but they could make the difference between success and horrible, abject failure. And if he incurred God's wrath, what did it matter? Wasn't he destined for hell anyway?

He closed his eyes . . . and shuddered at the cruel memory his brain conjured up: the shining look in Rachel's eyes when she told him she believed in him. A faith he hadn't earned, but had been granted anyway.

No.

He couldn't use void magic.

To Rachel, he was more than just an accumulation of his past deeds. She saw the potential in him to be a better man. She saw him as loyal and courageous and honorable, and he'd give anything to prove her right.

Using spells born of evil intent would disgrace her ... and the memories of his three children. The lure demon's defeat must be wrought from the depths of Lachlan's own character, not by the use of evil against evil. But to succeed, he had to truly believe he could win. He had to believe that one lonely warrior standing for justice could prevail over a demon of immense power.

The heavy silver cross, the one Lachlan had slipped from his dying brother's neck four hundred years ago, lay warm against his bare chest. Rachel had made a blind leap for him, and now it was his turn. He pictured Anselm Brucker's worn leather Bible, the quiet empathy in the old man's eyes, and the unshakeable faith in the old man's heart.

"There's only one way to know for sure," Lachlan said, smiling into the demon's arrogant face.

Done with the talking and more than ready to meet whatever the gods had in store, he tossed a restraining spell at Drusus and lunged with his sword.

18

To Rachel, the trek back up the sloping rock tunnel seemed to take twice as long as the journey down. Under the weak beam of the flashlight, the close walls and low ceiling enhanced the feeling of being trapped. Plus, the sharp upward angle and uneven ground took a physical toll. In no time both she and Em were breathing hard and clutching each other with sweaty palms.

Every step away from the cavern was harder than the last, and Rachel's chest burned. Fear for Em drove her forward. But thinking about that was impossible, because if Drew was hot on her heels, that would mean Lachlan was . . .

She pushed on, ignoring the ache in her legs and the pounding in her head.

By the time they reached the barrier spell, her energy was sapped and she was grateful there was no sign of demons. The men looked battered but triumphant. She fell to her knees as she shoved Em through the icy purple glow and into Brian's waiting arms.

Risking the bitter cold of the barrier, Stefan reached in, grabbed Rachel, and dragged her clear.

"Where's Lachlan?" Brian asked, as he rubbed Em's bloodless arms to warm them up.

"He stayed behind," Rachel gasped, struggling to sit up.

"Drusus let you go?"

She nodded. "But it's not over. We need to get Em somewhere safe. Somewhere he can't find her."

Brian glanced at Stefan. "Is there such a place?"

The mage scratched his head, thoughtful. "I think so. But I have to warn you, it's hardly the Ritz Hotel."

"It'll do. Take the rest of the guys and get the women to safety as quickly as you can," Brian said. "I'll wait here."

The mage nodded.

"Magnus." Brian turned to a burly warrior with wavy blond hair that grew past his shoulders. "I'm trusting you to protect these ladies with your life. Don't let me down."

Then he turned to Rachel.

"Don't bother. I'm staying," she said, unequivocal.

"Rachel." Brian frowned at her. "Lachlan will kick my ass if I let anything happen to you. I admire your courage, but what good will staying do? This is a battle that can only be fought by immortals."

Rachel's breathing had slowed, but her heart still pounded. And it was her heart that refused to let her dismiss the truth.

Yes, what she had discovered down in the cavern hurt—hurt bad. But the pain of betrayal had ebbed away on the endless climb up the slope, leaving her with one undeniable certainty—she loved Lachlan MacGregor—despite all his damned secrets, despite all his damned lies. His motivations for entering that cavern at her side might have been mixed, but they were good ones. Selfless ones. If he'd truly let Drew into the manor that night, the real blame lay at the feet of an ancient lure demon. Drew's sly words didn't change the facts: Lachlan had put his existence on the line to save Em—and her. How could she fault him for trying to save his family, even if it meant choosing them over her?

"I can't leave him to face Drew alone."

"He won't be alone," Brian pointed out. "I'll be here."

"*Here* doesn't really help him, though, does it?" Rachel scrambled to her feet. "You can't pass through the barrier. I can."

Stefan stepped toward her, shaking his head. "What can you possibly hope to accomplish? You are an ordinary woman."

"I don't know. I just know I can't let him do it alone."

The Romany mage exchanged a pained look with Brian, then sighed. "All right, return to him if you must. But I can't let you go unarmed. Repeat after me, *Irst am dol marga volumchis.*"

She mouthed the awkward sounds twice, just to make sure she got them right. "What does that mean?"

"It's an augmentation spell. If you get within a hundred feet of MacGregor, close your eyes, picture a thick shield encasing his body, and say those words." He shrugged. "Can't hurt."

His eyes dropped to Rachel's small leather purse, which by force of habit still hung over her shoulder.

"Any spare change in there?"

She shook the purse and numerous coins rattled.

"Good," said the mage. "If you get really stuck, toss some coins in the air, say, *Figa gi bovismir*, and imagine them whipping toward Drusus."

"And here's a couple of extra crosses," Brian said, draping more silver chains around her neck. "I just wish I could cover you from head to toe."

She smiled at the two men, grateful. Then, unable to

prevent a brief mental jag into the future, she grabbed the young Gatherer's hand. "Go with them, Brian, please. Save my little girl."

His gaze met hers over the flashlight. For once his eyes were serious. "If it's in my power, I will. Good luck, Rachel."

She took a deep breath, hugged her purse to her chest like a life preserver, and dove back through the barrier spell in search of Lachlan.

Lachlan scored first blood.

The powerful shade spell coiled around Drusus, pinning his arms tight to his body, allowing Lachlan an unopposed swing. Although Drusus leaned away, the *claidheamh mòr* sliced across the demon's upper shoulder, just under the cap of his leather armor, and a spurt of red escaped the parted flesh. The shade magic proved even stronger than anticipated, and he scored a second cut on the demon's thigh before Drusus shook it off.

All in all, a very successful start to the battle.

But he had no time to crow.

Drusus whipped a series of blistering white fireballs at him, each of them hitting the same spot in his shield, deeply pitting the charm, almost breaking through. Reflecting nothing but cold determination, the demon ruthlessly closed in, the sinews of his forearms flexing with every bomb. Lachlan had to dance back on the uneven stone floor to avoid the fourth and potentially fatal blow. At the same time, he parried a smooth and very precise downward cut from the demon's sword, one intended to break his blade.

Fireballs weren't the only weapons at the demon's disposal.

No sooner had Lachlan repaired the gouge in his shield than the demon raised a flurry of dead bats from somewhere in the caves. They flew at Lachlan's shield, unable to penetrate it, but blinding him with the sheer volume of their fluttering, ghoulish wings. His shield took another heavy pounding of fire from Drusus, and sightless, Lachlan dove desperately to the right.

He struck the wood-framed divan with his shoulder and grunted as he rolled back to his feet. Grateful for the freedom his plaid provided and temporarily free of the phantom bats, he parried yet another of the demon's masterful blade strokes and flung a summons into the shadows.

The eerie howl that immediately rose into the air gave him gooseflesh.

The shadows stirred, and a grisly chill descended like heavy dew. Long, inky fingers reached out from every darkened crevice in the cavern. Screeching loudly, the bats swerved up and over his shoulder in a desperate attempt to flee. The bone sappers he'd summoned slithered over the walls in rapid pursuit, eager to dine upon their spirit forms.

The battle was once again between him and Drusus.

And the battle suddenly became treacherous as the demon called down an icy rain from the countless stalactites decorating the ceiling. If that wasn't enough, a sluggish river of mud poured into the cavern through every open hole, sucking at Lachlan's boot-clad feet, slowing his movements.

Drusus was unfazed by the perilous ooze. His muscles were honed by a millennium of wading through the swampy water of the River Styx, and he maintained an easy stance, swinging his sword without pause.

Lachlan racked his memory of the *Book of Gnills* for some spell that might rid the room of the numbing and ever-deepening mire, but came up with nothing.

Instead, he tossed a spell at the mud, transforming

globs of it into bolts of frozen muck, which he tossed at Drusus in rapid succession.

Each invocation of shade magic came at a price, however. One by one, as Lachlan countered each of the demon's fierce attacks with a new spell, items in the grotto disappeared. The divan, the iron pot, the cushions, the curtains—all vanished. But that was not nearly as worrisome as the way the air inside the cavern began to distort, shimmering like water cascading down a glass wall.

The cavern was quickly growing unstable and Lachlan knew he had little time left to produce a spell that would bring Drusus to his knees. Small individual spells like cripple or blind would have no effect because they couldn't pierce the demon's powerful shield charm. It had to be something big, something overwhelming.

But, damn it, *what?*

The walls of the tunnel shuddered again and Rachel cringed, lifting her arms defensively over her head. Fragments of rock and plumes of dust rained down on her, stinging her skin and littering the path before her. By her best calculations, she had almost reached the cavern, but with every additional tremble of the earth, she fought a savage claw of fear. Her throat was so tight, it threatened to cut off her air supply.

Alone in the dark, she found it hard not to imagine the worst: dying in the tunnel, buried under a crush of rock, never having reached Lachlan. But it was that very same fear that impelled her forward: No way was she going to die without seeing Lachlan again.

The earthquake subsided. Rachel pulled in a thin, rattling breath and continued her journey.

She picked her way carefully down the tunnel, guiding her advance with a hand on the rock wall. Seeing

Lachlan again also meant seeing Drew again, a very uneasy thought. Two spells and a bunch of crosses would not hold a two-thousand-year-old demon off for long, and if she truly wanted to help Lachlan, she had to survive more than a minute.

How?

Brian's last words popped into her head. *I wish I could cover you from head to toe.* In crosses.

She halted, her pulse skittering.

He had smiled ruefully when he said it, assuming it was impossible, but was it? No. She dug into her purse and pulled out a handful of black markers. Not unless the crosses had to be silver.

Yanking the lid off one marker with her teeth, she bent and drew an outline of a simple cross on her white sneaker. Then she swiftly moved up the leg of her jeans, adding more crosses and smiling. This was one time when her talent for drawing fast would work to her advantage.

She had to peel off her blouse to cover the entire thing, front to back, and a ripple of worry ran through her when she realized the black ink was barely discernible against the purple cloth. Would they still work?

A sigh left her lips.

Only time would tell.

Her elbow scraped against the rock face as she buttoned her shirt, making her wince. In this one spot, for about ten feet, the walls were smooth and dry, worn flat by subterranean water that no longer trickled down its surface. The ceiling was close, no more than a foot and a half above her head, and the tight confines bred a strong sense of being trapped.

That's when the idea struck her.

A trap.

*   *   *

Lachlan sucked in a sharp breath and leapt back to avoid a wicked, two-handed slice that slipped through his battered shield charm. He needed something big, something shocking, something unexpected.

Something like ... shattered lightning.

The rough wall of the cavern loomed at his back, and Drusus continued to press at him, his muscular legs churning through the mud, his lean face tight with single-minded resolve.

Lightning was a dangerous choice.

Once the electrical charge fragmented, he'd have no control over the direction of the flying shards. The bombardment of fireballs and hacking sword blows had thinned his shield alarmingly in spots, and if a concentrated jolt of energy hit precisely the right spot ... the battle would be over.

But if several splinters struck Drusus at once and weakened the lure demon's defenses, and if Lachlan could take advantage of the short moment before the demon renewed his power by calling on Satan, he had a better-than-average chance at thrusting his *claidheamh mòr* right through the bastard's heart.

A lot of ifs.

But, honestly, he was out of options.

The river of mud was the only transmutable object left in the cavern, save the walls themselves, so he used it. Leveraging his core energy, he reached out, tapping into the physical fabric of the mud, seeing, feeling, and sensing the whole of the slippery goop. Every molecule of water and every grain of sand became familiar, became malleable, became *his*.

Flexing his heavy thighs to improve his stance, he gathered all of the raw energy seething inside the ooze, absorbed it into his body, and then drove it through his feet, into the ground.

The guttural words of the lightning spell rolled off his tongue, and instantly every hair on his body stood on end. Sparks of brilliant blue light licked over his body and snapped out toward the cavern walls, each fine strand bouncing and colliding with the others until a thick beam of white energy formed.

Then it exploded.

And at the height of the spectacular light show, Lachlan sprang toward Drusus, his shoulders bunched to deliver one last powerful swing of his mighty sword.

He got his moment.

But only through a miracle.

Five shards of shattered lightning struck Drusus simultaneously, causing his feet to stagger and his knees to buckle. His sword arm faltered, and Lachlan leapt for the kill, already seeing the coup de grâce in his mind—a fierce and decisive slash to the base of the demon's neck. But in midair he, too, was struck by a shard, one that ricocheted off the stone wall and shocked his shield with an eyebrow-singeing blast.

The bolt should have pierced his shield and knocked him off balance, but at the very moment his protection spell was about to collapse, it gained a vital, lifesaving boost from somewhere outside the grotto.

Lachlan completed his swing, and his blade dug deep into the flesh of the demon's neck, spraying blood in all directions. The *claidheamh mòr* glowed green and a fissure of power raced up Lachlan's arm, adding to the triumphant throb of his heart.

Success.

He snatched the reliquary from the demon's neck, breaking the heavy gold chain with a single sharp tug and a deep, triumphant roar that reverberated off the cavern walls.

Then he pulled his sword free of the demon's neck

and stared into a pair of shocked green eyes. "Die, you filthy bastard." His final thrust went straight toward the demon's heart.

But it never reached the target.

Even as blood spilled over the demon's lips and dripped onto his leather armor, Drusus batted away the sword and rose to his feet, the light returning to his eyes.

"Too little, too late," he snarled. Red droplets spattered on the floor, flung with each caustic word. "And I believe that's all you've got, MacGregor."

Before Lachlan's eyes, the horrific wound on the demon's neck began to mend, blood retreating, flesh merging, skin weaving together. The moment of opportunity had passed, and Drusus had pulled from the boundless supply of energy available to him in hell.

But there was one last ace up Lachlan's sleeve. The cavern was already unstable and the shattered lightning had created a substantial tear in the planar barriers. A focused spell could expand that rip and collapse the entire cave. Nothing would survive the destruction—not he, not Drusus . . . and not the souls of his family. But wasn't that preferable to letting Drusus win?

"Lachlan!"

He stiffened at the sound of Rachel's voice.

God, no.

Lachlan's heart dropped into his boots.

A perverse smile twisted the lure demon's thin lips. Menace radiated off him in furnace-hot waves, and the need to punish both Lachlan and Rachel with all the vitriolic horrors of hell shone with lethal promise in the miserable wretch's eyes.

This was not going to be good. Without waiting for his pulse to restart, Lachlan spun on his heel and raced for the mouth of the grotto.

*   *   *

As Lachlan turned and ran toward her, Rachel tossed a handful of coins in the air, murmured the second spell, and visualized the bullets of metal barreling toward Drew. Having seen the demon recover from the brutal damage of Lachlan's sword, she didn't have a hope that a few pieces of metal would stop him, but she prayed the distraction would give Lachlan the chance to reach her.

And it did.

Drew blocked the coins instead of shooting a fireball at Lachlan. Lachlan dove through the entrance to the tunnel with milliseconds to spare. The instant his warm fingers touched hers, her heart settled and her fear became manageable.

He barely paused as he tore up the slope, using his immense power to lift her clear off the floor and haul her against his side. Her flashlight and purse went flying, and the silver crosses cut into her skin, but she didn't complain. This was life or death. As the muscles in his body flexed and strained with every leap through the darkened stretch, she tried to compare the length of his stride to her tentative steps on the descent.

When she was fairly sure they'd reached the right spot, she dug her fingernails into his shoulder and shouted, "Stop!"

To her amazement, he did so without querying her decision. Instead, he twisted abruptly, tucked her behind his back, and faced the demon . . . who stood a mere three feet away.

"Running away, MacGregor? Surely not."

"Let her leave. This is between you and me."

Peering around the broad expanse of Lachlan's naked back, Rachel spotted the red glow of Drew's eyes and shivered.

"The time for generosity has passed," the demon

growled. There was nothing suave or smooth about him now. His skin was dark and mottled, and an odor of hot charcoal accompanied his words. "I let her go once. Not again. If she desires to spend her last moments in your company, so be it."

Lachlan's heart beat steadily beneath her hand, showing no sign of the terror shuddering through Rachel. With numb fingers, she pried his hand off her hip and guided it to the tunnel wall, pressing it against the outline of the cross she prayed was drawn there.

His fingers stilled, then slid along the wall of their own accord, tracing one cross, then two.

"It's no' her last moments we're discussing, Drusus; it's yours," he said. His warm hand squeezed hers. Then he placed the reliquary in her hands and pushed at her gently. "Back up a few feet, Rachel. Give me some space."

The demon's chuckle echoed harshly in the tight confines.

"I have to admire your bravado, I must say."

"Cease your idle chatter, hellbrat," Lachlan goaded. "Take up your sword and test my resolve."

"As you wish."

With his words, a furious gust of hot air tore through the tunnel, accompanied by a bone-rattling shriek that curdled Rachel's blood. Not quite human and not quite animal, it brought to mind some ancient evil crawling up from the bowels of the earth.

The swords of the two men collided in a brilliant flash of light, and Rachel closed her eyes.

Then, suddenly, there was silence—and fresh air.

She opened her eyes.

They no longer stood in the dark tunnel but high upon a stone wall that encircled a slate-roofed house, rolling hills, and verdant forests stretching out to the horizon in all directions. The sun beamed through the patchwork of a mostly cloudy sky, and the wind that tugged at their clothing was cool and damp. It was a hauntingly beautiful setting that begged to be captured on canvas.

Lachlan and Drew stared at each other, frowning. Both men had abruptly acquired shoulder-length hair and they looked strangely ... normal. Nothing glowed, and their lean, rippling muscles had turned a healthy pink color in the brisk breeze.

"Where are we?" she asked.

Lachlan's gaze dropped to the damp gray parapet beneath his feet. "MacGregor Manor."

Drew bent and picked up a loose stone, turning it over in his hand. "No, this rampart is too solid. Your ancestral manor has long been a moss-covered ruin."

"Don't be so two-dimensional." Lachlan's face twisted. "The condition of the wall would depend on *when* we were."

"When?" Rachel squeaked. "What do you mean, *when*?"

Lachlan stared at a large, dark stain on the stones for a long moment, then out at the lush green hills. A wistful look swept over his features, and then disappeared. "May 17, 1603."

"We're in 1603? How is that possible?"

"Obviously, he knows something we don't," Drew replied. His gaze returned to Lachlan's face. "What did you do, MacGregor?"

Lachlan stood tall and broad, his chest bare, his kilt hanging past his knees, his long sword steady in his hands. He was every bit the primitive Scottish warrior. Although her stomach was unsettled by the concept of jumping through time, the sight of him in his natural environment stirred her pulse like never before.

"I called upon the grace of God and prayed for a fair fight," he said quietly.

"The grace of God? You are no angel, *baro*, far from it. Why would he help you?"

"Because I asked him."

Drew snorted. "Why here, why now?"

"I should think that was apparent. This is the day the Campbells snuck in through the water gate at your urging, the day my wife and bairns were slain. This is the day you ran a sword through my brother's belly, intending to snatch the Linen from his lifeless hands. This is the day our miserable destinies became entwined. It seemed only just that they part here."

"And how do you intend to make that happen?"

"God has granted me the opportunity to meet you in battle as a mere mortal, Drusus. At this moment you are no' a demon, and I am no' a Gatherer. We are simply men."

A trickle of unease ran down Rachel's spine.

Mortal meant killable. That was good, wasn't it? Except for the part where Lachlan no longer healed with supernatural speed? She glanced down, her heart sinking as she realized her purse had not traveled with her. Not the best time to be without a Band-Aid.

Drew tossed Lachlan a grin. "Mortal or not, I'll still cut the heart from your chest, you heathen Scot, and fuck your woman atop your corpse. You're forgetting that before I died, I was the most feared centurion in the Roman army. Songs were sung about my victories. I cut a swath through my enemies, rejoicing in the spilling of their blood."

"You're forgetting that you died at the tender age of twenty-two," Lachlan pointed out softly. "You were no' as vigorous and hardy as you like to believe. You were defeated, if I'm not mistaken, by a mere politician, the infamous Pontius Pilate."

The grin fell away, replaced by a fury that burned

like a molten river in Drew's eyes. "That gutless fool. I warned him that sacrificing the Jew would make him a martyr, but did he heed my counsel? No. When he washed his hands of Jesus, he also washed his hands of me and my advice. Many blame the Sanhedrin for all that followed, but I do not. I know the truth. Pilate was a coward, a man ill deserving of his powerful position. I reported his poor judgment to the Roman Senate, and he, woman that he was, had me killed for it. But not on the battlefield. With poison."

"Then, you're in luck, hellget. This is your chance to die like a warrior. With a blade through your heart and a roar in your throat, instead of choking on your own puke."

Rachel grimaced. Men had such a brutal way with words.

And brutal was the only way to describe the event about to unfold. This fight would not be some pretty, well-choreographed dance across the movie screen, complete with politely regulated taps of blunted swords. Both men would be cut; both men would bleed. One man would fall to his knees, never to rise again.

"Lachlan."

He glanced at her.

"I love you."

Drew chuckled. "She's saying good-bye, MacGregor. She knows full well what the outcome of this battle will be."

"No." She glared at the younger man, her fists balled with anger. "He's going to win." Then her gaze, honest and open, returned to Lachlan, offering him everything in her heart. "But I don't know what'll happen when you do ... where we'll end up, or if I'll ever see you again. After everything that's happened ... I needed you to know how I feel."

He didn't make light of her fear. Serious and unsmiling, he rubbed a calloused thumb over her bottom lip and studied her face as if he were memorizing it. "Thank y—"

A shadow slid over his arm, and Lachlan abruptly shoved Rachel backward. Pivoting, he raised his sword to parry Drew's sneak attack.

Rachel stumbled back against the battlements, narrowly avoiding a painful fall. She hugged a crenellation, trying to stay small and out of the way.

Drew took advantage of Lachlan's imperfect balance and swung low, aiming for the exposed length of his calf. She cried out a sharp warning, but even before her cry rose into the air, Lachlan read Drew's intent and sprang adroitly to the left. He recovered his steady stance and aimed a powerful, two-handed slice at Drew's shoulder, which the Roman soldier easily parried.

The battle resumed as if it had never paused.

This time it was without magic, without firebombs, without misty swirls or brilliant lights.

Both men drew purely on their physical reserves. They grunted with their efforts and dripped sweat from their brows. Both men fought for their footing on the dew-laden walkway and stumbled over the occasional stone. Both men landed spark-inducing blows on each other's swords, and both men scored thin slices on legs and arms.

As blood began to mingle with the sweat running down Lachlan's body, the acrid taste of bile rose to Rachel's tongue. She had to force herself to keep watching.

The two men appeared evenly matched. While Lachlan stood taller and his sword sang through the air with an audible testament to his power, Drew had youth on his side and dodged several potentially fatal blows with

an agile leap. Lachlan's five-foot sword gave him the
longer reach, but Drew's leather armor stole away the
benefit.

Rachel had neither the talent nor the desire to interfere in the sword fight, but that didn't stop her stomach
from knotting with frustration at her helplessness. In
her world, in her time, where battles were fought with
dollars and job titles, she had options. Here, she could
only bite her lip and pray for Lachlan's safety. It hardly
seemed enough.

Nor did it help.

Under a bevy of aggressive blows from Drew, Lachlan retreated a step. But as his foot slid back, his boot
dipped into a rut, twisting his ankle. His arm jerked up
in an effort to right his balance, and Drew dove for the
opening with the speed and rapacious intent of a bird
of prey. Ducking under Lachlan's reach, he thrust his
sword with both hands. Despite a last-minute swivel of
his body, Lachlan failed to avoid the sharp edge of the
demon's sword.

Crimson blood spurted from his split flesh, pouring
down his side and soaking the belted waist of his kilt.

But Lachlan took it in stride, literally. A fierce growl
sounded deep in his throat and he leaned into Drew's
thrust, allowing the blade to slice cleanly across his ribs.
With their faces inches apart, he butted his forehead
against the Roman soldier's skull with a loud crack, then
pushed Drew away and spun to the right.

For the briefest of instants, rattled by the blow, Drew's
eyes clouded with confusion.

Lachlan showed no mercy. His shoulders and biceps
bunched as he gathered his strength and delivered a
strike of bone-shattering weight, right to the base of
Drew's neck. There was a loud crunch of resistance,
but the sword continued its straight swing with only

the slightest reduction in speed. For a moment Rachel wasn't sure anything had happened.

Then Drew's head tumbled to the dirt.

The solid thunk of it hitting the ground barely registered. Globs of something wet had flown off the tip of Lachlan's sword and spattered on her face. When Drew's body crumpled, her legs threatened to do the same. As she put a hand to her face and stared at the bright red chunk on her fingertips, a violent shudder ran through her.

"Oh God."

"Rachel?"

She lifted her gaze, dizzy with the realization that it was a strip of bloody flesh—Drew's bloody flesh. There was blood coursing down Lachlan's side from a wound that was deep enough to require stitches—a hundred probably, to stop all that blood. *Oh God. So much blood.*

Tossing aside his sword, he leapt toward her, concern in his eyes. "Put your head between your legs, Rachel."

But before he could reach her, before she had time to even consider bending over, there was a blinding flash of light. She closed her eyes to the glare and fell headlong into the abyss.

19

Lachlan caught Rachel before she hit the ground, grabbing her around the waist and hauling her against his sweat-dampened and gore-spattered chest. Heart still racing with his victory, and thrilled beyond belief to be able to touch her again, he held her tight and sure until he felt the dainty flutter of her eyelashes against his throat.

"It's okay," he said gently, ignoring the blood coursing down his side. "I've got you."

She drew in a deep breath. "Lachlan?"

"None other."

"Where are we?"

"In the tunnel, under the crosses you drew on the walls." As he held her, a vehement rumble shook the ground and bits of crumbling stone dropped on them from above. "We won. The bastard is dead. His body is over there on the floor."

She shivered.

"Sorry," he said. "Guess I shouldn't have mentioned that."

"We're in the tunnel? Did I just imagine that part where we traveled to Scotland?"

"No, you didn't imagine it," he said dryly.

Another quake shook the ground beneath their feet,

and she peered over his shoulder into the darkness. "Maybe we should get out of here. It feels like the tunnel is about to cave in."

"Good call," he said, lowering her until her feet were back on the ground. "The magic I used against Drusus caused some instability. This section of the plane is attempting to fold in on itself and there's no telling how much longer it will hold. Let's go find Emily."

"How? She's with Brian and Stefan, but I don't know where. They said they were going to take her somewhere safe, somewhere Drew wouldn't be able to find her."

"They gave you no clues?"

"Stefan just mentioned it wasn't the Ritz."

"Ah." A castle in the fifteenth century would certainly fit that description. Without letting go of her hand, he bent and retrieved his sword. Then he scrambled up the incline toward the cave mouth, tugging her along. "I know where they are."

Another furious tremble rocked the tunnel. Rachel stumbled and fell to her knees, gasping sharply. Breathing in a mouthful of dirt-clouded air, he lifted her into his arms and quickened their pace.

"You can't carry me," she complained. "You've got that terrible cut on your side."

"Back in the tunnel means back to normal." He quashed a sharp sense of regret as the ramifications of that sunk in. For an instant he'd simply been a mortal man in love with a mortal woman. His heart had beaten with the bittersweet vitality born of limited time and endless opportunity. But that had been a hiccup in time. "I'm healing already."

She didn't argue any further.

Not until they exited the tunnel into the cool night air and he began jogging down the mountain to where they'd parked the car, still holding her tight in his arms.

"We're out of the cave, and Em is safe with Brian. Can we stop and look at that cut now?"

"No." Not exactly sure how else to say it, he went with being blunt. "The mark on her cheek means Emily will never be safe again, Rachel. She'll need to be protected twenty-four-seven for the rest of her life."

"But"—she glanced at him in the moonlight, frowning—"you tried to do that for your brother and it didn't work."

"I was alone then; I'm no' now. Brian and the others can help."

"Can we really do it? Keep her safe forever?"

Lachlan was glad she couldn't see his face too well in the dimness. "I don't know," he said honestly. "But I'm around for ninety-one more years, and Brian, assuming he doesn't get himself into trouble, will be around much longer. It's possible. Don't give up hope."

"Okay."

She kissed him softly on the mouth, then wrapped her arms around his neck and laid her head on his shoulder, proof positive that her faith in him remained intact.

Faith he wasn't sure was justified.

Rachel stared at the mobile home with raw dismay. A good strong wind could blow the damned thing over. "This is the safest place on Earth for Em?"

"It'll surprise you," Lachlan assured her with a smile.

He parked the car and hustled her up the crushed-stone path to the door. When no one answered his knock, he flung open the door and entered.

The lights were off, the room empty. The kitchen sparkled with pristine countertops and the living room stood in uncluttered glory, the only visible sign of ownership a folded, hand-knit throw over the back of the leather sofa. Lachlan had eyes only for the floor-to-ceiling purple curtain hanging on the back wall. Crossing the room in three easy strides, he swept back the heavy velvet drapery.

And revealed a mildew-darkened, gray stone wall.

"Damn."

"What's wrong?" she asked, trailing him through the home. A cool, crystalline scent hung in the air, but she couldn't identify it.

"We need to get to the other side," he said ruefully, "but with no door . . ."

"Welcome to my world," said a crisp, female voice. "Forever stuck on the other side of where I want to be."

Rachel spun around.

The most beautiful white-haired woman she'd ever seen stood on the beige carpet not ten feet behind her, where only moments before there'd been no one. At least, she was pretty sure there hadn't been anyone leaning on that leather chair. But then again, the room was dim and the woman was dressed all in black, so maybe—

"Forever unwelcome," Lachlan added quietly. "The rejection must break your heart."

"Indeed." The woman laughed. "If I had a heart, it would surely splinter at being so sorely abused."

Lachlan didn't respond. He merely held out his hand to Rachel, inviting her to slip closer to him. She didn't argue.

Narrowing her eyes at his protective gesture, the white-haired woman said, "I'm most displeased with you, Gatherer."

"Why? Did I no' do everything you asked of me?"

"You embroiled a number of my other Gatherers in this affair—against my express wishes."

Rachel swallowed a thick lump of realization. *My*

Gatherers? This woman was Death? For some reason, she'd assumed a goddess who stole life from others would be older and . . . uglier.

"I merely protected the girl, as you demanded."

Death wrinkled her nose. "Well, it's of no consequence now. The job is done. Open the wall."

"I can't."

"Can't? Or won't?" The goddess stepped forward, a vision of lethal beauty in her inky black pantsuit and high-heeled pumps. She put a pale hand on the damp wall, the extra long fingernail of her right index finger tapping the stones. "A time barrier. The work of your sniveling little mage, I'd wager."

Again Lachlan said nothing. His breathing remained even, the strength of his chest solid and warm against Rachel's back, his arms a comforting wrap.

"The spell is easy enough to surmount," Death said. "Just tell me when and where he is, and I can break through."

"No."

She shot him a tight-faced look. Her blue eyes glittered like shards of glass. "Did you just refuse a direct order from your liege?"

"Aye."

"Then you must have temporarily lost your wits. Your soul is mine, MacGregor. I decide how long you serve me. How is eternal purgatory sounding?"

"Just fine. I'll be able to protect the girl until she dies a natural death at a ripe old age."

"Natural death?" A sneer lifted one side of the goddess's scarlet mouth. "A sweet sentiment, but sadly misguided. There is no natural death. All humans die, true enough, but the time and place and means are at my whim."

Rachel glared at Death. "If you have the ability to

choose when and where, then you can also choose to walk away. Leave my daughter alone."

Arching her thin brows, Death lifted her gaze to Lachlan. "Did you not explain to her what was at stake, MacGregor?"

He was incredibly still, and icy dread curled in Rachel's belly. Not another lie.

Death's gaze slid back to Rachel's face. "Did he tell you your daughter was the Trinity Soul?"

She nodded.

"Did he also tell you that if I consume the Trinity Soul, I acquire all of her power? And that with her power I will ascend to the status of a full deity and rule the middle plane with the same powers as God and Satan?"

"No." The word came out as a gasp. Consume? Death wanted to *eat* Em's soul? How gruesome was that?

"So you see, your daughter's death is my destiny. It may take me some time to break through this barrier, but be assured that I will."

Rachel's heart pounded.

"Romany magic is no match for primal energy," continued the goddess. "My triumph is inevitable."

"No' necessarily. Should you succeed in tearing down the wall, you'll still face the Gatherers committed to protecting her."

Lachlan's rumbled threat only made the goddess smile.

"You think they'll take up arms against me? Please. You're about to discover the other Gatherers aren't quite as noble as you, MacGregor. The threat of eternal servitude will cow them in an instant and win me back their loyalty. If it doesn't, I'll simply take their souls from my chest and offer them to Satan."

Crisp confidence hung from every word, leaving no room for doubt. Death would deliver on her promise.

Em would die—today. Rachel turned in Lachlan's arms and buried her face against his neck, breathing in his reassuring scent.

Maybe she should be angry he'd held back this part of the story, but she couldn't summon one ounce of bitterness. As far as she could see, the only reason for not confessing Em was going to die was to leave her with some hope, and how could she hate him for that?

His arms tightened around her.

"I'm sorry," he whispered in her ear, so gently the words were almost a caress.

"I know."

Death folded her arms over her chest. "Why not just tell me the year, MacGregor? You know you can't protect the girl."

"No." It wasn't Lachlan who answered, but Rachel. She spun around to face the goddess. "If you think we're just going to roll over and give her up, think again. If you're so freakin' determined to kill her, then work for it. We sure as hell aren't going to make it easy."

"By the gods, you *reek* of passion." Death's eyes widened. "Of course. It all makes sense now. All the while I thought it was the danger to his fellow Gatherers that sparked the fire in MacGregor's belly. But it was you. A warm, weak, needy woman."

"Go fuck yourself."

Death lifted her long white fingernail. "There's a real risk to annoying me, Rachel Lewis. Test me at your peril."

Lachlan's body suddenly radiated a dangerous, pulsing energy. He stood taller, firmer. "Careful, my liege. I've read the ancient tomes."

"You threaten me?" Death asked, amazed.

"You are no' invincible."

"Nor are you."

"But I *am* uniquely capable. My vow to protect the Linen gave me an unusual ability to tap into the power of faith. Combined with my natural talents as a warrior—which priest Protectors do not possess—it made me a Gatherer candidate unlike any other. You knew that the day you exchanged my life for my brother's. It's why you agreed to the trade. I didn't know the truth then, but I know it now. If anyone can defeat you, it is I."

The cant of her shoulders slipped a little, but her voice remained hard as ice. "Even should you strike a lucky blow, do you know the price of slaying me?"

He nodded. "If I kill you, I assume your role."

"And is that what you want? To be forever tasked with ending lives?"

"No," he admitted. "The notion turns my stomach. But I will gladly do it if you attempt to harm Rachel. Make no mistake."

She shrugged. "Truthfully, I do not care about your woman."

"My protection extends to Emily."

"Now that"—Death smiled coldly and with a wave of her hand conjured a dozen soldiers to her side, twelve skin-and-bone warriors with cloudy white eyes and sharp, shiny swords—"is a mistake. I think you underestimate my powers, Gatherer."

Lachlan gently pushed Rachel behind him and brandished his sword. "I think you underestimate mine."

A bright blue spark arced through the mobile home, crackling loudly, grounding itself in the television set. Another quickly followed, this time zapping the stainless steel refrigerator. Rachel peered around Lachlan's broad shoulders, wondering if he'd performed some sort of spell.

The tang of lemons filled the air, and her ears popped. An elderly man in a brown tweed suit and yellow vest suddenly appeared in the middle of the room, blinking with confusion.

"By the saints." Lachlan shuddered.

"Damn." Death stepped back, waving her ghouls behind her.

Rachel's gaze darted between Death and the newcomer as she tried to make sense of what was happening and tried not to panic at the thought of a man materializing out of thin air, from God knew where.

The elderly man smiled at Lachlan. "Ah, there you are."

Lachlan sighed, a huge, hollow sound of disgust. "I have no soul for you to collect, old man. You've made an error."

Death snorted.

The tweed-clad man favored her with a long, steady look, one brow lifted. "How very disappointing."

Her gaze dropped to the carpet, a flush rising on her pallid cheeks. "I'm not certain what you mean, Michael."

Rachel felt Lachlan stiffen.

"He put his faith in you, and you betrayed him."

Death's gaze lifted. "It was not betrayal. I merely wished to asc—"

The elderly man shook his head. "Do not attempt to minimize your actions. He's not the fool you take him to be. You will face his judgment and be duly punished."

"But—"

He raised his hand to halt her explanation, and she closed her mouth, reluctantly submissive. Then he turned back to Rachel and Lachlan.

"A fine muddle, this."

Lachlan fell to his knees. "My sincere apologies, Your Glory. My rudeness was unforgivable, but I had no idea—"

Stunned by the extremely reverent and apologetic

tone in his voice, Rachel stared at his bowed head. *What the f—*

"There's naught to forgive, my boy," the tweed-clad man said. "I play the part of a dotard to great success, do I not? Get up."

As Lachlan rose to his feet, his hand clutching hers, he whispered hoarsely in Rachel's ear, "God's most holy messenger, the Archangel Michael."

She blinked, then studied the peppered hair of the man standing before her. Had she heard that right? Did Lachlan just say this old geezer was an archangel? Weren't archangels supposed to be the most beautiful of all the angels?

The elder looked at her, his rheumy eyes twinkling. "Not quite what you expected, eh?" He patted his bright yellow vest. "All just an illusion, I'm afraid. But I rather enjoy this persona. He has a bumbling charm I don't actually possess."

The amusement faded.

In a flash, the short, plump old man was gone, replaced by a tall man with long, golden blond hair, who somehow managed to pull off a plain white suit with elegance to spare. His eyes, the deep blue of lapis lazuli, contrasted with the light tan of his face, giving him an air of unrelenting intensity—almost a glow.

"Step forward, Lachlan MacGregor."

Lachlan tried to shake Rachel's hand loose as he stepped toward the angel, but she wouldn't let him.

Michael frowned at her refusal to be parted from him, but otherwise ignored her. "I so enjoy being right. Since becoming a Gatherer, you've consistently made difficult but righteous choices. In the cavern you had the opportunity to use void magic to defeat Drusus, an opportunity many men would have found difficult to resist. You chose not to. Instead, you relied on your own skills and courageous heart." He paused. "The man you once were would not have made that same decision. You've proven yourself an honorable soul."

"Thank you, Your Glory."

The mightiest of God's angels held out his hand to Rachel. "The reliquary, if you will."

She handed him the tube.

Michael snapped the glass in half and a rush of white light left the vial, swirled around him several times, and disappeared into the air above his head. The reliquary fragments vanished.

"Your family now resides in the upper plane," he told Lachlan. "You've done them proud."

Lachlan's hand tightened around hers, a slight tremble in his fingers, and she squeezed him in return.

"Now," said Michael, "we have a mess to clean up."

He raised both hands and the gray stone wall disappeared. The occupants of the room spun around almost as a unit, staring past Michael to Death and her minions, horror on their faces.

But Death remained in her spot by the window, unmoving.

"Emily, approach me."

Rachel opened her mouth to prompt her daughter, but as it turned out, the urging was unnecessary. Although still pale and withdrawn, Em answered the summons, rounding a huge oak table and shuffling forward.

Michael made the sign of the cross on Em's forehead, and her eyes cleared and brightened, the last hints of enthrallment fading away. Her head tilted as she studied the tall man.

"Cool," she said simply.

He took her chin in his hand and examined her right cheek. Out of nowhere, a white spiral, thin and cruel, appeared on her daughter's pale skin.

"The mark of Death, how unfortunate." He glanced at Rachel. "It's a primal spell, dating back to the very beginning of time. I'm afraid even God does not possess the power to remove it."

Whatever hope remained in Rachel's heart turned to dust.

"However," he added, sighing heavily, "there is one thing he can do. He's reluctant, of course, because the solution has its own drawbacks, but there's little choice."

Rachel's heart began to beat again.

She crossed her fingers behind her back.

"By the power vested in me by Our Most Holy God"—Michael placed a lean finger upon Em's cheek, and almost immediately, the skin beneath began to glow a soft blue, like a robin's egg—"I bless you with the mark of Life."

Atop the pearly white spiral that Death had placed, another symbol took shape, the outline of an oak tree. When he dropped his hand, both symbols remained, blended together as if they were one.

"Are you mad?" Death surged forward to study Em's cheek. "Neither can be removed. One will forever balance the other."

He eyed her narrowly. "Indeed."

Death fisted her hands at her side, glaring at Michael. "Why? Why create a monster simply to tame my efforts to ascend? What sort of foolishness is that?"

"A monster?" Rachel stiffened. "What does she mean?"

Michael turned to her, his mouth opening to speak.

But Death snarled a response first.

"She can *never* die, that's what it means. She's doomed to walk the middle plane for eternity. And before you get excited, ask any of the Gatherers how they feel about that notion. It's not a gift; it's a punishment."

"Why?" wailed Rachel, suddenly overwhelmed by her daughter's bleak future. She spun to face the archangel. "She doesn't deserve this. Damn it. Why did he have to pick Em in the first place? Why the hell didn't he pick someone else?"

Michael's vivid gaze found hers. "He didn't pick her, Rachel. He chose you."

The blood left Rachel's head in a rush. *"Me?"*

He nodded. "Do you remember visiting the Louvre when you were in Paris? Sitting in front of the da Vinci painting *Virgin of the Rocks* for hours, studying the details?"

"Yes." As vividly as if it had happened yesterday. Those had been the last carefree hours she'd enjoyed before the phone call that changed her life.

"Da Vinci had a gift, rarely found. You were the only artist in a very long time who, like he, truly saw the connection between the elements—who knew the painting required the sharp contrast between the drab rocks, the beautiful Madonna, and the intricacies of the vegetation to fully come together. You were the only one who completely understood the balance between light and dark, and grasped the higher-level interdependency of it all. To unite the three planes, the Trinity Soul would require that same unique insight, so God chose you as her mother."

Rachel frowned. "Does that also mean he chose Grant?"

"For his intelligence, yes."

"So, basically, he put me through hell on purpose."

Michael tossed her a disapproving look. "He required the Trinity Soul to possess specific qualities. She has them."

"And she gets to keep them forever, apparently."

"It's not as bad as Death makes out," the angel

said, his expression calm, his eyes steady. "Emily is not trapped here. As the Trinity Soul, she can visit all three planes at will. Even God and Satan cannot do that. They are limited to their own plane and the middle."

"Still." Rachel glanced at Em, who didn't seem at all concerned by Death's pronouncement of her fate. "She's stuck forever as a fourteen-year-old, condemned to never grow up, never get married, and never have a child."

Michael shook his head. "She can age, if she desires. She can wed and have children, if she desires."

"Yes, but her husband and children will die before her," Death tossed in spitefully. "Ask MacGregor how good that feels."

"Now, now," Michael admonished, smiling at Em. "Even that is not as dreadful as it sounds. She will be able to visit them on whatever plane they reside. All worthy souls, of course, end up on the upper plane with him."

"Except the ones Satan steals because the angels are bloody well late." That gruff comment came from the group of Gatherers, but it wasn't clear which one.

Michael took no offense.

"We've been a trifle busy the past few months, patching up rifts in the planes and returning out-of-place creatures to their proper dimension. But with Emily finally gaining a measure of control over her new skills, the angels will have more time to meet with the Gatherers." The archangel turned his head. "Which leaves only one remaining item. What to do with you, Lachlan MacGregor."

"According to his indenture contract," Death said, "he still has ninety-one years in my service. Why do anything?"

"He's earned his soul back," Michael replied.

"But that's not—"

He raised a hand, and Death vanished.

After an instant of stunned silence, the Gatherers burst into applause.

"Be very careful, lads," Michael said, his gaze level. "I only sent her home to Antarctica. When all this is over, you'll report to her as usual, and it might not be wise to test her."

The applause died, but the grins remained.

"Now, Lachlan."

Rachel slid deeper into Lachlan's embrace, wrapping her arms around his waist. Earning his soul back sounded like a good thing, but she was suddenly afraid of what that might involve.

"God's given great thought to your future," Michael said slowly. "You would make an excellent archangel, and all of heaven knows we need more good people."

Rachel squeezed Lachlan tight and closed her eyes.

"But one sticky issue still remains."

Her eyes popped open.

"You have never recanted your decision to take your own life."

"No," Lachlan agreed.

"You know full well his stand on this matter: Life is very precious. A gift that is never to be taken lightly and never to be discarded willfully. Had you leapt in front of your brother to prevent a sword from piercing him, that would be one thing. Very selfless, no direct intention to die. Stabbing yourself on purpose is quite another."

"Aye."

"Knowing what you know now, understanding the full consequences of your actions, would you choose a different course of action?"

Lachlan was silent for a moment. Then he sighed and said, "No."

"We're disappointed in your response," Michael said, shaking his head. "You leave him with no choice. Since you've earned your soul back, he must force you to live a second life and insist that you spend those years proving how much you value the gift. Only if you live that life with the honor and dignity it deserves will he grant you a place in the upper plane."

Rachel's breath caught. A second life?

"Do I start anew, as a bairn?" Lachlan asked slowly.

"That's one option." Michael peered down the length of his nose, thoughtful. "Or he could leave you right where you are and let you make your way from here."

Lachlan's heart thudded heavily against Rachel's cheek.

"Do I get a choice?"

Michael smiled crookedly. "I'm afraid not. His decision."

The room was silent again, expectant.

"God has summoned the Trinity Soul now for good reason—to combat a rising tide of evil. Belief in God has fallen to an all-time low among the humans and, as sin spreads, more corrupted souls are entering hell than ever before. Each one adds fuel to Satan's fire, and their concentrated power is such that each one doubles his strength. But that alone would not have been cause to raise the Trinity Soul. Satan's interest in the Pontius Pilate Linen suggests these recent gains in power have incited him to consider the unthinkable. We believe he plots to overthrow God."

Rachel frowned. That really didn't sound good.

"To actively seek out and destroy the threat, we must be properly prepared," the archangel continued. "Emily will need considerable guidance in her role as the Trinity Soul, and he can think of no one better suited to take her in hand than you, Lachlan MacGregor. He's decided you will continue from here."

The room exploded into applause and hoots.

Rachel almost fainted with relief. Lachlan would stay.

Michael held up his hand to regain order. "One more thing. You are hereby offered the newly created role of Gatherer Trainer. We can no longer tolerate the preventable loss of souls. If you accept, you and your mortal progeny will train new Gatherers in the art of mystical war."

Lachlan slowly let the air out of his lungs and nodded. "I accept."

Michael nodded solemnly. "So be it."

Then he was gone.

20

Lachlan scooped a small blue-black rock from the shore of the windswept loch and ran his thumb over its smooth surface. *Slate, from Ballachulish, judging by the color.* Worn by the waves and faded by the sun, it was clearly old, perhaps an ancient fragment of slate roof. He tucked it in his sporran.

Climbing the rocky bank to level ground, his gaze automatically swung to the moss-covered lump of wall where Emily sat wrapped in her boyfriend's gray cotton hoodie. The damp May breeze tugged at the couple's clothing, encouraging a twining of bodies. He studied the pair for a moment, then glanced down at the image on Rachel's canvas, an image that successfully captured both the brightness of Emily's smile and the glowering clouds drifting across the west end of the loch. "I'm still no' convinced that's a prudent relationship."

"Leave them alone. They're good for each other."

He peered at his wife. "Pardon? Weren't you the one who insisted he was too old for her?"

"He is." She added a smudge of gold to the bottom of a cloud. "And the fact that he's dead doesn't win him any points. But look at them. Have you ever seen two happier people? Compare those expressions to the ones they wore seven months ago."

She had a point.

The darkness that had once haunted Carlos had eased. Whether it was because the lad had learned to forgive himself for his brother's death, or because Emily had a unique ability to soothe his soul, he couldn't be sure.

"Besides," Rachel added, rinsing her paintbrush in a tiny pot and standing, "we couldn't stop her from resurrecting him, so how the heck could we possibly stop her from dating him?"

"Paddle her arse 'til it's purple?"

"She's fifteen." She wrapped her arms around Lachlan's waist and pressed her body tight against the warm wool of his Aran sweater. Her hands were chafed and chilled from the hour she'd spent capturing the wild Scottish landscape, but not once had she complained.

"If you're suggesting that's too old for a healthy dose of discipline, think again." He planted a kiss on the top of her head. "Reacting emotionally—which she does all too often—is very dangerous for an immortal with the power she possesses. She snatched his soul from beneath Satan's nose. Trust me, that's no' the sort of deed that eases tension."

"He didn't deserve to go to hell."

"No, he didn't," Lachlan agreed. "But Satan is an immensely capable primal being, no' an enemy to be trifled with. He's stirring up enough trouble as it is. The demon attacks may be fewer these days, but they're more purposeful and more dangerous. The last thing we need is to have Emily incite him into anger. She needs to gain some self-control."

Rachel was silent for a moment. Then she said, "There's such thing as having too much self-control, you know."

His eyes met hers. "Pointing a finger at me, are you?"

"Yes. This is a pretty momentous day, but you've barely said ten words about it."

He lifted his gaze to the bluebell-dotted green hills above the loch. The only hints that a fortified manor house had once stood in this spot were two crumbling pieces of wall, both overgrown with moss and bracken. But on a thin crag of rock overlooking the choppy blue water, a twelve-foot granite statue of an angel now gazed up at the sky, wings spread.

Four simple names were etched into the wide base, no dates.

"I'm pleased," he said. "It's a fine marker."

"Wow, we're up to sixteen."

He sighed. "What do you want me to say?"

"I don't know. More. You carried the weight of their deaths on your shoulders for four hundred years, and here we are on the anniversary of their murders and you feel nothing?"

"I feel plenty. Thanks to you."

With her cheek resting against his heart, he felt her smile. Then he heard her say, "So, share."

"This is the first time I've set foot on this spot since the raid," he confessed, "no' counting those brief moments with Drusus. I couldn't bear to return, knowing what I'd done. But the guilt has eased. I'm no' very comfortable acknowledging I played the puppet for a demon, but I am . . . accepting."

"Okay. But something still fills your chest when you look at that monument, right? What is it?"

The memory that had swamped him down by the edge of the loch—of his two eldest children giggling with delight as they skipped stones on the water—surfaced again. He could finally open the pages of his inner photo album without being ripped apart by regret. He gave

Rachel a quick squeeze. "Nostalgia. The bittersweet tug of old memories, nothing more. I promise."

She stiffened. "I'm not jealous."

"Are you sure?"

"I *was* jealous. And hey, no offense, but I had good reason. You looked me right in the eye and swore you only went down in the cave to rescue them, not Em and me."

"I was lying. To protect you from Drusus."

She smiled up at him. "Yeah, I know. And you've made a very impressive effort to make up for that lie since we got married."

"I can do more." He deepened his smile to a leer. "Much, much more."

"Hmmmm. That sounds promising." Grinning, she unwrapped herself from his body and bent to her painting supplies. "Let me pack up my stuff and we can head back to the hotel."

"Nay, no' the hotel," he objected. "Everywhere you look in the village, you see the stamp of the Campbells. The MacGregors of the mist are long forgotten there. I may have forgiven the past, but I'll no' make our future in a Campbell bed, pretty as it may be."

"Uh, the brochure says the village is Victorian in design. And the hotel isn't owned by a Campbell."

"Brochure be damned. When I was a lad, the Campbells had full reign of the village and their stench still fills my nose. *This* is MacGregor land. Right here."

Her eyebrows soared. "You're not suggesting . . . ?"

"I am."

She glanced around, wide-eyed. "Outside? With Em and Carlos within hearing range? Are you crazy?"

"No, I'm no' crazy. Just madly in love. With you."

Her eyes softened. "Yes, but—"

Giving in to the urge that had assailed him from the moment he first met her, Lachlan scooped her up and tossed her over his shoulder, oblivious to her squeal of protest. Sometimes the old ways were best.

"Carlos," he called out, "pack up Rachel's things and take Emily back to the village. Rachel and I are going sightseeing."

Emily's snort was audible.

"Sightseeing?" Rachel hissed. "Is that the best story you could come up with?"

"It'll do." Leaving the dirt road, he trekked north through the sweet-scented bluebells, up the glen, toward a large patch of forest.

"I don't think ... this is such ... a good idea." Her words came in gusts, her breathing impacted by every surging stride he took up the hill. "The grass is wet."

"It'll be drier under the trees."

"I can't believe ... I'm letting you do this."

He smiled as he ducked under an arching willow branch and entered the tranquility of the forest. "Are you letting me?"

"Don't be a smart-ass."

Stopping beneath an ancient elm, he lowered her to the ground, sliding her very feminine body along the length of his as he did so. Enthralled by the notion that she was his wife, he stared into her lovely eyes. Every time he thought about how lucky he was to have this incredible woman in his life, he was humbled. She made him feel clean and worthy and honorable. She made him whole. "There are moments when I'm weak-kneed with the knowledge that we're wed. This is one."

A smile erased the grumpy expression on her flushed face. "See? Now that's why I love you. You don't talk nearly enough, but when you do, you say absolutely wonderful things."

Taking her hips in hand, he pulled her against him. Hard. A jolt of delicious heat went in all directions, licking through his veins like warm brandy. "I want to make love to you right here, in the country where I was born, under trees that sprouted when I was just a lad. Are you game?"

She glanced down at the bed of moldering leaves and fallen pine needles and wrinkled her nose. "Uh . . ."

He kissed one side of her mouth. The taste of her, still faintly flavored with her early-morning coffee, was sweet to his tongue. "Say aye, Rachel."

"But I'm wearing my brand-new cashmere sweater."

He kissed the other side of her mouth. "Say aye, Rachel."

The stiffness of her shoulders told him she still wasn't convinced. She needed a little more . . . motivation. His hand slipped under the edge of her cream sweater and found the soft, bare skin he was craving—smooth as satin, a delightful contrast to the rough skin of his fingers. He brushed his knuckles along the underside of her breast, deliberately teasing.

Her breath caught.

His lips wandered along her jaw and down the tender slope of her neck to the pulse that beat a little faster now. With his tongue, he adored that indisputable evidence of her desire for him, evidence that his own body responded to with brain-fogging enthusiasm.

"Say aye, Rachel," he pleaded hoarsely.

"Aye."

It was a raspy, almost-choked response, but it was all the encouragement Lachlan needed. His hand popped the clasp on her bra, freeing her breasts to his touch.

He groaned.

Delightful. But not enough to satisfy him. Not nearly.

Grabbing the edge of her sweater, he tugged the soft wool up and over her head, baring her to the cool Scottish air . . . and to his avid stare. "Have I mentioned that you're incredibly beautiful?"

"Yes, but feel free to say it as often as you like."

"Be forewarned." He tugged his gaze away from her puckered nipples and up to meet her eyes. "I'll say it with such frequency, you'll tire of hearing it."

"Impossible."

The dampness in the air made the tips of her hair curl and her skin glow. She had that same fresh-faced look she'd worn the first time he saw her.

"You're beautiful."

Under his intent stare, she flushed. "So are you. Honestly, I never thought I'd find a man's knees sexy, but you in this kilt sure get my vote for best-dressed man. When we get back to the States—"

He unfastened the button on the top of her jeans.

"Uh, Lachlan?"

"Aye?" He slid the zipper down and parted the denim until the lace of her black panties saw daylight.

"I just remembered. Nigel called this morning, begging me to help him out with a new project—" His fingers grazed along her delicate skin and slipped beneath the lacy edge. She tensed a little, her voice gaining a subtle edge of desperation. "Now that the MaskWeave product has finally shipped and Celia's been fired, he says he can hire me back as a contract designer. He needs me to call him. What time is it in San Jose?"

He bent his head and kissed the pale arch of her neck. Using his tongue, he painted a filigree pattern on her flesh. The sweet spice of her skin was ambrosia to his senses, inciting a fresh tide of hot possession. The woman of his dreams was his.

Suddenly, with a gusty sigh, she relaxed. "Damn. I'm doing it again, aren't I?"

He blinked, then pulled back to look in her eyes. "What?"

"Being somewhere else instead of being with you. Letting the world and all its problems rate a little higher than my happiness." Her smile was wry. "Old habits die hard."

"That's why we're learning new ones." His hand dipped lower and found the dampness between her legs. A slick, warm welcome that made it incredibly difficult to remain on his feet. The thought of sinking into her became a dizzying drumbeat in his head.

He opened his mouth to demand her full attention, to seduce her with every coarse promise of pleasure he could muster, but he never got a chance to speak. She reached up, dug her fingers deep into his hair, and tugged his head down until their lips met.

It was a kiss unlike any he'd gotten from Rachel before—aggressive and possessive. Her lips swept over his with brazen demand—hot, wet, and insistent. She didn't just taste him; she ate him up, pressing hard, chewing on his bottom lip, thrusting her tongue in and out of his mouth in an impossible-to-miss suggestion of what she wanted next.

The rush of blood to his groin was so swift, he actually thought his legs had turned to jelly. His hand slipped out of her pants as he grabbed her hips to stop the world from spinning.

"I love you," she said when she surfaced for a breath.

Her words cut through the haze of his excitement and tunneled their way right into his heart. She sounded so fervent and sure, so utterly convinced. He scooped her up, dropped to his knees in the perennial layer of fallen leaves, and laid her out before him.

"Lord, Rachel, I love you, too. In ways I couldn't have imagined before I met you. One look from you and I'm on my knees. My heart pounds as if it will burst from my chest. You make me feel unbelievably alive, *mo cridhe*."

He buried his face against the tender flesh of her breasts, drawing in her scent, memorizing it for eternity.

"Lachlan?"

"Aye?" He glanced into her eyes.

"I'm tired of being on the bottom."

He grinned. "Are you?"

Gathering her in his arms, he rolled over in the leaves. Sunlight streamed through the canopy overhead, the lacy pattern painted in the shade a perfect foil for her dark beauty.

"Better?"

"Getting there." She stood and quickly shucked her jeans. Wearing nothing but a silky scrap of black panties, she straddled his hips, wriggling suggestively against the hard ridge of his erection. The wool of his kilt rasped against his bare flesh. "Mmmm, much better."

Lachlan could barely think. Between the pleasure rocketing through his body with every grind and the wondrous sight of her breasts bobbing in front of his eyes, there weren't a lot of brain cells working.

"Much," he agreed hoarsely.

"I have a question." She danced her fingers up the ridges of his belly, over the planes of his chest, and down his arms. Everywhere she touched, he trembled.

"Christ. Whatever it is, my answer is yes."

"You're alive now."

"Aye." So bloody alive, it was killing him.

She wriggled again. "It feels different, right? Different than when you were dead?"

He grabbed her hips to stop her from moving. It was a question that deserved a coherent answer. "Aye. When Death held my soul, I was still me, but I felt mildly disconnected. I could see and touch and feel, but something was missing."

"And now?"

"Colors are brighter, food tastes better, and all my senses are keener. Everything is more vivid, more real. I'm alive." He let his eyes darken suggestively. "In every possible sense of the word."

"Really." She licked her full lips, then smiled slyly. "Well, then. I'm thinking we need some quantitative data to prove just how *alive* you are. How 'bout I do a test-drive?"

"Test-drive?"

"Uh-huh." Leaning over to nibble his jaw, she let the tips of her breasts brush across his chest. Unbearable. "Pedal to the metal stuff. To check you out. See if you moan louder, breathe heavier, last long—"

"Finish that sentence on pain of death," he warned.

Grinning, she pressed a quick kiss to his lips. "Come on, it'll be fun."

"What exactly does a test-drive involve?"

"Me at the wheel, pushing you to the very limits of your endurance, making you see stars, making you beg for mercy. If you're real lucky, I'll let you explode. What do you say?"

Lachlan looked into her face.

She'd changed subtly over the past few months. In losing her job and nearly losing Emily, she'd found herself. She was back to painting, less concerned with rules and doing everything by the book. She smiled more often. Best of all, the worry lines were long gone, replaced by a playful, carefree look that made her eyes dance.

The notion of being teased to the point of begging for

mercy was a little disconcerting, but that sparkling look in her eyes was worth any sacrifice, even his rigid self-control, which was already dangerously close to snapping, anyway.

"I'm game." He cupped her head in both hands, tugged her down, and kissed her, hard. Because warriors who'd once been immortal should never be soft—at least, not on the outside. "Go ahead, love. Drive me wild."

Read on for a glimpse at the next
sizzling paranormal romance in
Annette McCleave's Soul Gatherers series,

BOUND BY DARKNESS

Available in May 2010 from Signet Eclipse

In the dim stairwell, he pulled his sword out from under his suit jacket. Freed from its mystically warded scabbard, the fifteenth-century Oakeshott was visible to the human eye, but witnesses were the least of his worries. A single explosion could have been caused by a havoc demon, one of those sick bastards who occasionally broke through the barrier for the simple joy of causing freak accidents. But havocs were like sparks from the fires of hell—they had only moments to execute their sorry-assed deed before they fizzled out. Once depleted, they were sucked back into the lower plane. They definitely didn't have the juice to hit a joint twice.

This was something else.

He murmured a quick shield spell and then slowly descended to the landing. Debris littered the stairs—chunks of concrete, a fallen sign, and a thick layer of gray dust—but overall, the enclosed space seemed intact. Which made the crumpled body all the more confusing. A middle-aged woman with a huge gold lamé purse lay between him and the next floor, her limbs bent at awkward angles, almost as if she'd dropped midstep.

Brian scanned her limp figure. No blood, no burns, no visible injuries of any kind. His gaze traveled outward, along the floor to the gray-painted cinder-block walls, where a series of scorch marks danced over the concrete, culminating in a black spot near the corner. The burn pattern was familiar, a perfect match to the forks of electrical energy that preceded every visitation from another plane.

The poor woman had simply been in the wrong place at the wrong time. The demon materialized right on top of her. Sighing, Brian put a hand to her throat. Immediately a warm, soothing sensation flowed into his fingers, fluttered up his arm, and wrapped around his heart. The tickle of a transitioning soul. The good news was this one was destined for heaven.

The walls oscillated mortar dust into the air as another explosion hit the building. More screams floated up from the floors below and a piece of concrete the size of a bread loaf dislodged from the stairs above, crashing to the ground a half inch from his toes.

Fuck this.

He tucked away his sympathy for the dead woman and leapt over the metal railing, dropping four floors in a blur. He landed at the bottom in an easy crouch, then sprang to his feet.

Sword in hand, he strode into the smoke and fragmented masonry that had once been the ladies cosmetics section. The scene was bad. The first floor tended to be one of the busiest spots in the store, filled with gawking tourists and trend-worshipping teens. Tonight was no exception. Broken bodies lay everywhere, some piled three deep. Strewn about like garbage, dampened by a barely functioning sprinkler system. Men, women and . . . children.

Brian tore his gaze away from the devastation, searching the hazy interior for any sign of movement. Emotional reactions could come later. Right now, dealing out justice took priority.

The thin wail of sirens rose and fell in the distance. Reassuring, but not the sounds he needed to focus on. Filtering out emergency vehicles, electric crackles, and low moans of the injured, he homed in on the noises that typically haunted a Soul Gatherer's nightmares: the raspy murmur of hellish incantations and the whoosh of fire bombs in the air.

And he found the bastard.

Left. About a hundred yards through the haze.

Most of Satan's henchies wore a glamour to disguise their presence among humans. But not this one. It was a mottled red and gray colossus, twice Brian's height and probably three times his weight, horns and talons everywhere. A long ooze-dripping tail extended in his direction, writhing with a life of its own. Giving the flexible appendage a wide berth, Brian advanced through the rubble, visualizing his attack. Spotting his opportunity, he leapt atop the remnants of a display counter and dove at the hulking figure from behind. His target was the heavily muscled neck. An unlikely win, perhaps, but possible. The Oakeshott was a very fast blade.

Just not fast enough.

The demon pivoted as the arc of Brian's swing gained full momentum. Red eyes glaring, it raised a platter-sized palm, muttered a single word, and blasted Brian in the chest with a fat glob of red-hot lava. The missile sent him flying, and he landed on a display case in a splash of splintered wood and tinkling glass. Worse, the lava bomb ate right through his shield, gnawed through his Jay Kos jacket, and drilled deep into muscle. Breathing became a serious chore.

What was this thing?

He surged to his feet, conjured a fresh shield, and brandished his sword, prepared to fend off another fireball. But nothing came at him. The behemoth demon had turned away, wading through the rubble toward the Fiftieth Street doors. It wasn't interested in him, couldn't care less about the angry Soul Gatherer determined to send its ass back to hell.

And that made Brian's heart skip a beat. What demon could resist an opportunity to steal a soul? Especially when the odds appeared to be in its favor? It didn't make any sense.

Unless it was after something else.

He peered through the smoke, past the demon's massive frame, and frowned. The surprisingly intact door to the outside world was swinging shut. Someone had just left the building. Judging by the smear of bright red blood on the glass, an injured someone.

Not pausing to sort out the whys, Brian dashed around the demon, narrowly dodged a vicious stab of its tail, and pushed through the door into the late-May evening. The sun was just beginning to set, leaving thin ribbons of tawny light falling between buildings. The traffic on the busy street had slowed to a crawl, and heads popped out car windows, wide eyes locked on the wafting smoke several floors above.

Brian panned the gawking bystanders, looking for his wounded escapee.

There. A bloodstained T-shirt-clad figure climbing the stairs of St. Pat's cathedral.

The door at his back exploded in a thick moil of fire and greasy black smoke, pitching Brian and a million shards of glass and metal halfway across the street. He rolled over the hood of a yellow cab, bounced to his feet, and raced for the church entrance. New screams were abruptly silenced as the demon swept aside a parked car and seared everything in a fifty-foot radius with a mouthful of furnace-hot heat. Brian shoved the ugly thought of fried bodies to the back of his mind and kept going. The demon never varied its pace, but every step gained it fifteen feet. It wouldn't be far behind him.

Brian's eyes adjusted instantly to the dim interior of the church.

The last afternoon mass was over, but a few map-carrying tourists lingered in the pews and in the gift shop. Spotting his fugitive was easy. A bone-thin blond girl, no more than twenty, limped up the nave toward the altar, one arm hanging by her side, the other clutched to her chest. It was a testament to the awe-inspiring beauty of the cathedral's arches that no one noticed the blood trail she left behind on the marble floor.

Brian leapt over two rows of pews and sprinted for her.

He reached her just as the demon hit the church with a marble-crumbling blast. The girl was on the verge of collapse. Deep cuts laced her arms and neck. The front of her threadbare T-shirt was soaked with blood, and her lips were chalky white.

Each passing minute was killing her.

Behind him, the heavy bronze doors exploded inward, sailing twenty feet before landing on pews that buckled under the weight. The tourists ran blindly for the main entrance, far less interested in what had caused the explosion than in escaping the mayhem. Not bothering with introductions, Brian scooped up the girl in one arm and dashed for the Forty-ninth Street door.

She didn't make things easy. Despite her weakened state, the girl flailed.

"No," she gasped as she pummeled him with her fist. "I can't leave."

"Honey, if we don't leave, we're going to die," he told

her grimly, his fingers struggling to keep their hold on her blood-slicked skin.

"Let me *go*."

A fireball hit him in the lower back—a teeth-rattling jolt that disintegrated his new shield as easily as the last. He stumbled, but kept running. Conjuring another shield, he leapt left over a pew, and dove behind a marble column. Just in time. The wrought-iron chandelier above his last position crashed to the floor, sending a spray of fine glass and chipped tile in all directions.

Unfortunately the dive allowed the girl to slip free of his hold. She slithered under the nearest bench and peered at him from her dim hideout. Her face was ashen, her eyes dark and wide. "This is a church; this is sanctuary. It can't hurt me here."

He stared at her. *Damn.* She believed that shit.

The column protecting them took an indirect hit, cracked, and partially crumbled. There wasn't enough time to explain how things really worked, so he reached for her again.

She flinched away.

"Sweetheart, *please*," he begged. The marble floor trembled under the advancing steps of the demon. "This whole place is about to fall down around our ears."

But she pulled farther into the shadows and shook her head, refusing to be swayed.

Which left him with only one option. His original choice. Fight.

He closed his eyes, finding and focusing on the throb of power that lay deep in his chest. Drawing hard on the cool white energy, he shoved off the floor. His muscular legs flexed with practiced ease and he flipped over ten pews, landing in the nave with his sword ready for action. The demon again ignored him, maintaining its relentless pursuit of the girl. Perfect.

Brian ducked under the creature's long whipping tail and went for its Achilles tendons.

Were they still called that if the creature had cloven hooves?

The magical enhancements on his blade cut through the demon's shield, and he sliced deep. Unfortunately the demon's thick, scaly hide served its purpose and his swing fell short of success, unable to sever the tendons completely.

The demon issued an angry roar that blew out every stained-glass window in the cathedral. It spun around, splintering a dozen pews into matchsticks with its tail, and released a gust of thousand-degree breath in Brian's direction. Benches all around him licked into a fiery blaze, then disintegrated into ash. But Brian's shield survived the attack, and so did he. Dripping with sweat but still vigorously alive, he rushed the demon again, leaping high and scoring two slices—one across the beast's massive chest and the other across its bicep.

Before he could regroup and deal another blow, however, the demon's tail slid around his waist with anaconda strength and flicked him aside, tossing him a hundred feet with incredible ease. Brian smacked into a marble wall, the air in his lungs expelled in a sharp puff. He slid to the floor, dazed, an easy target for the huge chunk of marble the demon tore from a wall and flung atop him. His shield repelled the worst of the blow, but Brian's sternum took the rest. He scrambled to his feet, sucking in a breath.

Shunting aside his misery, burying his pain beneath a layer of fierce resolve, he sped back toward the demon. He zigzagged around pillars to make himself a more erratic target, but the demon managed to lock onto him in spite of his defensive maneuvers. Molten lava hit him at the hip, tore through his shield as if it were made of tissue paper, and burrowed into his skin. Brian staggered.

A dozen hot, hungry worms chewed through his flesh, right to the bone. Every nerve ending howled. Black spots crowded his vision, a vain attempt by his mind to shut out the pain. Nausea clawed at his belly, and his arms and legs turned to rubber. He might well have fallen to his knees were it not for the feeble words that filtered through his agony-induced haze.

"Hail Mary . . . full of grace . . ."

The girl was praying, using her last breaths to beg forgiveness for her sins.

Damn it. *No.* He couldn't let her die here, not like this. There hadn't been a mark on her cheek, no sign that she was destined to die today. At least none that he could see. And she was just a kid, barely a woman. She was a lot like . . . Melanie.

Brian reached deeper, found a last reserve of strength, and forced his legs to move. This fucking demon had to go down. *Now.*

He pumped his legs again and again, each step firmer than the last, each step taking him closer to his quarry. Another fireball hit him, but he kept going, the pain an ever-tightening cinch around his chest and yet, somehow, hollow and distant. As if it were happening to someone else. Adjusting his hold on the leather-wrapped hilt of his sword, he envisioned his attack, right through to a successful conclusion.

Then he leapt.

Using the creature's flexed knee for leverage, he launched himself upward, ducking around its massive arm and swinging at the bulging cords of its neck. His blade, the marvelous creation of a very talented mage, had gained new energy from the drips of demon gore sliding down its length. It hummed with supernatural strength, and the glowing blue edge broke through the demon's shield. Out of the corner of his eye, Brian saw the angry, undulating tail lash in his direction, but his attention remained focused on his target—the base of the neck where a fat jugular vein pulsed with undead life.

The cutting edge of the sword bit deep into the demon's flesh, carving through hide, sinew, and nerves alike. Thick crimson blood sprayed everywhere. *Success. Sort of.* The demon's tail whipped around his torso, encircling him. It slithered all the way up to his shoulder and then ... squeezed. Ribs, collarbone, shoulder blades—a dozen bones snapped under the pressure, a sickening series of crunches. Only when a death-throe shudder racked the demon from head to toe did the pressure ease. Thrashing mindlessly, the tail flung Brian into the air.

The demon lurched, fell to its knees, and collapsed face-first in the rubble.

Brian only vaguely noted the fall. Agony had him firmly in its grip. He'd ended his flight thirty pews to the left, atop his mangled shoulder. His immortal body, aware that the battle was over, threatened to shut down for repair, but he fought the siren call of blackout. The job wasn't done. He had to reach the girl.

Bile in his mouth, his vision distorted by a red film, he pushed unevenly to his feet.

His blood pounded at the exertion, filling his ears with an angry rush. Hearing anything else was impossible. But he located her anyway, still huddled beneath a pew near the doors. Pale and bloodless. Her eyes were closed, her prayers silenced. He knew long before he took her slender hand that she was dead; he just didn't want to believe it.

Gently, he tugged her out of her cave and into his arms. The movement jarred his arm, but the pain felt right and just. He let his chin sink to his chest. He'd failed her.

The sudden crackle of electricity didn't rouse him. Nor did the pop of his ears or the light scent of lemons. His body howled for sleep, and he almost gave in to the demand.

"I came as soon as I heard her prayer," a quiet male voice said. "But I see I'm too late."

Fueled by a wave of frustration, Brian lifted his head to glare at the angel—a lean, casually dressed young man with a cascade of light brown curls falling to his shoulders. For someone so pretty, he exuded a robust intensity. "You guys are always too late."

The angel crouched beside him. "Not true. I've battled my share of demons."

"Since when? I thought psychopomps only collected souls?"

A half smile curved the angel's lips. "I'm no psychopomp. My name is Uriel."

Brian frowned. "As in *archangel* Uriel?"

The glorious one nodded offhandedly, as if archangels dropped in on Soul Gatherers every day. An attitude that matched his baggy blue jeans and skater-boy sneakers. His gaze wandered to the fallen demon. "Congratulations on your victory. It couldn't have been easy."

Yeah, he was reminded of how *not* easy it had been every time he took a breath. "What is that thing? Bastard ate through my shield with one blow."

Uriel stood. "A martial demon. You're lucky to still be around. Only a handful of Gatherers have survived an encounter with one."

Brian blinked. Rumor had it his buddy MacGregor had once battled and defeated two martial demons singlehandedly. His estimation of the guy went up twenty points.

"I'd best get rid of our large friend," the archangel said. "He'll be a little difficult to explain to the authorities. When you're ready, I'll collect your souls."

Brian's gaze dropped to the limp girl in his arms. Brushing a blood-crusted lock of hair away from her face, he studied the keen angles and sunken eyes of an unhappy life ended way too soon. "Sometimes I hate this job."

Uriel squeezed his shoulder. "We'll take good care of her. I promise."

Then the angel left him to his thoughts.

Brian gently laid the girl's body on the broken tiles. *Barely weighs anything, poor kid.* About to put his hand on her throat and collect her soul, he paused. A *martial* demon. One of Satan's most able-bodied warriors, sent to snuff this little slip of a girl, a ninety pound threat. How did that make any sense?

He explored her face again, taking in the big eyes and sharp cheekbones. Was she someone important? Someone powerful? The cheap clothing hanging off her starved frame said otherwise. His gaze slid to her fisted left hand. Maybe she had an item they wanted? Seemed unlikely a street kid would own a keepsake the devil himself desired, but she'd clutched that hand tight, never once loosening her grip, right up to the moment of her demise.

He uncurled her fingers.

In the center of her palm lay a dull silver coin. Uneven edges, stamped with the image of some curly-haired guy, no date that he could see. It looked old.

A ripple of unease swept through him as he stared at the coin. He had the sense he recognized it, yet he was equally convinced he'd never seen it before. Laughing at himself for being superstitious, he picked it up with the edge of his shirtsleeve. The back was engraved with some kind of weird bird.

"Uriel?"

In the midst of working some heavenly magic on the demon's body, the angel glanced over his shoulder. "Yes?"

"This look familiar to you?" Brian held up the coin.

"It's a Tyrian shekel, once used to pay temple taxes in Jerusalem."

"Think it could be what the demon was after?"

The archangel turned back to the creature's corpse. A casual flick of long fingers, a brilliant flash of white light, and all that remained of the beast was a pile of red sand. Releasing a heavy sigh, Uriel faced Brian once more. "Is there a tiny star stamped on the back?"

Brian looked closer. "Yeah."

"Then sadly, yes. Peter marked all thirty coins with a star when he retrieved them from the potter." He seemed a little disappointed that Brian didn't immediately understand the reference. "It's one of the silver pieces Judas received for selling out the Son of God."

"Okay." That made it infamously ancient, not just old. "What do I do with it?"

"Keep it, for now." Uriel raked a hand through his long curls, a furrow marring his perfect brow. "I'll consult with Michael on how to best proceed. But by all that's holy, do *not* let Satan get his hands on it. My guess is he's already acquired some of the others. Seventeen of the coins were under the care of a Protector here in New York."

A Protector? "Are you telling me these coins are like the Pontius Pilate Linen? That they're some kind of dark relic?"

"Yes."

He studied the coin again. "What evil mojo do they stir up?"

"They fuel betrayal on a grand scale. Touch the coin

and you're sucked into a web of manipulation that will soon have you betraying even those closest to you. The more coins held, the stronger the influence, and if the wrong person secures the complete set, multiply the nightmare by ten."

Brian did some quick math. "If seventeen coins were here in New York, where are the other thirteen?"

"No one knows. They were lost during the fall of the Knights Templar in the fourteenth century. On the positive side, it's unlikely Satan has them."

"Yeah?"

"Everything is too calm. But if I'm right and he has sixteen of the New York coins, that will quickly change. A wave of corruption and scandal will hit the news within a day or two, generating the first sparks of fear. If he acquires the other thirteen, he'll topple governments and send major corporations into turmoil. The fear will escalate. There will be riots and possibly wars. And if he gains the last . . . well, I'm sure you see where I'm headed."

An invisible weight settled on Brian's shoulders. "So, let me see if I have this straight. This coin in my hand may be the only thing standing between the devil and a cataclysmic butt-fuck of humankind."

Uriel's brows soared, but a glimmer of amusement shone in his eyes. "Those wouldn't be the words I'd use, but, yes. That's the gist of it."

"Great, thanks." He tucked the coin in his pants pocket.

The minute he got back to San Jose, he'd do the right thing and hand the silver piece over to MacGregor. The last thing the world needed was Brian Webster tasked with saving the day. That would turn out bad. Guaranteed.

"Let's move swiftly," Uriel urged. "We have less than a minute before the New York Fire Department comes charging through the door."

Brian nodded.

His gaze dropped back to the lifeless girl. How wrong was it that he didn't even know her name? Hell, she was the hero in all this. She might not have understood what she was doing, but she'd given her life to protect the coin. And no one would know but him.

Damn it.

If a fragile little girl could make that kind of sacrifice, the least *he* could do was make sure the rest of the coins stayed safe. The poor kid's death should mean something. Life had kicked her in the teeth—repeatedly—by the look of her. She'd spent months, possibly years, on the streets, lost, starved, and beaten. And in all that time, no one had come to her rescue. No one had saved her.

Not even him.

Putting a hand on her pale throat, he gathered her soul.